PRAISE FOR THE
LEAGUE OF GALLIZE SHIFTERS SERIES

GRAY WOLF MATE

"Gray Wolf Mate is a brilliant start to this epic new series."
~Clare & Lou's Mad About Books

"Dianna Love once again gives us another wonderful series for us to savor and follow." ~ The Reading Cafe

"The League Of Gallize Shifters is definitely original in many areas, and I was totally intrigued during every compelling incident." ~ Always Reviewing

"Gray Wolf Mate is the first in an exciting new shifter series by the fantastic Dianna Love. There are shifters and then there are Gallize Shifters." ~ In My Humble Opinion

"The Gallize shifter is an intriguing and innovative new twist and I absolutely love this new book." ~ ChelleMB, Amazon

LEAGUE
OF
GALLIZE
SHIFTERS

MATING
A GRIZZLY

DIANNA
LOVE

*Len you rock!
Dianna Love*

MATING A GRIZZLY
League of Gallize Shifters series

MATING A GRIZZLY is book two in a series of unusual shifters.

JUSTIN IS AN ELITE BLACK ops warrior on a unique shifter team. He's as deadly as they come and determined to succeed on every mission. He turns into a monster grizzly and rushes into danger without hesitation to do his duty ... but he's having second thoughts on his current assignment. If there's one thing he can't tolerate it is arrogant people like the jerks he grew up around who acted superior to him. Justin can't believe he's stuck playing bodyguard for a Russian shifter princess. He'd rather face down a pack of armed terrorists alone than spend time with a cold-hearted prima donna. Except, Elianna turns out to be unlike anything he expected. She's hot, but he'd like to see her smile. He's on a mission to get that smile—and more. First he has to stop the assassin trying to kill him and kidnap her.

Having lived her life as an outcast among her own kind, Elianna hates being called princess. She's the ugly mistake of a Russian grizzly shifter who got her polar bear mother pregnant while on a sabbatical from his mate. With the exception of the little boy she saved after his clan abandoned him, men are the bane of Elianna's life. When she makes a miscalculation under duress, her biological father coerces Elianna into accepting a deal with high stakes if she fails.

Justin is unlike any other man, human or shifter, she's ever been around. He makes her want things she can't have—like mating—because the deal she struck prevents a relationship with him or she'll never see the little boy again who is everything to her. Her plan was simple and doable, but meeting Justin complicated everything.

"GRAY WOLF MATE is a truly ground-breaking paranormal romance. Ms. Love is a writer who can conceive an innovative idea, and then cleverly bring it to life for readers to enjoy." Always Reviewing (League of Gallize Shifters book 1)

Note: All the League of Gallize Shifters books are stand-alone paranormal romances.

DEDICATION

Thank you, Candace Fox, for your friendship, your help with my online events and all the ways you support my books. You are a generous soul and just all round wonderful person.

CHAPTER 1

Petropavlovsk-Kamchatsky, eastern border of Russia

ELIANNA SQUATTED IN A DARK cranny between two build-ings, which was as good a place to hide—or fight—as any. Not a good place to die, though. Her little brother, Nico, needed her alive. She forced herself to calm down and stop sucking in noisy gulps of cold air as if the Grim Reaper was hard on her trail.

That wasn't far from the truth.

"Where wolves now?" she muttered softly and kept watch for any movement. Even alone, she practiced her English and French for the day she hoped to use those languages.

Her hands hadn't stopped trembling since she'd hidden Nico.

The cold didn't bother her. Low forties in early May was nor-mal and her body generated more heat than a human's.

It was fear, driven by the vision she kept having of a grizzly shifter standing between her and Nico—*that* chilled her to the core. Not just any bear shifter, but a powerful one.

Her visions always came true. Her mother knew that, but still had ignored her warning.

At the moment, though, wolf shifters were Elianna's main threat and they were hunting only her.

Crazy shifters probably hopped up on Jugo Loco. Their Black River pack had brought the drug, originally made from a halluci-nogenic tea in South America, to Russia. It affected supernatural beings in different ways, and never good ones.

Her mother had picked a bad group to cross and died for her mistake. If only her mother had listened when Elianna warned of her vision.

Her mother had refused to take the vision seriously, though, and now an innocent six-year-old child was in danger.

Elianna tried to recall the last time her mother had been happy. Too many years to count. Her mother's mind was broken, thanks to Elianna's biological father. The poor woman dragged strange men home more and more often lately, anything to make her feel loved, but it was false love. Elianna had begged her mother to stop until she found a place to live with Nico.

Then her mother could put out a sign for men if she wanted.

But no.

Her mother, a polar bear shifter, had gone to her regular Friday drinking hole last night and turned down a wolf shifter. She'd believed that by sleeping only with humans, she was being true to Elianna's father, a man Elianna had never met and never would if she had any luck left.

He was the most powerful grizzly shifter in this part of Russia, which was why the vision weighed heavily on her mind.

In the vision, Elianna had seen wolves all around her mother, but not what happened in the end. That vision had ended with blurry darkness.

Sadly, she now knew how the end of that vision played out.

The rejected wolf's pack had paid her mother's crappy little third-floor apartment a visit just before dark.

Wolves did not accept no, especially from a shifter who took a human to her bed.

Elianna could still smell the fresh blood. She'd scented it as she neared the apartment building over an hour ago with Nico's tiny hand in hers. She'd asked a friend to watch him today or he would have been with Elianna's mother and would also be dead. Standing out of sight near the apartment, Elianna had listened as the wolf shifters descended the stairs and laughed about killing that 'bear bitch.'

Then one of the wolves brought up smelling a second female and young male in the apartment.

He still had a taste for bear. The wolves howled, ready to hunt.

Elianna had gone into protection mode.

She'd taken her coat off and wrapped Nico in it, then carried him as she ran to a restaurant dumpster filled with table scraps.

Disgusting, but it would camouflage his scent. She'd rubbed her hands on everything at the entrance to the alley, then left to find the wolf shifters. When she did, she found an upwind spot and lifted the tail of her shirt to give them plenty to smell, then started walking away.

When she heard a wolf howl, she'd taken off running.

Now she waited a kilometer from Nico, hoping to survive.

How close was that pack of five shifters?

Glancing around, she familiarized herself with the area she'd chosen to take a stand. Moonlight danced over large, earth-moving equipment, creating long shadows across the open space in this fenced-in storage lot behind a construction business.

Any other shifter in her shoes would probably consider changing shape right now.

Her bear would be of no help in a fight.

Also, even though she'd be stronger as a bear, she could blend in better and escape more easily as a human if she had to run. Having had no chance to change clothes for her night job, she still looked like every other dockworker in her dull-gray pants and long-sleeved pullover stained with diesel oil and mud. Smelled like them, too.

A shifter could identify her true scent, but humans had no idea she was anything more than a low-paid laborer like they were. They *would* have known about her if a bear clan had accepted her.

Invisibility among humans was the only benefit she'd derived from being an outcast among her own kind.

Shifters were first revealed to humans in America eight years ago. Elianna suspected many of the old-timers had been aware of the Romanov Kamchatka bear shifter clan even before then. Elianna's genetic father ruled that clan. His family had descended from royalty and had been in power long before the general human population of this country found out that monsters walked among them.

With her father's reputation as a powerful alpha and his family's royal ancestry, no one in this part of the world dared cross him or his clan.

Living on the remote Kamchatka Peninsula on Russia's lower Pacific coast offered her father a perfect location. Alexandre Romanov was treated as the king he believed himself to be.

As for her, she was fair game to any threat, be it human or shifter.

Something clanged close by.

Lifting her nose, she sniffed for wolf scent mixed in with the aroma of stew being cooked in a nearby tavern and the smoky tinge of burning logs. She trusted her extremely sharp sense of smell over any other sense. Nothing yet.

The waiting was nerve-racking.

She was not known for her patience.

Maybe she shouldn't have run across the tops of two buildings, then shimmied down the water drain and through a small window into a ladies' bathroom that opened into a bar and ... she smiled at the obstacle course they'd been forced to take to follow her.

She knew this town inside and out.

They were the outsiders.

A tabby cat stalked by, explaining the noise. If it looked her way, the cat would see only a dark figure, if anything. Elianna still wore a navy-blue rag tied around her cinnamon-colored hair, hallmark of being the bastard in her mother's family of polar bear shifters. Her hair was only one difference between her and others in a polar bear clan that possessed shades of blonde hair and eyes so dark brown they looked black.

Once the polar bears had seen Elianna's mixed-blood bear, it hadn't taken long for them to boot Elianna and her mother from their clan fifteen hundred miles north of here.

Among the bear shifters in *this* town, her pale-blue eyes marked her as not belonging to her father's clan.

She missed living in her first home, a cold wilderness where, as a child, she had survived on the land and faced few real threats.

Miss fish. Eat fish. Swim.

Of course. Her bear says nothing about being threatened by wolves, but let Elianna make the mistake of reminiscing, and her bear starts whining.

Speaking to her bear with her mind, Elianna said, *Please sleep. I fight bad wolves. No interfere.* She'd been speaking to her bear in English for a while now, but still added, *Understand?*

Her bear grumbled and pushed at her, but settled down, which was as much acknowledgment as Elianna would get.

Twice a month, she shifted into her animal abomination to allow the bear freedom to run in a remote section of the mountains west of the city.

After a last, half-hearted snarl, the bear ignored her.

They had a relationship of tolerance. It was unlike those of other shifters who actually enjoyed friendships with their animals, but it worked.

Elianna accepted half the fault for the wall between them, but who could blame her? Should she be happy to have a bear inside of her that her own clan found disgusting? Her father had never even tried to meet her, and her mother had refused to share much about him.

Ironic, considering the fifteen hundred miles through rugged mountains her mother had forced Elianna to travel to be close to the man she wanted as her mate.

But he already had a mate.

Small details often escaped her mother.

Like humiliating a wolf shifter.

Elianna and her half-breed bear would forever be outcasts here. She had to find a way out of here with Nico.

Swim, swim, swim. Eat fish, her bear grumbled.

No, Elianna replied. *Go sleep.*

No fair.

"Life not fair," Elianna muttered softly. She studied everything she could about life outside Russia, always preparing for any chance to leave a land where she no longer felt welcome. In Canada, she could vanish with Nico into the wilderness. She needed no clan and no man. As a bear shifter, she would never have a life in PK, the name locals used for Petropavlovsk-Kamchatsky.

She refused to turn twenty-three in this place.

Of course, losing to the wolves would take future birthday concerns off the table.

Her thumping heart could handle the demand of running through knee-deep snow and scrambling over boulders to outrun her enemy, but it couldn't take anything happening to Nico. He might not be her blood brother, but he was hers to protect.

A sharp smell on the wind yanked her head to the right. She sniffed again to be sure. Wolf.

The pack was close by. Just as she'd planned.

Good. Nico was safe. He had to be.

But ... what would happen to Nico if the wolves killed her?

Her bear rumbled at her, attempting to convince Elianna she had options if she'd let her bear out.

Elianna rolled her eyes. She had never put her bear in a life-and-death situation, because the silly animal would rather swim—or chase that tabby cat to play with—than fight a pack of wolves. Did her bear think she actually believed this attempt to help?

Me swim, me swim, me swim, her bear said in a singsong voice.

See? Her bear was never serious. Even if Elianna could bring a bear to this fight, being exposed as a shifter in this city could blow up in her face if humans found out her true identity.

She and Nico would be hunted to sell for experiments.

The Black River pack was rumored to pay top dollar.

Shaking off that thought, Elianna sharpened her attention. Survive tonight first, then figure out how to leave this place immediately.

She'd met Lubov, a merchant ship captain, when she'd been hired at the docks to unload the smaller vessels, and the old guy liked her. As a walrus shifter, something she'd never heard of before she'd met him, he would understand her dilemma better than a human would.

He'd once told her if she was ever in trouble to come to him.

She was in much trouble.

He might let her owe him for the fare.

With each breath she drew, icy air spiked her lungs and stung like tiny needles, but still, she preferred the cold.

Her nose twitched. The stink of wolf came from the left this time.

They were surrounding her, hunting as a pack.

In fact, this particular bunch was rumored to pass a woman around, which meant they'd probably done the same to her mother. They must have drugged her mother or they'd have faced a polar bear who would have crushed their skulls. Elianna wouldn't shift, but these wolves would lose body parts, favorite body parts, before she went down.

She looked longingly at where moonlight dusted the mountains and volcanoes in the distance. She could have led the pack out there where she would have had the advantage of knowing the land better than a visitor, and also of shifting if she'd decided to make that gamble, but the wolf shifters might have lost patience and come back to hunt for Nico instead.

No, this was it. She would make her stand here.

Rising to her full height, all five foot eight inches, she prepared for the attack.

Then she heard them moving in.

They weren't being quiet. They didn't care that she heard them coming. They wanted to terrorize her.

She stepped out of her cubbyhole and put her back to the brick wall, which felt like a block of ice.

Two figures emerged from behind one of the frontend loaders. They'd probably jumped the fence on that side.

Two more dropped to the right of her from the roofline, like demons spit from the night. Fifty-gallon, steel drums were stacked in a three-high pyramid on her left.

The wolves smelled of her mother's death.

Blood splattered their faces and clothes where they'd ripped apart her body.

Elianna's heart quivered at the horrible pain her mother must have suffered.

She hadn't been the best example of a mother, but she didn't deserve to be shredded by a pack of lunatic shifters.

Sharp fingers of worry clawed at Elianna.

Where was number five?

Not that she wanted one more wolf shifter to take on, but she *did* want every one of them here, far from Nico.

"Come on little cub," the bald one with tattoos all the way around his neck taunted in English with a Spanish accent.

"Who is leader?" she demanded while she tried to think her way out of this alive. She began to doubt the possibility unless some guardian angel hanging around wanted to perform a miracle.

Nope. No flutter of wings.

Elianna had been taking care of herself for a long time. This was no different.

The wolves looked at each other, then at her with confusion.

Stressed, she had reverted to Russian.

She repeated the question, but in English this time so they

would understand her.

"Me. Call me Varga. I am in charge," bald guy replied, laughing as he pretended to introduce himself.

Looking past their baggy pants and nylon jackets, she could see that they were skinny, dangerously thin. Also, she had one to two inches in height on these guys, but hungry shifters of any size turned into vicious killing machines.

She'd bet their lack of muscle was due to drugs and not to going hungry.

Regardless of their size, they had soulless eyes that glowed more yellow than the amber color she'd have expected.

Plus, there were four.

"We are good guys. We give you chance to do this easy way, bitch," Varga said without a bit of sympathy in his tone.

Lies. Always lies from men.

The pack began easing forward.

She sidestepped to the left.

They smiled, clearly happy to herd her toward the stacked barrels. She wasn't as fluid as a wolf at jumping high, so they could reach the top of the barrels ahead of her. She had only one choice and that was brute strength.

She fisted her hands to hide any tremors and asked, "Why kill woman?"

Varga shrugged. "We like to kill. She deserved it. Consider her death service for community."

"She harmed no one," Elianna countered.

He sneered. "She was slut, which I would not hold against her, but she refused wolf shifter. She was whore for humans." He spit on the ground. "Worse than slut."

Elianna said, "Mistake to kill that one. She was under Romanov Kamchatka alpha protection." That might be a complete lie, but Elianna had always wondered why Alexandre Romanov had never sent a bear shifter to demand her mother declare herself to their clan and king.

She'd asked her mother about his clan once and received no answer, only a sharp warning that Elianna avoid asking questions about that clan or their alpha.

Elianna had done as her mother asked.

Just look where that had landed both of them.

The half circle her attackers formed pulled closer every second. With Elianna's next step back, her heel bumped a metal drum.

"No shifter king protects a whore," Varga scoffed. "If he did, he would mark territory."

She was running out of anything to say, but had one more critical question, one that required arrogance to get an answer.

"Where is other wolf? Is he coward, afraid to fight female?" That came out sounding like she had a sick stomach instead of ringing with confidence.

She had no play left. She smiled in the face of death.

Stupid, maybe, but it made her feel better to not show the bone-cold fear inside her.

One of Varga's pack members answered her. "That one? He has best nose of pack. Someone had to find brat we saw in picture with you."

Nico! "You all die!" she yelled.

The one on the far left attacked first.

CHAPTER 2

a

THE WILD-EYED WOLF SHIFTER DOVE at Elianna.
She made a fast move to one side, bringing her fisted hands down on the back of his neck while he was airborne.

He landed beside the steel drum stack. Bone cracked loud enough to ensure he was out of commission until he healed. Pity she hadn't killed him.

Had that missing fifth wolf found Nico?

Every second she'd wasted talking to these shifters might be costing Nico. Whipping around with her hands up, she ordered, "Move or die."

They must have sacrificed the first shifter to test her.

This time, all three came at her, snarling.

She had those two inches in height on all of them and used her extra arm length to slam her fist at the first head. As he was on his way down, she kicked, connecting with his hard skull.

But one ducked the fists she continued to whack at anything that moved. He came up behind her, landing a blow on her back. That drove her forward and off balance. Still, she kept jabbing her elbows and using head butts to fend the others off.

It didn't matter.

In less than a minute, they wrestled her to the ground and booted her in the side. She coughed and spit up blood. Her bear growled and bumped, still wanting out. She was tempted, but she and her bear had never fought together. If her bear turned and ran, the wolves would gut it.

Then they would both die without even attempting to fight. Her bear had no idea what it was up against.

It was Elianna's job to protect both of them.

One of the wolf shifters had his arm across her throat. He was wheezing too much to be a shifter.

Had that drug made this pack so mentally and physically unfit?

Varga sat on her middle and the last wolf pinned her legs.

Varga's slick head had a few new gashes and his eyes were bright with crazy.

She didn't need him to tell her that she would die more brutally than her mother, but ... Nico. Her heart cramped. She'd failed him.

Varga leaned so close to her face she couldn't avoid his disgusting breath or body odor. Shifters normally prided themselves on being clean.

To be told they smelled bad was an insult.

She couldn't insult someone who didn't care.

"I warned you," Varga said, still dragging in deep breaths. "Now, you will regret making me teach you respect. We put you in chains and take you over and over. You will not die soon. I may keep you that way for months." He shrugged. "Until you bore me."

Reaching deep, she heaved her chest up one last time. Nobody moved.

Varga slammed her head on the ground.

Everything blurred and spun around her. Her skull felt cracked open. Warm liquid wet her hair. She imagined her life force trickling away.

Sadly, she would rejuvenate and heal the damage.

Someone snatched the cloth off her head and grumbled. "Fuck, must have hit her too hard. Damn rag is soaked with blood."

She didn't care for herself, but Nico would suffer without her to protect him.

One of her attackers howled, but ... not a victorious sound. That had been more like the pained cry of an animal caught in a trap. The heavy bodies piled on her started moving around, jumping up to face a new threat.

Boots stepped on her chest as they moved across her.

More blood gushed from her mouth.

She opened her eyes and saw only blurred images so she closed them.

Had the last wolf shown up? Did he have Nico? Why were they fighting? Snarling, hitting, yelping. What was happening?

When the sounds died off, silence closed in.

Elianna blinked awake. She must have passed out. She could still feel the hard ground beneath her, but someone had propped her head on a wad of soft material. Her head throbbed, though less now than before.

Peeking through her thick lashes, she discovered it was still night, but even darker with the group of massive men hovering around to stare at her.

Squinting, she focused her eyes, but leave it to her nose to identity them first.

Bear shifters.

"You are Elianna, yes?" The largest man had a deep voice, better English than hers, and spoke with a refined edge, but he was clearly Russian.

"Yes." She drew in air to speak and hissed at the pain in her chest before she squeezed out, "Who are you?"

"Alexandre of the Romanovs."

"You are—"

"Yes," he said, cutting her off.

Evidently he did not want to be identified as her father in front of his men. She would not do so, for now, only because they had clearly dealt with the wolf shifters.

That didn't make him her ally.

He stared at her with deep interest. She didn't hide her curiosity either as she took in the man who had made her a pariah among all bear shifters.

His men watched the staredown, but didn't dare say a word.

Someone who must have thought her eyes needed help flicked on a dim light off to the side. She could finally see her father clearly, and did not enjoy admitting that she now understood what had attracted her mother.

Alexandre possessed the high forehead, sharp cheeks, slightly curved nose and smooth mouth of an aristocrat. Dark hair fell around his shoulders and he appeared strong enough to lift one of the buildings surrounding them. His eyes were the most startling of all. At the moment, they were glowing like gold nuggets under bright sunshine.

Nico often commented that when she became angry, her gray-blue eyes lit up like diamonds on fire. Adult bear shifters were not meant to have eyes like hers.

All she'd inherited from this man, other than the grizzly blood that ruined the color of her coat, longer claws than a polar bear's and a shorter snout in animal form, was that her eyes glowed when something infuriated her.

She did not have this man's rich brown hair, but a reddish color between pale brown and blond. Nothing that would belong to a pureblood Romanov Kamchatka bear shifter. Her face had more fullness than his narrow one. He even had a pretty mouth.

Elianna was as plain as this man was beautiful.

The bastard.

No, she was the bastard, thanks to him.

She had no way to stop him from doing as he pleased with her, but she would not stand by and let him harm Nico.

Her brains snapped back into use.

"*Nico!*" She struggled to sit and fell back, ribs broken and one arm refusing to work.

Alexandre ordered, "Calm yourself. My men found the child when tracking the other wolf. Child is safe, but could have died. Wolf was sniffing dumpster when my men showed up."

Immediate relief took her breath.

Should she thank this man when he had failed to protect her mother from that same pack?

She was at Alexandre's mercy, but nothing could stop her from asking, "Where were you before? They rape and maul my mother."

His lovely eyes showed true sadness. "If she had listened to me, she would still live. I offered a safe home away from here for all of you. She knew when we met I could not mate her. I never lied to her. We searched for wolf shifters who dare to enter my territory without permission and found her remains. You are fortunate we found *you*. I would have saved your mother if I could."

Why did he have to sound so reasonable?

She needed to rail at someone and unleash the anger chewing up her insides.

But this man had Nico.

Elianna remained silent, especially since every breath hurt to draw. One of the broken ribs had to be piercing her lung. She would heal, but without shifting it would not be quickly and she was in no shape to hike up mountains to release her bear.

Me heal. Swim. Fish. Heal.

Her bear had no sense. Elianna silently replied, *Not here. Be quiet or no run for you for long time. I try to save me, you and Nico.*

Surprisingly, her bear actually did as asked, thankfully, since she had to keep her attention on the man she hated with every part of her being.

Elianna had no choice but to heal without shifting.

The one time she'd made the mistake of turning into her bear in front of other bear shifters had been enough humiliation to last a lifetime.

"You and I must make decisions," Alexandre said, gripping his chin in a look of serious consideration. "You cannot live among my clan. You would suffer daily at their hands. My mate would eventually kill you."

Judgmental glares bore down on her, reinforcing his words.

She had done nothing to these people.

She had stayed out of his way and watched her mother wither into an empty shell of a woman.

That pushed Elianna's temper. In Russian, she asked, "Your pack would disobey orders?"

The men around him made a collective sound of anger on their leader's behalf.

She'd insulted all of them.

Alexandre lifted a hand to quiet his men and silence fell immediately. He sighed and answered her in his native language. "I would never force my mate or clan to face my mistake daily and I would never ask them to accept an ursid hybrid as a member."

That hurt, but not because she expected anything more from this man.

But he'd called her an ursid hybrid in the same way her attacker had called her mother a whore.

Elianna had never wanted to be part of Alexandre's clan or any other. No polar bear or grizzly clan would accept a half-breed.

But she would choke on her pride before she admitted his words had cut her.

Seeing no other way out, she kept speaking in Russian to move this along faster and asked in a civil tone, "Please allow me to heal and leave on my own. In a show of appreciation for your help tonight, Nico and I will go far away from your territory."

Sure, she had pride, but she was not going to allow Nico to suffer over something she could swallow to save him.

"Actually, you are thinking the same as I. I agree it would be best for all if you go far away, but you and the child would not survive traveling north on foot through hundreds of miles protected by small shifter groups."

"I survived a trip through the mountains once," she claimed, sure she could do it again.

"That is only because I received word your mother was determined to cross them with a teenager. I asked that she be given safe passage."

So many things she did not know about this man, but he'd just admitted a way for her to succeed. "Then give me that same protection so we may go north."

"I have a better idea."

Bones were trying to mend in her body, but they weren't properly set. She shifted to ease the pain, but she had to move this along for her broken arm.

"I am starting to heal. I have bones that need to be set."

Nodding his understanding that she needed him to hurry up, he spoke quickly. "I have made an agreement with a grizzly bear clan in North America for me to accept one of their females and send him one of mine so that we may crossbreed and keep our bloodlines strong. I think you would be the perfect woman to send to the United States."

He wanted to send her to a grizzly clan. Had he missed the whole point about her bear being unacceptable to any clans?

Arguments rolled up her throat, ready to burst forth, but when she heard him say United States, her mind changed direction. She'd been studying English and French since turning fifteen, so that she could one day leave here for Canada. If he made the deal with full knowledge of her being a half-breed, then any complaint would be laid at his feet.

Cautious, she rattled off her concerns in Russian. "How can you do this? I would need papers."

"I have already arranged for documents."

"Legal documents," she clarified.

"Yes, legal. I know someone in that country who has a unique relationship with the US government. He can clear a shifter coming in with something of value to offer. You speak English and French, if I am correct."

"Yes." She frowned. How did he know that?

He continued, "If you fulfill the agreement I have negotiated with him and show that you can be useful as shifter translator, your full citizenship would be processed after one year. You would be allowed to remain on special visa until then."

Her heart picked up its thumping, but with a renewed sense of hope. Then that little voice piped up, the one reminding her how men had never been trustworthy.

"To expedite your healing, I will send my healer to you tonight," he added.

Would the healer expect her to shift?

Her bear growled. *Yes. Hurt.*

She would pacify her irritable bear once this was done. She could not make a mistake and end up in a strange land with a child and no way to care for him.

Elianna said, "I will need our clothes and money."

"Everything has been gathered from your apartment and your clothes will be delivered tonight to a location I have where the healer can tend to you. I will make arrangements for ... your mother."

She studied his face for any sign of regret or remorse.

The hard eyes of a ruler, who would show no weakness in front of his men, stared back at her. He asked, "Do you wish to be present when we burn the body?"

No, she did not want the stench of burning body to be the last reminder of her mother. She already knew the smell of her mother's blood and death, and would carry that with her forever. But she chose to think of her mother as the young, happier woman she'd been when they'd lived in the north, long before coming to this place chasing this man.

That woman had been gone for a long time.

Holding her head as still as she could so the pain did not blind her, Elianna said, "I do not. I accept your generous offer. Now, if you will help me to this protected location where I will meet your healer, and bring Nico to me, you will not have to ever see me again."

Alexandre became suspiciously quiet, so much so that his men were sending guarded glances his way. He said, "It would be dishonorable for me to allow us to part ways before you understand all the terms of our agreement."

That worried her, but Alexandre was known for his word being unquestioned in business deals. He had no reason to lie to her since he held all the power right now.

What had she missed?

CHAPTER 3

Bighorn National Forest, Wyoming

"THIS IS A BAD IDEA."

"You worried the Big Bad Wolf gonna get you, Rory?" Justin asked the more conservative of two teammates walking with him through Bighorn National Forest in northern Wyoming. He shook his head at the jaguar shifter, who could take down one of the bull elk roaming this area.

Rory needed to chill out. It was only Thursday afternoon and they'd probably be here the entire eight days.

Justin couldn't wait to shift. His grizzly bear, Herc, would be in heaven once Justin turned him loose. May had rolled in with plenty of sunshine, but he still welcomed the chill at this elevation.

Herc chuffed a happy noise in agreement.

They both liked it cold.

But in truth, Justin couldn't tamp down the worry niggling at him that this trip would not end happy.

Rory's gaze cut over to Justin when he added, "Even a big-mouth grizzly should be concerned about Adrian's wolf."

Justin sighed. Rory was not helping with all these negative waves, but Mr. Doom and Gloom couldn't tackle a problem until he had pointed out every potential failure.

Justin would not fail Adrian. Neither would these two, but Rory's harping was not helping Justin get past his own concerns.

"Rory's got a point," Cole muttered. The wolf shifter had been on his mobile phone with his mate most of the trip since leaving

Spartanburg, South Carolina, which was understandable. Cole had only recently been mated and grumbled every time he had to leave Tess.

But much as Cole wanted to be snuggled up with his sexy new mate right now, he was just as committed to saving Adrian as Justin and Rory were. Failure meant their boss would have to put Adrian's wolf down, and Justin couldn't face that loss.

Neither could the other two, especially the wolf shifter.

Not after Cole had tried so hard to save Sammy, a Gallize grizzly shifter they had all respected and considered a brother, before the mating curse killed him.

That wasn't entirely true about the curse ending the big grizzly's life, though it had been at the core of Sammy's problems.

The Black River pack of degenerate wolves had accelerated the effects of the curse when they'd used magic and drugs on Sammy. Cole was the last person to talk to Sammy telepathically before Sammy died. They'd both been in animal form. Against their wills, they fought as adversaries in a bloody battle.

Cole had been suffering the mating curse, too, but he'd managed enough control over his wolf to spare Sammy's life even though the big grizzly shifter admitted he couldn't change back to human.

Seconds after that, a Black River wolf killed Sammy.

Losing Sammy had gutted all of them.

As Gallize shifters, they were apex predators at the top of the shifter food chain, with only their boss, the Guardian, above them in power for the most part. He actually called up every Gallize shifter's animal for the first time. Usually that happened after the shifter turned twenty-one. Cole and Sammy had been exceptions. They had been younger. Gallize lived longer than humans, but they were not immortal—or invulnerable.

These days, humans knew about shifters, but very few people of either type knew Gallize shifters existed.

Things had been chaotic enough before five mages joined forces to position themselves as Power Barons, a group not to be crossed. It had been a smart move, and those magic-wielding jerks had manipulated their way into alliances with many countries.

That would be like a hawk forming an alliance with a bunch

of chipmunks. The Power Barons smiled and played nice with humans just to have exclusive access to the databases on any other supernatural beings. If a shifter or some other nonhuman went missing unexpectedly, humans wouldn't look twice at the Power Barons. In fact, they'd probably celebrate thinning the numbers of *others*.

One day, they might realize that to mages, everyone else was classified as *others*. Including humans.

Justin would never want to deal with the scheming Power Barons in person, which was not a problem as long as the Guardian ruled Gallize shifters.

In an attempt to push everyone back in a better mental direction, Justin asked, "Either of you have any idea at what age Adrian met his wolf?"

"No," Rory said. "Adrian never said much to me about his early days."

Cole interjected, "Sammy once told me he'd been the first one to train Adrian, like Sammy trained me. He claimed Adrian had been full of himself at twenty-one, so I'd guess he shifted into his wolf by twenty at the latest."

"Sammy would have been the one to drop that wolf a notch," Rory said in his quiet way, always a bit of reserve in his voice.

After a quiet moment passed, Cole's grim look eased with a smile born of memories. "No doubt. Sammy kicked my wolf's crazy butt over and over until I finally gained control." Cole's throat bobbed with a hard swallow. "I do miss that bear."

"Me, too," Justin murmured and Rory nodded.

Sammy had been the one to save Cole, who had fought against his wolf from day one. Cole had no idea he was anything but human until he took off in a panicked run one night during college. The Guardian had been keeping tabs on Cole and ordered him brought in. Then the Guardian called up Cole's wolf and forced the change, as he had for all of them. Cole had not reacted well, completely opposite to how Justin viewed meeting his bear.

Justin had experienced a sense of peace for the first time in his life upon shifting to Herc, because he'd been the odd Gallize actually born into a grizzly shifter clan.

That had sucked big-time.

Where his clan mates had shifted the first time as young children, he couldn't. He'd tried over and over again. He'd had no idea he needed the Guardian's help, since most shifters knew nothing about the Gallize. Day after day of being ridiculed as the only male in Clan Boudreaux who could not shift had slowly destroyed his confidence.

Teenage grizzly females snubbed him, unwilling to even date. What was the point when they would never mate with someone like Justin?

No man had been happier than Justin to join the League Of Gallize Shifters when he changed for the first time, not only to a super-sized grizzly bear, but one with extra power when he needed it.

But Cole had wanted no part of being a shifter, and his wolf hadn't liked him any better.

The Guardian had faced the unenviable task of putting down Cole if Sammy had not stepped in to save the wolf shifter.

That was how they all rolled. They had no clan, pack or whatever. The shifters in their group watched out for each other in their brotherhood.

"Why'd you ask about Adrian's age when his wolf was called up?" Cole asked. "Adrian is closing in on twenty eight. You worried about the mating curse?"

Rory kicked a rock and kept walking. "That would be the cherry on top, wouldn't it?"

"I think we're good with that for right now," Justin countered, hoping to diffuse any new negative suggestions on Rory's part. "I'm just thinking if we could get Adrian close enough to function out in the world, maybe a mate would help him over the last hurdle."

"I don't know." Cole stared into the distance. "Meeting a mate is amazing ... and stressful. With very little information available after the Gallize females lost their guardian, it's hard to know what the hell is going on when you meet a potential mate. I'm not sure putting Adrian in that position would help him any time soon."

Justin found that comment interesting, and would press Cole later for more information about his first encounter with Tess.

Every Gallize male faced a curse placed on him by a pissed-off dark witch. That had happened many centuries ago, back when a Gallizenae druidess was handpicking five pregnant women whose male babies were blessed as the first generation of Gallize shifters.

She also chose five women carrying female babies to birth the first Gallize females, who were *not* shifters, though they did receive powers from the blessing. But not even Justin's Guardian could tell his men what abilities to expect, so Cole did have a point.

The curse was no myth.

Justin had seen it firsthand.

Over a period of weeks, Sammy and Cole had both deteriorated, with their animals gradually taking control.

Cole's mate saved him, which had not been as simple as it sounded.

Still, now that Justin thought about it, he questioned whether the torture and abuse Adrian had suffered at the hands of an enemy overseas might have triggered the mating curse.

Damn, he hoped not.

Cole said, "We need to find mates for you two and soon."

Rory made a scoffing noise. "I'm in no hurry."

"Why not?"

"I like being a bachelor with no ties."

Justin glanced at Cole, who met his gaze with a frown because Rory had just lied. But neither of them would call him on it.

The introspective cat shared nothing until he was ready.

Shrugging as if Rory's comment hadn't mattered, Cole said, "You're missing out. I love every minute of having a mate."

"Oh, sure, rub it in our faces that you're getting laid around the clock," Justin teased. He'd love a mate, too, but he had serious doubts about ever bringing Herc to the table for that decision. He wouldn't choose one his bear didn't accept, and Herc hadn't liked any Justin had met.

Stretching his arms over his head, Cole muttered, "It's taking forever to get inside the ward this way."

"Hey, what are you complaining about? I'm the one toting a loaded backpack," Justin tossed out.

"Like you even notice that weight," Cole countered. "If you can't manage, ask Herc to carry it. He probably needs the exercise."

"Let's get inside the ward and shift so Herc can show Gray Wolf how his claws and fangs are in top shape."

"Bring it, bear." Cole grumbled, "Whose idea was it to park half the world away and walk five miles to get to the ward entrance?"

Rory actually snickered. "My idea. Being mated has made you soft."

"Fuck you, cat."

"Take him up on it, Rory," Justin quipped. "That's the only action you're gonna get with your sour attitude."

Cole suggested, "Or you could pour whiskey over your hand to get your usual date drunk."

Justin laughed.

Rory called Cole a colorful name and gave Justin his middle finger, then chuckled.

Justin warned, "Don't be saying I'm number one to you, or you'll make your left hand jealous."

Rory huffed out a long breath. "I deserve bonus time off for putting up with you two. I can't wait to see the woman who can put up with your shit, bear."

Justin grinned, just to piss off the cat. At least Rory had stopped complaining about Adrian's wolf opening a can of whoop-ass on his jaguar. "You two girls still shaking in your boots about Adrian's wolf?"

Rory didn't answer. Instead he made a gravelly, rumbling sound deep in his throat.

Cole gave Justin a you-just-have-to-be-a-dick look.

Laughing, Justin said, "Damn, when did the two of you turn into pussies?"

Cole sent him a repeat glare.

Rory let out a loud snarl.

Just to poke at their pride, Justin said, "'Cause if you're having second thoughts, just say so. Herc and I can whip Adrian's wolf into shape."

That brought on even louder cursing. Cole said, "I'm not bailing out, asshole."

Rory mumbled, "What he said, dickhead bear."

Now that he had their full attention, Justin stopped kidding around and asked, "You do think Adrian can fix his wolf, right?"

Cole cut a steely gaze over at Justin, then shoved his hands in his pants pockets and looked forward again. "I don't know, man. I'm in all the way to do whatever it takes to save him, but I still remember when we brought Adrian to this place and how he looked when we left him here. I've sent messages for the past ten days and gotten no replies. It's not like he can't get them. The Guardian set up a satellite link so he'd have internet service for his mobile phone and he's got a generator with plenty of fuel."

Justin hooked his thumbs in the corners of his front jeans pockets and walked down a slope to the ward entrance that had been set between two old oak trees. "I hear you, Cole, and agree Adrian should have answered you. He might not have spent much time in the cabin, though. He spent three years overseas without creature comforts and I'm thinking he might not like being inside a building even for a little bit."

"Especially after being held prisoner," Rory said, then added a sobering point. "It's time to stop dancing around the topic and just say it out loud. If Adrian has remained in his wolf form this whole time, we may be facing an impossible task."

True, but Justin had sensed a longing in Adrian when the Guardian had granted him this time to regain control of his wolf. Of course, that had happened only after the three of them argued on Adrian's behalf and asked for a chance to work with him.

Adrian had been ready to submit to the Guardian.

In his shoes, Justin would have been, too, but that's why they were a brotherhood, more than just friends.

Adrian had been on a mission when he infiltrated enemy territory alone to rescue a female fox shifter hostage, but it had been a trap.

The enemy used a missile to hit the helo extracting them just as the bird lifted off.

Everyone died except Adrian.

When he came to a day later, he'd suffered major broken bones and internal damage besides bleeding external wounds.

Even worse, he had no way to shift and heal.

They'd locked him inside a cage three feet on all sides and constructed of titanium. They fed him just enough raw meat to keep him alive.

His claws and fangs would extend then retract. He said sometimes his limbs would partially shift into a hideous half form.

The Guardian had warned all of them to never stop partway into a shift, going either direction, or they faced the possibility of being stuck and turning their animal rabid.

Cole and Rory had grown up thinking they were human and had not known about that potential problem until after they shifted the first time. On the other hand, Justin had grown up being taught to never shift partway. It hadn't mattered, not until meeting his bear.

He would never do that and put Herc at risk.

They were a tight pair. Herc had covered Justin's butt more than once while they were overseas in military operations.

But Adrian had no choice in the partial shifting, which erupted unexpectedly while he'd been captured. The only good news about his body shifting just one part at a time was that Adrian had survived. His wolf had been far too big to fit inside the tiny space. If he'd shifted fully inside that small titanium box, he wouldn't have made it back to human.

The result, though, had been severely damaging his wolf.

Justin got sick to his stomach with guilt every time he thought about what had happened to Adrian.

It was Justin's fault. He should have been on that mission, not his wolf shifter teammate. But Justin's mother had died and the Guardian felt it was important for Justin to attend the funeral held by Clan Boudreaux. His boss knew Justin had turned his back on that clan after years of misery among those people, a lot of it from his mother.

Justin went to the funeral.

Adrian got captured.

Adrian's wolf went mad the first week of being in that cage.

When Justin and the team finally tracked down the rebels holding Adrian, they annihilated the entire camp and got their Gallize brother back. Transporting him home required heavy sedation. During the flight, he shifted every few hours while still knocked out. Rory worked on setting bones and monitoring his health, but nobody could touch his mind.

Upon seeing the Guardian again, Adrian immediately demanded to be put down or freed.

He would not accept being locked in a Gallize training facility to work through control issues.

The Guardian refused to allow any Gallize shifter with no control and capable of massive slaughter to move among unprotected humans.

Justin and the guys argued at the top of their lungs on Adrian's behalf.

The Guardian finally agreed to allow Adrian to run free on these twelve hundred acres of federal land in Wyoming. Their boss had a unique relationship with important humans high in US government as well as counterparts in other countries who knew about the Gallize.

That would be a very *small* number of humans even though, as of eight years ago, the world was aware that shifters existed.

Those officials trusted the Guardian to ward this area in a way that put no humans at risk.

Justin walked up to the twenty-foot-wide space between two imposing oak trees that stood tall as natural guards.

He passed through first, feeling a tingle from the ward magic. Cole and Rory entered right behind him.

The ward shimmered when it recognized them. Any Gallize and natural animal could enter, and Justin's group could leave, but Adrian couldn't. Humans would avoid this area and not realize why they'd altered their paths. Supernatural beings who were not Gallize couldn't pass through the ward.

Rory rubbed his arms. "Makes me itch every time I go through that magic."

"Might not be the magic. Maybe you need a flea collar," Cole said in a deadpan voice.

Justin grunted out a laugh, encouraged to see the return of Cole's humor.

He doubted Rory had been born with any.

Rory said, "My cat is itchin' to sharpen his claws when you least expect it."

"Gray Wolf needs the exercise," Cole tossed back. "I hear cat fur makes a soft pillow. Might take you a while to regenerate that though."

"This is gonna be one long fucking week with you two," Justin said, smiling.

"What are you so happy about?" Rory asked. "We have a week

to do the impossible and not even running water. I'll rough it when need be, but I don't mind a nice bed, flat-screen TV and hot meal at night."

Justin argued, "This place is beautiful and full of wild game. We're gonna run and hunt and save a good friend. What's not to be happy about?" Before Rory could answer, Justin added, "Do you good to rough it for a bit. Never know when we'll have to go somewhere nasty again."

"True," Rory conceded.

The breeze carried a fresh evergreen smell and a nice touch of cool air Justin liked *far* more than the hot bayous of Louisiana where he'd spent too many unhappy years. He'd loved this place the minute he saw it. So much natural beauty across the land, with timber sprouting all around them and streams full of fish, then it opened up to an occasional bald hill like the one where the cabin stood.

Mountains climbed to the skies for a breathtaking backdrop.

Justin really hoped Adrian had soaked up the peacefulness here, but even he had doubts about Adrian being ready next week.

When the Guardian agreed to this deal, he added one caveat. Their boss had said, "Adrian has three months to prove he can control his wolf, which is predicated on his showing significant improvement by the time I make my first visit."

That initial review was coming up next week.

Cole stopped with a fist in the air, a sign for all of them to pause. He lifted his head, sniffing.

Rory paused and slowly turned around, taking a closer look at their surroundings.

Justin frowned. "Adrian's scent is everywhere. What're you smelling?"

Rory uttered, "Smoke."

Of the three, Justin had the best sense of smell, seven times that of a bloodhound. "I picked that up way back. Smells like someone burned logs in a fireplace."

"I don't think so," Rory said and pointed.

Following Rory's gaze, Justin saw a tendril of smoke swirling above the treetops. He said, "Shit, that's where the cabin is," and took off.

CHAPTER 4

J USTIN LEAPED OUT IN FRONT of the guys, racing toward the cabin where they'd left Adrian.

Rory passed him. Damn fast-as-hell cat.

Justin called on more energy, powering up his legs to hang with Rory, but Cole pulled ahead, too. That wolf was quick, but he now benefited from the power of being mated.

Bears weren't built to be speedsters.

Justin managed to keep those two in sight. Since Cole and Rory had exceptional shifter hearing, Justin didn't have to yell when he said, "No one made any plans for a damned forest fire. What if this place had burned to the ground before we showed up? Adrian couldn't get past the ward."

"The Guardian would know," Rory answered over his shoulder, then swatted branches out of the way when he peeled off the winding path that stretched another mile. Instead, he cut through the woods, taking the straightest route to the cabin.

"How could the Guardian know?" Justin understood his powerful boss had gifts and abilities they had yet to see, but to know what happened here when the Guardian was normally in a suite high above the Baltimore coast was crazy.

Cole answered, "When we got back from dropping Adrian off, I asked the Guardian if ..." He jumped over two trees fallen across each other, landed in a gully and bounced up out of it.

Damn limber wolf.

Justin did a respectable job of leaping over the same downed trees, then shoved two small saplings aside to clear the way. He might not be cat or wolf fast, but he could plow through practically anything.

When Cole didn't finish his sentence, Justin pressed, "And what, wolf?"

"I asked if there was any danger for Adrian being here alone. The boss said no, that he would sense a significant disturbance in the land."

Always something new to learn about their boss.

Rory and Cole burst through the trees and stumbled to a stop with echoes of, "Shit."

Stench of burned wood clouded the air.

Justin caught up and slowed to pause next to them. His heart sank. Only a pile of charred wood remained where the cabin had been on top of a gently rising hill with a stunning view.

Rory suggested, "It could have been lightning."

Cole shook his head. "Nope. See that charred fuel can? This smells tainted like petroleum was involved."

"Good thing the Guardian had the land cleared far enough away to not start a massive forest fire."

Justin rubbed the back of his neck where it twitched with a bad feeling. If Adrian had actually been inside and kept a fire going, his wolf *could* have dragged that fuel can to the flame. "This pretty much screws next week's meeting with the Guardian."

Always the levelheaded one, Rory said, "Let's not jump to conclusions. There may be an acceptable reason for this."

And there was the about-face from Rory's earlier doom-and-gloom attitude, because that was classic Rory. He'd first list out all the possible negatives to a mission, then jump in to figure a way around them.

Justin walked to his right and uphill, for a better view of what was left. He couldn't imagine any acceptable reason for this destruction and knew Adrian was not there.

First of all, he couldn't smell burned flesh or fur.

Plus, over the past few years, Adrian had preferred sleeping outside.

All of that led to one conclusion. Justin said, "He burned it. You know he did."

No one argued.

"Where do you think he is now?" Rory asked.

That would be the million-dollar question. Justin had been

scenting Adrian's wolf even more heavily in the woods they'd raced through, which meant Adrian had probably been spending a lot of time in animal form.

A sick feeling tumbled through Justin. What if Rory hadn't just been hung up on negative possibilities and Adrian really had remained in wolf form the entire time here?

What if he couldn't shift to human?

Of course, that would mean Adrian *hadn't* burned the cabin.

The approaching sound of thundering hooves suddenly pierced the calm.

Cole jerked to his left. "What the fuck?"

Rory started yanking off his shirt. "Whatever it is, I'm not ... "

A herd of cow elk stampeded up the dirt road that belched out right before the hill where the cabin had stood. Justin and the guys would have entered from there if they hadn't pulled off the trail.

The minute the herd burst into the open space, they spread out, turning into a blob of gray-brown fur and pounding hooves.

Justin had seconds to dive to the right and roll out of the way as the herd parted around the cabin ruins.

Cole and Rory had taken off and shifted on the run. They split up, leaping to top speed ahead of deadly hooves.

The chaos pounded away as quickly as it had appeared.

Justin dusted himself off and walked over to see where they all went, but caught a sudden strong scent of Adrian's wolf, Red.

He turned slowly to see the wolf chasing a straggler into the clearing, which answered any question about who had started that stampede.

Red had once possessed a deep-rust-colored coat, but after the torture, his coat had changed to a lighter champagne hue, as had Adrian's hair. In human form, he now had silver locks mixed with his natural auburn even though he was only twenty-seven.

Cole had a beast of a wolf known as Gray Wolf, but Adrian's was no slack at two hundred and seventy pounds, and standing four feet tall at the shoulder.

Adrian's wolf snapped at the hind legs of a young cow that was half the size of the herd mates who had left her in their dust.

Guess elk don't hold to the no-man-left-behind rule.

In a lunge, the wolf locked his jaws on the hindquarters of the cow, pulling it to a stop.

Justin remained perfectly still as Adrian's wolf battled with a two-hundred-plus-pound female elk unwilling to give in.

Everything was going fine until Cole returned in wolf form and came trotting around the burned structure. He'd had no way to see Adrian and the elk until it was too late.

Justin couldn't warn the other two unless he shifted to his bear. The Gallize shifters could talk mind to mind only when in animal form.

Adrian's wolf released the elk and snarled viciously at Gray Wolf for daring to enter his territory.

Damn. Justin walked forward one slow step at a time and kept his voice soothing. "Easy, Red. Easy, Adrian. You know us. We're not intruders."

Thankfully, Cole's animal had frozen the minute he realized the problem.

The ravaged, but still alive, cow limped off, now forgotten by Adrian's wolf, which continued to stare at Gray Wolf with dead eyes. Tufts of the light gold fur along Red's shoulders continued to stand in a sure sign that this was going downhill fast.

"Adrian," Justin kept trying in a calm voice. "Look at me, buddy. We're your friends."

When Red turned his head to Justin, eyes filled with rage met his.

No one home.

Gray Wolf advanced slowly. Cole would be doing that with intentions of watching Justin's back, as they all did for each other.

But that small motion yanked Adrian's wolf back to his initial target. Growling an unholy sound, Red launched himself at Gray Wolf, who accepted the challenge and met him halfway.

"Fuck! Back off, both of you!" Justin yelled.

No one paid him any attention.

Claws and fangs ripped up muscles on both wolves. Cole had only recently regained control of his animal and probably figured Red needed a beat down, but if no one stopped them, one would die.

Red would not pull back from a kill though, where Cole would. Sammy's death was still too fresh for all of them, but especially Cole.

He wouldn't let Gray Wolf kill Red, but Red wouldn't be as accommodating.

Ripping clothes half off, Justin called up his grizzly.

He was not losing two friends this way.

Shifted, Justin's bear lifted on his hind legs to stand over ten feet tall. Herc unleashed a roar that would send most animals running for their lives, but these two didn't even pause. Fuck.

He stepped forward, hoping he didn't have to kill one to save the other.

CHAPTER 5

Ⓐ

WITH HERC IN THE LEAD, Justin let his bear choose where to enter the fierce battle between Cole's and Adrian's wolves. Herc dropped down to walk on all four legs as he approached the brawl.

Now that they could speak telepathically in animal form, Cole called out to Justin. *I can't stop Red unless I go for his jugular.*

I know. Back off and let me have a go at him.

Gray Wolf snarled and still fought, snapping his jaws, but it was clear *that* wolf was under control, where Adrian's wolf battled like a rabid animal. When Red spun around and slammed Gray Wolf hard, knocking him sideways, Justin shouted at Cole, *Now!*

Gray Wolf continued to roll away from the hit, then came up on all fours, head down, fangs still bared.

Justin sighed.

He hadn't expected Gray Wolf to just saunter off, but that action demanded a response.

Adrian's wolf dropped back on his hind legs to leap at Gray Wolf for round two.

Time for a workout, Herc, Justin silently told his bear. Herc was the shortened version of Hercules, which Sammy had named the grizzly the first time he met Justin's bear.

As Adrian's wolf lunged up and out, Herc picked up speed and crashed into the wolf, knocking Red into a ball of legs and bloodied fur bouncing over the ground.

Lifting his head, Herc roared a challenge.

Justin approved. He and his bear had been through difficult battles together that most people couldn't imagine. They worked as one with Justin taking the lead when the human side held the advantage and Herc doing the heavy lifting when muscle and power ruled.

Adrian's wolf shook off the vicious hit and rounded on Justin, who called out to his friend mind to mind. *Adrian, it's me, Justin. Have you forgotten your friends?*

Silence answered him.

Shit, yet another bad sign.

Herc remained standing on all four legs, rocking his head back and forth, huffing.

That only meant he was ready to brawl.

If Herc started popping his jaws and snorting, well, that was a polite warning for his opponent to throw in the towel.

Unfortunately, none of them had a towel handy in their animal forms and Adrian's wolf didn't show any sign of backing off.

Justin, Cole called to him. *You can't trust that wolf not to rip your throat out. I sent word to Rory to go back to the truck and get a tranq.*

Herc kept his gaze pinned on the wolf creeping toward him as Justin replied, *By the time Rory can get a tranq and return, this will be over, so call him back, but tell him not to walk out here as a jaguar. We may need his medical expertise to keep one or both of us alive.*

I'm coming back into the fight then, Cole warned.

Stand down, Cole. I got this.

That sounded pretty damn good for a bald-faced lie.

Justin wasn't sure how he was going to manage preventing Adrian's wolf from ripping all of them apart, and at the same time, not kill his friend or get Herc's throat torn open.

Herc made a rumbling noise Justin had come to think of as his bear chuckling, if bears chuckled.

Herc was just letting Justin know he had no intention of dying today.

Justin tried once more to reach his friend. *Adrian, make your wolf stop attacking so we can ...*

The wolf in discussion went from zero to sixty in seconds, snarling as he dodged to the side and leaped on top of Herc.

That was a bad idea.

Reaching around with jaws that could crush the wolf's head, Herc snapped at the wolf that was digging claws into his back.

Fuck, that hurt.

Justin's bear lifted up on his hind legs, shaking back and forth to loosen the wolf's hold. It seemed to work as the wolf slid down, dragging his claws as he did.

When the wolf landed on the ground again, Herc dropped back to all four legs and lurched around to face his attacker.

Adrian's wolf had been ready and ran in a circle, chasing behind Herc and avoiding being bitten. When the bear stopped to turn in the other direction, the wolf locked his jaws on one of Herc's hind legs, crunching hard, trying to break bone.

Herc bellowed with anger, kicking at the wolf's head, but that wouldn't make him let go. Jerking his huge bear body around in a circle, he dragged the wolf, which kept his jaws clamped hard on Herc's leg.

But that left the wolf's hind legs exposed.

In a move Justin considered one of Herc's signature counterattacks, the bear latched onto the wolf's outstretched leg.

Where Adrian's wolf couldn't break Herc's bones, the bear had no trouble cracking bones in the wolf's leg. A howling scream broke loose when the wolf released Herc's.

Adrian's wolf whined, howled and hobbled around on three legs, but still not giving up.

Justin's bear waited, huffing in short breaths from the exertion, but Herc had yet to fully tap the load of power he possessed.

When the wolf didn't attack again immediately, Justin kept trying to reach Adrian's mind. *Talk to me, buddy. I know you're in there and your wolf is hurting. Let's stop and fix your leg.*

Limping forward, the wolf had his head slumped down in submission.

Herc waited as the whimpering wolf crept closer.

Justin's bear stood much taller than the wolf, which allowed the wolf a perfect position to rip out Herc's throat.

Justin, back off! Cole shouted in his head.

He ignored Cole, letting Herc handle it.

His bear dipped his head to one side at the same second the wolf lunged. Herc swung that massive head right back and whacked the wolf's head with a sickening crack.

Adrian's wolf sidestepped, shook its head and tried to stay upright.

That damn wolf had a death wish.

It started forward again in a stuttering gait, holding its rear leg off the ground.

Herc lifted up on his hind legs and roared an even louder warning that he ruled this battle.

The wolf wobbled and fell onto its side, bleeding profusely from when he'd fought Gray Wolf and now with a crushed back leg plus a possible concussion.

Did that matter to Herc?

No. Justin's bear dropped down again and stepped over to place a foot on the wolf's neck, drawing a weak snarl from Adrian's wolf. Herc kept up the pressure, pushing just short of crushing the wolf's throat.

This time, when the wolf whined as if begging, it was an honest sound.

Herc removed his massive paw from the beaten wolf and sat back on his butt.

Rory came striding into view, wearing his jeans and no shirt. He tossed a pair of jeans at Cole.

Justin thanked Herc for a good job and for not killing the wolf, then he asked to shift back.

His bear snorted. *Play time.*

Only Herc would think that had been an easy battle. The change flowed over Justin, which sounded simple and smooth, when in truth it sometimes hurt like a bitch. Like now, when his back had been clawed and his leg was bleeding and already starting to swell, though thankfully not broken.

Cole had shifted back to human form and put on his jeans.

He stepped over to give Adrian's wolf a long look.

Rory took a spot on the other side of Justin and said, "I don't think there's enough of your jeans left to make jorts."

"Jorts?" Justin gave him a look of confusion he normally reserved for human guys who tried to pick a fight with him.

"You know. A cross between jeans and shorts."

Another deep voice said, "You should be embarrassed to admit even knowing that term, Rory."

Justin looked over to find a naked and bloody Adrian lying on his side, with a bushy beard and head of hair that belonged on Big Foot.

He winced at Adrian's mangled leg and asked, "How's your

head?"

"Feels like someone used it as a wrecking ball."

"That's because you're so damned hardheaded," Justin growled.

Rory dropped down to look at Adrian's leg. "Leg looks like it went through a blender."

Adrian gritted out, "Yep."

"You should shift back to heal it faster."

"Nope. If I do, that fucker will attack all of you even without a fourth leg."

Rory cursed under his breath. "Stay stretched out and I'll do what I can."

"Yep."

Justin exchanged a quick look with Cole while those two talked, if you considered Adrian's one-word answers conversational. From the sick expression on Cole's face, he was having the same thoughts as Justin.

Adrian was nowhere close to being ready for his meeting with the Guardian next week.

Cole asked, "What's going on with Red?"

Adrian hung his head, staring at the hard ground. "There's still a big disconnect between us." Looking up, he said, "I've been letting him run free and have his head. I thought we were starting to find a happy medium, not fixed, but one step toward getting better. The minute my wolf scented Gray Wolf, he shut me out. I tried to stop him. That lack of control ... sucks." Glancing over at Cole, he said, "You know what I'm talking about, right?"

"What do you mean?"

"Dude, you were showing signs of the mating curse when you were here that first week with me."

Cole nodded. "Oh, yeah, you're right. It does suck, but I didn't realize you knew."

"I wasn't sure, but you were guarded about releasing your wolf when we got here. That's why I told all of you to leave. If you had issues with your wolf and mine was insane, we might have bled everyone dry."

Cole rubbed his forehead. "I was jacked up back then, but Gray Wolf and I are connected now in a way we've never been."

Adrian gave Cole a long look. "I'm guessing you're mated."

"Yes," Cole acknowledged, sounding uncomfortable to talk

about Tess.

Justin got it. Cole didn't want to make a big deal out of it when none of them had a potential mate on the horizon.

"Don't, Cole," Adrian cautioned.

"What?"

"Don't feel bad about the rest of us. I'm glad you've got someone. It gives everyone hope."

Giving a nod, Cole said, "How'd you know about the curse starting for me, though?"

"I couldn't figure out, at first, why you wouldn't let Gray Wolf run when you were here. But then I remembered you guys kept trying to talk my ear off on the flight here and—"

"You could have talked," Rory pointed out.

"I would have if I'd wanted to." Adrian stared off, then came back to what he'd been saying. "Anyhow, right before you dropped me off, Cole said Sammy was suffering the mating curse and had gone dark on everyone. Considering how Cole and Sammy had unusual situations when their animals were called up and adding that to Cole not wanting to let his wolf out to run ... I made an educated guess." Casting a sharp look in Cole's direction, Adrian said, "Your wolf is tougher than before. What beefed up Gray Wolf? The mating?"

Cole lifted an eyebrow and smiled. "What? Worried I'm going to let Gray Wolf kick Red's ass?"

Justin frowned at Cole's use of the nickname for Adrian's wolf. Adrian hadn't called his wolf by name since being rescued overseas.

Maybe Cole was doing the right thing and it would be good to start using Red's name.

Adrian gave a dark chuckle. "Nope. My wolf doesn't have the sense to fear anything, because he's in kill mode twenty-four seven. I was fighting my wolf just as hard as Gray Wolf was. If I had let go of the reins, my beast would have slaughtered everything in sight." Adrian cut his eyes back at Justin. "He'd have a harder time with Herc, but you have no idea just what I'm holding back when he's in the lead."

Shit, that sounded even worse than Justin had thought.

Still, Adrian cocked a quizzical look at Cole. "But you're packing—" He jerked and sucked in a breath. Muscles across his body bulged.

Rory murmured, "Sorry, man."

Adrian caught his breath, then let the air out. "It's fine." He finished telling Cole, "You've got more punch than before and your wolf is ... intense. That happened with just mating?"

Justin spoke up before Cole could. "That miserable fucker got himself a mate all right. A Gallize female no less."

If Justin hadn't been sitting right in front of Adrian, he'd have missed the subtle shift in his friend's face. Cole stood to the side and Rory was focused on the crushed leg, so neither of them could have seen the moment when something unexpected bloomed in Adrian's face.

Hope.

His friend had been ready to end it all when he came home.

Did he think a mate would help him heal?

"How'd you find her?" Adrian asked, that slim shimmer of optimism brightening his eyes.

Cole sat down on the ground and crossed his legs. "I met her in college, fell in love back then, and you guys found me the night I was going to ask her to marry me. I had no idea she was a Gallize. Then I ended up captured by her SCIS team in the middle of a mission."

"You're not saying she works for that stupid Shifter Criminal Investigation Service, are you?"

"Yep. The very one."

"How'd they catch you?"

"I walked in on a bomb. It blew and I woke up locked in their facility."

Adrian muttered a vile curse.

Justin added, "We're gonna need beer to give you all the details."

"You're SOL then," Adrian said, sighing when Rory sat back from fooling with his leg.

"Guess again, sucka." Justin laughed and pointed at his back-pack. "You didn't think I would waste space to haul something like food up here, did you?"

That brought out a smile, not the real one Adrian used to wear when they were clanging mugs in a bar and talking about women, but better than Justin had seen in a while.

Evidently, Adrian wasn't done with Cole. "Is bonding with a Gallize everything we've heard about for years?"

Cole eyed Adrian with a solemn expression. "Yes. It was enough to bring me back from death."

"No shit?"

Rory nodded. "It's true. I saw it. She's just a little bitty woman, but she stood up to the Guardian—got all up in his face, even— and *refused* to let Cole die."

Adrian studied Cole with a bit of awe.

Cole said, "All true, but I don't recommend the dying part. Hurts like a bitch. Still, I'd go through that and more just to be with her."

There was a man who had everything he needed when he looked at his future wife. If Justin didn't care so much for this group, he could enjoy a good bout of hate. He'd admit to a twinge of envy, but he could not be happier for Cole and Tess.

Sadly, he didn't hold out much hope of finding that perfect mate.

Cole had never talked about Gray Wolf's opinion when it came to mates, but his wolf clearly accepted Tess.

Herc, on the other hand, had a definite opinion on mates and narrow criteria for acceptability.

They were all quiet a moment and Adrian said, "Good for you. Maybe the rest of you will find one, too."

Cole's smile fell at Adrian excluding himself.

Justin said, "The rest of *us*, asshole. Stop counting yourself out."

Making a snorting noise, Adrian said, "We all know I have to face the Guardian next week. He's allowed me time to get my wolf straightened out. Believe me when I say I've tried, but I'm not going to sit here and lie to you three. I'm not making progress. If I can't stop my wolf from attacking you, I have no hope to keep him from going after the Guardian's throat. We all know that will last about a half second."

"That's why we're here," Rory interjected. "We're going to get you in shape."

Adrian took in each face. "You guys ... I, uh, shit. I can't undo what was done to me in that cage. You can't either."

"Don't make me wake up Herc," Justin warned. "I'm not here

to lose. We. Don't. Lose." That was a motto the four of them had repeated when shit got deep in war zones.

"You're stuck with us for eight days," Cole said, giving no room to argue.

"I have some research," Rory added. "I've got a couple ideas I want you to consider."

There was the Rory that jumped in to save everyone.

Frowning, Adrian asked, "What about the Black River Wolf Pack cases? When you left here you were headed to Spartanburg."

"We shut down one division and the Guardian pulled in another team specifically to flush out channels the Black River pack is using to distribute Jugo Loco," Cole explained, referencing the crazy juice the Black River pack was giving to shifters. "After we busted the group in Spartanburg, we all realized this network is even larger than we suspected."

"So instead of being with your new mate, or these two off looking for mates, you're here?"

Rory stared off at the horizon where low clouds floated by. "It'd be easier to find a unicorn."

That damn Rory. Justin turned to him. "Not true, dickhead."

"The Guardian can't find them," Rory argued. "The females no longer have a guardian overseeing them the way ours watches over us. There may be hundreds or there may not be ten females in the whole world. We have no way to recognize one."

Man, talk about a downer. Lifting his hand to count, Justin said, "Sure we do. Their eyes could be two different colors. They're always born in a true blue moon month. They're always the second born in a family. They have ... gifts."

"See? You don't even know what that means. What kind of gifts?"

Justin looked to Cole, who lifted his shoulders in an I-got-nothin' response until Justin gave him a darker glare.

Growling, Cole said, "I haven't wanted to say much about this when all I have is speculation, but there *were* some noticeable signs if I had recognized them. Until I had time to think about it over the past few weeks and talk to Tess, I didn't realize that my mate's Gallize power was actually calling to my power back when I first met Tess. We both thought we were humans then.

How would we know?"

"That is crazy," Rory murmured.

Cole said, "Even when I was reunited with Tess, I thought it was just the mating bond trying to connect, but it was more. I think you'll get a sense of a Gallize woman's power when you're around her ... *if* she's to be your mate."

Adrian rolled over on his back, still naked and not caring any more than the rest of them. He tossed an arm over his eyes. "I don't need all three of you here. Why don't you draw straws and see who gets stuck. The other two can go back."

Justin, Cole and Rory said, "No."

Cursing, Adrian said, "I can't unleash my wolf with more than one of you shifted at a time. The other two are going to be sitting on their butts. Don't ask me why. I'm telling you it's worse to have more than one of you in animal form."

The satphone holstered on Rory's hip played an alert tone. He answered, paused and said, "Yes, sir." Then he handed the phone to Justin.

Lifting the receiver to his ear, Justin said, "Yes, Guardian," because that was the only person who would be calling on this phone at this moment.

"I'm sorry to interrupt your retreat with Adrian, but something has come up that I need you to do."

"Yes, sir. Whatever you need." Justin had no doubt it was important, because the Guardian was good for his word when he allowed them the time to work with Adrian.

"I've sent one of my company jets to the airport in Sheridan. You need to take it to San Francisco."

Justin knew the airport east of here, from when they'd flown Adrian in, but what the hell was going on in California? Before Justin could ask, the Guardian said, "You'll find a file on the jet to study before you arrive. Are you familiar with the Romanov Kamchatka Clan?"

"The one on the east coast of Russia?" Justin asked, already digging around mentally for information. All he came up with was that the Romanov alpha running the largest grizzly shifter clan in that part of Russia had descended from royalty.

"That one, yes. Their alpha, Alexandre Romanov, is someone I've known a long time and he's handled difficult situations in the past for me. He's sending his firstborn daughter here and has asked for security to escort her to Clan Boudreaux."

Was his boss kidding? Justin managed to keep his voice calm when he asked, "Are you sure I'm the best one to do this?"

"Is there a problem, Justin?"

Answering that the wrong way would not go well.

The Guardian added, "I know you have issues with your clan."

"Former clan. Sir."

"Fine, but this woman will be in a strange country and will need someone familiar with shifters and particularly bear shifters. In addition to that, I considered all three of you and thought you would want Cole and Rory to remain. If I've missed something, please explain."

Justin took in his friends. Cole would be more help than anyone due to being a wolf shifter and having gone through a lack of control. Rory had more medical skills than all of them put together.

Justin's only reason for staying was because he needed to see Adrian succeed.

But he had to trust his team. Clearing his throat, Justin said, "Sorry, sir. I failed to take everything into consideration. I have no problem with delivering her."

"Excellent. I have given my personal guarantee that no harm will come to Romanov's daughter. I believe you're the best suited to handle this task."

"Yes, sir. One more thing. Will she have documents?"

"Absolutely. I have arranged for her entry on this end. You will have her shifter paperwork, plus additional papers such as a shifter ID that identifies Clan Boudreaux as being responsible for her while she is in the US. She's being sent from *Petropavlovsk-Kamchatsky* by ship, which will hand her off to a fishing vessel in international waters. Then she'll be ferried to a personal craft, which will deliver her to docks on the San Francisco Bay."

No one checked a privately owned boat that came and went from the US coast on a regular basis to fish or pleasure ride, unless the owner had raised suspicion at some point.

"What about entering San Francisco territory? Doesn't a wolf alpha run that entire area?" Justin had heard of a wolf pack which had been established in San Francisco long before humans learned that shifters existed. Supposedly, that alpha maintained the city as wolf shifter territory for his pack only, and allowed no other shifters to enter without his permission.

"Yes. I've also made arrangements for you to have twenty-four-hour access without interference from the local shifter group. Contact information is in the file for when you arrive."

Justin knew of other, similar, ways for shifters to enter a new country. He'd used a few of those insertion methods when under-cover.

The Guardian would utilize a network of people above reproach and very likely to be human. The documents Justin referenced were for shifters only, as they had their own set of rules.

With the Guardian making arrangements on this end, she should arrive with no problem.

Great. The sooner she got here, the sooner Justin could dump her at Clan Boudreaux.

"I'll leave right away," Justin said, finishing the call. He handed the phone back to Rory, then stood up. "More beer for all of you, but I'll reload on my way back. You got rid of one of us for a couple days, Adrian, but that's all."

The wolf shifter rolled over on his side again, propping his head on his hand. "You don't sound excited. The Guardian send-ing you back overseas?"

"No, it's worse. I'm escorting a freaking bear clan princess coming for a visit." Justin would rather face a band of armed terrorists than be stuck with a woman who would look down on him the same way his own family had for eighteen years.

Rory grinned. "You're complaining about getting stuck with some hot bear shifter? What if she's the *one*?"

"Trust me. She's not."

"How do you know?"

"She's a Romanov princess and I'm security. Her daddy would lose his mind if she ate a meal with me. Besides, I don't deal with high maintenance women," Justin joked, but that wasn't the real reason he would never end up with a grizzly shifter.

Herc had made it clear long ago that he detested female grizzly shifters. Justin would never take a mate his bear didn't like, so he had little hope of ending up with a mate who could accept the power she'd receive with his bond.

CHAPTER 6

LAND. SOLID AND UNMOVING LAND.
The shore was in sight.

Elianna couldn't wait to stand on firm ground. Her head still swam from being on a ship for six days, then handed off to a fishing trawler, then to a private boat. She'd always loved the water and had never expected to be seasick, but two days out to sea the weather had turned vicious.

She'd thrown up so much that her bear had just hunkered down and gone to sleep. She couldn't have shifted into her animal if the world was coming to an end and that had been the only hope for survival.

At least she'd crossed the ocean with her friend, Captain Lubov, who had explained how she'd be transferred from his ship to two more vessels so that she could arrive in a private craft.

She'd tried to listen to what he said, truly. But they'd been in rough waters already when he started talking, and all she recalled of that conversation was that she'd arrive in the US on Friday.

The water had smoothed out now, but her head still twirled around, unhappy with her.

Now this nice man named Arthur, who said he grew up as a mountain lion but preferred the water to mountains, had spent the day fishing. His deep tan supported his claim to be out on the water every chance he got. He'd chatted all day, explaining how he had to keep up appearances even during times he wasn't out strictly for fishing. Once he caught what he considered to be enough fish, he headed for shore.

His thirty-five-foot boat was nicer than any house Elianna had lived in and he'd told her to make herself comfortable.

She'd curled up on the padded bench seat out in the open and kept quiet as he fished.

Her bear didn't even stir when the man pulled in a nice, fat salmon.

Elianna had eaten crackers earlier. Those came back up.

Late in the afternoon, Arthur said, "I believe we're safe to go in now. Before we reach the docks, I'll slow down so you can change to clothes delivered to me. I was told you would want to blend in."

She didn't care about how she looked, but would not be impolite to this man who functioned as part of the transfer network. People were doing their part to allow her entry to this country.

For them she could be nice. "Thank you."

Alexandre, on the other hand, deserved a claw across the throat. "You're welcome," Arthur said. "I wish you could eat."

"I am fine." Either that or she would die and right now she didn't care. She had been glad to find jeans, running shoes and a lightweight knit pullover to wear.

By the time he motored slowly under the Golden Gate Bridge, which she recognized from pictures as an icon of San Francisco, and maneuvered his yacht into a slip, his boat became a puzzle piece inserted into a marina filled with pleasure boats.

Her heart lifted at being so close to standing on a sturdy dock.

He opened a doorway in the hull and jumped out onto the dock, then offered his hand.

She accepted it, shaking all over. When she turned to take a step, her head and legs had not agreed on which way to weave. Standing there for a moment, she inhaled a deep, calming breath. Her head appreciated it, but her body thought it still moved back and forth in the water.

She didn't care. She was on firm ground again.

Arthur hurried back into the cabin area and retrieved her small suitcase, which held all she had left in the world.

All but Nico.

Her heart squeezed into a painful knot every time she thought about him, which had not stopped since leaving Russia. Alexandre had allowed her to see Nico one last time before boarding the ship.

Her throat closed up, recalling the tiny tears streaming down his face. She'd sworn to him she would not let him down and she would die before breaking that vow.

"Are you okay, Miss?" Arthur asked with a load of concern.

"Yes," she answered, making a point of speaking her English words clearly. She'd soon find out if all her language studies would pay off.

"Need me to carry the case for you?"

"No. I am strong," she said with a smile.

"I know. Just wanted to make sure you're set. I can only dock here for a short time."

She needed no help with lifting something so light, but she owed this man her appreciation. So few men had earned it. "Thank you for smooth ride and help me arrive. All was good."

He beamed. "I'm happy to do my part. I was radioed that your driver is waiting at the top of this walkway. They prefer us to not interact with the next transfer unless there's a problem. Do you want me to walk you up?"

"No. I will find driver."

She glanced around as if searching, but they were over a hundred feet from where people milled around on a walkway above the marina. Seeing between docked boats was not easy.

But Arthur would not leave until she gave him a sign that she saw someone.

She narrowed her eyes even though she saw no one and said, "He is here." She gave a little wave at no one and picked up her suitcase.

"That's just great. Have a good trip." He watched her walk fifteen feet, then climbed back on his boat and started cleaning it up.

Pulling a cheap pair of plastic sunglasses out of her small shoulder bag, Elianna slid them in place. Under different cir-cumstances—and if she felt better—she'd be struggling to hide her excitement over getting her first look at America.

Instead, she was working to quell her anxiety. Taking in a deep breath of the salty air, she moved down the walkway toward the shore.

Halfway there, her legs shook. She stopped and put the suitcase down to gather herself now that she was finally alone.

As she stood there and looked in earnest for anyone who might appear to be waiting on an arrival, she searched the people meandering around an upper walkway that ran along the shore.

Her gaze was drawn to the corner of a building where a large man leaned against the wall with his arms crossed.

He'd been looking out over the marina, but at that moment his gaze latched onto her and would not let go. He stood away from the building, studied her another second, then started straight for her.

Was that her escort?

How could he know she was the one he waited for?

It had to be the clothes she'd put on.

She lifted her case and started moving again. Had the clan sent one of their grizzly shifters for her, or had they sent a human? Some clans had associations with humans, which came in handy for times when they couldn't enter another shifter's territory.

She maintained her calm exterior, but her hands began to sweat and her nerves sent warning signals throughout her body.

She'd agreed to do this.

No going back now even if she could.

The more of the man that came into view, the more she realized he was much larger than she'd first estimated. He had at least eight inches on her, which wouldn't concern her, but someone had found it necessary to fill him out from toe to head with as much muscle as possible. The gray T-shirt and black pants he wore ... fatigues? Yes. They belonged in a military movie.

He held himself and walked as one not to cross or he'd make someone pay.

Above all of that large body, he had short, dark-brown hair. His whiskey-colored eyes were staring holes through her.

Some would say he was pretty.

No. Wrong word. Pretty did not fit him. He was too hard and tense for such a soft word. To call such a man pretty could end with walking away limping.

She dug the word out of her new vocabulary. Attractive.

Yes, that would suit him.

Or it would if not for his angry gaze.

Did he know about her? Had Alexandre told his contact here that she was his bastard and a half-breed on top of that?

No, the Romanov alpha would not admit the bastard part. Only time would tell if he had shared the rest. When there was twenty feet left to reach this man, she put her suitcase down and waited. She would like to find out immediately if he had any prejudice against her.

She had no intention of putting up with being snubbed or talked down to while on her way to the bear shifter clan.

Alexandre must have told them she was not pure grizzly.

This driver did not know her. He should not judge her, but she had yet to meet one grizzly or polar bear shifter who had not.

She inhaled and answered one question.

He was a bear shifter. That made sense. He was probably from the Boudreaux Clan. Had he been informed of her plans?

She'd had only one stipulation as part of this deal.

Alexandre gave his word to her in front of his men and said that he would make sure everything was set when she arrived.

The bear shifter approaching her offered a polite smile that had no heart as he got closer, but he didn't stop several steps before reaching her as she'd expected.

When he was next to her, he leaned down slowly, close enough for her to take in a deep breath of his earthy scent. His distinct smell woke up parts of her that had missed contact with a man.

Her sea-tossed brain did nothing to help her.

She couldn't think of what she'd intended to say only a minute ago.

Grasping the handle on her suitcase, he lifted it and announced, "I'm Justin. I assume you're Elianna."

"Yes." That was a terrible reply. She barely spoke the word. No confidence came through.

An energy hummed through her core with him so close. What was that about?

He lost his smile momentarily, cocking his head to the side, then shook off whatever bothered him and said, "Welcome to our country. Ready?"

His words were polite, but cool.

Motioning with his arm for her to go ahead, he waited for her to move.

She managed a nod and walked forward, feeling like a fool for being rattled so easily. But she had not caused the vibration she still felt tingling in her body.

In Russia, women pulled their own weight, but men carried luggage for a woman as a sign of respect.

She had expected no male bear shifter to do that for her in this country. Clearly her driver had been instructed to show his best manners.

If he treated her politely, she would do no less. Maybe riding with him would not be as stressful as she had been thinking. She could feel him behind her as if his heat reached out and touched her.

She stopped short.

What was she doing, allowing a predator at her back?

"Whoa." He sidestepped past her, swinging the suitcase wide or it would have struck her.

She braced for his anger, which she deserved for almost sending him off the dock.

He looked off into the distance, took a breath and asked her nicely, "Is something wrong?"

When he didn't snap at her, she felt embarrassed and wished for a good night's sleep so she could get her head in a better place.

She owed this man the truth. "I do not like someone behind me."

"Fair enough. What if I walk beside you?"

She didn't understand why he was being so polite when she had sensed that he was not happy to be here. But he had been cordial and she would, too. "Yes. Thank you."

He waited until she took a step and fell in next to her.

She had no trouble staying with him. They both had long legs that covered ground quickly. What did he call himself? Justin.

She hoped he had been informed that she really had to keep to her schedule. If not, his manners might disappear.

Men, especially shifters, cared only about their own schedules.

If he argued, she would ... what would she do? Threaten to return to Kamchatka when she had no way home?

She should not ask for problems before they showed up.

If Justin hesitated to do as she asked, she would simply request to speak to his alpha and clear up any confusion. He would tell Justin that she was in charge until they arrived at the Clan Boudreaux.

Alexandre had said the American alpha was desperate for new blood, especially female.

But would he want tainted blood?

Elianna shoved that thought away. There were many miles to go before she would allow any discussion of mating.

Was that why Justin had been chosen to be her escort? Had he volunteered to retrieve her so that he could get first look at the new female bear shifter? He'd looked at her as if he'd been curious at first, but after a few words he'd said nothing.

Maybe he'd taken a good look and decided she was not for him.

She was not attractive like Justin, but she was not ugly.

Why did she care?

In truth, she wanted no one as a mate, but that decision would be out of her hands soon.

A hand wrapped around her arm, pulling her to a halt. "Careful there," Justin murmured.

At the second he'd touched her, images flew through her mind in a blur of ... running from him.

Or had she been running *with* him?

She jerked her head around to face him, but her gaze had fogged from the momentary vision. She mumbled, "Do not touch me."

He immediately released her, lifting the offending hand as if he'd been scalded. "My bad. I know you'll heal, but I didn't think you wanted to bust your ass out here."

Confused, she blinked her eyes until they cleared, then looked around and realized a set of three stairs rising to the main walkway were inches from her shins.

She'd been so lost in thought about her future, she almost walked into the wooden stairway and would have fallen, just as he said.

What had that vision about the two of them meant?

Was it connected to the one she'd had before leaving Russia, where a bear shifter stood between her and Nico? The images were too confusing and she was too tired to figure out anything.

She would have to think on that later.

Right now she'd made a fool of herself.

What could she say and not admit to being distracted by thoughts of him in a flash of images, which would mark her as even more strange than being a half-breed? The longer she weighed her words, the fewer she came up with that were of any help.

Blowing out a sigh that sounded heavy with hidden frustration, he said, "No big deal. Just be careful walking and I promise not to touch you."

She mentally kicked herself. The people she'd known back home liked her and considered her a nice person.

They would frown at her in disappointment now.

Turning to Justin, she debated taking off her dark sunglasses, but seeing him stare at her odd blue eyes would not help. "I am sorry. It was long trip and big seas. Very bumpy on boat. I am not think clear now. Thank you for make me not bust ... bottom."

He snorted and almost smiled. His mouth didn't want to join in, but his eyes twinkled and in that moment she changed her mind.

He was not attractive. He was beautiful.

She felt like the weathered boards on this dock next to him.

"Apology accepted. Let's get you to the hotel so you can grab a hot bath and something to eat, then sleep in. How does that sound?"

She wanted to argue that she would rather get moving on her schedule, but he was correct. She needed at least one full night's rest to best accomplish her goals, plus he was being very understanding.

That was more than she deserved after snapping at him.

But he was also the man running with her or chasing after her in that vision.

"Yes, I would like," she finally said and turned to take the steps up.

The image played through her mind again, filling her with a sense of unease.

It had only been for a second, but she'd learned the hard way to never ignore any vision.

CHAPTER 7

JUSTIN COULDN'T BELIEVE HE HAD a luxury hotel room on a Friday night in San Francisco. He couldn't appreciate the perk. All he could think about was getting back out to the country with his team.

Any other time he'd check out the ladies.

Not when he had to play bodyguard to a Russian princess.

About that princess ...

He stared at the worn and faded gray suitcase he had placed in the middle of Elianna's beautiful room, which connected to his via a common door.

She'd stepped into the bathroom as soon as they walked in and it sounded as if water ran in the sink.

What kind of princess was sent on a trip with that piece-of-shit bag?

Romanov was a freaking alpha shifter king. His clan had to be loaded.

On the flight here, Justin recalled the time he'd heard all about Romanov and his clan. That was years ago and had been Rory's fault. That egghead lived for research. During a typhoon when they were hunkered down in a Quonset hut in some unholy country, Rory started talking about bear shifter clans. When he hit on Clan Boudreaux and began drilling Justin for information, Justin warned him off the topic of where he'd grown up.

He did not want to relive one minute of his life in that place before he'd turned his back on them and vowed to never return.

Unfazed, Rory had gone off in another direction, talking about the clan on the Kamchatka Peninsula and how it had been the best-kept secret within a royal human dynasty. Evidently, one of the sons with a roaming eye got involved with a woman who turned out to be a grizzly bear shifter. She gave birth to a son and raised the boy in secret, but with the father's knowledge. When it came time to battle the king's enemies, the first Romanov alpha bear shifter became the king's best weapon, with no one knowing the truth about him except his mother and father.

Fast forward a few hundred years and humans learn of shifters among them. As soon as that happened, Romanov declared his clan and that he ruled the Kamchatka Peninsula.

Yep, the princess Justin had to play bodyguard for came from royal blood, which showed. She carried herself with the haughtiness of royalty, but she'd managed to be polite after all.

That was more than he'd expected.

He still didn't understand that ratty suitcase.

The bathroom door opened and her skin had more color, but she still wore sunglasses. He couldn't even see her eyes. Why would it matter? They had to be brown.

She asked in a worried tone, "You are sure this is place I stay?"

Damn, was he going to have to find a suite to appease her? He'd actually asked about one when he arrived, just in case, but the hotel had a conference going on.

Justin explained, "These reservations were made by my boss. I have no say over the type of room you get, but if this is not ... acceptable or big enough or whatever then—"

"What? No. Not what I say."

Justin had been up thirty hours by the time he reached Junction, Wyoming, but he'd planned on drinking beer and trading lies with his buddies tonight.

Instead, he'd jumped on the jet, arrived in San Francisco and taken off in the SUV rental the Guardian had arranged to have waiting. The rush had been due to Justin's need to meet with the local alpha of a powerful wolf shifter pack in San Francisco, to confirm he had entered the alpha's territory. This particular alpha was deadly serious about no unauthorized shifters entering his area, regardless of the animal. Especially wolves from another pack were not allowed.

With being short on sleep and worrying about Adrian, by the time Justin had reached the dock he was not at his best.

But that wasn't the reason he hadn't been his usual jovial self when he met Elianna. He'd carried a preconceived notion about her and now felt guilty over being less than charming.

When he was on his game, women loved his charm.

Pretty women brought it to the surface without him even trying. In spite of being a princess and not showing her eyes, this one was every bit a serious babe.

But that whole royalty crap had screwed with his head.

It wasn't Elianna's fault that everyone had treated him like day-old scraps while he was growing up, and she was obviously trying to be polite.

His screwed-up attitude changed now.

Softening his tone, he addressed her point that he had misunderstood her words. "Okay, then I'm confused, which is my fault for not listening closely. So help me out. What's wrong with the room?"

Her expression would be comical if not for leaving him even more confused. Damn, he really wanted to see her eyes so he could better read her.

She stared at him as if he'd asked whether she wanted to eat a live gator for dinner.

"Nothing wrong. This room ... too much." She glanced over at the door to the large bathroom with a walk-in shower. "I do not share bath?"

Okay, this whole gig was getting weirder by the moment.

And the brains in both of his heads leaped to the idea of sharing a bath with her. She might be polite to the help, but getting naked with him would never happen.

Justin wanted to ask her what kind of palace or home did Romanov run if a princess had to share a bathroom.

Maybe he had a pile of daughters.

Instead, he kept his tone easy going and said, "No, you don't have to share the bathroom while you're here."

The image of water rushing down over her as she lifted her arms to wash her hair flooded his mind. Then she'd turn and smile at him.

Not the time for fantasies, Justin reminded himself.

There was no explaining the way the male brain worked other than admitting to its simplicity. He was in the presence of a sexy woman who had yet to curve her lips up at all and he wanted to make her smile.

And scream.

Stop. Right. There. That thought was way out of bounds. Not for another woman, but he wasn't touching a princess even if she offered it to him, which she clearly wasn't. Also, he did not intend to face the Guardian and explain how he couldn't keep his pants zipped on an assignment.

Hell, this was the most conversation they'd had since he grabbed her arm and she barked at him. That was another thing. When he touched her skin, his hand had tingled. No, it actually *buzzed* with energy like a mild electrical shock.

Not painful, just ... stimulating.

"Do you wait for me?" she asked.

How was it that yet again he felt like an idiot around her? He was just standing there, staring at her as if he'd never seen a woman before.

No wonder she probably thought he was a jerk.

He had been, but no more. "No, I'm not waiting on you, but, uh, I was wondering, uh ... " *Think, moron. Say something intelligent for once.* "Oh, yes, when would you like to eat?"

Whew. Not brilliant, but a decent recovery.

"I am good for five minutes."

"What are you going to do in five minutes?"

"Take bath and dress."

Five minutes? What woman at any point in time had ever showered and been ready in five minutes?

She wouldn't be thinking about rushing if he hadn't made her feel as though she'd been imposing on his time, which this assignment was, but not her fault.

He smiled. "No, you should take at least an hour."

Her eyes narrowed to slits and her mouth did a great impression of a heart monitor display when it flatlined.

Now what had he said wrong? In a hurry to leave before he made it worse, he took a step away. "I'll knock on your door when it's time to go eat."

He stepped out, but before he closed the door, he reminded her, "Please don't leave the room without me. I'm responsible for your safety."

"You guard body?"

She just had to say body in that lush accent.

His eyes—all on their own he wanted to point out—tracked north to south along that curvaceous frontier.

"I do not need guard." Her abrupt comment brought his gaze back to her face and reminded him he was on a mission he could not screw up.

Or do any screwing around during, period.

He must not have replied fast enough, because she said, "Is local alpha shifter?"

"Yes."

"He knows I am here?"

"Yes."

"He approved?" she asked.

"Yes," Justin said, repeating his answer like some damn canary with a one-word vocabulary." He explained, "I sent him a text as soon as I saw you arrive to start the twenty-four hours we're clear to move around his territory without any restrictions. He assured me his people would give us a wide berth." More like the alpha had warned his people not to cross Justin due to whatever the Guardian had told him in their discussion regarding the princess.

This was getting complicated and didn't need to be.

Justin cut to the point. "Whether you think you need protection or not, I *am* your bodyguard until I deliver you to the Boudreaux Clan."

"Why do you frown?"

He had to start saying that name without grinding his teeth. Sticking a fake smile in place, he said, "Muscle cramp."

She gave a terse nod, which he took more as dismissal than acknowledgment, because she continued to just stare at him.

Getting the royal cold shoulder was all it took to push his mind back on track to treat this as a job.

He pointed at the deadbolt lock on the door. "Turn this when I leave so no one can come in."

"Know what lock is."

That sounded like he'd just stepped on her last nerve.

He backed out and shut the door before he had no feet left to walk on at the rate he was shoving them down his throat.

He waited for the lock to click.

When it didn't happen, he said, "Elianna."

She made some muffled noise that sounded like a Russian curse, then the lock snapped in place as if flipped hard.

He actually laughed.

That woman had some piss and vinegar in her royal veins. If that hadn't gone so awkwardly, he'd have departed her room through the adjoining doors to let her see that he was only a shout away.

But his gut told him she would take exception to a strange man having access to her room.

Once she took a long, hot bath and had a meal in her, he'd give her the sealed packet with her name on it. Justin had found one for him and one for her on the Guardian's jet.

Beyond that, the Guardian did not expect to hear from Justin unless something came up that he couldn't handle on his own.

Seriously?

The boss knew Justin would never live it down if he called for backup to escort a woman to a clan. With the exception of having to walk into a bear shifter territory he'd sworn to never enter again, this mission registered as nothing more than a nuisance.

In fact, calling this side trip a mission was a stretch, but if he thought of it in professional terms then he could stay on track and approach her with the polite respect she deserved.

Nothing more. Nothing less.

Definitely no eyeing her lush princess body again.

He also couldn't allow his irritation over being pulled away from Adrian to spill over onto Elianna. This was probably no more than a vacation for her, but it was her time and Adrian was not her problem.

Justin just couldn't brush off the worry hanging in the back of his mind.

While Rory and Cole were more than capable, being in San Francisco with a pretty woman felt like farting off while his buddies were getting bloodied.

Adrian had to make the cut.

Justin had lost human and shifter friends in some nasty ways, but he couldn't live with losing that wolf.

But Adrian would be the first to tell Justin to focus on what was right in front of him, which meant delivering Elianna safely.

Feeling every long hour of grime clinging to him, Justin headed for his own shower. He scratched his chin, noticed the start of a beard, and grabbed his shaver. Pausing, he listened as the shower ran next door. Their rooms were mirror images, which meant his and Elianna's bathrooms were side by side.

That water had to be running down her sweet body and touching places he ...

Shit. Stop it, right now, dickhead. She doesn't even like you.

Maybe that was a good thing.

He peeled clothes off, already thinking of how he could up his game and do a better job of interacting with her during dinner.

Who knew, he might get a smile out of her.

She'd had a rough sea crossing, which could explain why she'd gotten a little cranky as he'd left her room. Still, after thinking back over everything he'd said, he honestly couldn't pinpoint what had been wrong.

He'd be ready much sooner than an hour. Should he go back early?

Why not? She'd been the one to say she needed less than ten minutes to get ready.

If that was true, she was a woman after his own heart.

Good mate.

Justin froze with his hand on the shower controls, trying to decide if he'd heard Herc correctly.

Herc, the most obstinate bear in the world, that had never liked *any* female bear shifter Justin had shown an interest in.

Ever.

Herc had even told Justin once, *Grizzly mates no good.*

Still, that had sounded pretty clear. Pausing, Justin listened again then asked, *Herc? Did you say something?*

His bear snuffled as if Justin had disturbed him. Herc liked his sleep.

Shaking his head, Justin spun the controls to blast hot water and snorted at his imagination.

That's all it could have been.

He wanted a mate at some point, but he wasn't up against a deadline like Cole had been with the mating curse. Around ten years after having a Gallize animal called up by the Guardian, the mating curse started activating if the shifter was not mated.

Cole's wolf had been going mad until Cole reunited with Tess. Lucky bastard. Few women could accept the Gallize power during bonding, but a Gallize female or a strong female shifter with their own power would survive the mating bond.

The female guardian who'd been charged with watching over Gallize females had vanished two hundred years ago.

The odds against finding one of those women to mate without that guardian involved were mind-boggling, just as grumpy Rory had pointed out.

But Herc didn't like female bear shifters.

That meant Justin's chances for flying the next spaceship scheduled to launch were better than him finding a suitable mate, but the desire nudged at the back of his mind.

Attacking his body with a bar of soap, he snorted again at the *good mate* comment.

He'd simply misunderstood his animal.

CHAPTER 8

ELIANNA BRUSHED HER DAMP HAIR back, yanking each
stroke with vengeance until she caught a tangle. "Ouch."

She put the brush down on the hotel bathroom sink. "Hair did
not insult you, foolish woman," she told the mirror.

That arrogant bear shifter had been the one to tell her she
needed to take more time.

Did he think scrubbing harder and washing longer would wipe
away her natural look and turn her into some hidden beauty?

Staring at her reflection didn't improve her mood. If she could
be honest, he had a point, and that annoyed her even more.

She had fine hair in an unfortunate reddish, pale-brown color,
plus her face was too long. She might improve her looks with
makeup, but she'd never had money for frivolous things back
home, and makeup would not hide her greatest flaw of being an
ursid hybrid.

She hated those words.

Now would be an even worse time to waste money on her
appearance with so little in hand until Alexandre sent her the
money he promised for when she arrived. Then he would send
more later. In Russia, she'd saved every bit of money to put
toward an apartment for her and Nico, but extra rubles hadn't
come along often.

With one last look in the mirror, she scoffed.

Mascara would not change her pale blue eyes.

She stood out like a lost grizzly on fresh snow.

Justin's eyes should have been dark chocolate, too, but his were
more like dark syrup that caught the light and brightened to gold

at times.

Take at a least an hour.

Why would his words not leave her alone?

Slapping the brush down, she said, "I can not fix face or body. I do not care, grizzly."

But, sadly, she did and being told she needed to spend more time primping stung. It felt like a rejection.

It should not matter. She must worry about what she had to do, not about making any grizzly shifter happy. Like her father, who had smiled and acted as if she should be thankful he had given her a great opportunity.

He was as dense as every other man she'd ever met.

Men would never understand her, because they thought only of their own needs and assumed she would, too. He probably also thought she'd arrive in this country and be so intimidated she would do what every man told her.

Alexandre had lived a long time and everyone around him probably changed to suit his needs. She'd learned to adapt at an early age, which had not been fun, but because she was flexible, she feared nothing except losing Nico.

Not a new land. Not the unknown. Not a man.

She made a grinding sound of disgust. She had only one thing on her mind and that was to prepare for Nico's future with her. The Boudreaux Clan alpha had to carry out his end of the deal, because no bear clan wanted a Romanov for an enemy.

She would fulfill her part as well, but on her terms.

Men lied to her all the time.

She owed the full truth only to Nico.

With her usual efficiency, she dressed in her jeans again, but feeling cleaner this time. She pulled on a lightweight shirt with long sleeves, then tied her hair back into a ponytail at her neck. Glancing at the digital clock on the nightstand, she scowled. She had taken her time and still there were forty-eight minutes until her keeper returned.

Sitting hard on the edge of the bed, she slapped it.

Go out. Play. Go out. Play.

Her silly bear had risen from its rest.

Elianna spoke to her bear telepathically. *Cannot go out.*

Why? Bad air. Go out.

I am tired of being in boats and buildings, too, she replied.

Go out. Now, now, now.

No, I must wait for guard, Elianna explained.

Why?

She didn't have an answer this time. She had no reason to fear humans who would not know she was a shifter. If she didn't appease her bear in some way after the animal had rested so long, Elianna would not hear the end of complaining for hours.

Maybe all night.

Maybe tomorrow when they were stuck inside a vehicle.

Elianna told her bear, *We will go out, but no shift.*

She expected the animal to sulk, but instead heard, *Yes. Out.*

Now she felt bad. Her bear rarely went along without griping, which meant the poor animal needed to get out soon and run. That would not happen for at least a week, maybe longer, until Elianna could find a place where no one would see her bear.

Pulling out a scarf from her case, she wrapped it around her neck. She would not allow this Justin to treat her as a prisoner. He was her escort.

It was time to begin learning this new land.

Justin had said the local shifters would not bother her, just as it was in her father's country when he gave permission for another shifter to visit.

She left the room, feeling lighter of heart than she had in days. By the time Justin came for her, she would be back.

CHAPTER 9

JUSTIN HAD PACED FOR THE last ten minutes and finally gave up.

Elianna had only wanted five minutes. If he showed up at her door thirty minutes early and she wasn't ready, he'd wait in the hallway, but he had to get out of his room.

Maybe he should knock on the connecting door and show her how close he would be if she had any problem.

Herc chortled. *Lie.*

Justin started to argue with his bear, but arguing with the doorknob would give him better results. He just ignored the joker and decided he'd point out the additional room access later.

When he reached her door, he listened for any sound.

Nothing. Maybe she was sleeping.

Damn. He was starving. She had to be hungry, too, so he should wake her, right?

Herc came alert. *Gone.*

Justin forgot food and knocked. "Elianna?"

No answer. Dammit. He dug out the extra key to her room and opened it.

Herc had been spot on.

Where the hell had she gone? It was clear she'd left on her own. There was no other current scent in the room, just a tinge of smell left by humans in the past.

Rushing out, he was halfway down the hall by the time her door snapped shut behind him. He allowed Herc to come forward enough to take the lead, but not so much that a human looking into Justin's eyes would see a change in his gaze. A shifter would know, but according to the alpha, he wouldn't see any shifters while they were here.

Each of the Gallize shifters had a little extra power of one kind or another. For Justin, he could exert a push of energy that caused humans to avoid him, much as an alpha of a pack could do at will. He didn't do it often in public, because that same energy alerted shifters to a predator in their midst.

They wouldn't know he was a Gallize, but their hind sense should warn them to avoid him unless they were too stupid to pay attention to their instincts or carried a suicidal ego on their shoulder.

When he stepped through the hotel doors, he sniffed late-day air that held a blend of salt, city, and chocolate, because the hotel was in the Ghirardelli Square district.

So far, so good, because the only fresh shifter scent he picked up was Elianna's and it headed toward the boardwalk along the waterfront.

He ran a hand over his head, trying to not lose his temper. She was in a new country and probably just wanted to explore.

He'd explain to her—again—how she had to do what he told her. He would do it calmly and show his patient side.

Lie.

Justin growled at Herc's censure and whispered under his breath, "What's with this running commentary?"

When Herc didn't answer, Justin said, "Well?"

Stupid words.

That meant either Herc didn't understand what Justin had said or wanted to insult him.

Usually the latter.

Using Elianna's scent to determine his direction, Justin got busy tracking her. He and Herc generally got along even if his bear could be one stubborn son of a bitch. This was one of those times he needed the bear to work closely with him and get this woman off their hands in a day and a half, then Justin could drive back to Wyoming.

Simple task. One the Guardian expected to be performed without any drama.

Now, he just had to get that across to one misbehaving princess.

Justin more often spoke to Herc with his voice instead of his mind, but either worked. Keeping his voice down, he said, "We need to keep this woman safe and deliver her on time. Once we drop her at the Boudreaux Clan, we're free to get back to Adrian's land where you can have your way."

Bad clan. Wrong.

Not that Justin disagreed, but getting off on that topic would not solve anything. "Not up to us. We're just the delivery service."

Not go.

"Herc, why are you fighting me on this?"

Follow scent.

Justin snapped his head up and inhaled.

Herc was right. He'd gotten off track, because he'd assumed she would be headed toward all the lights and crowd noise. Swinging to his left instead, Justin wove his way through a loose trail of humans walking in the opposite direction toward San Francisco's famous Fisherman's Wharf.

He was headed toward the bridge.

Twilight eased in from all sides with the sun now out of sight.

The boardwalk ran east and west, fronting San Francisco Bay where it reached the Pacific Ocean via the Golden Gate Strait. The smell of fried fish hit Justin in the next block and his mouth watered.

When he did find his missing body-to-protect, first they'd eat, then he'd have a talk with her.

He continued west on Bay Street where the Golden Gate Bridge stood tall in the distance.

Maybe she'd stayed near the water and hadn't gotten off into some dark side street.

In the next four blocks, his nose pulled him to the right, where he crossed an acre of groomed land between the road and a marina further west than the one where she'd arrived. Gravel and dirt gave way to a paved surface that eventually ran parallel to the water.

She had been keeping on the path that ran closest to the bay.

He searched ahead. Where had she gone?

But that wasn't the only thing bothering him.

Why hadn't she waited for him?

Was she trying to get away from him? He rarely had an increase in heart rate, short of being in a tight battle, but that organ was pumping extra hard.

Don't overreact, he reminded himself.

Maybe she just needed to walk after being on a boat for so long.

With the bay on his right, he picked up his pace.

He couldn't explain it, but he felt that odd sensation he had when he'd grabbed her arm. His skin had tingled as if he'd touched a live wire. An odd energy he hadn't forgotten.

It was buzzing through his chest right now.

Elianna's scent still floated on the salty breeze, brushing across his face and bringing his dick to life. That part had no business in any of this. He could handle being turned on around a client as long as he kept his head straight.

Wolf, Herc huffed.

Justin caught the new scent at the same moment he felt Herc growl. Another shifter was on this path.

That local alpha had better not cross the Guardian.

If any of the wolf's shifters bothered Elianna, the alpha wouldn't have to worry about meting out punishment.

Justin wouldn't leave enough of the wolf to face his alpha.

Herc growled again, letting Justin know they were in full agreement. Justin wasn't about to ask his bear why he was playing nice with this female bear shifter. He would just thank his stars that he might not have to deal with a grumpy Herc while they were around her.

Some wolf was about to get his ass handed to him.

Rules were important in the shifter world, especially in the powerful packs and clans that wanted no part of being sent to an enclave.

That was a nice word for the equivalent of a reservation. When humans found out about shifters, they did not want those abnormal beings living around them.

Justin ground his teeth. Abnormal beings. They were supernatural beings.

Yes, like, Herc said, which meant he agreed.

When Justin reached the west end of the marina, he noted the humans out and about. They were all calm, which meant nothing noisy had happened like an attack or kidnapping.

The two scents he followed twisted together on the next breeze that slid past his nose. Overhead lights had come on by the time he exited the hotel, but they did little to illuminate where the shore met black water.

Fog continued to build until half of the bridge was nothing more than a translucent looking shape.

He picked up his pace, staying alert to everything in his field of vision. He could not shift around all these humans.

Neither could the other shifter *if* he was part of the local pack. Rogues followed no rules, but neither did they survive long when they trespassed into a local pack's territory.

Even worse if they crossed into this particular territory.

Didn't matter.

As a Gallize, Justin packed more power than the shifters most humans knew about, and he could actually handle those shifters in his human form.

Herc snarled, *Hurry.*

While in human form, Justin's bear came up hard and strong when he sensed danger. As the trail passed the end of the marina, Justin reached a small park with a parking lot and trees casting long shadows.

He had an idea where she might have gone.

San Francisco had an attraction created at the end of a jetty called the Wave Organ. An artist and master stone mason had created an acoustic structure made of material from a demolished cemetery, and organ pipes made of PVC. When waves struck the structure, it emitted different sounds.

With darkness swallowing him, he pushed his speed. If a human saw him, they wouldn't see him long enough to identify him.

Herc growled a warning. *Two wolves!*

When he got Elianna back to the hotel, he was packing her up and driving her straight to Louisiana.

CHAPTER 10

α

SWIM NOW.

"No. How many times must say that?" Elianna asked her bear out loud, but not loud enough a human would hear her. She should have walked into the city instead of here around San Francisco Bay, but she'd wanted to smell fresh air and enjoy some peace before her world got complicated.

On the streets, she'd heard a woman talking about the nearby rocks that made music.

Shifter hearing could be very handy.

After asking directions of a uniformed man working at the front door of a fine hotel, she found her way with no trouble to their Wave Organ.

Even with her bear complaining, Elianna found her little adventure enjoyable.

The marina had been right where the gentleman had said. Once she reached it, she continued all the way down until she made what he called a big U-turn that brought her to this jetty.

Odd musical sounds were definitely coming from the rocks below. Somebody had constructed this with stone steps and parts that reminded her of cemetery stone.

She sat on the top step, finally alone.

Leaning back on her elbows, she turned her face into the breeze blowing off the water. Lights glowed through fog hovering around the beautiful bridge. She had seen pictures of this city often in magazines left in the hotel rooms she cleaned on weekends.

She should head back soon. Her bodyguard would be upset

when he had no body to direct. She wished she'd brought her sunglasses, but they would have looked stupid in this dark.

Once Justin saw her blue eyes, he'd be done with her. He might even call in someone to take his place.

She didn't care.

Do care, her bear argued.

"Would like some peace. You mind?" she asked her bear, but still kept her voice soft with the wind blowing in her face. Someone walking up might hear her and think she was crazy.

Yes. Swim.

There was no winning with her bear. She tried to placate her animal. "Be good five days and you run in woods. Promise. I have plan."

Her bear made a sound Elianna recognized as her sigh of impatience. She did that often, because her bear was never patient with Elianna.

Feeling guilty, Elianna said, "I tell truth. If you—"

Her bear said, *Wolf.*

That was the only warning Elianna got before a rough hand covered her mouth. Her attacker's other arm wrapped around her chest, yanking her up to her feet. She jerked and fought, trying to get her feet on the ground where she could better deal with the attack.

He yanked her up higher, keeping her off the ground, which was not easy at her height. He ordered, "Stop it or I'll knock you out and drag you over these rocks."

She didn't care if she got banged up and bruised, but she couldn't escape if he knocked her out. If he took her out of here asleep, she'd have no idea where she was upon waking.

At least here, she had Justin.

Now, she regretted the trouble she'd given her bodyguard over not needing protection, but she was supposed to be safe from shifters in this area.

Or had she left the boundaries of her safe area?

Her kidnapper must have believed her act of compliance, because he put her feet on the ground again and turned her to walk ahead of him. "Make a sound and I'll knock you out, then kill anyone who interferes."

She would not harm an innocent, but she would not concede

either. If this man wanted money from Alexandre, he would get none and kill her when he found out.

In three steps, she let her leg fold as if she'd stepped in a hole.

He hadn't expected that. His weight fell forward with her.

She reached over her head, grabbing for shirt, hair, anything she could find. She bumped her butt into him and yanked hard, using momentum to roll him over her as she ducked forward. He cursed as his shoulders and back slammed the ground. She jumped up, ready when he also leaped to his feet. She hadn't thought flipping him would harm the wolf, but it now put her equal to him.

His face was covered by a stocking cap, barely. She'd nearly torn it off.

He lifted hands with human fingers that ended in sharp claws that could slash her open.

How could he show those claws in public?

The wolf shifter started forward, eyes glowing more yellow than amber in the night.

"You make mistake," Elianna warned the wolf as she circled defensively. He would not kill her if he had plans for ransom.

She considered the spot she was in and did not want a repeat of what happened during her last night in Russia. For that reason, Elianna grasped at something her mother had tried to teach her, but that she'd never attempted with her animal in a defensive situation.

Elianna asked her bear, *Give me power, yes?*

Want out.

No.

The wolf lunged and slashed a claw at her.

She jumped sideways, but still could not get past him.

This was why she never involved her bear. Her mother could call *her* bear's power forward in human form. As an adolescent, Elianna had tried to get while in human form for her bear to lend power the way her mother had explained many times. Her bear always refused unless Elianna agreed to shift.

Desperate to survive this wolf attack and tired of being vulnerable to other shifters, Elianna warned her bear, *I die, you die.*

Still nothing. *This* was why she hadn't asked her useless bear for power back in Russia.

She kept moving her feet side to side, but she had no chance of getting past that wolf with the crazy eyes.

This would not end well for her.

The wolf shifter swiped at her and she dodged again.

She wanted to scream in frustration, because this wolf was strong. Not weak or thin like the ones back in PK. This one would win unless she had help. So she prepared to fight to the death.

Her eyes must have glowed bright blue, because the wolf hesitated and stared at her face.

She took advantage of the distraction, spun around and ran toward the water.

Two steps from the edge, the wolf shifter caught her and yanked her back.

She came around slamming fists one after another and twisting her body to break his hold. In their moving back and forth, he ended up on the end of the rocks with his back to the water.

Perfect. She relaxed her arms and breathed as if beaten. His grip eased a tiny bit.

She yanked her arms free and put all she had into knocking him backward with both fists. With any luck, he'd hit a few boulders in the water, six feet down.

He lost his balance, waving his arms.

It was a good plan. A sound plan.

Until he locked the fingers of one hand tight around her wrist and shot the other hand out with claws extended, digging a gash across the shoulder she had leaned into him.

No wolf was that fast.

Pain lashed through her shoulder.

Claws ripped shirt and skin, burning a path across her shoulder. She shoved him harder while leaning her weight away from him, struggling to stay out of the water.

His clawed fingers clamped harder around her wrist while he tilted backwards more and whipped his free arm around, trying to regain his balance.

She pushed her heels down, struggling to break free and stay upright. In spite of the pain, she slammed a fist at his jaw, cracking it.

He still held on and dragged her over with him.

They both went over the side and hit the water with a loud splash. People probably thought they were fighting a fish or feeding them.

She broke loose from him and lunged for the low-water side of the rocks.

Splashing followed her.

Not slowing when her foot hit the first stone above the water, she scrambled up the steps. Water ran down her face and her soaked clothes clung to her. She jumped up the last two steps and landed forward on her knees. Breathing hard, she pushed to her feet and took a step.

He grabbed her ponytail and yanked her back to him. She struggled, hammering fists when she could, but he finally wrestled her into his hold. When she looked up through wet hair, she was staring out to the bay. He stood behind her with her body and arms locked in his grip.

Never had she heard of a lone wolf shifter that could overpower a bear shifter in human form.

His gritty voice snarled into her ear. "I gave you a chance to do this nice and simple, but no. When I knock you out, I'll let you make it up to me. I'll take my time and enjoy you."

Chills ran up her spine that had nothing to do with the cold air hitting her wet body. What was it with men who thought a woman should go along quietly to be mauled and raped?

She heard a roar of fury right before the wolf was snatched away. She stumbled backwards before he let go. When she turned, she heard the distinctive sound of bones breaking right before he went airborne, and landed far out into the bay.

Justin's strength stunned her.

She'd been around powerful bear shifters, but she wasn't sure her alpha father could have thrown a wolf shifter that far.

After some splashing, everything got quiet.

She asked, "Did you kill him?"

"No." Justin covered his eyes. "Maybe. I shouldn't have thrown him out there, but my bear was too furious. I had to do that or turn my bear loose." Justin dropped his hand, stepped over to her, and turned her face to the ambient light bleeding off the shoreline. "You're gonna have a bruise."

Why did he sound so disappointed?

He knew she could heal. Not as quickly as when she shifted, but she would survive. Besides, her shoulder was far worse.

He touched her so carefully it stole her breath. No one except Nico had touched her with care since she'd first shown her bear.

"I want to turn you around so I can make sure you're not hurt worse."

Before she could say anything, he placed a hand on her shoulder as if to turn her, but touched her wound.

She hissed at the pain.

His eyes widened. He pulled his hand back, which was covered in dark liquid. Her blood.

"Shit, Eli. Why didn't you tell me he clawed you?"

"I will heal." Eli? Her name was not Eli, but she did not want to sound unappreciative at this moment.

A look of concern flowed over his face. "I know you will, but you can't shift until we get back to the room."

"No shifting."

"Not out here with humans, but you can do it in the room. I'll make sure you're safe."

She sighed. This was when the complicated part started. "I do not change to bear."

That seemed to throw him. "Not at all?"

"No."

"I don't understand why ... "

To stop a string of questions, she leaned into him as if she were faint. She had never been faint in her life, but she understood decent men, at least the few she'd met. Justin was one.

And to be honest, she was not at her best strength.

"Hold on, Eli." His big arms went around her and pulled her close to his chest without hurting her shoulder. No more than it already ached. She put her hand up to keep some distance, but her fingers had no sense.

They tangled in his shirt, gripping him.

Something strange happened that she'd never experienced anywhere else. Never with a man.

She felt safe in this Justin's warm embrace.

It was then she noticed how very tired losing blood had made her. If she did not start walking, she would not make it back on her own.

Lifting her head, she looked up at his nice face. "I am good."

His eyes wouldn't give up their hold on hers.

Her bear made noises she didn't recognize. What was her bear up to now?

A sizzle of energy buzzed in her chest.

No, not only in her chest, but also between her chest and Justin's. He finally broke that endless gaze and glanced down to the spot where she could feel the hum building.

This had to be her bear's fault.

Elianna pressed a little against Justin's chest to make more space between them and he eased his hold on her.

Now she wanted to swat her bear.

That had been nice in Justin's arms.

Couldn't her bear allow her even a small enjoyment once in a while?

"Can you walk?" Justin asked.

"Yes. Bleeding will stop. I am not fragile woman."

He just gave her a long look that made her wish he'd tell her what he was thinking, but he didn't. Instead, he took off his outer shirt, leaving him in a gray T-shirt that showed powerful biceps and forearms.

Her body noticed, and that was not a good thing.

The last time her body noticed a man this way, Elianna had ended up naked, then disappointed when he backed off after seeing her bear.

Justin pulled his shirt around her. "You're still going to be feeling chills from shock in human form. Let's put this on you so we can get back to the hotel without being stopped." He gently eased her arms into the sleeves, then tugged the sides together in front.

He put his arm around her and began walking them back. "Was there another shifter?"

"No. Why?"

"No big deal. Thought I smelled a second one."

She would have lost to two shifters. What had happened to the other one?

It didn't matter.

Justin was here and she was thankful for that.

Surprisingly, her bear was being quiet. Elianna silently asked her bear, *You sleep now?*

Yes.

She didn't trust her bear. She asked, *Why?*

Swim sleep. Swim sleep. Happy.

She should have realized her bear had gotten her way after all and gone for a swim. Had her bear been the reason she went flying into the water with that wolf?

Probably.

Mean animal.

Me nice. You mean.

With that last word, her irritating bear finally quieted down and Elianna prepared herself to answer questions. Justin had been understanding out here, but back in the hotel room she had a feeling he was going to be one demanding shifter.

Grizzly shifters, in particular, expected to get their way and have their questions answered.

It should be interesting since she had no intention of shifting or of explaining why she would not.

CHAPTER 11

a

JUSTIN HAD NEVER MET A pure grizzly with blue eyes.

Elianna had to be grizzly, right?

She couldn't be mixed blood, could she? She was the alpha's firstborn daughter. Justin kept Elianna close to him and constantly glanced over to see if she was still holding up.

She'd suffered a vicious clawing. Even if the bleeding had slowed, she would not heal fast unless she shifted.

As soon as he had her stable, he was calling the wolf pack alpha. Someone was going to explain why Elianna had been attacked in what was a guaranteed safe zone. He was known for ruling his land with razor sharp claws.

Back at the hotel, Justin kept her close enough to shield any view of the blood still seeping through her shirt.

Wasn't she healing at all?

Inside his room, he sat her on the commode seat in the bathroom. He got his shirt off of her and said, "We need to take your blouse off."

"Go. I can do."

"If you're not going to shift, then I have to see to your wound."

She didn't budge on the shifting part. Dammit.

He unbuttoned her shirt and worked it slowly off her shoulders. The blood had dried in some places so it meant first soaking a towel to wet the area so he could slowly work the material away from her skin. He wouldn't have been so nervous working on one of his teammates, but Eli's skin was delicate.

Her white bra had blood on it. That could be washed out later. Shifters were used to naked bodies, but a woman was a woman.

This one had been attacked and the last thing he wanted to do was make her uncomfortable.

He knew she could heal, but seeing her creamy skin raked by claws infuriated him all over again.

Who was that bastard?

Justin slowly cleaned the wound, grinding his jaw teeth every time she flinched. He wanted to pull her to him so he could hug her once more and take some of the misery out of her eyes.

For a princess, she was tougher than he'd thought.

She didn't make a sound the whole time he cleaned her up, but her lips were pressed together tight and pebbles of perspiration broke out on her forehead.

She was clearly in pain.

Next, she started shivering. Shock had taken its sweet time setting in.

Finished doing all he could to clean the ravaged skin, he was heartened to see the blood seepage had actually slowed.

Now that she was somewhat stable, he spoke quietly. "That's a nasty clawing. You need to shift and get it healed."

"No."

"Why not?"

"No explain. Is my decision."

Why would she fight that?

Trying again, he said, "I know you don't know me well, but I swear to you that you'll be safe to shift."

She looked at him. "You are fine. My bear not ... well behaved."

Was this a case of a princess who couldn't control her diva bear?

Could this crap get any worse?

Justin wanted to be pissed, but he considered how she'd seemed fragile earlier, whether she thought so or not, and all she'd been through since being dumped at the dock.

She didn't know anyone.

Nobody from the Boudreaux Clan had come to meet her, which still bugged him. Not because he wanted to see any of that bunch, but this whole delivery thing just seemed ... off.

Raking a hand over his hair, he assessed his options and said, "Okay, fine, but if you're not going to shift, you have to eat a hearty meal and help your body heal."

She lifted those crystal blue eyes to his and really looked at him.

"Thank you. I will eat."

Finally, a win of sorts.

He took a clean towel and folded it up, then placed the pad gently against her shoulder. "If you'll hold that in place, I'll have them send up a first aid kit now and the food right behind it." He had a great kit in his truck, but he was not leaving her.

She put her hand over the towel compression, but covered his fingers as she did. He had leaned close to her and could feel that freaky energy zinging through his fingers and around in his body.

What the hell?

But he couldn't make himself pull his hand away and break the connection.

This close, he could see flecks of silver in her blue eyes. He'd never seen anything like those eyes on a grizzly bear shifter.

She held his gaze without blinking.

Her tongue slipped out between rosy lips for a second, then disappeared.

Damn, he was getting hard.

She whispered, "Blood will stain towel."

Like he cared? "It's not a problem."

"I do not want make trouble for you."

Too late. He was staring at trouble with gorgeous blue eyes.

She leaned forward. All he'd have to do is meet her in the middle to kiss her ...

Herc said, *Like?*

His bear's voice broke through the fog of sensual heat clouding his brain.

Oh, hell. Justin pulled back and eased his fingers out from under her hand. "Uh, while I make those calls, why don't you, uh ..."

"I need second bath."

Yeah, talking about bathing that body wasn't going to help the fever she'd stirred up in him. Now he had perspiration on his neck.

"Wait for me to bandage your shoulder first. Okay?

"Yes, okay." She gave him a half-hearted nod.

He backed out of the bathroom and hurried to call downstairs. He offered a tip no one would turn down for the person who showed up in sixty seconds with the first aid kit.

Then he called room service and placed their order, adding more incentive.

A knock sounded at the door as he hung up the phone.

Nothing like motivation.

Justin paid the promised tip, receiving an exuberant thank you from the woman who delivered the bandaging kit.

When he walked back into the bathroom, Elianna sat there with her stoic face. He'd get her patched up, a hot bath and some food in her. She should be showing signs of healing by the morning.

She peeked under the towel bandage. "Not much good."

That kicked him back into motion. "I'll be the judge of that. If you aren't going to shift, then I'm the doctor tonight."

She arched an eyebrow at him and Justin's chest eased. There was the snappy attitude she'd first displayed. He didn't want to see a wounded look on that face.

Pulling out all the materials from the first aid kit, he did a job of padding and taping Rory would be proud of, even making sure to tape in different directions to allow her some mobility.

Antibiotic ointment was unnecessary. Shifters didn't get infected.

When he was satisfied with her shoulder, he kneeled next to the tub and put the plug in, then started the water running.

"What do you do?" She sounded appalled.

Don't lose your patience with her. She's tired, hungry and injured.

"I thought you wanted a bath," he said as he checked the temperature of the water. Should be good.

"I can do."

"I'm sure you can, but it's easier for me to do it right now."

When she didn't answer, he turned to find her staring at him in shock. "What?"

"You should not do."

"Why not?" He was dying to hear this answer.

"You are alpha bear. I can tell. You do not serve woman."

Okay, that floored him.

She didn't think he should be doing this because he was an alpha? Well, he wasn't actually an alpha, but as an apex predator he trumped most alphas running packs and clans.

Justin couldn't explain that he was a Gallize so he tried to make light of it. "Running your bath is sort of an honor, princess."

Her mouth dropped open until she recovered to say, "I am not princess." Looking down she said, "Water full."

What? He swung around and stopped the water in time before the level was too high for her to step into, but he didn't understand why she denied her birthright.

When he stood to leave, she said, "I am sorry. I do not mean to not appreciate you. I ... please do not call me princess."

"Okay, I won't." He was as confused as a bear with two honeycombs. "Can you manage?"

"Yes, okay."

"I'll be right outside the door if you fall."

"Will not fall. Told you. Am not fragile woman."

No, she wasn't, but she seemed wounded in spirit as well as body.

Justin closed the door and walked to the balcony overlooking the bay as he called the local alpha. "Justin here. You've got a problem."

"What problem, bear?"

Were all alphas assholes? This one addressed him the same way the alpha of Clan Boudreaux did. Justin and his buddies used the terms bear, wolf, cat or whatever in the interest of good kidding, but his Louisiana alpha had called him bear as an insult back when Justin had no bear.

Justin ignored the slight and said, "You either have a rogue wolf in your territory or one of yours is not behaving ... *wolf*."

This time, the alpha's voice changed from surly to pissed. "None of my wolves would dare cross me and a rogue knows the price of entering without permission is death. Did you step outside the area I set as a safe zone?"

"No. The body I'm guarding was attacked by a wolf at the Wave Organ."

Justin waited through three beats of silence then the alpha said, "Where's the rogue wolf?"

Shit, this wouldn't go well. "He's at the bottom of the bay unless he figured out how to regenerate a broken neck and swim to shore."

"How'd he end up out there?"

"I threw him about thirty yards out."

"That's not possible, even for a bear."

Justin smiled to the empty room. "I can show you how it's done if you want to donate a wolf."

"Not funny, bear. If you'd given him to me, I could have found out where he came from. Why'd you kill him before we could get a look at him?"

Because I lost my mind when I saw him attacking Elianna.

Justin said, "I had to get him as far from my client as possible and that seemed like the quickest way. I didn't have time to hold him until you showed up, during which time humans would have probably come by and noticed all the blood."

"What'd he look like?"

"It was dark and he wore a black stocking mask. His eyes were more yellow than amber. I saw him maybe two seconds."

"I can account for every one of my wolves tonight. He had to be a rogue. I'll put my wolves out immediately to track any scent left and they'll bring me an answer. It may not be immediately, but I will know who defied me."

This guy hadn't asked the condition of Justin's injured patient, but that fit his ruthless reputation. Justin could call the Guardian and let him arrange for the alpha to make amends, but he decided on a better idea.

Justin suggested, "If you'd let me know who it was when you find out, we can consider this situation satisfied."

He must have surprised the alpha, because the wolf's tone changed again to one more congenial. "I'll let you know as soon as I have an identity, Lebeau."

I rank being called by my last name now, huh?

Someone tapped at the door as Justin ended the call. His nose told him room service waited to get in.

He checked the hole and opened the door. "Smells good."

"Would you like me to set up the food on your table?"

"Sure."

As the young man wheeled his cart across the floor, he glanced around. "My order noted two place settings. Will you need more?"

Justin smothered a chuckle. He'd ordered enough for four husky men, because he and Elianna had expended a lot of energy and shifters ate plenty.

He was concerned about her more than himself.

For a human, it would appear to be too much for two, but Justin covered by saying, "I'm a big guy. I get hungry during the night. You can just set up two places and leave the rest on the cart for now."

His server finished placing a small vase with flowers in the middle of the table and turned to Justin with a professional expression that hid any surprise. "Yes, sir."

Justin scribbled his signature on the guest check and handed the guy a cash tip. "Thanks for getting this delivered quickly." He locked the door behind the happy server.

The bathroom door opened an inch. "I need clothes."

Damn. He'd overlooked that one small detail. "Hold on. I'll be right back." It took him less than thirty seconds to access her room via the connecting door.

He appreciated the expedience of having her case packed and no clothes lying around, but it seemed odd that she had left the case ready to go.

Placing the worn out luggage next to his bathroom door, he didn't tap on it since he knew she could hear every sound. "Your bag is outside the door and I'll be over at the table. Our food is here."

"Yes. Good smell."

He smiled. Food might just be the way to this little bear's heart.

He had to stop thinking that way.

She was a client. Why was that so difficult to program into his mind?

At the table, he kept his back to the bathroom. Everything had been duplicated, so he lifted two of the four silver lids covering the food on the table, enjoying a whiff of each one.

Rare, thick-cut steak with baked sweet potato plus brown sugar and butter. Moving the other covers revealed asparagus and sautéed spinach.

He scrunched his nose, but had ordered the greenery because some women liked green stuff on their plate. The last lid had hidden two slices of some dessert he couldn't pronounce, but the description sounded like chocolate fig honey cake. And they had a basket piled high with honey biscuits.

He'd never known a grizzly or any other brown bear that didn't have a sweet tooth.

If that didn't do it, the other silver covers protected grilled fish.

At the sound of the bathroom door opening, he stilled, trying not to move too quickly around her.

When he turned, he really meant to check out her shoulder first, not the way her tank top clung to her curvy body or those workout pants covered sweet hips. She'd twisted her wet hair into some kind of knot women created with a stick.

It was probably not called a stick, but the thing was five inches long, thin and pointy.

A plastic stick.

When his eyes finally made it to her face, blue eyes too large for that face hid some dark thought.

Was she angry with him? Why?

She was the one who went strolling around in a strange city after he'd told her to wait for him.

"Hungry?" That was the only thing Justin could come up with to break the silent standoff.

"Yes."

He had to get more than one-word answers of out her or tomorrow would be the longest day of his life, stuck in a car with someone who he was starting to think really might not like him.

That was the rub.

Women liked him. A lot, dammit.

She stepped toward a chair and Justin moved quickly to pull it out.

See? I'm a good guy. He smiled.

She frowned at him, shook her head at something she didn't share and started for another chair.

What the devil? "Eli."

"What?"

"I'm pulling the chair out for *you.*"

She stared at the chair, then him. "Why?"

What kind of men had she been around? She was a freaking princess. Didn't they treat her like a queen? "It's what we do here. At least, men who treat a woman properly will pull out the chair."

Again she looked embarrassed, then accepted the chair. "Sorry."

Wanting to loosen her up, Justin joked, "No problem, but it

does make me wonder about the manners your alpha's men are taught."

She answered offhandedly. "I am sure they are nice to women they like."

Justin studied her reply, trying to understand it.

He mulled over "women they like." That sounded like they didn't care for her, which raised the question why?

Since his goal was to find some happy middle ground, he would not ask that question. He got busy lifting lids out of the way and the rich smell of good food intensified.

Sucking in a deep breath of aroma that had his stomach jumping up and down, he said, "Dig in. Nothing like steak to get you healing faster."

"Okay, yes." She started cutting a perfect square of steak. "But not need all this. I heal soon."

"Hey, this is only the first course. Once we finish the steak and a killer dessert, we also have fresh fish."

She finished chewing that first bite and wiped the linen napkin over her mouth. Placing both wrists on the edge of the table, she sat there.

Justin chowed down. He had no idea what was going on with her now, but he needed to eat. He dug in, trying to ignore her, but gave up. When he couldn't take the quiet any more, he sighed and put down his fork.

Counting to ten did nothing, so he couldn't help the exasperation in his voice. "What's wrong now, Eli?"

Her blue eyes were fierce. "Where is money from Boudreaux Clan? They promise to me when I arrive."

"Money? What has that got to do with anything right now?"

Her lips firmed. "You spend on fancy room and food?"

She thought he'd spent money intended for her? What fancy food?

"No. My boss is paying for the room and the food. Well, he's paying for the first course. I'm paying for the rest, because I figured we'd both be hungry after burning all that energy and you getting slashed. As for anything due to you, it's probably in the envelope I was given for you, but we haven't had time to go through anything like that yet." Just a bit irritated that money was so important to her after he'd started to think she might be a normal person after all, he added, "I have the envelope so you can look through and count all your money."

"Oh."

One word.

It said very little, but the sound had been coated with shame.

That dampened his irritation.

He stood up. "I'm sure things are confusing. Sit tight. I'll grab the envelope and put your mind at ease that whatever you're expecting should be in there."

He pulled a thick, nine-by-twelve-inch envelope out of his duffel.

Still, wasn't this more like a princess to be worried about her money? He'd never been interested in a woman who cared about living high and the almighty dollar.

That alone should cool his fever around her.

He sure hoped so considering how long a drive he had ahead of him.

Returning to the table where his silent guest waited, he handed her the envelope.

She met his gaze. "Thank you. Sorry. Did not mean to ... "

"No big deal." He waved off the apology, still willing to give her space to be tired and injured. "My boss said everything you should need is in the envelope and to let me know of any special requests on our way to the Boudreaux Clan tomorrow."

She had nodded and taken the envelope to her lap, intent on opening it until his last words. "Tomorrow?"

"Yes. Unless you're not ready to travel." He hoped she was up for it.

"I will be ready." Still appearing confused, she dug through the envelope. First, she pulled out a black credit card she gave a long look and turned over, then set aside. Next came a stack of hundred dollar bills secured with a paper band, which Justin estimated to be a thousand dollars.

She placed the money beside the credit card.

Then she withdrew a black folder the size of her hand that looked like a passport and even had PASSPORT embossed in gold on the front, but it was actually a US National Shifter ID. Most shifters used a driver's license for identification, so few people would recognize the difference between a shifter and human passport.

Once a person passed the inside back cover of this ID under a black light, the shifter stamp would appear.

Shifters worked within the laws of humans, but they weren't considered citizens of the US. For that reason, this ID would not have allowed Elianna to pass through customs or surely she'd have flown over in first class.

Maybe she carried an old beat-up suitcase as a cover.

That made more sense now.

Her eyes sparkled as she looked at everything, but still no smile.

Not even after the clan gave her a black card, which probably had no limit, and a wad of cash? What was it going to take to make this woman happy?

She put it all back in the envelope, which she placed by the leg of her chair, and started eating.

Okay. Evidently getting her hands on shopping money set everything right.

Justin let it go and returned to his meal. It took more than a glass of wine to get a shifter intoxicated, but he liked the taste of sweet wine. He poured them both a glass, which she sipped.

She finished eating first, only pecking at her dessert. If she left that, it was fair game.

He pushed back and folded his hands over his chest. "All better now?"

She nodded.

Now he was down to less than a one-word answer. "Let's talk about tomorrow if you're up for the drive?"

"Yes, okay. I am good."

Now she was the anxious one to hit the road? That tweaked his nose, but whatever. Hadn't he been saying he was in a hurry to get her delivered?

He kept his voice upbeat. "Great. If we hit the road early and stop only for food and gas, we can ... "

"Must shop."

Of course she wanted to shop.

That money probably wouldn't last the week. He was not going to follow her around a mall like a lackey.

But arguing with her might be as fruitless as it could be with Herc, so Justin offered, "I'll find a mall on the way out of town and we'll stop for an hour. Sound fair?"

"What is mall?"

"A big building with a lot of stores in it so you can find everything in one place. Plenty of shops with dresses and shoes."

"We have shops."

Good. She knew what he was talking about. "So we'll hit the mall first then get on the road."

"No."

He mentally watched the fraying line of his patience unravel a little more. "You're gonna have to give me more than a no. I don't understand the problem."

"No dress. No shoes."

Bewildered, he asked, "Then where do you want to go?"

Studying him, she said, "Your store."

"Me? I don't shop."

She took in his clothes and arched an eyebrow.

"Okay, fine. Yes, I buy clothes and gear when I need it, but I don't go to malls."

"Good."

Don't growl, he told himself. That would only stir up her bear, which had to be a bit on edge. "Good ... what?"

"Good. Your store."

He sat back and imagined her trying to find something fancy where he liked to pick up clothes.

Smiling, he said, "Sure." If she complained, he'd remind her that he offered the mall first.

Then he'd drive as hard as he could for thirty-five hours and drop her at the Boudreau Clan where she would be their problem.

"Leave early, yes?"

"Works for me," he replied. "That way we should reach Louisiana by midday Sunday."

"No."

That word was back. Did she think it automatically explained anything? He worked his jaw, which had become tight from clenching and unclenching his teeth, then sighed hard. "What are you saying no to?"

"Five days, then meet clan."

Oh, hell no. He deserved a medal for shouting that only in his mind.

Herc chortled.

Justin didn't want to know what the fucker found funny in all this. He told her, "Sorry, but that's the plan."

"No."

One more no and Justin could not be held responsible for his actions. He dropped his hands to his knees and leaned forward. "We need to get a few things straight. One is that I am in charge of delivering you to that clan. Two is that I am not your fulltime driver for a vacation. Three is that it will go much easier if we can have a real conversation and that isn't going to happen if you just keep saying no. Understand?"

"I know English."

"Great. Now try using all your words."

She sat straighter and pinned him with a hard stare. "No. Is not plan. Both alphas agree five days before meet Clan Boudreaux. I am told you make my requests."

"Not make. Fulfill," he corrected out of annoyance.

He noted she hadn't called the alpha of her Russian clan father, but Justin put that aside mentally to dwell on later. For now, he needed to fix this somehow.

Trying again, he explained, "I said I would take you shopping. Tomorrow. I did not say I would spend five days—and before you argue about it—what exactly do you need five days to accomplish?"

"Plan each day."

That meant she did not intend to share her plans in advance, which only upped his irritation.

He got up and walked around the room, scrubbing his face with his hands. This was crazy.

Pulling his phone out, he hit speed dial for the Guardian who answered, "Hello, Justin. Did Elianna arrive as expected?"

"Yes, sir, but she's confused about something."

She said, "No confused."

He waved a hand at her to be quiet and continued explaining to his boss, "She thinks I'm going to drive her around for five days doing I-have-no-idea-what before I deliver her to Clan Boudreaux."

"I did tell you to take care of any special requests on the way to her drop-off point."

Justin's stomach hit his feet at realizing the file he'd received from the Guardian *had* said to do that, but Justin had assumed his boss meant only during the drive tomorrow.

Had the Guardian known about this and withheld information until Justin was neck-deep in this mess? Why? It hit him. His boss felt he was too close to Adrian's problem and wanted Justin to gain some distance. This would definitely give him space, but he didn't like it.

Needing to confirm his guess, Justin asked, "Don't you want me to give the guys in Wyoming a hand?"

"They'll be fine. I have known the Romanov alpha for many years, which is why he asked that I oversee his daughter's security and delivery. It is my responsibility to fulfill the terms of his agreement with Clan Boudreaux." The Guardian paused then added, "If I thought Adrian's healing depended on your presence, I would not have asked you to do this, but I needed you in particular, and I believe you'll be more useful to Adrian after this assignment."

Yep, Justin had failed to hide how much Adrian's problem was affecting him.

His boss had given his word to the alphas.

Now it was Justin's responsibility to make good on that word.

Without waiting on Justin to comment, the Guardian said, "Elianna knows the limit of those terms. From what I understand, of all parties involved she is the one most determined not to deviate from the agreement. Is there anything else?"

"No, sir."

"If you need anything or support of any kind, call me back."

No way in hell that was happening.

The Guardian's casual offer of help was the same as asking Justin if he had doubts about handling his mission.

Herc made a huffing sound again, poking at Justin.

Stuff it, bear, Justin muttered mind to mind.

"Thank you for meal," Elianna said, standing.

Justin put his phone away and turned to her, now in an entirely new mindset. "You're welcome. Keep in mind that I didn't tell my boss what happened tonight ... yet."

She went very still.

It might have been the new tone he took with her, or her normal reaction. He had no idea with this woman.

He continued. "I'm expected to report everything that happens to my boss." That was a stretch, because the Gallize shifters had a certain amount of autonomy. On the other hand, if anything went wrong after today, Justin's ass would be in a bind for not reporting the wolf attack.

What could Justin say? That he couldn't protect her from a rogue wolf shifter?

Unfortunately, he hadn't, but that wouldn't happen again.

Elianna's face went from soft to angry. "You would tell and ruin plans?"

"I don't want to ruin your plans."

Herc said, *Lie.*

Justin ignored his irritating bear so he could deal with one conversation at a time.

He told Elianna, "But the minute I report that attack, my boss is going to change my orders to deliver you either to a safe house for the next five days or to Clan Boudreaux, who will take over your protection." Considering someone else taking over bugged him. Why?

"No." She came alive, stepping toward him with her fists clenched. "We make deal. All agree. *Must* have five days."

Justin had thought she was starting a diva fit at first, but her voice quivered and that last sentence pinged with importance. She could have said no one was being fair or she would call someone and demand a new driver.

No, she had said she *must* have five days.

Must. Very little emotion had entered her face until now, but Justin picked up the scent of her fear.

Not just fear, but terror.

What was going on with this female bear shifter?

Then as if this reaction had not been unexpected, she surprised him again when she said, "Please."

One word filled with anguish that had come from somewhere deep in her soul. From a place where she locked away her worst pain.

Justin knew that spot. He had his own.

His gut argued that she wasn't telling him everything, but his instincts told him she kept her emotions and her secrets tucked close out of a need for self-preservation.

If she had smiled sweetly and teased him to get what she wanted, she'd have come up empty-handed. Justin had been with all kinds of women and he could spot a manipulative one a mile away.

This one had fought him at every turn and rolled out the word "no" as if it were a universal bargaining chip.

Her frightened eyes and softly spoken plea did what nothing else could have. It made him fold faster than a gambler with a bad hand.

"Okay."

Her eyes brightened. No smile, but he held out hope that over the next five days he could coax one happy face out of this woman at some point.

But he was not taking any more chances with her safety.

He offered, "I'll wait to report the incident until after I've delivered you."

"Thank you."

Justin held up a hand. "We need to have an understanding. First, we roll at o–six–hundred." He shook that off. "Six in the morning local time. You need to be dressed and packed."

"Yes, okay." She started for the door to the hallway and Justin reached it first, blocking the handle.

"What?" she asked, eyes flashing with warning.

Really? She thought that look would scare him?

Moving on, he said, "You're staying in here tonight."

Her anger fell away. "No." But this no came out soft and unsure.

"Yes."

Once again, she got her grit back quickly. "*Stay in my room!*"

"Actually," he said, pulling his phone out and hitting the redial for the hotel, "it's *my* room under my name." When the front desk answered, Justin gave them her room number and said that party had decided to check out.

She gasped. "No. Can *not* do."

He ended the call and shoved the phone in his pocket. "I just did. Before you get all jacked up, you're the one who broke the rules and ended up attacked. If we're going to spend five days together, you're going to be where I can keep an eye on you the entire time. It may not seem important to you, but my boss expects me to keep you safe until I deliver you. I do not let that man down. Until we arrive, I'm not chasing you down again and I'd just as soon avoid fighting other shifters as well."

"Not nice."

True. Herc found that amusing and snorted.

Fucking bear. Justin said, "That's not a fair statement, Elianna." That was her name. Not Eli. She was a client. "I'm making sure you get the five days. That's nice, right?"

Her face fell. She muttered as if the words might choke her. "Yes. Thank you for duty."

She was turning his insides into a pretzel.

One minute she shouted angry words at him, the next minute she turned him into putty with her pleading, then she went back to demanding and now insulted him with her backhanded thank-you for performing the job that he'd been assigned.

The wiring got crossed in his brain, because he still found her hot. Even more so the few times she let go of that tight control and yapped at him.

Five days.

He shouldn't do this, not with the way she affected him, but he'd said he would.

He kept his word, no matter how much anyone annoyed him while doing so.

Unlike the Clan Boudreaux alpha, who Justin didn't consider high on the integrity ladder.

Justin had done everything he could to distance himself from that bunch, starting with being a man he could face in the mirror every night.

Now he had to go back to the place he never wanted to visit again. Five days from now.

"Am tired." Turning away, she dragged her suitcase into the bathroom and shut the door.

Justin's stomach growled. He was still hungry so he went back to the table, determined to enjoy the rest of his meal while she did whatever had to do to get ready for bed. He normally stayed up late, but the last two days had been long and it was closing in on eleven locally.

When she didn't emerge in twenty minutes and Justin didn't hear any water running, he tapped on the bathroom door. "Elianna, please come out."

"No."

"I thought you wanted to go to bed?"

"Yes. Sleep here."

He thunked his head against the door.

CHAPTER 12

E LIANNA HAD A STIFF NECK from trying to sleep in the bathtub, but it felt better now as she stretched.

How could she stretch in a tub?

She curled her fingers into the soft linen beneath her and realized she was no longer in the bathroom.

Opening her eyes, she allowed them to adjust to the dark room. With the bathroom door left ajar, the night-light inside gave off a soft glow. Enough light slipped through the crack in the door for her to see clearly with her bear shifter eyes.

Directly across from her in the bed closest to the door, Justin lay on his back wearing only a pair of shorts. He had an arm draped across his face.

Beautiful male creation even from the side.

His whole form was a work of art, carved exactly how she would create a man's body. Long legs wrapped with cords of muscle. On each exhale, she got a nice view of more across his stomach.

Six pack. That's what she'd heard an American woman call the hard ripple of muscles.

Elianna counted. Justin had eight, not six.

She had almost ruined her chance at five days of exploration by going for the walk. Her bear had better not give her any more grief after that. She felt her animal sleeping, but once the bear stirred it was like an active child wanting to do everything Elianna couldn't allow.

Her shoulder still ached, but had healed enough for her to use her arm. Her bear wanted to shift so she would heal faster. Elianna would like that too, but it could not happen.

Her bear did not understand her life.

Just a little patience and she'd free her bear, but not until these five days were over. She mentally counted from today, which was Saturday to Wednesday.

She could do this. She would not show Justin what her bear looked like. It bothered her that she should care what he thought, but ... he had agreed to the five days.

He had been nice. She had been angry.

Five days close together would be bad. Very bad.

Because she liked the way he looked at her even if it could go nowhere.

If she shifted to her bear, Justin would be polite, but things would change between them as it had between her and a polar bear she'd met two winters back.

She'd taken a three-day break and went up into the mountains after weeks of being unable to shift and free her bear. She'd met a man four years older than she was, who followed her the entire first day as she hunted a spot to spend the night.

He hadn't been threatening, just curious.

That night she called out in the dark and invited him into her camp. He was nice and said he'd been traveling alone for months. He sounded as lonely as she felt. She could not date humans and she was not welcome at the local clan back home, which left few choices for companionship.

That night, she soothed years of feeling rejected in the arms of a generous lover who made her laugh and tremble with need. She awoke the next morning to his happy face.

They decide to shift and hunt breakfast together.

She started believing she could have someone in this world who did not judge her as inferior.

But as soon as she shifted, her bear sensed something was wrong. This man's beautiful white polar bear shied away from her bear, choosing to hunt for fish downstream.

Her bear didn't like him either.

Once they'd shifted back to human form and dressed, her sweet lover came to her with disappointment in his eyes. He said, "My bear and I are one soul. I would like to find out if we could be more, but without his approval it isn't possible."

She'd choked back tears and nodded. "I see."

He had hugged her and kissed her, thanking her for the wonderful night and apologizing again for not being able to stay.

Not even a stranger bear shifter would accept her.

Justin was just as close to his bear. She could tell.

Over on the other bed, Justin made a deep inhale. He didn't move his arm, but he said, "Mornin'," in a sleep-roughened voice.

How had he known she was awake? "Yes, morning."

Lowering his arm, he rolled toward her and bent his other arm to prop his head.

She got a full shot of his chest and ... there were no words. She knew what powerful male shifters looked like with few clothes, but other than that fleeting night with the polar bear shifter, no others had ever raised a hair of interest from her.

To be honest, the polar bear shifter could not compare to Justin.

Licking her lips, she realized her mouth was dry.

Justin groaned and yanked a pillow from behind him that he placed over the front of his shorts.

She looked from that to his face where his mouth twitched with a smile. How could a smile cause her body to heat and her breasts to ache?

His eyes darkened and her heart skipped a beat.

Where the polar bear shifter had been teasing and enthusiastic, the look buried in Justin's dark gaze warned he had far more than teasing on his mind.

"Stop worrying, Eli. I'm not going to do anything, but I can't control a natural reaction to waking up across from you."

She struggled to come up with a reply.

She should be correcting him about calling her Eli. That was not her name, but it sounded so nice when he said it. She wanted to wrap his words around her and hold them close.

Her polar bear shifter had been nice, but the words he'd spoken had been used so often for other women that Elianna could hear the worn edges when he teased.

"Cat got your tongue, Eli?"

"No."

He sighed. "You're gonna need a bigger vocabulary for me to spend five days with you."

There was that twisted humor of his, but she was still stuck on

I can't control a natural reaction to waking up across from you.

Had he meant that as a compliment or just a statement of his situation?

She chose to call it compliment. There had been so few in her life she would not give this one up.

Justin's words were unpolished and gruff, but he said what he meant. She liked that in a person and had met few men who possessed that trait. Her ship captain friend had been one.

The reason she thought this might be true of Justin was the way he hadn't tried to gain her cooperation last night. Instead, he said what he had on his mind, which irritated her beyond belief.

In fact, he'd behaved like a grumpy bear as opposed to a normal man, especially a shifter, who would have tried to manipulate her.

In hindsight, she wanted to chuckle at the memory.

But where she came from, people did not laugh at such foolishness. Her people were a serious breed who faced the hardships of life with a stern face and iron determination.

She would bet Justin laughed as much as he breathed, and she envied his lightheartedness.

"What's going on in that head of yours, Eli? You plotting my death the minute we drive away so you can shove me in a ditch and take the car?"

See? He said the most outrageous things. "Would not hurt you."

He rolled his eyes up and back down. "Chill. I was joking."

"You are strange man."

"I've been called worse." Then his grin appeared again when he added, "But not by a prettier woman."

Her heart flipped around in her chest again. He was giving it more work than when her bear ran through the mountains.

Speaking of which, her bear was fully awake and said, *See bear.*

Her bear wanted to see Justin's? Why?

The only thing Elianna and her bear had been in agreement on since moving to PK was that neither of them had ever been interested in any grizzly bear shifter.

What was Justin doing to her bear that it wanted to meet his?

"How's your shoulder, Eli?"

"All fine."

"You're sure?"

Why did he question her? She could not make the wound heal faster.

Not true. Not true. I heal us, her bear chimed in.

Elianna silently told her bear, *No. Be quiet.*

Not nice.

Yes, yes, yes. How many times had her bear said that, even though Elianna would work day and night to get ahead so she could get a half day off to climb into the mountains at home and let her bear run?

Her bear made a soft growl and let it go.

Elianna searched for something to say because Justin watched her as if he waited for a reply.

What had he last said? That she would kill him and take the car. He had no worries.

She told him, "You and car safe. No drive in Kamchatka. No driver in ditch."

His eyebrows lifted at that, but then he asked, "Wait. You don't drive? Why not?"

"No place to drive."

"You live in one of the largest countries in the world. I'm sure it's a long distance between major cities on the east coast of Russia, but being a bear shifter I'd think you'd like to roam some."

Her bear said, *Yes. Run now.*

Elianna silently said, *No. Do not interfere. Busy day. Be good if you want run and swim soon.*

Swim with bear.

Ignoring that, Elianna said to Justin, "I walk much." She could see no clock, but figured she should get dressed so she would not make him late to leave.

"Why five days?" he asked in a soft voice. "Why did they agree to that?"

She considered all the things she could say and dismissed them. Justin was being nice, but men were the reason she was in this bad spot in life.

With nothing better to say, she shrugged. "First time in this country. I want see much before stuck at clan."

From the solemn look on his face, he weighed her answer.

Would it come up short?

He asked, "How much has your shoulder healed?"

She moved it a little and felt the twinge of healing. "Is fine. Shirt will cover."

"You can have the bathroom first, and take your time."

She growled at that before she could stop herself.

His eyes widened. "*What* did I say now?"

"Nothing."

"Did you make a big word out of no? That's new."

Aggravating bear! She had slept in her clothes, which were wrinkled badly, but no worse than the rest of her things in her suitcase so she slid out of bed.

Her gaze went to her open—and *empty*—suitcase. "Where are clothes?"

"Calm down. Your clothes are hanging in the closet and the rest of your stuff is sitting on a shelf next to them."

She could not understand this man. "Why would you hang clothes?"

"They were wrinkled. Would you prefer them that way? If so, give me a minute and I'll wad them up," he countered in a calm voice with that little smile at the corner of his mouth.

"No wrinkles." *Crazy man*, she silently added.

"Then we're all happy, right?" He gave her a big smile.

"Yes, okay." She found a button up shirt and jeans in the closet, admitting to herself that he had done her a favor. Too many years of being shunned and the butt of jokes had destroyed her ability to accept anything at face value.

She would have to show her appreciation today. She didn't know how, but with many miles in front of them she would find a chance.

For now, she turned to him, holding her clothes. "Thank you."

He said, "You're welcome ... Eli."

She took her time in spite of being annoyed at once again being told to not rush through dressing. Not that it should matter, but she did take a long, hot shower and a few extra minutes to comb her shoulder-length locks to a shine. She pulled her hair into a ponytail at the nape of her neck, hissing at having to raise her arm so high.

When she finished, she gave herself an honest assessment and decided she did look better than when she stepped off the boat yesterday.

She would not scare people. Justin might have been right.

Still, it seemed rude to point out she could use improvement.

When she stepped out of the bathroom, Justin had on a green long-sleeved pullover and worn jeans. He stood just a bit taller in his boots and his short hair glistened with water.

She asked, "You shower?"

"Yep. All set. I'm ready to eat."

"Where?"

"In your old room."

Her mouth dropped open and he put a finger under her chin, lifting gently.

That stalled whatever she had been about to say.

Stepping back, he said, "Hungry?"

Now she remembered what had been on her mind. "Room was closed?"

"I had a key, but I actually used the door connecting both rooms."

"You called to close ... "

"Oh, I called back and got the room again."

She crossed her arms and paid for it with a sharp pain in her shoulder. "You lied."

"No, I didn't. I did cancel the room, but I called back after you decided to sleep in the bathroom and said I needed the key to remain active until eight this morning since the room had already been paid for."

How could she argue with that?

She wanted to, but she didn't. Instead, she made a mental note not to trust anything he said from here on. Just another man who rearranged the truth to suit his own needs.

The same man who must have carried her from the bathroom to the bed. Why did he have to be so confusing?

She would not go off on her own again while they were in the cities, but neither would she live under his thumb.

These five days were hers.

She paid for them with her freedom.

"We eat and shop," she declared, letting Justin know he was not in charge of her.

"I can't wait." His grin widened.

Why was he so happy about that? What was he not telling her? "What?"

"Why am I excited?"

"Yes, that."

He stepped close, causing her brain to quit working again. Probably because all the blood ran away to her bottom half. He whispered, "Because I'm going to give you exactly what you want."

What did he think she wanted?

CHAPTER 13

G

Clan Boudreaux, Louisiana

"IS IT DONE, WOLF?" T-BONE asked, gripping his mobile phone in a tight fist. He knew the answer to that question, but he was always willing to give someone a chance to prove him wrong. This wouldn't be the first time he'd been disappointed, but it would be the last time this Black River pack managed it if this wolf screwed his plan.

"No, T-Bone. In fact, I'm seriously considering giving this contract back after you lied to me," Mateo said, not sounding as if he bluffed.

T-Bone paced his upstairs home office and kept his voice low. He shouldn't have to worry about someone hearing, but you could never be too careful in the Boudreaux Clan. He'd soundproofed the walls in his two-story house against any shifter listening in on his conversation from outside. He'd tested it with his hearing and television turned up gradually to know what worked.

That's why he took calls above the ground floor, but he still worried about someone who might have found a way to listen near the windows on this level. He couldn't remove the windows to replace with better soundproofing without alerting others.

No precaution was too much.

He couldn't be connected to the Black River pack in any way once this wolf did manage to finish the job for which T-Bone had already paid a sizeable deposit.

Torn between wanting to tell this jerk, Mateo, to piss off and worrying that the wolf might not be bluffing, T-Bone asked, "Why? Is one female bear shifter that hard for your people to take down?"

"She won't be a problem, but her bodyguard killed my wolf. You said she was being escorted by *humans*."

Ah, shit. What had happened? "Hey, man, that's what I was told."

Who had T-Bone's alpha sent to collect Elianna in San Francisco?

His alpha said he was calling a friend who was not connected to any shifter clans or packs, to ensure she would arrive safely. His alpha couldn't send a bear shifter from their clan due to bad blood between him and the wolf pack alpha who ran San Francisco, or T-Bone might have been sent to pick up the Russian princess.

He'd dodged a titanium bullet there.

In the past, his alpha had tapped humans he'd known for many years to do the occasional side job. He'd been doing that long before one of their own had revealed the existence of shifters to humans eight years ago.

Shit got acquainted with spinning fan blades.

A damn jackal shifter had sold them all out. Humans didn't deal with that well. They considered shifters to be on the same level as animals.

That wasn't true.

Humans liked their domestic animals but would run a shifter down in a minute.

Mateo broke into T-Bone's thoughts. "What do you intend to do about my wolf?"

Here we go. Everything came down to money. "You want me to pay for a wolf that got his ass kicked by a bodyguard? What kind of people are you hiring, wolf?"

"I *expect* to be compensated for losing a very capable operative from our Black River pack, who trusted me not to send him in blind. The shifter protecting her is stronger than most shifters."

T-Bone paused in his stomping around. "Hey, I'm a bear shifter. Don't go lumping me into that weak mix."

"Really? Can you pick up a wolf shifter that weighs over two-fifty in human form, and toss him thirty yards through the air?"

Exaggerate much? "Not unless I grew another three feet taller.

Are you trying to tell me someone tossed your wolf into the San Francisco Bay?"

"Yes."

No joking or hedging, just a straightforward answer that had T-Bone fidgeting more. Could that be true? He walked to the window, searching outside.

Nothing there.

Could a person die from an overload of paranoia?

T-Bone took no one's word on something that sounded like a rumor. "How do you *know* this bodyguard did that?"

"I had backup close by, but not close enough to reach my first wolf before the bear shifter jerked him up and hoisted him out into the bay."

"Your wolf couldn't swim to the bank?"

"Not with a snapped neck."

That sucked. Hold everything. "Did you say the bodyguard is a *bear* shifter?"

"That's what my second wolf told me."

No shifters from T-Bone's clan were unaccounted for, so who had his alpha sent?

That wasn't T-Bone's problem.

This wolf was being paid well to make sure Elianna did not show up in five days. T-Bone had no intention of ever meeting her, much less in his territory.

If she did manage to arrive, his life would no longer be his own.

He hated to spend the money, but he said, "If I double the fee, are we good?"

The wolf didn't jump at that offer.

T-Bone despised having to deal with this bunch of slimy wolves. "What's it going to take to smooth this over, wolf?"

"Double the fee *and* Jugo Loco distribution rights."

"No. Shit no. You think I want our shifters losing their minds on that jacked-up tea your bunch cooks up? Stick to hooking smaller packs on that drug. Not ours."

"I'm not suggesting we supply your people. Your alpha rules most of Louisiana. We have to go around that state to make deliveries to the east. I simply want the ability to drive across without being detained. That's not a lot to ask in exchange for bringing in a highly skilled shifter from our army."

These wolves were the only group capable of handling this issue with Elianna quietly and without leaving a trail leading back to T-Bone.

But he trusted them as much as he did the rest of his own clan. Not one bit.

If he granted this wolf pack access through his alpha's territory, the Black River pack would deal that Jugo Loco inside the state.

He knew it as he stood here.

You'd think gaining a Russian bear shifter of royal bloodline, and in her prime, would be bonus enough for the Black River pack.

Greedy bastards wanted more.

T-Bone was up to his neck in trouble if he backed out at this point, so he said, "Done. But you have to run your people through when I tell you. I'm not in a position to personally clear every shipment on a daily basis. I'm going to have to select a handful of our shifters who will look the other way for the right amount of money." More money to pay out.

This bitch was costing him a small fortune.

"Understood, but we start moving our shipments through tomorrow."

He hated the smug note in the wolf's voice. T-bone added, "Now that you know all you need to know about this job, I don't want any more excuses, Mateo."

"We deliver results. With our new agreement, I can spend more money on this. I'm assigning the task to a wolf that specializes in difficult cases and who knows how to handle magic. Using magic is another expense, so you're getting more than your money's worth. You'll be notified as soon as your female shifter is off the radar. I'd intended on keeping both of them, but we may have to kill her bodyguard."

"Like I give a shit what you do with him, wolf? Just don't leave any trail that leads to me."

"Don't insult me."

Touchy wolf. T-Bone said, "Where are they now?"

"She and her bodyguard returned to their hotel. Evidently my wolf clawed her before the bodyguard showed up. My second wolf observed the bodyguard being chummy with her."

As if T-Bone cared? He'd spent years working his way up the ladder in the Boudreaux Clan, but never expected his alpha to *reward* him with a mate.

He didn't want a mate.

Not until it was time to take over as alpha. To satisfy his voracious sexual appetite, he took what he wanted from human women outside of his home territory who didn't expect to see him again.

No cubs or any other bullshit family crap in the way.

What man would give that up for some damn Russian princess who would consider herself equal to him? *Dream on, bitch.*

His alpha had been seriously happy to inform T-Bone his life was about to go straight to hell.

Taking all that into consideration, if anything bad happened to this woman and her bodyguard, it was his alpha's fault.

T-Bone grinned. Felt good to get that off his conscience.

But that damn wolf was still yapping about how his people operated.

Losing interest, T-bone asked, "How long will this take?"

Mateo paused and said, "Sometime during the five days you said she'd be allowed to travel first."

"You can't nail the timeframe down any better than that?" It was Saturday and T-Bone didn't want to step away from the clan until this was done so he'd have the perfect alibi, but he hadn't planned on screwing up his entire week.

"We're successful because we don't rush in without a plan. The only time we aren't successful is when our clients fail to give us all the information."

Just had to keep bringing that up, didn't he? Ready to end this conversation, T-bone let the wolf get his say done.

"My people will wait for the perfect opportunity to neutralize the bodyguard and snatch her. Don't call in the meantime. Wait to hear from me. Don't interfere in any way, bear. Only a seriously suicidal person would intentionally become my enemy."

T-Bone could turn into a nine-foot-tall monster that crushed anything in its way. He'd faced shifters of all sizes and types in battle, but that wolf's warning sent ripples of concern across his skin.

Those Black River pack dicks were crazy fuckers.

He hung up his phone, thinking over it all to see if he'd missed anything. Felt like this was getting out of hand.

But the Russian alpha couldn't blame Clan Boudreaux with failing to fulfill their end of the agreement if his daughter never arrived. The bodyguard's employer had to know his business came with the chance of losing a man on the job, which left the female bear shifter as the only innocent in all of this.

It wasn't Elianna's fault that she was going to be in the wrong place at the wrong time. On the flip side, she shouldn't have agreed to join the Boudreaux Clan sight unseen and she knew she lived in a dangerous world.

What female shifter wouldn't in today's anti-shifter climate?

Elianna was about to find out just how deadly it was once the Black River pack got their hands on her to use as one of their lab rats.

CHAPTER 14

JUSTIN HELD THE DOOR OPEN for Eli, who had an unsure expression in place. He wanted to say, "Be careful what you wish for," but he doubted she would understand the reference.

"What is this?" she asked, her eyes taking in the very tall, two-story, open floor plan filled wall-to-wall with anything a person could want for hunting, fishing and camping.

"Jackman's Outpost," Justin replied. "It's similar to a Bass Pro Shop or a Cabela's."

"What?" she asked as her wide eyes continued taking in everything in the busy store. Saturday was prime-time shopping here.

He had to keep reminding himself that she'd come from a place that probably didn't have big-box stores. He asked, "Don't you have a store for buying fishing and hunting supplies?"

"Yes."

"What's it called?"

She told him, but the words didn't make sense.

He frowned at her. "Are you saying *avocado*?"

"Yes."

He spelled it. "That's a fruit here."

"No. Avokado. With k, not c." She looked around. "Why are we here?"

He tried out a new smile on her, hoping to crack that serious shell she lived inside. "Last night you said you would go shopping at my favorite place. This is it. I don't get here often since it's not near where I'm usually working, but I'm glad you suggested it."

He'd been smiling for the last couple hours since leaving San

Francisco and heading north. This store had always been a treat for him.

She glared at the stuffed brown bear standing upright near the entrance. "You like dead bear?"

The taxidermy structure did creep him out these days, but he hadn't been able to shift when he first walked into this place. Later on, he fantasized about seeing the bear shifters who taunted him as a child turned into one of these.

Not a healthy thing for a kid to think, but he'd lived in an unhealthy state for one his age.

Still, Justin was not admitting any of that and giving her an opening to argue her way out of this place. He dismissed the stuffed animal as, "It's not one of us. Okay, let's get a buggy and get you shopping."

"Okay, yes."

He got a kick out of her new reply when she agreed with anything and pushed the buggy into the center of the store to get this show going.

An hour later, Justin was ready to admit defeat.

He had first steered her to women's clothing where she surprised him by not selecting something she'd look good in walking a runway. Instead, she chose flannel shirts in muted colors, cargo pants and hiking boots. From there, she continued selecting items only an outdoors enthusiast would want, which included a pup tent.

When Justin tried to explain it would be too small for her, she gave him one of her what-is-wrong-with-you looks and said, "I know."

From that point on, he withheld his opinion since she never asked for it, but he began to figure out that she was buying for someone younger than her as well. Whatever she bought for herself in clothing, she chose a mini-me version in the boys' department.

He guessed the kid had to be around five to seven years old.

That explained the pup tent, sort of, but not really because she was a bear shifter headed to a bear shifter clan.

Did she think shifter kids in this country would need a tent? Was it for a kid back home?

For that matter, who *was* the kid that would receive the clothing?

Justin had to hand it to her, though. She was an efficient and frugal shopper, only turning to him for clarification of a price or tag description.

Hell, if he was really honest, he'd admit to having fun watching her shop.

She turned to the buggy Justin had manned while he followed her. Instead of shock over all she'd bought, she seemed to be taking inventory to determine if she'd missed anything.

When she finally caught his eye, she said, "Am done. What do you want?"

A smile.

He'd pay for all she'd picked out if she'd just smile.

No, he wouldn't. He wanted to get an honest one given freely.

Shaking his head, he said, "I'm good."

"You said this was favorite store."

"It is."

"But you did not enjoy."

"You don't think so?" he asked, expecting that to throw her sideways mentally.

She started to speak and stopped, clearly at a loss.

She was wrong about him enjoying himself. He'd become engrossed in watching how her mind worked and seeing her choices. Eli wasn't at all what he'd first expected, and yes, he had given up trying to make himself call her Elianna.

That name was too formal for the woman before him.

There were layers upon layers of Eli he wanted to peel back one at a time until he found the person inside who showed her real emotions.

The one who laughed.

She had to be in there.

He did love a challenge and had yet to find one quite as intriguing as this bear shifter.

If he could get her out in the woods, he'd convince her to shift so he could see her bear. The one that Herc had been showing an interest in as well.

That was strange. Herc didn't like female bear shifters.

Two bears, Herc murmured.

What are you talking about, Herc? Justin replied silently

Not one.

What in the world was Herc saying? Justin let it go and pushed the cart toward the checkout, where he suggested Eli use her credit card.

"Yes, okay," she muttered as she dug into her pocket. She pulled the card out and handed it to Justin. "Here."

Justin shook his head. "You do it."

"Woman busy. You are more fast."

He crossed his arms. "You are just as fast."

"Why ruin good day?" Eli snapped at him.

"I'm not. I don't know how often we'll be shopping together and figured you'd want to know how to use the card later on by yourself." He stopped short of saying after he dropped her off, because he wasn't in such a hurry to do so anymore.

Gifting him with a loud sigh, she turned to the woman running the register and waited for directions. With some pointing and explaining, the woman walked her through processing the charge and requested Eli's ID.

Thankfully, the shifter ID looked just like a passport and even had a decent image of Eli for comparing, right down to the disgruntled expression.

Justin wished Eli had been given a driver's license instead, but thankfully not all cashiers could immediately tell the difference between a shifter passport and a human passport with just a visual check.

If Justin had to guess after watching Eli shop meticulously, which probably included keeping a running total in her head, he'd say she was the type who wanted to be good at what she did.

Not to appear as a clueless foreigner.

Once the transaction was completed, a smiling cashier handed over the credit card and thanked Eli for her business.

His little hedgehog politely thanked the woman for excellent service.

If Justin hadn't picked up all the bags and made for the exit, Eli would still be standing there in a mutual admiration contest with the woman. But all joking aside, he was starting to see new pieces of Eli and liked what he'd observed.

She sure hadn't turned out to be a diva princess.

Had she bought all of this for something she had planned once they reached Clan Boudreaux? Why not wait until then to shop? Half of this would be too hot in Louisiana for a shifter, even in the winter.

More for him to figure out, but the largest puzzle piece was why Eli had refused to shift into her animal last night.

Her bear had to be ready to run after that long sea trip and Eli's injury. Herc would have been upset with Justin if he stayed human for no obvious reason after being wounded.

Justin seethed every time he thought about that wolf shifter attacking her. In hindsight, he'd let the predator off too easy. The San Francisco wolf alpha had better come up with a name and origin for that rogue soon.

With the bags stuffed into the back of his big sport utility rental, he shut the rear gate and told Eli, "I have a surprise for you."

Her face fell and her eyes narrowed in suspicion. "No surprises. More shopping."

What the hell? He repeated his mental mantra of not losing his temper and asked, "What are you looking for?"

"Maps. Want maps of ... country."

"This entire country?" he asked.

"No." She concentrated a moment and said, "Forest and mountains. No cities."

"It's a big country. Do you have a specific place in mind?" Hopefully mentioning mountains ruled out Louisiana.

"North. Snow in winter."

Damn, that just played into his hand. "I know exactly where to find what you're looking for and the maps won't cost you a penny."

Her face softened with relief. "Yes, okay. Free good, but no steal."

He scowled at her. "Why would you think I meant we'd steal them?"

"You change words and trick me."

"Like when?"

"You lie and close room."

She had a point. "Okay, I might have misled you a little about the hotel room, but I am not going to lead you into trouble like stealing."

"Maybe." She turned for the passenger side.

He stepped past her to open the passenger door.

Those crystal blue eyes lifted to his and threatened to pull him in so far he'd never be able to climb out.

"Thank you for best store and shop with me. You nice."

He didn't get a smile, but her words were sincere and hearing her say he was nice at this point carried more weight than other women fawning over him in the past.

Spending so much time with this one could be dangerous.

CHAPTER 15

Glacier National Park, Montana

ELIANNA WOULD NEVER HAVE THOUGHT she could spend this much time inside a vehicle with a strange man and like it.

They had left San Francisco two days ago, visited Justin's favorite store, which was now her favorite, on the way to Oregon and explored beautiful giant trees along the way.

Redwoods. She wanted to show Nico. He would look like a bug in that forest.

Justin never tired of any request she made.

He did not change his mind about staying in the same hotel room, but she had no complaint. How could she, when she woke to see so much of him sprawled on the second bed every morning?

That never got old.

Feeling safe was nice, too.

He called today's travel a "Sunday drive" through amazing national forests in Idaho. She would like to take Nico on Sunday drives some day.

Every stop Justin picked had been perfect.

She felt better about coming to this country even if she only had now three and a half days left to travel.

This was no vacation. Justin might think so, but she needed to know this land for the future.

From the passenger seat, Elianna studied the map of Idaho

spread across her lap, amazed at how many roads connected every place here. She stopped trying to figure them all out and just enjoyed the view as they rode through beautiful country. Now she understood Justin's confusion when she told him PK had no roads connecting it to anything else in Russia.

If there had been even one road out, she would have taken Nico and ridden a bus north.

Maybe she could have saved her mother, too. She doubted that, but she would have tried.

Her mother would not have left Alexandre even though it sounded as if Elianna's father had not misled her mother. Still, every time Elianna recalled how her mother had died, her chest ached.

"You doing okay, Eli?" Justin asked from where he drove this big vehicle with one hand. So at ease and happy.

Silly man would not stop calling her Eli.

She should correct him. Next time.

He wore his confidence as he wore his jeans. Comfortable. She would like to be that secure and to learn how to drive. "Okay, yes."

He chuckled.

"What?"

"I like the way you say yes. Might be my favorite two words, especially spoken in that hot accent of yours."

If he had been making fun of her, she might have taken offense, but he called her hot. She knew what he meant, just not as how that word applied to her. "Not true."

"You don't believe me?"

"No."

"*Annnd* ... my least favorite word is back. Why don't you believe me and don't say it's because I tricked you in the hotel room."

She lifted her eyebrows at him. "Ah ha."

He stopped grinning. "Hey, I'm not admitting to tricking you."

"Sound like yes."

"Stop changing the subject. Back to you. If I say you're hot, you *are* hot."

"Not what you say first day."

Scrunching his forehead, he asked, "What are you talking

about?"

"You tell me use one hour to fix self."

He drove along on the smooth highway that felt as though she were floating over land. When he cut his eyes at her again, he asked, "Do you mean when I told you to take an hour to freshen up that first night?"

"That."

He started laughing and scratched his chin. "Eli, I wasn't saying you needed an hour to get pretty. You're already pretty. Hot, in fact. I just wanted you to have extra time to relax."

"Oh." She turned away, studying the tall signs and trees that flew past her window.

"Is that why you were so mad at me the first night?"

"Not mad," she muttered, embarrassed at facing the truth.

"Don't forget that I'm a shifter. You can't get that past me," he said, calling her on the lie. "Okay, so now that we're clear, you're hot. Got it?"

"Crazy bear." But her heart lifted with knowing he had not been criticizing her appearance.

Ignoring his foolishness, she lifted the map, intending to get out of this topic. While his ridiculous comments made her insides melt, she had to stay on track and beat down this attraction she felt for the grizzly.

She could shift and that would end all flirting.

But she liked his flirting, so no shifting.

Run. Run. Run, her bear chimed in.

She spoke to her bear silently. *Please, no trouble. You run soon. And swim. Be good, please.*

Her bear grumbled, but settled down.

She had to keep her attention on gaining as much information as possible.

Justin had been very helpful, answering her million questions, but she had not asked about the one thing she'd been avoiding. "Do you know Clan Boudreaux?"

The relaxed look on his face slowly tightened into one of no emotion unless that muscle twitching in his jaw counted. Why was he angry?

"Yes, I know about them."

"How much?"

"Lots. I grew up there."

He had not sounded happy about it. "Bad clan?" she asked, growing concerned about the deal she had made in blind faith.

"Not bad for everyone else. I just ... didn't like it so I left at eighteen."

Maybe not so bad. He had been a young man wanting to go out on his own, but she still wanted to know more. "Why leave?"

He didn't answer her at first. When he did reply, he said, "We had a difference of opinion on some things. I decided to part ways instead of staying, which created conflict. There was nothing in Clan Boudreaux for me."

If this powerful grizzly shifter who had carried himself as an alpha had no place in that clan, what kind of mate would she end up with eventually?

Thinking about that made her stomach hurt.

Seeing Justin unhappy made it worse. She looked around, realizing they'd been rolling for a while. "Is Idaho?"

His shoulders visibly relaxed. "We left that an hour ago. We're in Montana. Look for the map in the door pocket."

She found it and opened the map, then started checking signs. "Is Glacier Park?"

"Yep. Glacier National Park and we're almost there."

She got excited every time they went around mountains, especially this far north. She had a map of the entire country and Montana was next to Canada.

In the next few minutes, they drove along a river that was one long picture she would keep in her mind forever.

This reminded her of the home she loved.

"What is Go To ... " she read out loud, trying to figure out the strange road name.

"Going To The Sun Road. If we stay on this highway it will climb to the top of the mountains. Really spectacular views. We'll drive out that way when we leave and exit on the other side of Glacier so you can see what I'm talking about."

As he usually did when they visited new places, Justin pointed things out to her, explaining history behind the names and locations.

She had been so busy taking it all in, she lost track of where they were when he pulled off on a dirt road.

Before she asked why they were stopping, he said, "I'm going to show you one of my favorite spots. I was born just over the border in Canada and we migrated through these mountains."

"Not Louisiana?"

"My mother's brother was down there. My dad died in an accident so my mom moved south. Louisiana is beautiful, really. Don't misjudge it because I left. It had nothing to do with the territory. I'm just not a hot-weather person and I like the mountains."

The importance of this place was evident in the longing Justin didn't try to hide.

"Is special?"

He leaned forward, looking for something and murmured, "Yes."

Slowing down, he crept along, leaning forward and squinting at everything until his expression changed to one of relief. He sat back and turned off the dirt road, then drove carefully through a path that had not been evident at first.

He found a place and parked. Giving her a sly smile, he said, "I worked as a guide at one time for a group that was gathering evidence of the natural grizzly bear population decline. We used this spot to park and hiked out of here, rather than tourist trailhead areas. I figured you might like to do a little hike."

"Okay, yes," she said in a voice much like Nico's when he got to go fishing. She shoved the map away and scrambled out of the truck, meeting Justin at the back.

He was already opening the rear entry and pulling a backpack to him, which he began stuffing with packaged food, water, and a long-sleeved shirt for each of them.

"So much," she mumbled.

"It's going to be much cooler at the top of these mountains and we have to drink lots of water."

She would not be cold, but he had done everything she'd asked since taking off yesterday morning and he'd never complained. She could do this without pointing out he wasted his energy carrying so much.

Instead, she asked, "What mountain?"

Looping the straps over his arms, he closed up the truck and locked it, pocketing the key. "We're headed to Heavens Peak. You'll love it."

"Yes, okay." In her excitement, she almost repeated her words as her bear had a habit of doing. Inside, Elianna was jumping around and clapping her hands, but outside she kept her pleasant, but controlled, profile. To do otherwise would be inappropriate and make her out to be a silly woman, which she was not.

After watching her for a minute, Justin shook his head.

"What is wrong?" she asked,

"Nothing." He stepped back and looked up at the sky.

She felt certain his nothing was something.

Did he think she was unhappy with this choice? She said, "Good place to walk."

He said, "Uhm-hmm," but his answer got muffled by him facing away.

She added, "Glad for break."

She got a grunt in reply. He was quickly ruining her good mood. "What wrong?" she grumbled.

He replied without facing her. "I don't think you're ready to hear the answer to that question."

She gave up. "Why backpack? My backpack."

"Yes, it is yours, but I'm going to carry it so you can enjoy just looking around and be careful to watch where you step. I know you're a bear shifter that can climb this terrain, but I also know this area like the back of my hand and you don't. The backpack is because I thought we'd spend the afternoon up on that ridge," he pointed in the distance. "Maps can't give you a true sense of the land."

He was right. All mountain areas looked the same to her.

He kept explaining, "We may be shifters, but we're going to expend energy reaching that altitude. We'll need food and water as we burn calories. I only packed fruit, energy bars and water we picked up at the last gas stop."

She definitely wanted to explore this area. "Good."

"Ah, so that's two things I've done right today."

"Yes."

From the way he stopped talking, she assumed he waited for something else from her, but she didn't know what it could be.

Then he gave another headshake as if to himself and suggested,

"You might want a jacket once we get up there."

"Am good." What was that all about? Why did he keep waiting for her to do or say something, then act disappointed when she couldn't guess what was going on inside his hard head?

If he wanted something, he should say so.

An hour later, she glanced around to find they had covered a lot of ground and the view got more breathtaking with every step. Based on what Justin said when he slowed to point out an eagle soaring, they still had a ways to go to reach the spot he wanted to visit.

She no longer thought about the miserable voyage to this country, the wolf attack or the confusing man walking ahead.

Lie, her bear muttered.

Elianna was surprised her bear had left her alone this long, but the demanding animal was correct.

She wanted to ignore Justin, but he would not allow it.

His very presence swarmed her senses, making her notice everything from the scent of man and outdoors intermingled to the nice view she'd had of his backside on this climb.

She would like to follow Justin with him wearing shorts.

And maybe no shirt.

Her bear said, *Want see bear. Play, play, bear play.*

No, Elianna told her animal silently, not surprised it still wanted to meet Justin's bear. She pleaded, *Please wait.*

The only reply she got was, *Now.*

She mentally sent back, *No.*

Mean.

Elianna couldn't stomp and shout out loud at her bear without Justin wondering if she'd lost her mind, or asking questions she didn't want to answer. Holding her patience, she told her bear, *Yes, I am mean. You should have picked better shifter.*

When she heard nothing after that, she considered it a positive sign. Maybe her aggravating bear would sulk in silence for a while. She had too much to do over the next three days to lose opportunities like this where Justin was willing to teach her more. Her bear would have plenty of time to play as soon as she had Nico and control of her life.

Once Clan Boudreaux got a look at her bear, Elianna would be sent on her way.

Then her bear would be able to run every day.

Justin paused and Elianna ran right into him, which was her bear's fault for distracting her. She bounced off his big body and started sliding back down the sharp incline.

Moving faster than she thought even a shifter could, Justin grabbed her shoulders before she slipped back down the last ten feet they'd traversed.

Her shoulder had not entirely healed, but Justin had been careful not to touch the damaged area, yet he still managed to keep her from falling.

He pulled her up to him and stared down with panicked eyes. "Hey, I'm sorry, Eli, babe. I should have given a hand signal that I was stopping. Damn, you could have tumbled down the mountain."

Her heart raced as if that had actually happened.

She should be calming down now that she was safe, but the feel of his hands on her encouraged her heart to beat even faster. Of course, her hands clutched his upper arms, which were almost too large around for her to manage a strong grip.

That was different. She had big hands for a woman.

She told him, "I am fine. I would roll like ball. Not break neck. But I like not fall."

She was ready for him to release her, though she was in no hurry to give up his touch.

Next, he did something she never expected.

Lifting her in the air, he turned and walked up six more steps to a flat area and set her down.

Too shocked to speak, she could not move her gaze from his face. Her heart continued to show how fast it could race.

His heart thumped just as quickly.

She realized her hands had moved from his arms to his chest. When had they done that?

Energy rifled through her body again, unlike anything she'd ever experienced near another shifter.

Justin lost his worried expression, but the one that replaced it now worried her. Hunger burned in his intense gaze.

The kind of hunger that had nothing to do with a meal and would normally send her running.

Not this time.

The longer he stared at her as if she was everything he needed in this moment, the more her body came awake, wanting what that gaze promised. Deep in her mind, a voice warned her to back away, that she had a goal and it did not involve an irresistible grizzly shifter.

One that would be appalled the minute he saw her bear.

Justin leaned in and she panicked, backing out of his grasp.

He let her go without argument, but that heavy gaze didn't let up.

Her skin felt too tight. Everything inside her wanted to step up and take what he offered, but she could not make a mistake right now. This was the only chance she had to find a place to hide when the time came to take Nico and run.

She must be careful and make good decisions. Every one of them would affect her and Nico.

Why did it feel as if she were turning her back on something amazing that she'd never see again?

The moment disintegrated when Justin looked out over the mountainside and said, "We have a little farther to go and we'll take a break to eat."

Half of her was thankful he acted as if nothing was going on between them, but not the half that felt abandoned. She couldn't blame that on him.

The choice had been left in her hands.

"Ready?" he asked in a sober tone that left her feeling chilled.

"Yes."

He struck out again, but took a more easterly direction over rolling terrain with tall trees and cool air.

She could not keep her mind on hiking. Not when she fantasized what it would be like to throw off all caution and give in to this aching need that ate at her more and more, the longer she was around Justin. Her breasts felt heavy and wished for his touch. That was nothing compared to the need between her legs.

She had lived without a man's touch for close to two years after the one time she'd let her guard down with the polar bear shifter.

Hadn't she learned anything from him?

The minute his bear had seen hers, his polar bear had turned his back, disgusted by the mixed-color coat of Elianna's bear.

Back in human form, the man had tried to blame it all on his bear, but after he walked away she realized the human side had been just as put off.

It was a simple fact of nature to desire your own kind.

She had no kind. She was other.

Polar bear and grizzly shifter males wanted the cubs that represented their dynasties to be pure.

She couldn't blame them, but it didn't make her feel any better to know she'd be rejected over and over again, except for whatever mate she ended up with in Clan Boudreaux. Had the alpha there already chosen someone, or would he allow Elianna to choose?

What grizzly shifter would accept her bear once he saw it?

The Clan Boudreaux alpha, and her father, wanted strong blood for expanding their clans and allies. They didn't care what anyone else wanted, certainly not a bastard female shifter.

She felt sympathy for the poor male stuck with mating her if he could not refuse her, but that would be disastrous. Still, she felt more sympathy for herself and Nico. She wanted Nico to have a good life. She wanted that for herself as well.

How could she mate someone who would despise her from day one?

How could she mate someone she cared nothing for?

Watching Justin move smoothly ahead of her, she wished he was still at Clan Boudreaux. He would be a strong mate.

What was she thinking? As nice as Justin was being, he would also step back as soon as he saw her bear.

She had no hope for a happy future with any mate and wishing she could have Justin would only make it more difficult to accept someone else.

A smart woman would prevent Justin from continuing to flirt. Moving this mountain would be simpler than stopping Justin from something he was determined to do.

Still, she was the one who could end this attraction before they turned around to leave.

Swallowing against the thickness in her throat, she made up her mind and searched for the perfect spot to ruin a wonderful day.

CHAPTER 16

*S*HE MAD, HERC GRUMBLED.

Not ready to shift into his bear and let the grumpy animal run off some of his attitude, Justin gritted his teeth.

Did Herc think he needed to be told that Eli was irritated at him for almost kissing her back there?

You stupid.

Enough, Herc. You're not helping.

Always help.

Ignoring his mouthy bear, Justin pushed branches out of the way and held them until Eli walked past. For the first time since they'd started this hike, he had a great shot of her sweet derriere as she strolled into the semi-shaded spot he figured would be a nice time out.

As the trees thinned out higher up this mountain, the air had cooled as well. Not that they didn't both have the stamina to keep going, but it was time to eat and drink more water.

Pointing at a small boulder, Justin suggested, "Why don't you sit there, Eli?"

Turning to look where he designated, Eli sat on the rock and offered him her standard content expression, which lacked any real emotion.

In fact, the only obvious emotion she had shown so far had been anger.

She hadn't even seemed frightened during the attack in San Francisco. She'd been more resigned than anything else, and just thinking about it riled Justin again.

Did she think female shifters were attacked at random all the time here?

Who knew what she thought, when the strength of her vocabulary depended upon yes and no?

Mostly no.

Justin sat cross-legged on the ground in front of her, but remained a reasonable distance away.

She moved to the ground to sit in front of the boulder and mimicked his position. "Told you. Not fragile woman."

"Uhm-hmm." He got busy unpacking the backpack and handing her first water, then two energy bars and a handful of grapes. She'd have to eat a lot more once they made it back to the truck and drove to a restaurant.

This hike hadn't been as demanding as he'd expected for her though. She'd stayed with him step for step to the point she'd run into his back when he stopped to get his bearings.

That had scared the crap out of him. As he turned, he expected to see her falling backward down the side of the mountain, breaking every bone in her body.

He shouldn't have touched her with his adrenaline pumping. That touch had ignited a fire in his body that hadn't died down yet. It was the strangest thing he'd ever experienced around a woman. He'd gotten hot and bothered with sexy and fun women, but he'd never had one flip his switch so easily, especially one that had yet to smile at him.

He'd been so surprised at the scent of her arousal in that moment, he'd just stood there like an idiot until his brain finally said to move her to a safer spot.

He might have chuckled at her surprise when he lifted her so easily, but his dick was hard and he couldn't have pushed a word past his lips when all they wanted to do was kiss her.

What kind of male bear shifters were in her clan?

From the way she'd reacted, you'd think they took her at her word about not being a fragile woman. She was no wilting flower, but she was a still a woman. Even though the shifters in her clan were not as powerful as a Gallize, they weren't weak like humans.

Those males should be able to pick up a woman Eli's size without a major effort, unless they were a bunch of pussy bears.

Herc snorted. *Pussy bears.*

Justin's bear had the same attitude as he did when it came to a male making a woman feel safe.

They didn't have to be an alpha to protect a female.

Justin was starting to seriously question the kind of men Eli had been around growing up. Why else would she act as if she had to constantly fend for herself?

Just another puzzling part of her that did not make sense.

She was the alpha's firstborn daughter. She might not like being called a princess, but coming from a royal line meant that title was her due.

"Why angry?" she asked after a swallow of water.

Her question caught Justin off guard. "I'm not angry."

Pointing at her chest, she said, "Shifter. No got lie past me. All time you smile. Not now."

"I could say the same about you, but you *never* smile to begin with." The words were out before his brain kicked into gear to tell him that had probably sounded better in his head than it had falling out of his mouth.

She paused in chewing on an energy bar and gave him a wounded look. "Not angry."

"I didn't mean that you were. Just ... never mind."

Herc said, *Be nice. Good mate.*

Justin had just taken a big bite of his energy bar and choked on it. He started coughing.

Eli jumped up and ran over to pat his back, and hand him her water. "Drink."

He took the bottle and downed a big swallow, embarrassed to be choking on a damn energy bar.

He said, "I'm good." Lifting his hand as a signal to stop, he repeated more firmly, "I'm good."

Her hand snatched back as if he'd bitten her.

She returned to her spot, but kept her eyes cast down at the energy bar she nibbled on.

Herc growled, making the kind of vibration inside that Justin normally felt just before his bear was ready to break out and kick someone's butt.

His bear was not upset with Eli, but Justin.

To calm Herc and make up to Eli, Justin handed a fresh bottle of water to her and said, "Sorry. I didn't mean to snap at you. I was just ... uh ... " Justin struggled for the right word.

Herc supplied, *Pussy bear.*

Fuck. Shut up, Herc.

Now his bear chuffed in humor.

Eli asked, "Who is Herc?"

Shit, had he really said that out loud?

Now Justin understood what Herc had found so funny besides insulting Justin. "My bear. He's an annoying son of a gun some days."

Her eyes rounded. "You name bear?"

"Sure. Didn't you?"

She glanced down. "No."

Why not? Thankfully, *those* words did not spill out of Justin's runaway mouth.

Lifting her head again, she asked, "Why tell bear shut up?"

Relief smacked Justin at the hope he hadn't said fuck out loud. "Because Herc has an opinion on everything, including things that are not his business," Justin said, hoping his bear caught that message.

Mate my business.

Eli nodded, evidently content with that explanation, and went back to eating her bar while tossing occasional glances at Justin.

He closed his mouth before he started ranting at his bear, who had clearly said mate again and more than once. Justin had not misunderstood Herc back at the hotel after all, but what the hell?

Mind-to-mind, Justin said, *What's with this mate stuff, Herc? She can't be our mate.*

Mate.

Justin reminded Herc, *You do realize she's a princess from a royal line of bear shifters and we're delivering her to Clan Boudreaux?*

Bad clan.

Damn, Herc could be persistent. *What the hell, Herc? You don't like female bear shifters. You told me a long time ago you didn't. What makes this one all of a sudden different?*

Not grizzly.

Well, shit. Did that explain Eli's blue eyes? *What is she?* he asked Herc.

Change and run.

His bear had a point. If Eli shifted, that would clear up all confusion. Had his bear forgotten that Eli still had a not-yet-completely-healed wound because she refused to shift?

Justin wouldn't force her to shift even if he had any idea how to do such a thing. He would never push a woman to do anything she didn't want to do.

But what about this mate thing?

Was Herc just being curious, or was there more to this primal reaction Justin was having to Eli?

She handed Justin the wrappers and empty bottle.

Justin put his second bar away, no longer hungry. Not for food anyhow. He wanted to find out one way or another what was going on between him and Eli before they got off this mountain.

He was a man on a mission he intended to accomplish.

Packing up the backpack, he stood and prepared for an argument. "I don't know about you, but my bear needs to get out and run. It'd be nice to have company."

She brushed invisible crumbs off her clothes and looked around, spotting a cluster of bushes. When she turned back, she said, "Need bathroom."

His excitement at possibly seeing her bear deflated. "Sure. I'll keep my back turned."

This woman was twisting him into an emotional pretzel. He always let his pleasure show, but not what went on inside. He kept unhappy feelings and uncertainty out of sight.

The world was tough enough without sharing his disappointment, but he was having a hard time stuffing it away this time.

He kept hearing the word *mate* in his head.

Herc's fault, no doubt, but it wasn't Herc's fault this wouldn't work between Justin and Eli. He should be glad she didn't want to shift.

She had a destiny that didn't involve Justin.

That was just the way life worked sometimes.

Our mate, Herc demanded.

Before Justin could reply, he heard the brush rattle in the direction she'd walked and instinctively turned to greet her.

No Eli.

A bear almost as big as Herc, with a winter white coat on top that blended down to brown legs, faced him. The shallow-faced shape said grizzly, but this bear had no hump on the top of her back. She had a polar bear shape.

That was the most unusual bear he'd ever seen from a shifter.

She took a tentative step toward him, then another.

Herc pounded at Justin for release. *Out now.*

Justin was too busy sorting through his thoughts to pay attention to Herc's antics. The blue eyes and mixed coat all came together in Justin's brain.

He said, "Ursid hybrid?"

The bear that had been moving steadily toward him froze.

She spun around and took off running.

CHAPTER 17

Elianna let her bear go. They both needed to run until neither one could move.

Ursid hybrid.

Justin couldn't have hurt her more if he'd cursed her.

She'd expected him to ask about her coat or why she'd finally decided to shift, because the Justin she knew would be nice to her.

Not utter the words she could not escape.

She thought he liked her. Maybe even more than liked her.

Not that she had returned his interest even though she'd wanted to, but calling her an ursid hybrid was the same as saying bastard.

Her bear's coat and her mixed-up body shape marked her as the king's betrayal of his own kind. In her case, her father had also betrayed his mate by his infidelity.

That's why Elianna could never be accepted in his clan.

Any clan.

She dropped back and gave her bear the lead.

Her bear ran, happy as a bumblebee bouncing through the woods.

Elianna would use this time to nurse her wounded heart and get her head together so she didn't act like some weepy woman when she was in human form again.

Deep down inside, she'd hoped Justin would be different. He'd be that one shifter who would see that she wasn't damaged goods, but just unusual. He'd proven to be a decent man, better than the ones she'd known. If someone as good as Justin could not look at her without contempt, no male bear shifter ever would.

This would prepare her for meeting her future mate in bear form, but she would not hurt so deeply over that one. Not the way she felt now.

She had solved her problem of Justin flirting all the time.

No more silly comments or smoldering looks.

This was awful.

Something bumped up against her bear, throwing her sidestepping. Her bear chuffed and came around, ready to see who it was, then quieted and backed up a step.

What? No back away from anyone. Elianna had never been submissive to any bear and would not allow her bear to do it now.

Those words fizzled in her mind as soon as she got a look at the largest shifted grizzly she'd ever seen. She was very big for a female, but that grizzly had to be another head taller, flatfooted.

Justin shifted into a monster bear.

If he attacked, he'd slaughter her.

Changing her mind in the hope of staying alive, Elianna instructed her bear, *Drop head. Do not antagonize. We cannot win.*

Her bear remained with her head up and fixated on that breathing mountain covered in a deep brown coat Justin had called Herc.

The giant bear lifted his head and opened his big jaws, roaring loud enough to make the trees tremble in fear.

Elianna's big bear heart thundered with excitement. Her foolish bear clearly did not recognize a danger right in front of it.

Bear mate.

What did you say? Elianna asked.

Bear mate.

What was going on with her bear? *No. You do not pick mate.* They couldn't choose one like that. Could they?

Yes, her bear answered.

Elianna might as well share her pain. She told her bear, *Does not want bear like us.*

Mate.

She and her bear had been communicating more than ever since arriving here, but Elianna could not get her bear to listen until she figured a way to pull her bear's attention away from Herc.

Yes, Herc mate, her bear confirmed.

The Herc they were discussing had lowered his head from that almighty roar and padded toward them. He wasn't frothing at the mouth or making deep sounds of impending attack.

Elianna had no way to make her bear move at the moment, so she prepared herself to be bloodied. Maybe Justin could stop his bear before he killed her.

When Herc reached them, he lowered his head and rubbed his cheek against her bear, who returned the affection.

Lost in the moment, Elianna became very still and soaked in the happy emotion rolling off her bear. That was when she realized she had never known her bear to show this kind of joy since being a cub.

Things had gone badly after Elianna's first shift. She began noticing dirty looks from polar bear shifters in her mother's clan once they saw Elianna's animal form. She'd hidden her bear ever since.

Now, she felt shame over withholding joy from her bear.

When the grizzly nipped her bear's neck, the party began.

The bears chased each other and played, sometimes tumbling over each other. The happy sounds coming from her bear warmed Elianna's heart and made her take stock of their relationship.

She had to do a better job of keeping her animal happy. Elianna had spent so many years suffering shame and rejection, she'd lost sight of how much her pain affected her bear.

For the next hour, she let her bear have her head and romp through the woods with Herc, who appeared just as happy. When her bear finally found a spot in the shade and dropped to the ground, Herc settled right next to her, but kept his head up in a protective way.

Her bear placed a paw over Herc's big paw and he licked her ear.

Climbing up the mountain and running all over the place had worn Elianna out as much as her bear. She closed her eyes and slept soundly, like she'd never rested before.

When she woke, someone was brushing fingers over her hair.

Hair? Her eyes came open and she stared up at Justin leaning over her, smiling.

He said, "Hi there, Eli, babe." His voice reminded her of warm mornings snuggled under a thick blanket with the snow falling outside.

She felt so relaxed. Whisper soft, she said, "Hello."

It felt so good to lie here on the thick grass her bear had pressed down. Oh, no.

His smile dimmed. "What's wrong?"

"My bear not here. I am." She took in his body that no longer had a shirt, and looked down to see she wore his shirt. Thankfully, it went to halfway down her thighs. "I wear wrong shirt."

"A trained observer, are you?" He grinned again.

Was everything funny to this man? "You are wise mouth."

"I think you mean a wiseass."

"Yes, that." She drew a shallow breath, enjoying his scent that surrounded her

His eyes lit with more amusement. "Better a wise-ass than a dumb-ass."

"How did clothes come?"

"I had Herc grab the backpack as soon as I shifted. He dropped it close by once we found you. I knew I could keep you corralled in this area, but I had to go back to find your clothes. You were tuckered out so I just let you sleep." His finger kept toying with her hair.

What had changed from when he saw her bear? "Why I wear your shirt?"

"Because I like seeing you in my clothes, but I'd like your smile more."

He acted so happy. She wanted to give him a smile, but she could not when he had called her a name she hated.

Her brain pounded with two words that gave her a headache. She had to address what he called her and find out why he was acting nice now.

Loading her words with plenty of accusation, she said, "You call me ursid hybrid."

"Yes. Why did that upset you?"

"You know meaning?" she asked, unable to hide her anger. Was he intentionally acting dense or turning her into a joke?

"Of course, I do. It's a cub that came from the cross between a polar bear and a grizzly mating. I just never expected to see one in my lifetime. You have the most beautiful bear I've ever seen. It's like seeing a unicorn that is as magnificent as it is elusive."

Tears pooled in her eyes.

His face fell. "What'd I say wrong, Eli, babe?"

She smiled and he stared at her as if she'd shocked him. Her lips trembled as she forced words out. "You ... you call my bear pretty."

His eyes softened and his voice turned gruff. "No, babe, I didn't call her pretty." When her face crumbled, he explained, "Pretty doesn't begin to describe you or your bear. You're beautiful and your bear is spectacular. But your smile can bring me to my knees."

Her heart thundered, pounding her chest.

She lifted up and kissed Justin, sharing all the happiness he had just gifted her.

He jumped in right with her, bringing her body up to him. His arms wrapped around her and he dove into the kiss, taking everything she'd give him. He had no idea how much she had bottled up inside her just waiting for this moment.

Not with just any man, because Justin wasn't just any man or any shifter.

He was ... spectacular. She liked that word.

When a hand reached between them and slid up inside the shirt that smelled of him to touch her, she shivered in reaction. "Yes, that. I want that."

"I love it when you talk dirty."

She started laughing and his hand fell away.

He leaned her away and looked at her with such awe, she stopped laughing and asked, "What?" She was still happy.

"I've been waiting for you to smile, but your laugh." He swallowed. "I can die a happy man now that I've heard it."

She couldn't contain her smile that got bigger and bigger. "No die. I smile more if you not stop."

"Yes, ma'am." He lowered her down and gently pushed her arms to the ground on each side of her head. "How's your shoulder?"

"Is good."

"Glad to hear it, Eli, babe. I plan to put a smile on that face you can't wipe off for weeks."

"I like you talk dirty."

He chuckled as he got busy unbuttoning the shirt he'd covered her in, but his humor fled as the cloth fell away and exposed her all to him. Moving slowly, he eased his hands to her breasts and massaged them.

She closed her eyes and moaned.

Then his fingers played with her nipples, gentle then a small pinch of teasing pain that she hissed at, but begged him not to stop.

"Not unless you tell me to, babe," he said. "It would kill me, but I will always do whatever you want."

She opened her eyes, struggling not to cry out as he continued to mix sweetness with the seductive torture of her nipples. "I want ... you."

He muttered something wicked and dropped his head to one breast, using his tongue and teeth as he had his fingers.

She felt that in her womb and clenched her legs.

His free hand now moved to those legs, easing them apart and running his finger through her moist center. She could not take this forever.

Sliding his finger across the sensitive bud, back and forth, he then dipped inside her. He had big hands and the feel of that thick finger took her breath as he slowly moved it in and out, then drifted his fingers over the heat building between her legs.

She was panting. Muscles in her body were taut, anticipating something just out of her reach. Justin would not let up, but neither would he go ahead and give her relief.

Her body begged to be released from the tension twisting through her. Blades of grass snapped off in her fingers, but she kept her arms in place.

He swept his mouth from her breast to her lips and kissed her, in no rush to finish. Healthy shifters did not suffer heart attacks, but she might.

Her tongue had a mind of its own when his slipped between her lips. They seemed to know each other.

Justin pushed his finger insider her again and she forgot to keep her arms down. Her hands clutched his powerful shoulders. She shook hard as he drove in and out of her, then pulled out one last time and his finger stroked her perfectly.

She lost herself when everything broke apart inside her. The coil of need unleashed, lashing through her like an out-of-control whip of pleasure.

She clung to him, sure that she was safe in his arms.

He would not let her fall far before he pulled her back to him. Every time he touched her, she felt the zing of energy inside her race to meet his fingers as if recognizing him.

His head lifted up a few inches. "Better?"

"No."

He dropped his head to hers. "Dammit. What is with that word and you?"

She laughed at him. "You funny."

Picking his head back up, he said, "That's not what a man wants to hear after making love to a gorgeous woman."

He tossed words like "gorgeous" around as if they were so easy to attach to her. She brushed her fingers over his cheek and he turned to kiss them.

When his dark gaze returned to her, she said, "You want hear how good you do?"

"I wouldn't complain if you said that."

"Not good," she managed to tell him with a straight face.

He frowned. "You're joking, right?"

Fighting to stay serious, she said, "Not call what you do good. It would be insult. More like maestro with simple instrument you make sing as angels do." Smiling up at him, she said, "Your kisses make me lose mind."

There was the grin of a proud man whose ego might blow off half the mountainside if it continued to grow, so she added, "But not finish."

"Huh?"

Now that his head had shrunk back to normal size, she explained, "I see great promise in pant bulge."

He lifted his eyebrows up and down. "Liked what you saw, huh? I'm not one to brag, but it's impressive."

She chortled. "You crazy."

"About you."

She would truly lose her mind if he kept saying such things. "If so mighty, why not show?"

"Because I didn't have any idea this would happen. I don't have a condom, babe, or you'd get the full Monty."

"Who is Monty?" Her eyes widened and she gasped, "You name that, too?"

He barked a laugh. "No. I'll tell you about the full Monty later when I can demonstrate."

"Need no condom. I know body. One week before can make cub. Now, more excuse?" she challenged, enjoying the banter.

"Hell, no." He jumped up and had his pants shed faster than her next breath.

She stared up at the most incredible man. He was a vision of excellence from head to toe. The short dark hair fit Justin's no-nonsense side, but with his clothes off and his signature grin in place, he was nothing short of delicious.

And he had not been exaggerating.

She licked her lips and said, "Hello, Monty."

He dropped his head back and bellowed a laugh. When he caught his breath, he lowered himself to the ground and propped his big chest up with those formidable biceps. Then he dangled Monty down, teasing the small triangle of hair where her legs met.

"I wonder ..." she murmured then reached down to grasp him.

"Holy mother of ... " Justin shouted.

She paused in her first stroke. "No like?"

"Are you kidding? I love it. I was surprised, but in a good way."

Always with the sweet words, this one. She moved her hand again and he let out a sound of such happiness that it made her feel special to give this man pleasure.

"I use mouth," she suggested.

Justin made a deep groan. "No way."

"What?" She paused with him in her grip.

He was breathing hard. "Babe, I would love your mouth on me, but I want this to last more than a few seconds. I've wanted you twenty-four hours a day since coming back from your walk to the beach."

"Oh." She knew he meant the wolf attack, but he would not bring that up now.

"Hey, don't say 'oh' like I can't last, but not this first time. I want you so much I'm barely hanging on."

She gave him what she hoped was a coy look and kept stroking him, reveling at the velvet feel of his skin. She nipped his chest and he kissed her neck, mumbling words she couldn't understand but they sounded sexy.

When she quickened the pace, he lifted up out of her reach. She asked, "Now what?"

"Now ... this." He watched her until he lowered his mouth to kiss her stomach, then moved further down until his lips touched her in the most intimate way.

Opening her legs gently, he did things with his mouth she didn't think possible. She arched, clinging to her sanity and pleading for him to keep going.

He did and stars burst into her vision.

Her climax rushed through her this time like a flash flood of heat. When he finished, she was limp all over.

Then Justin began kissing her all over as he worked his way up her body, massaging muscles and loving each inch of skin. He did not bypass her breasts and they thanked him for the extra attention.

As his face came into view above her, he eased Monty inside her just a bit. He kissed her thoroughly and she lifted up her hips to take more of him.

There seemed to always be more.

For that, she was thankful and appreciative.

He was next to her ear when he whispered, "Ready?"

She said, "Why ask? I fall asleep if ... "

He filled her to the hilt and she sucked in a breath.

"You okay, Eli, babe?" his voice murmured next to her ear.

"Yes. Much okay."

His voice was tight, but still held a smile when he said, "I love the way you talk, especially when you leave out the word no."

"Less talk. Move," she ordered, unable to stop smiling at this crazy man.

He did as she'd ordered.

His hand cupped her bottom and lifted her to him where he pulled out and slid back in deeper this time.

She dug her nails into his arms.

He grunted, but it sounded like a happy grunt.

Her legs shook from the strain of another climax building. Justin started moving faster. He gritted out, "Still okay?"

"No. More!"

"Waiting on you."

"I help." She reached down and touched herself.

That must have been all he could handle. He slammed into her over and over. She cried out a second before he shouted her name.

She would never get tired of hearing him say Eli, babe.

Little by little, he slowed, but even when he stopped he was still partially hard inside her. She had a feeling he could do this for many, many hours.

Being careful not to put his full weight on her, he lowered his body and rolled, bringing her over on top of him as he breathed deeply in and out. Her hair draped over his chest.

She wrapped her arms loosely around his neck.

His arms had never let her go. He held her in a possessive way.

She did not want to open her eyes and have this all vanish.

He had seen her bear and liked what he saw.

Justin held her as she came completely back into her body, because she was sure she had left it at some point.

Those were not normal orgasms. Not one of them was like being with the polar bear guy. She did not even recall his face now. The only face she saw in her mind was Justin's.

No, this did not just *feel* different.

It *was* ... different.

Could her bear be right?

Could Justin be her mate?

Her sleepy mind drifted into a happy place. She walked the shores of PK picking up shells and talking to her sweet Nico. He laughed at a bird and ...

Her eyes flew open. *Mate?*

No, she could not take a mate. What was she thinking? She had to save Nico and could only do that with a Boudreaux Clan mate.

Closing her eyes tight, she held back the tears threatening to burn down her cheeks.

She wanted Justin as hers forever.

But if she stayed with him, she would break her end of the deal with her father.

She would lose Nico.

That could never happen. Then she thought on all Justin had told her. He had grown up in Clan Boudreaux. He did not like them, but he was a male bear shifter of that clan. Her heart lightened at realizing she could have Justin, but ... only if he wanted a mate.

Her eyes blurred suddenly and the world twisted.

The vision she'd had in San Francisco occurred again, but with more detail. A wolf shifter chased her through the forest. He was much faster than her. Another wolf showed up. They ran her into the ground. She could see Nico in the distance, but she would not get to him in time. He started fading. She reached for his little body and grasped air. Howls followed close behind. Turning to take a stand, to call up her bear would make her vulnerable to the wolves. At the last minute they lunged and ... the image blurred and turned dark.

Elianna squinted, trying to discover the last part.

What did it mean?

She should tell Justin, but if she did he might take her straight to Clan Boudreaux or the place he called a safe house.

Not yet. The vision could be for much later when she and Nico left the clan. For now, she could not give up control. Not yet.

CHAPTER 18

JUSTIN COULDN'T WIPE THE RIDICULOUS smile off his face as he packed up the backpack while Eli stepped away for a nature call. A real one this time.

He'd found his mate.

She was a pistol and a half. She'd shifted just to get his reaction. His happiness dimmed a bit when he realized she'd been shunned for being an ursid hybrid and had expected that from him.

Were those shifters in Russia crazy?

They rejected her for being mixed blood?

Smiling to himself again, Justin shook his head. Their loss and his gain. He couldn't be happier than he was at this second ... except for convincing her to be his mate and finalizing their bond.

They would have beautiful cubs with winter-white coats, brown coats, but hell, he didn't care what color. He'd love to have a little female cub that looked like her mama.

Cubs? Was he ready for that?

He'd never felt such a sense of peace. Yes, he was ready for a mate and a family. He couldn't wait. He had never been in a hurry to get tied down, but damn he wanted to make Eli his in the worst way and see her pretty stomach bulge with a cub.

Reality stepped in to disrupt his happy parade.

There was still the small issue of Clan Boudreaux expecting Justin to deliver Eli to them. That might require some serious negotiating, but the Guardian would never expect Justin to give up a mate when he had no doubt she could accept his power when they bonded.

Finding mates for the Gallize shifters was near impossible.

Wouldn't the Guardian do all in his power to make this happen?

Justin was going to do this right. First he'd take her to the Guardian who he believed would immediately recognize they were destined to be mates. They had some intense energy flowing between them. Hadn't Cole said that was another sign of meeting a mate?

The Guardian had rocked around for three hundred years. He'd seen a lot. Justin put his faith in his boss. The Guardian would know how to make everything work out.

Justin thought about that energy again.

Could Eli be a Gallize?

Wouldn't that be the jackpot? He didn't give two flips about her being Gallize as long as she could take his power. Supposedly, a non-Gallize bear shifter could survive the bonding and he knew from touching Eli she was far more powerful than the average shifter.

He heard her walking into the clearing they'd stomped down earlier. She'd taken a bottle of water and rag with her to clean up, but nothing short of a long bath would remove the lingering succulent smell of their lovemaking. He pulled in a deep breath, soaking up that scent.

"Need help?" she asked.

He finished stuffing the bag and turned to find her smirking at him. His new goal in life was to keep her lips curved up and that twinkle in her eye, which was only there at the moment because she enjoyed taunting him.

"Sure." Without warning, he tossed the bag in her direction, but not at her. He'd never risk harming her even if she was a shifter.

Her left hand shot out fast as a snake on attack and snagged the bag in midair. She didn't even look at it that whole time, confident in her ability to catch the bag.

Alpha woman through and through.

What more could a man like him want in a mate?

Not a damn thing, but he still had to ask, "When were you born?"

She cocked her head. "Do not know. Why?"

She didn't know? He asked, "Not even the year?"

"Oh." She looked up as if calculating and said, "Think I am twenty-two. Born in winter."

He calculated the months in his head, because every Gallize shifter he knew had memorized the true blue moon months, which was a month with a second full moon in a twelve month period. He didn't think she fit the birthday criteria and she had blue eyes, not mismatched eyes.

"One more question, Eli. Do you have any older siblings?"

"Brother. Ten years more than me. Never meet."

Interesting, but not something Justin would sweat right now. He also noticed that over the last two days of conversing with her that Eli's English was improving in spots. Beautiful and bright, but most of all sweet.

His Eli was no diva.

She unzipped the side of the backpack, pulled out an empty plastic bag which she put her rag into, then stowed that and appeared to be dropping the pack to the ground.

Justin was turning to check for anything left behind when he sensed a missile coming his way. In a swift move, he swung completely around with his hand already out to retrieve the flying backpack.

She'd tossed it at him. Straight at him. He grinned. "Gonna be like that, huh?"

Her eyes sparkled with mischief. "Like you. I test reflex."

Opening up the bag, he started toward her, but he didn't fool her for a minute. She didn't hesitate to spin and run.

Tossing the bag to the ground, he was after her.

Justin would never be as fast as Cole and Adrian, wolf shifters, or even Rory since he was a jaguar, but he could hold his own with any other non-Gallize bear shifter.

When Eli broke out of the trees, she had fairly level area to run across if she didn't hit a hole or stumble over a rock.

A ledge that dropped off forever was fifteen feet away on her left.

Worry intruded on his fun.

He didn't want her hurt.

He closed the distance between and started to shout at her to slow down when her bubbling laughter reached him. His heart skipped a beat.

It just paused right there to hear that musical sound.

At the other side of the clearing, she slowed from the hard sprint to stand with her back to the next tree line and showed him a face he wanted to see every day of his life. He gave up jogging and walked, taking his time to enjoy this moment with his future mate.

As he passed a large outcropping of boulders, a bee flew up in his face.

He jerked back, twisting and waving his hands.

A bullet slashed across his forehead and struck the rocks.

The rifle report followed.

He screamed, *"Get down, Eli!"*

Good advice. He should have hit the ground himself, but he hunched over instead, holding his head and raced toward her.

She still stood, looking confused.

He yelled again. *"Get down!"*

She squatted, looking around then zeroing in on him. Blood oozed between his fingers.

"You are shot?" she called out.

Shit, she wasn't low enough. He wanted her flat on the ground.

The second bullet struck the ground in front of him. Blood leaked into his eyes. He kept going, but something was very wrong. Much more than just getting shot. His vision distorted and his head was on fire, ready to explode.

The wound burned as if they'd stabbed his head with a hot poker, which meant ... titanium bullets.

He was fifteen feet from Eli when she stood up again and started toward him.

"No!" he shouted, but the sound came out raspy. His vision of her warped and vertigo spun his world sideways.

He couldn't tell if he'd reached her.

His legs gave out.

He hit the ground hard enough to knock him out.

CHAPTER 19

ELIANNA WATCHED IN HORROR AS Justin hobbled toward her.

Blood ran through one eye and over the side of his face. He wanted her to stay down, but he started to crumble to the ground. He was not going to make it.

Ignoring Justin's orders, she raced over to him as he hit the ground. Catching him under the arms, she lifted and groaned. He weighed more than she had expected.

What made him so fast, so strong and so much heavier compared to other bear shifters she'd known?

It didn't matter as long as Justin could also heal better.

She hadn't realized at first that someone was shooting. She'd heard a muffled crack and dismissed it. Who had shot at Justin?

She barely moved him a foot. Desperate, she begged her bear for help. Suddenly, her arms and legs flooded with additional strength she'd never felt in human form. If anyone looked her in the eyes at this moment, she would bet they'd see her bear staring back at them.

After the attack in San Francisco when he bear refused to offer aid, she wasn't sure her bear would send her help, ever. Elianna sent a thank you.

Her bear growled low, sounding concerned.

Dragging Justin, she pulled him to the bushes next to where she'd originally decided to give up their foot race and claim the win.

She would forfeit all future races if he only lived.

He was breathing in gasps. Blood poured from the gash across his forehead and his shirt was getting soaked. The bullet had been so close to ripping through his skull. And it smelled funny.

Where had she smelled that metallic odor?

Titanium. She had heard about it, but had never encountered the metal until she found a dead Amur leopard in PK and sniffed the foul odor. Later, when she told her ship captain friend about it, he scowled and explained someone had probably mistaken a natural animal for a shifter and used titanium.

If she had lost Justin, she would have unleashed her bear with no rules. Her bear had never fought, but neither had her bear ever claimed a mate.

Had Herc chosen her bear, too?

Elianna would have to ask Justin later.

When she finally had Justin behind cover, she was heaving breaths, shaking with terror over his condition and that she'd be shot any second, too.

But there had been no more shots even when she was exposed. Why?

Had they only wanted to kill Justin and not her?

If that was so, did these people know she was Alexandre's daughter and thought to get money? They could not know unless the Boudreaux Clan had told them, which made no sense.

The Boudreaux Clan had gone to a lot of trouble to bring her to this country.

Rolling Justin to his back, she arranged his head in her lap. What she would give for a bottle of water.

She yanked off her shirt and bit an edge to start a tear, then ripped off a strip she used to put against his head.

Had he been hit anywhere else?

She checked as best she could, but saw no other blood.

Using the rest of the material, she wiped the extra blood from his head to give her a better look at the wound.

Ugly, but not as bad as it could be except for the skin around the wound that had begun to turn gray.

That was not normal.

Why hadn't she studied medical treatments or asked more about titanium?

With trembling hands, she folded a second strip into a bandage and pressed it against his head.

He groaned.

She gave a prayer of thanks for that pained sound. It meant he lived. "Justin, wake up."

All the time she tended to him, she kept searching the area around them for a threat. She expected armed men to come running out of the trees any minute, but those bullets had probably been shot from far away.

Did those people fear Justin so much they shot him from a distance? They would have to know him ... or maybe these people were connected to the wolf that attacked her.

If so, that would mean the one in San Francisco was not a lone wolf. He had been trying to drag her away. She'd thought he intended to kidnap her at first, then it changed to sound as if he intended to rape and kill her.

Had he been truly kidnapping her instead?

Why would any wolves care about her? Again, why would they even know she was here?

Justin's hand lifted to his head.

She caught his fingers with her hand. "Do not touch. Need shifter doctor."

"No." His voice was rough and dry. "We have to move. Hide." His eyes opened, but he had to blink a few times. "Help me sit up."

The blood seeped through both of her rags. "No. Change to bear."

"Not yet. I can't talk to you in that form. I need to get you somewhere safe."

She said, "Not shoot me. Think they want kill you."

"Agreed." He growled a sound of pain then took a deep breath. "That means they want you ... but realize they'll have to kill me to get you. I'll be okay once I know you're safe. Let's go."

"Wait."

"Please, Eli, don't argue now. This is critical."

"So is wound. Skin gray."

"That makes sense. Pretty sure they shot me with a titanium-coated bullet to slow my healing. If it hadn't been so close to my head I could fight past it. They're probably shifters. The sooner we get to a hiding place, the sooner I can deal with my wound."

"Yes, okay."

"Remember, I like those words," he said, clearly trying to get her to smile.

She gave him a smile in return, but it was weak from fear over his injury. After looking up and around, she said, "Must go more this way." She pointed in the direction they'd been running.

"You're right. Let's move out."

Helping him sit up, she tried to keep him on the sheltered side of her.

He drew a couple of breaths as if stabilizing himself. "Don't try to put yourself between me and that rifle."

She argued, "I told you. Not shoot me."

Without replying, he pulled her to his other side where he shielded her body with his bigger one.

She grumbled, but hooked her arm around him to share his weight when he hunched over and started forward, keeping step with him.

It seemed to take an hour to reach the next thick copse of trees, because Justin struggled to keep his balance. Between the few trees and spotty bushes along the way, they had a little cover, but she doubted that deterred anyone from shooting.

Her guess? They didn't want to risk hitting her.

Everything about this was odd, and now she included the wolf attack in San Francisco in that "odd" category, too.

Justin had locked his jaw and breathed through his teeth.

"Few more meters," she encouraged, hugging him more in an effort to will him her power. She spied a place where he could sit with his back to a wall of rocks. Good spot unless they had to climb those rocks to escape, since she worried he would become dizzy and fall.

Now his face had also turned a pale gray shade.

What could she do? She had no medicine and no phone to call anyone. She said, "You have phone?"

"It's in the backpack."

She cursed in Russian.

He squinted at her through blood-encrusted eyes. "What'd you just say?"

Her face warmed with embarrassment. "Not nice words."

"You cursed? In Russian?"

"Yes. Bad to do."

He grinned in spite of his obvious pain. "I think it's hot."

"You think all is hot," she chided him with an indulgent grin.

"Only all things about *you*, Eli, babe. You're hot." He hissed and touched his head.

"Must clean. Need water."

He waved off her concern. "It's in the backpack. I'll fix my head soon. Looks bad, but I'll survive."

She scowled at the way he pretended the pain he had to be in as nothing more than a headache. "Stubborn man."

"When it comes to protecting you, yes. Get used to it. No one is touching you." He took the shirt she'd used to wipe his head and handed it back to her. "Put it on."

"Why? Have bra. You bleed."

"Much as I love seeing you in fewer clothes, I want your skin protected as we go through those woods. I don't need the any more of your clothes to patch me up. The bandage pad you made from a scrap is sticking to the blood as it dries."

She marveled at this man who cared only about protecting her.

His words touched an empty place inside her, because no man had helped her when she struggled and none would ever have stepped between her and danger.

Guilt climbed up her back. She had to tell Justin everything about her agreement with Clan Boudreaux and hope he saw the light in all this that she did. Would he consider talking to the alpha and asking her to be his mate? She owed him all the truth about that and Nico. But now was not the time for long conversations when Justin could pass out at any moment.

She announced, "I am bear. I protect us, too."

"I have no doubt, Eli, babe, but for now please do as I ask. I have been here longer and have been trained to deal with threats like this."

If he had demanded that she obey him, she would have balked, but he made a logical argument and had requested she work with him.

This was a man worthy of a woman's love.

Love? She waited for panic to hit her over that thought, but she had never lied to herself. She could no sooner stop herself from loving Justin than she could from loving Nico.

That didn't mean she deserved someone like Justin, but she would do her best for him.

Men had lied to her many times over and now she felt guilty for not sharing more about her situation. She had not intentionally tried to deceive him.

Had she known what would happen once they came up in the mountains today, she would have told Justin everything first.

If they survived this, she would explain what she had not before.

That she could not stay with him unless they could convince the alpha to allow them to mate.

Her bear roared with fury at Elianna and she felt the same way, but she would not mislead this man who meant so much to her.

CHAPTER 20

FUCK, FUCK, FUCK. JUSTIN NEED to be up and moving. Like right freaking now! He leaned against the rocks and let his silent curse pound mentally at his raging, migraine-level headache and the stomach-churning sensation of constantly feeling off balance.

He had to get control of his body before they took off again, to keep her safe. Dammit, what a time to deal with titanium, but a minute or two now could make the difference in staying upright the harder they ran. Honestly, a triple-fuck didn't even cover this situation.

He wasn't going to spew those bad words around Eli.

He *did* intend to have her teach him Russian cursing, though.

That little rant had sounded cute coming from her.

The bullets shot at him had been specifically intended to kill a shifter. Titanium inside a shifter body worked like a poison, slowly killing cells faster than he could regenerate. If he didn't get this crap out soon, the skin would start dying around his wound and rot away.

Titanium would do more damage, and faster, this close to his brain, because it would begin to impede his thought process soon.

Very soon. Thinking right now hurt like a mother and he had to fight to stay alert. If he closed his eyes for a minute, they might not ever open again.

He considered the terrain options he had and was glad those bastards hadn't attacked him in unfamiliar territory, but they had clearly been following him.

That had to have started in San Francisco, which pointed at the damn wolf shifter attack. Not a rogue after all.

The last thing he wanted to do right now was end up lost.

In addition to losing his man card, he'd put Eli in more jeopardy.

A hundred to a hundred and fifty yards from here they should find a stream running down an indentation in the mountain that was decently shielded from view. It might be dry or it could be pouring water. He hoped it was wet, and they had to get to it soon.

Eli still fussed over his head.

If not for the obvious danger they were in, he'd enjoy her attention, because he knew she would not worry over anyone unless they were dear to her.

He liked being in that circle, but he couldn't take the time to bask in her caring. Whoever had shot him was tracking Eli.

Who was that wolf from San Francisco? Herc had caught a second wolf scent the night she was attacked. Had wolf number two been a sidekick who reported back to base?

Was this a revenge hunt for losing a wolf, or something else? If this was about the dead wolf, Justin would have expected them to shoot at Eli, too.

He was so damned glad they hadn't.

No time to waste what little mental power he had until they were in a better position for defense. First, he needed to give Eli a way to protect herself in case the next shot hit its mark and took him down.

"Eli, babe, I need you to do something."

Her face dropped to eye level with his. "Yes, okay."

He liked the fierce sound of her voice. "Lift my right pant leg. You'll find a gun strapped to my ankle."

"Why?"

Cocking an eyebrow at her, which he immediately dropped when it caused new shooting pains in his head, he said, "Because I was sent to be your bodyguard. I carry a weapon all the time. I want you to carry it now."

"Why?"

"Is that word going to replace no?" he asked, sounding as grumpy as he felt.

"Maybe." She gave him a serious look, but her voice had

betrayed her teasing.

He couldn't rise to the bait. Trying to think and plan was demanding all he could handle until the titanium was out of his system.

Telling her that he was concerned about being killed and leaving her defenseless would only get her back up more. His woman was a fighter who would face an enemy straight on.

Instead he said, "I might get woozy. If you don't know about the gun, it is of no use. If you don't carry it then you have no chance to defend us against a group of humans if that's who is after us."

"Ah. I see." She looked under his pant leg and fished out his Detonics .45 caliber pistol.

He took a moment to explain the gun to her, keeping it simple so that all she had to do was point and shoot.

Now, on to the next step. He nodded in the direction he wanted to go. "If we head that way, we should reach a stream."

She looked around and frowned. "Much woods."

"Yep. We may have to knock down some small saplings, but that will slow up whoever is tracking us." Those shots had come from far below them, so the shooter had to climb to their elevation, but that might only give them a small lead.

Jerking around to stare at the way they had come, she asked, "How long?"

"I don't know, babe, but we need to keep going."

She came back to him and held his face in her hands. "Must shift."

"Not when we can't talk—"

"No talk. You are strong as bear. You lead. I follow. My plan better."

He stared into the eyes of a woman who would always have her say around him even if he didn't like her opinion.

That's the woman he wanted, one who had a mind of her own.

Not those flirty females he'd been around who cooed at him, saying what they thought he wanted to hear.

This woman would stand next to him and their cubs, ready to take on the world to defend her family. An alpha mate through and through.

How had he gotten so lucky?

He didn't have her completely yet, but he would. She couldn't hide how much she cared for him.

They belonged together.

He said, "I will shift, but not here. We need to get past one area where it could be too tight to squeeze through as bears. Once we're safe to shift, I'll let you know."

Sighing and clicking her tongue in thought, she finally said, "Yes, okay. For now."

Herc said, *Kill enemy.*

Justin silently told him, *I agree, but we have to stay human so I can figure out the best way to reach a safe place.*

Then Justin told Eli, "Thank you for dragging me away from the shooters. I have no doubt you could kick their butts, but they aren't getting close to you. As soon I clean out my head wound, I'll start to heal." Not exactly true, because the titanium wouldn't be entirely out of his system until Rory got his hands on Justin.

He added, "Herc and I will not allow anything to happen to you or your bear. He took to your bear right away."

"Mine is same. Has affection for Herc."

Our mate strong, Herc murmured.

Damn right, Justin answered only for his bear. He had to hand it to Herc, who had recognized their mate so soon.

Once Justin was upright again, the throbbing in his head climbed into high gear. He could not waste any time getting to the stream where he could wash out as much of the poison as possible.

The going was difficult and slow for eighty yards, but a narrow opening in the rocks appeared right where he expected it. He said a silent prayer of thanks.

Clouds closing in on this part of the mountain threatened precipitation. There was normally snow at the higher elevations in spring, but he didn't want more dumping on them.

He welcomed the cool air on his fevered body, but if they didn't get off the mountain by dark, which wasn't looking possible, this cold would double down after the sun set.

He didn't want to spend the night in bear form in case he had to move them again, but he'd figure that out later.

After showing Eli how to tuck the weapon behind her in her jeans waistband to free her hands, he led the way and squeezed through an opening between two walls of rock. He held her hand, pulling her through gently to avoid scraping her skin.

When they exited on the other side, she reminded him of his promise to change into his bear.

He kissed her forehead and stroked his hand down her damp hair. It felt icy already. "I'll change if you say so, but look about twenty yards that way," he said indicating an area where a narrow waterfall spilled down the rock face. "If I can clean out the wound, I have a better chance to heal faster."

"I see. Go," she ordered.

"Yes, ma'am." He took her hand, searching all around them for any threat. This area was more exposed, but someone would have to make a shot from straight below for any chance of hitting them.

Not realistic.

Besides, if the enemy were wolf shifters, they were tracking Justin and Eli, which was even more of a worry since they could move fast in this terrain.

When he reached the water, he started splashing it on his face, trying not to throw up at the ragged pain only getting worse. He pulled off his T-shirt and soaked it in the water then ripped the padding off his forehead.

If Eli hadn't been there, he'd have cursed a blue streak. That fucking hurt.

She made a noise.

When he glanced over, her face was pale. "Is bad, Justin."

He loved hearing his name on her lips, but not the worry thickening her voice.

"I'm gonna be fine, babe. This water will really help." He twisted water out of his shirt, wrapped it around his hand and soaked it again, then gritted his teeth, accepting what he had to do.

Sucking in a deep breath, he clamped his jaws shut before scrubbing that rag hard across his forehead.

That took the starch out of his dick.

He would not make a sound and expose their location, but inside he bellowed.

Herc moaned.

Justin's eyes burned and his stomach wanted to revolt.

Then he felt Eli's arms come around his chest, holding him from the back. Her warm skin touched his and blended as one body at that point. He could swear he felt her energy seep through his back and radiate through his body.

Slowly, the pain receded to a dull throb.

The lack of sharp edge to each pulsing ache in his head meant he'd washed out the titanium he could access.

He patted her arm. "Okay, babe. I'm good."

"In pain."

"You made it better."

"Really?"

Giving her hand a squeeze, he said, "Always. Just being near you makes me happy and whole." The blood had stopped trickling into his eyes. "Let me rinse out my eyes and we'll shift."

She released him, then stood with her back to him with the gun in her hand pointed out as she guarded them both.

He was feeling better already.

He could live with a high level of pain and function as long as the residual titanium didn't stay in his body too long.

"I'll take the gun back," he told her.

She turned around with the business end pointed at him.

"Oh, shit, babe." Justin jumped to the side. "We have got to spend time getting you familiar with a gun. Rule number one is not to point it at anything you don't want to kill."

She looked at the gun as if it had crawled up her body and climbed into her hand. She dropped it on the ground.

Do not yell at her for dropping a loaded weapon, Justin told himself. Most modern handguns could take a far worse beating without accidental discharge, but still, never a good idea. He picked up the weapon and returned it to his ankle holster.

Then he pulled her to him and kissed the daylights out of her. This right here was all he'd ever need or want.

When he let her take a breath, she said, "Not time for play." But then she kissed him back even harder.

Her hands went around his neck and he savored a moment of holding her. It might not be the time, but he'd needed this from the minute he'd been shot and thought he might not live to keep her safe.

Finishing the kiss with a peck on her nose, he said, "See? We did have time. Now, I'm ready to shift and get over the next ridge to a place I have in mind."

Nodding, she started unbuttoning her shirt and looked up over her shoulder. She noted, "Is snow up there."

"Our bears can handle it. Think you'll be cold?"

She gave him a wicked smiled. "Me? No. Part polar bear. Maybe grizzly cold."

"You wound me, woman. I can take anything you can."

"We see, yes?"

He gave her an affirmative nod.

Justin had a couple of energy bars he'd shoved in the back pocket of his pants for easy access on their hike back down to the truck, but that was all he had for food. They could eat it now, but he'd rather wait until they made the climb and needed to rejuvenate at a rest stop.

It would be nice to have a container to fill with water from this stream, but who would have thought they'd be making a survival run?

When she stood naked except for her bra and panties, he told her, "Once you shift, take a good drink of water before we leave."

He took a minute to explain signals Herc would give her bear once they were shifted.

Listening intently, she said, "I understand. Same thing when I was child."

She'd used hand signals when she was a child? He had so many questions he intended to get answered.

Justin said, "I'll wrap up the clothes and carry everything. You just keep an eye on your surroundings."

"Yes, okay," she said with conviction.

If wolf shifters were tracking them, they would likely shift at some point too. If so, those wolves could catch bears in a foot race.

Justin glanced up at the snow-capped peaks.

Crossing snow was the worst place to try to hide, because it was easy to be tracked.

Resigned to no better option, Justin said, "Go ahead and shift, babe."

She handed him her bra and panties, then dropped to all fours. Her transformation was fairly fast compared to a lot of shifters, and he was sure it had to be that weird energy she possessed. He'd felt the magic brush through the air.

In the next minute, Justin got his second look at a beauty of a bear.

What idiot had not thought that was incredible?

Eli's bear—that had no name—made a low, chuffing sound.

Justin wanted her to name her bear, but he had a bad feeling that Eli was not one with her animal the way he and Herc were.

That could put Eli and her bear at a disadvantage in a fight, but he and Herc would be there to cover their mate until Justin could figure out what was wrong.

Her bear sniffed around and moved as if anxious to get going.

Herc growled, making it clear he wanted to be out with Eli's bear.

"I hear you, Herc," Justin muttered, then shed his clothes. First, he wrapped them all around the weapon and energy bars. If Justin needed his gun, he'd shred the clothes before he shifted to human form.

But the gun wouldn't save them against a pack of wolf shifters with rifles and titanium bullets.

Especially not a wolf pack hell-bent on knocking him out of the way to reach Eli.

Who was after her? The only people who were supposed to know about her, other than Justin and his boss, were Eli's father and the alpha of Clan Boudreaux.

Now he had even more reason not to hand her over to that Louisiana bear clan and he expected the Guardian to back him up.

CHAPTER 21

Q

WOLVES HOWLED FAR BEHIND THEM.
If Justin had to guess the distance, he'd put it at over two kilometers back, which was slow going in these mountains. He'd spent many hours roaming Glacier National Forest and specifically Heavens Peak.

He hoped those wolves weren't as familiar with the other side, where a line of timber undulated all the way down.

Staying in bear form, Justin continued to lead Eli's bear higher and higher, fighting the waning sunlight.

Once he got them out of here, he'd find some place to call the Guardian, but that would not happen tonight.

Justin would normally suck it up and figure his way out of this mess on his own if he were alone. He'd definitely double back to hunt his pursuers, but not when it put Eli at risk.

If he were doing this with his Gallize teammates, Justin wouldn't hesitate to consider every potential route or counterattack. He and his teammates worked as one when dealing with the enemy. He suspected Eli's bear could hold its own in a battle, but his insides kinked at the thought of her in any danger.

Was this what having a mate would be like?

Yes and no, he figured. He would never stop being on alert to keep her safe, but once they bonded he could share his power with her. That would add another level of protection.

A human might die while bonding with Gallize power, but Justin had never heard of a shifter that couldn't handle the blast of energy. Eli might need time to adjust to the surge, but she packed her own power, and he couldn't wait to find out more about it.

Still, he would discuss it with the Guardian first and be very sure.

Justin trusted the Guardian to assess Eli's power and strength. If anything, his boss erred on the side of caution when it came to protecting his Gallize shifters.

That included the women they chose as mates.

Damn. Justin grinned.

He was getting used to the word *mate*.

Herc leaped over a fallen log and paid for it with a dizzy wobble sideways that took the bear to his knees.

Justin grumbled, *Stupid jump.*

Eli's bear came around quickly and locked gazes with Herc, who immediately forgot about any pain.

His bear stood up on all four legs so fast Justin snarled at him. *Fuck! Don't jump up so fast!*

Ignoring Justin, Herc sniffed Eli's bear and licked her cheek.

Justin warned, *We don't have time for flirting.*

His bear said, *My time. All good.*

No, it's not, Herc. We need to get to safe ground.

Soon.

Dammit, Herc. Don't give me a hard time about this. Let's get moving. Didn't you hear those wolves?

After licking Eli's bear again and allowing her bear to snuffle along Herc's jaw and neck, Herc made a heavy sighing sound, then moved out.

Padding along like the king of the woods he was, Herc didn't slow again until Justin had him alter course. Justin hoped the path hadn't changed much in all these years.

He had Herc angle east and head uphill again, climbing higher with every few steps.

Herc went in that direction, but asked, *Lost?*

Justin told him, *No. We need to get those wolves off our trail before we get to a cabin.*

He didn't add *if* the cabin was still there.

Good. Herc added, *Or kill pack.*

You and I could, Justin assured him. *I just don't want to risk our mate, because I don't know that she can handle herself in a fight. We can't do our best if we're distracted.*

I like.

That was as close as Herc came to saying Justin's ideas were solid, but Justin knew his bear well and appreciated the vote of support.

They wound their way up, then down, the backside of the mountain and kept moving until they reached timber again. Moving deeper into the forest, Justin was relieved to find a wide, but shallow and partially frozen, stream he'd played in as a cub. He'd been to this spot many times in the years since.

Due to the shallow water in stretches, this part of the stream had never been a good area to find fish or they could find something to eat while traipsing through the stream.

He had Herc turn to Eli's bear and lift his jaw.

She moved her head up and down, letting Herc know she understood to follow exactly in his steps.

For the next thirty minutes, they walked up and down the wide stream, drinking their fill, and stepping out on both sides. In and out, walk more, in and out.

When Justin felt they'd done it enough, he instructed Herc to wade upstream two hundred yards to where water spilled across boulders and rocks. The walls on each side could be climbed, but only by a skilled climber with professional gear. Justin had spent afternoons letting Herc laze in the sun, then making a game of figuring out how to reach the narrow plateau above the waterfall by letting his ten-foot-tall bear climb the boulders.

Herc leaped out onto a massive boulder at the side of the water.

Then he climbed up to the next tall rock and turned so they could watch Eli's bear make the same leap. Herc chuffed approval as her bear, slightly shorter but amazingly agile, made a sure-footed jump. He kept picking his way up the rocky incline, which rose over forty feet. At the top of the rock pile, Herc dropped down on the other side where snow had accumulated on the forest floor, though there wasn't much timber at this point.

When Eli's bear landed right after him, Herc pounded the ground twice with his paw.

Eli's bear sat.

With Justin directing Herc, his bear spent the next fifteen minutes pushing huge rocks down the incline until it was not passable for either wolf or human.

The wolves would have to backtrack a long way to reach this elevation, and that was only if they knew this mountain well enough to locate the exact point to turn uphill again.

At each little sign Justin recognized as familiar territory, his worry lifted more and more.

The woods had changed in the three years since he'd been here, but not so much that he couldn't find his way. Now to see if anyone else had been in the cabin he'd discovered many years ago. Public hunting wasn't allowed on these protected lands, but a backpacker might have happened on the spot. Justin had never seen it marked on any map, and even satellite images seemed to miss it because of the heavy tree cover.

A lone wolf's howl echoed.

Herc paused. He and Justin listened for the direction.

The howl came again, but this time in duo, which meant there was definitely a minimum of two as Justin had suspected. He judged the sound to come from far down the mountain, back before the spot where he'd cleaned his wound and they'd first shifted.

Satisfied, Herc kept moving.

That escapade would throw the wolves off their trail for now, but it was only a temporary delay.

If those wolves had enough reason to kill Justin, they wouldn't quit at the first obstacle. If they were trained as he was in black ops, they would have high-tech tracking devices to use in addition to their noses.

Justin's head was no longer on fire, but the dull ache that should be gone by now was not a positive sign. He had no way to purge that metal from his body. He only hoped he could fight off the titanium effects long enough to keep Elianna safe until he could get in touch with his people.

Herc paused. *Den?*

Justin saw what had stopped Herc.

The cabin where he'd been hoping to keep Eli safe tonight had been burned to the ground. Some charred trees had also fallen, but new sprouts were evident, so it had been a while.

Justin's best guess? Unlike the Guardian's cabin, this *did* appear to be caused by a lightning strike. Acres of woods hadn't gone up in flames along with the structure, though, probably due to the wide space he'd cleared around the cabin.

He told Herc, *That's gone, but let's find somewhere around here to bed down.*

Safe?

Justin considered all they'd done to cover their tracks. *We should be good here for the night.*

Herc angled his head around and made a low huff at Eli's bear, the signal that they were safe.

Eli's bear's ears pricked up.

She ran past Herc and pounced on the pockets of snow, then began to play and prance around.

Herc took off to catch up to her with Justin cursing him every step.

When he got his breath back, Justin stopped yelling at Herc and eased back, letting his bear do as he pleased. Justin enjoyed the vision of Eli's bear happily playing in the snow. The pretty bicolored bear snapped at snowflakes drifting down. The joy in the bear's face made him wonder when her bear had last been free to run.

That peninsula in Russia where she came from had plenty of snow. Wouldn't she have taken her bear to romp there?

He let the bears have a moment of downtime, but Herc was slowing down. He might be fascinated by Eli's bear, but the titanium was affecting him as well.

Justin suffered a wave of dizziness.

Herc shook his head, feeling it too.

Nudging Herc to get walking again, Justin had him check on Eli's bear. She was right behind him, so they plodded through occasional piles of snow. If the wolves found this place, tracking them would be no trouble.

Justin racked his mind for a second option.

The only caves he knew of were too far away going west, but they had wolves between them and safety if they headed east. Nope, neither direction offered a better option. The nearest camping was Avalanche Campground. With dark closing in, he wouldn't risk either of them falling into a hole.

There were drop-offs that didn't stop for hundreds of feet.

Enough to mangle even a shifter, or bash a head.

With a slim amount of moonlight building, he and Eli would

have some night vision, but not as sharp as a wolf's.

Herc's sense of smell topped his vision by a long way.

Justin searched everywhere, but couldn't find a place with enough shelter to allow him to return to human form so he could keep an eye on both of them tonight. In bear form and with the wound they had, Herc might go into a deep sleep and Justin would not be able to wake him fast enough.

But his human form was not resilient enough to go through a night here in the cold without any gear. He'd probably survive, but he didn't like the *probably* part of that equation when it came to protecting Eli.

She could remain a bear.

He wanted her rested. She had to be exhausted and would need her strength tomorrow, because they had only power bars for food tonight. That wasn't much for rebuilding their strength.

Looking through Herc's eyes, Justin searched ahead, then back-tracked to fallen trees he'd seen downhill.

Herc slowed at the crest of the hill, waiting for direction.

Justin guided his bear to where trees and branches knocked over in a storm had piled up in one spot. He nosed around, pushing debris out of the way.

With a little work, that could be a makeshift lean-to large enough to shield even two bears their size if Justin had to shift for short stretches to stay warm.

Justin had Herc back up and shake off the clothing pack looped over his head, then he called up the change.

Cold air bit his skin.

He told Eli's bear, "Don't change yet."

Snow continued to float down. Not heavy, though.

Rushing to unpack the bundle, he dressed in record time, hoping nothing got frostbite.

Monty topped that list.

Dressed, he wrapped his hands in Eli's clothes and dug out the snow piled under the angled cover. When he backed out, there was a small bunch of branches inside which he started tamping down for a mat to keep them off the ground.

He looked around and Eli's bear was dragging more evergreen branches over.

Justin took them as she made a pile, adding some of the branches at the top to create a slanted roof that went from tree to ground. When he finished with that, he used the other branches she'd found to cover the inside floor.

It would be cold, but that gave them a little layer of insulation between their bodies and ice-cold ground.

Just fine for a pair of bears.

Who was he kidding?

He might have an internal furnace that ran far hotter than a human because of sharing a body with Herc, but if he stayed in human form tonight he would freeze his nuts off. Sleeping next to Eli's bear, they could generate heat, but they had nothing to hold that heat in close.

He hadn't seen new branches in the last ten minutes.

Where the hell was Eli?

He didn't want to yell because sounds carried out here. If she didn't show up soon, he was shifting to Herc and tracking her.

He waited thirty seconds.

That was enough.

Just as he unbuttoned his shirt, he caught the sound of Eli's bear huffing on her way back. Damn, but she had scared him. He had to remind her that although she was part polar bear and part grizzly, she didn't know these woods.

She shouldn't go anywhere without telling him first.

He buttoned up his shirt and crossed his arms. Yes, he was getting ornery, but he was tired and still had the headache from hell.

The closer she came, the more he realized she was dragging something again, but not tree parts.

When she reached him, her bear grinned around a mouthful of nasty canvas that trailed behind her fifteen feet. It looked like what was left of a tent from a storm. Maybe the same storm that had taken down these trees and blasted his cabin with lightning.

He'd seen wind strong enough to flip a ship over blow uphill out here in a blizzard. That tent probably came from the campground, but from the looks of frayed edges and holes, it had been blown here a long time ago.

Justin dropped down and hugged her bear. "That's a hell of a find, babe." He wanted to use her bear's name.

They would fix that next.

Eli's bear rubbed all over him. He loved this woman and her

bear. Loved them more than he'd ever thought possible.

The only family he'd known had treated him as a leper.

It had taken a woman from across the ocean to tear down his walls one word at a time, to see past his constant joking and find the man inside.

Her bear bumped his head and nodded at the shelter.

Justin stood up. "I get it. Finish my chores first then I get some lovin'." He reached for the canvas. "What you got here?"

It had tears and no sign of structure, but it looked to originally have been ten by fifteen feet. Now that he thought about it, a hunter might have had this tent. He'd get word out to scout this area for someone hunting illegally once he was back to a phone.

On the other hand, it could be wildlife photographers. He'd run across his share of those, too.

Darkness had set in completely before he figured out how to create a free-form tent structure using the slanted roof, but shafts of moonlight offered enough illumination for their bear vision. In the end, he used thick limbs to prop up the inside in different directions. He gathered all the excess canvas inside to pile on top of the branches.

All in all, not too damn bad.

The canvas wouldn't have been as good without the lean-to construction and vice versa. A beneficial combination.

"Good place."

He swung around to find Eli butt naked. "Damn, woman. You're gonna freeze." Not that he wasn't enjoying the best view he'd had since the last time she'd been naked, but he didn't want her suffering frostbite on one inch of that body.

"Polar bear blood. Strong in cold."

She dressed and put her boots on, then stood up and faced him with her arms crossed. Her nose was red and her cheeks were pink, but she'd made her point.

She was no fragile woman.

She arched an eyebrow and leveled a challenging look at him.

"You are so damn hot."

That sent her into a fit of laughter. When she caught her breath, she said, "You funny."

His heart started beating like it wanted to join a marching band. "You're beautiful."

She ducked her head then raised those big blue eyes at him.

He knew the first time he saw them he was in deep trouble, but he wouldn't change a thing about her.

"Night here. Get in," she ordered.

"Yes, ma'am."

"Not old woman. Not ma'am," she complained as she climbed through the opening created when he pulled overlapping flaps back.

"We say ma'am out of respect whether you're five, twenty-five, or a hundred and five."

"Oh. I like."

She made it to the opposite side of their accommodations for the night.

Justin stood there thinking about how she'd just used Herc's words of compliment.

This was the perfect match.

He and Eli could spend a lifetime getting to know everything about each other, but he knew all he needed for now. She was loyal to a fault. She said what she thought. She was a woman he could trust with his heart and his future.

He would never settle for anything less than her.

Easing inside, he closed the flaps and tried to prevent upending their shelter. His headache was down to a dull throb, but he could feel the poison seeping into his body. The cold might be helping him since his blood flow would slow down.

He'd watched a Gallize shifter die in a war zone. Losing one of their shifters was rare because they were so tough.

But titanium affected all shifters adversely, including Gallize. Justin's unit had a medic that could have saved the shifter, but they didn't reach him in time to irrigate the multiple wounds and apply a neutralizer to offset the effects.

The warrior had shifted into his mountain lion form. By the time they found him, his tail and one leg had rotted off. He couldn't shift back to human, which left the bullet holes not lined up, because he'd been shot in human form. Even if the medic could irrigate every opening, too many areas had moved during the shift and some had healed enough to close off access.

Eli was on her side, curled up and watching him.

Justin pulled her to him, kissed her sweetly, then rolled her over so he could bring her back against his chest. He wrapped his arms and legs around her, shielding her every way he could.

Tomorrow was critical.

He had no idea how much titanium was still influencing him or the amount of damage it would do overnight, but he'd always been warned not to go beyond twenty-four hours with that crap in his system.

He had to get them off this mountain tomorrow and find a way to contact the Guardian. He couldn't risk Eli being left alone up here facing those wolves if the titanium won the battle and killed Justin.

CHAPTER 22

Q

"SHE'S A WHAT?"** Cazador held his mobile phone out from his ear, pissed at the wolf shifter's shout. He spoke *at* the phone. "Just so you know, Mateo, my wolf hearing is possibly better than yours. Don't do that again."

"Sorry," Mateo, his contact at the Black River Pack headquarters in South America, muttered. "I'm just ... hell. An ursid hybrid is like ..."

"Finding the impossible," Cazador filled in calmly. Unlike his South American client, Cazador didn't speak with a Spanish accent. He'd been born in Florida, where natives had no accent. He said, "While natural ursid hybrids definitely exist, ursid hybrid *shifters* are perhaps the rarest form of shifter imaginable. That makes this one extremely unique and adds significant value to the contract on her."

Cazador had pulled off the hunt tonight and returned to his truck, parked at the trailhead, for one reason—to cut a better deal. Those two bears didn't have his wolf vision, which normally drove him to hunt relentlessly at night.

His guess? They would be bedded down until first light.

"Decide soon, Mateo," Cazador warned.

Mateo had to be careful or Cazador would keep this ursid hybrid. Cazador had been brought in to do what the Black River pack wolves operating in the US could not—capture one female bear shifter.

For that he had demanded his usual high sum, but this new development ... deserved a fitting price tag.

"Do you have pictures?" Mateo asked.

"That is not the kind of shooting I do. When I deliver her, you force her to shift and you will have proof of purchase. Which brings me to the point for this call. This is no usual job."

Mateo's tone switched gears from surprised to annoyed. "You're getting paid five times what anyone else would be paid, plus expenses."

"True, but I'm ten times better than anyone *you* could send after them, which means you're getting a hell of a deal just for a pair of bear shifters. She is a jewel worthy of high price. Before you stroke out on me, keep in mind the reason I'm paid so well is because I have the patience to always deliver the goods. When dealing with deadly or unusual shifters, not many hunters can say that," Cazador finished with a smile.

He wasn't bragging, only stating his value.

His moniker, El Cazador, translated to The Hunter. He'd earned it in South America when he tracked down a huge Andean condor shifter.

Natural vultures had a ten-foot wingspan.

This one could carry off a full-grown man.

The condor shifter had been attacking Black River pack wolves, because one had killed his sister.

Sixteen dangerous wolves had died before that condor shifter picked Cazador off the ground. The condor shifter was never seen again.

But Cazador didn't have to argue the point of his value. Mateo already knew it.

If this pack didn't pay him, Cazador would send them the money they'd wired in advance, plus the outstanding balance they had not yet paid. He'd include a note to consider the contract canceled and the money as payment in full for the ursid hybrid.

Any mercenary contractor would do the same in his shoes.

Many would do far worse to walk away with Elianna, when a Power Baron would hand over an insane amount for this bear shifter.

Myths regarding ursid hybrids might all be hogwash, but myths usually grew from some grain of truth.

"How much?" Mateo asked in a guarded voice.

Cazador gave him a figure and smothered a grin at the wolf's intake of air.

Mateo said, "We will pay that, but this may adversely affect your opportunity to do business with the Black River pack in the future."

"No, it won't. You run drugs that target our kind and kidnap shifters to use as experiments. Your pack will always need contract shifter help. What you've just done is ensure that I continue to offer my services to your pack."

Silence followed. Not an uncomfortable kind, at least not on Cazador's end. He had preparations to make, so he moved to the next item on his list. "I need a magic spell."

"I do not have magic to hand over."

Sighing, Cazador said, "My time is very valuable and you're wasting it by lying. Your headquarters in South America provided me with a spell in the past." He rattled off the name of this man's superior within the Black River pack. "If you can't supply it, I'll contact your upper management directly."

"You're a fucker to deal with."

"There's no need to get vulgar," Cazador said in his usual congenial voice.

"You should have negotiated that in your contract. It will cost extra."

"I will trade the bodyguard grizzly for the magic spell. See? I'm saving you money."

"What if you are unable to deliver him alive?"

"Then I will pay for the spell. I know what they cost. You just get the spell to me in the next six hours or the entire contract will be null and void."

Cazador would ideally deliver the male bear shifter in trade for the magic, but he would not tolerate a headache to do so.

Not when the ursid hybrid had just tripled his take.

CHAPTER 23

ELIANNA PEEKED THROUGH HER LASHES.
It was still dark outside the shelter she and Justin had built from forest debris. She'd napped on and off. Was it early morning?

She had thought by today she'd be making great progress on her plans for when Nico arrived, not to wake up on Monday in the middle of nowhere and being hunted.

All she wanted now was to survive this ordeal with Justin.

Her boots were next to the slit they used for a doorway to this tent. Not a real tent, but she was proud of the way she and Justin had created a haven for the night.

She knew he'd intended to stay up in his human form and that had worried her. The inside smelled of fresh pines and Justin. His scent surrounded her.

Nothing stirred outside.

He slept with his body turned toward the opening, with her in front of him. Sometimes a man put himself between a woman and the door to protect her. She had no doubt Justin trusted his ability to flatten her to the ground and protect her with his whole body if anyone approached.

She had never felt safe like this.

It was strange, yet wonderful.

She could protect him, too, if she and her bear worked together. Her bear had never been serious until yesterday when Justin and Herc were wounded. Then her bear had helped her with power, and demanded to be let out to kill wolves.

Her bear.

Elianna did not know what to make of that, but she was happy. She'd like to be able to hold her own in bear form.

The air still had a bite to it, so she snuggled back against Justin ... and woke Monty.

"Mornin' babe," Justin said in a rough voice.

She liked that sound.

Rubbing her rump against Monty, she stifled a laugh at his muttered comment about how he couldn't help it.

How she should just ignore the thick length prodding her.

Foolish man to think she hadn't intended to wake Monty.

She turned to face Justin and slid her hand between them and down inside his pants where she got a good grip and stroked him.

He hissed. "Jeezo mighty."

"What is jeezo mighty?"

"A lot nicer than the words I was thinking," he groused.

Did he think she had never heard bad words? She wouldn't tell him. It was nice that he cared.

She kept her hand moving slowly up and down the thick shaft. When he groaned this time, she tried to sound innocent when she asked, "This hurt?"

"Yes, but not like you think. Hurts because I want you."

She paused and he held his breath until she stroked him again. "I hurt, too. Want, too."

Justin's body shuddered, then he pulled her hand gently from him. "Music to my ears, babe, but you need to rest. Tomorrow will be long."

Why didn't he want to play? Had she been doing something wrong? "Is tomorrow now, yes?"

"Guess so, now that you mention it."

She pressed her hands on his chest and asked, "Head hurt?"

"Not bad. I didn't plan to sleep so that was fine. I got up a little while ago and took a walk."

He was lying, but men would be men. "Why? You hear noise?" Her breath sent frosty clouds billowing in the air.

"Nope. Me and Monty needed a nature break."

"Oh. Is safe here, yes?"

"Yep, this location worked out. I thought it might. Wolves hunt at night, but being wolf shifters who function all day as well, they had to stop at some point. I'm thinking hitting that rockslide did it or they'd have been here before now if they'd kept going. We do need to be out of here soon though, because they'll be already moving again."

"How long?"

"Dawn should start in maybe thirty or forty minutes. We'll have enough ambient light for our bear vision. I want to get rolling then."

She sighed on a smile and changed her tactic. "Is cold. I want warm."

He hugged her to him in a tight bear hug, which squashed her against his still unsatisfied Monty. "Ugh. Squeeze too much."

"I'm keeping you warm."

"Need more heat."

He chuckled. "Babe, I'm a furnace. Just stay still and I'll warm you."

She had to know if he was in too much pain to play. "You lie. Much pain."

Releasing his grip on her body, he said, "No, really. I'm fine."

Taking advantage of the opening she gave him, she pushed herself up on one elbow and gripped him again. "Good. Be still and I make better." This time when she stroked him he didn't talk. The only sound she heard for a moment was his ragged breathing that also blew out puffy white clouds.

His arm muscles got tighter and tighter as he breathed faster.

She watched his face in fascination, thrilled at the power she held in her hand.

He grabbed her arm and held it still and spoke through clamped teeth.

She was breathing hard herself, excited watching him. "What?"

"I want to feel you all around me."

"Yes, okay," she told him enthusiastically. Shimmying her pants down and out of the way, she pushed him over and freed Monty. Then she went up on her knees and positioned herself above him.

He said, "Wait, you're not ready."

"Yes. Much ready."

"Damn, that is so hot."

She laughed softly and lowered herself onto him, then lost her smile at the feel of Justin. With all the control in her hands, she took her time lifting up to almost slide him out of her. His chest rumbled with a growl that would make her laugh again if not for how she tortured herself.

His fingers touched between her legs and she flinched at the surprise. He didn't stop there, continuing to tease the folds with her hanging on, so close.

She picked up speed, driving him in and out.

With one touch, he brushed over the nub that sent her body and mind spiraling with her orgasm. His big hands gripped her hips and he took over.

Good thing because her legs were not so strong any more.

It took very little for her to join back in, meeting him with each fierce stroke. She fell into his rhythm and told him, "More. Much more."

He pushed hard two more times.

She clenched around him and he stroked deep, curling his body up to hers, his arms hard with pumped muscles. The sound that came from him was as flattering as it got for a woman.

She slumped against him and his warm arms held her.

They were both covered in perspiration.

He mumbled, "Warm enough, babe?"

"Yes. I like."

"Herc says that."

She pushed up to look at him. "What?"

"He says, 'I like,' which means he approves or sometimes it's a compliment."

"I would like to hear Herc."

"You could if ... " He broke off what he was saying.

"If what?"

"Nothing, just rest until we have to get going."

As he stretched out again, she draped her body over him.

"Eli?"

"Yes?"

"You should name your bear."

She'd never thought to do that, but seeing Justin and Herc made her regret not having a relationship like theirs. As an adult, Elianna hadn't spent time with other shifters besides her mother, and her mother had not named *her* animal either. Elianna had no friends to talk with about things like naming a bear.

She'd had no one like Justin.

Looking back now, she realized her mother's clan had probably never named their bears, but that wasn't the reason Elianna hadn't. She'd witnessed so much connection with Justin and his Herc, that it made her want more with her bear.

She said, "I will think on this naming." With her post-love-making euphoria wearing off, her mind got busy bothering her. She'd like to just enjoy this special time, but her conscience was pitching a tantrum.

She said, "Must talk."

"About your bear?"

"No."

"You should rest, babe. We can talk later."

"Why? You need sleep?" she asked in a teasing tone.

"Not really. I won't sleep soundly until we're out of here."

"Pain?"

He toyed with her hair. It had to look a mess. Justin explained, "Pain isn't keeping me awake. I was trained for military operations. Sometimes we went days without sleeping. When that happened, we slept in short bursts of a few minutes here or there. I'm not going to sleep hard when we have wolves tracking you."

She knew what she had to say, but she was stalling. A selfish part of her did not want to give up the way Justin looked at her right now, as if she was his future.

Maybe she just wanted to think those were his thoughts, because that was how she looked at him.

"What is it, Eli, babe?"

"You said you were young boy in Clan Boudreaux."

His finger stopped twirling her hair for a second, then started up again. "Unfortunately, yes."

"Not bad clan?" She hadn't considered the fact that she might be going to an abusive clan, but Justin's obvious dislike of this clan had made her think twice about where she was headed.

"Not exactly." Justin continued to play with her hair as he spoke in a dull monotone so unlike the man she'd come to know who was full of life and energy.

His growing up there could solve everything. But she needed to know why Justin did not like this clan.

She asked, "How long?"

"How long did I stay with them?" he clarified.

"Yes."

"Until I turned eighteen. I told my alpha I was leaving and he didn't care."

"Why not care? Herc powerful bear."

A sad smile overtook Justin's mouth. "Not back then. I never shifted into my bear until after leaving the clan."

She pushed up, shocked. "How? You meet bear as child."

"Normally, yes, but I was an unusual case. I kept waiting to feel this animal everyone told me about, but I never felt anything. They thought I was damaged."

She could only imagine how awful that must have been for Justin. "Clans not nice to ... "

"Weak shifters. You can say it. I heard much worse growing up."

"But ... you are bear now. How?"

"That's an interesting story I can't wait to tell you, and I will share it very soon, but not yet. I can't explain a lot about my time after that right now." He stopped talking and looked up at her with a longing that squeezed her heart. "I work with a secret group and can only share what I am and what I do with my mate."

He put his hand on the side of her face and she leaned into it with her eyes shut.

Her heart cried out, because she could see he wanted her as a mate. She had never expected any shifter to want her and never one so honorable as Justin.

But she could not let him ask her if she had not told him everything yet.

"Eli, babe, I think you and I—"

She grabbed his hand. "Stop."

"Why?" He was still just as calm as he had been, but his heart pumped hard beneath her other hand.

"I must talk. Need truth."

Justin's throat moved with a swallow. "I'm listening."

"Must go to Clan Boudreaux."

"I know that." He frowned as if she confused him. "I understand you probably plan to go back to Russia soon, too, but—"

"No. Not to Russia."

"Ever?" he clarified.

"Ever."

A peaceful happiness overtook his face. "Really? Then there's nothing else that matters."

"I wish is so, but ... I must make agreement."

Frowning again, he said, "You keep saying that like I've forgotten it's my job to take you to Louisiana, which I will. I just don't promise to leave you." He winked and grinned.

She looked away, trying to find the right words.

He turned her chin back to him with his finger, and now his face reflected the seriousness she felt.

"What is it, Eli, babe? We can figure out anything if you're not just visiting and going back to Russia."

Her voice shook. "Not visit. Must join clan. Part of deal."

"Join? You're serious?"

"Yes. Must do."

"What are they making you do?" His voice vibrated with anger.

She put a finger on his lips. "Wait. Hear first." When she felt the muscles in his body ease beneath her, she explained, "I leave Russia. My alpha make deal with US alpha. Each send female shifter for clan ..." She couldn't think of the right words when she was nervous.

Justin helped her. "Most shifter clans and packs have a hard time introducing new blood into the group, so this has been done before. But the females have to go willingly," he added in a firm voice. "Are you being coerced?"

"What is coerced?"

"It means the same as twisting your arm to do something you don't want to do."

"Ah. No, I plan long time to come."

Surprise lifted his eyebrows. "I'm confused. If this is what you wanted to do, why didn't your father just send you here? Why use you as part of a trade? What is he holding over you?"

Her throat squeezed at what she had to explain. "Small boy. Six years. His name Nico. I claim as brother." She explained who Nico was and how she was the only person who would ever care for this child. As she told him about Nico being left by his clan because he was too small, she could see the understanding dawn in Justin's eyes.

She strayed from the topic when she started telling Justin stories about her Nico, then took a deep breath and finished what she'd started. "Romanov not want bastard he made with polar bear. My mother. Had trouble with mate and took trip for six months."

"Did he know he'd gotten your mother pregnant?"

"No."

"What happened next?"

"I am born in far north."

"Where?"

She told him about the beautiful country in the northeastern corner of Russia where she had miles to run, mountains to climb and so many fish to eat. "Meet bear at six. She like swim. No one see bear until nine. We stay far from clan, but mother want mate. Polar bear shifter see my bear and tell clan. They tell mother take bastard cub away. We move fifty kilometers, find place to stay. Same problem many times. Mother much lonely. Like me. Too much. They leave when see my bear."

Justin stroked her face. "That had to be hard."

Elianna shrugged, but could not deny how difficult it was and that she blamed herself. Her mother had been content to stay up there and find a mate until the clan and other shifters turned on her.

They did not want Elianna around to shame them with evidence of breeding with a grizzly.

"Mother miss grizzly alpha," Elianna said, determined to get this all out. "She drag me over mountains many months. I am maybe nineteen. On way to PK, we find Nico. Tiny boy. I save him." Casting a look down at Justin, she said, "I keep him. Always."

He nodded, which was enough for now.

She said, "I hide bear always."

Justin's hand stilled. "Are you saying you've been keeping your bear hidden out of shame?"

Dropping her head, feeling the shame he was talking about, she whispered, "Yes."

"Oh, Eli, babe, you can't do that. You and your bear need to live as one."

"Bear not like me."

"She does," Justin argued. "But she might be hurt. That's changing now. You don't hide your bear from anyone ever again."

She felt the years of exhaustion wash over her from constantly hiding among both humans *and* shifters. "You are special, Justin. You like my bear."

"Love your bear. You have to use the right words."

Her heart jumped at the word love, but it had been for her bear. "Others hate. If you with me and I shift, they shun us."

He cupped her face between both of his huge hands. "I will never allow anyone to make you feel uncomfortable or to shun your bear. Ever. They will respect you for the incredible gift to our kind that you are or they will pay a price."

Her eyes welled up, but she was not a crier. She would not show a weakness in front of this man who was ready to stand up for her and her bear.

He lifted up and kissed her with so much love, she felt it in her chest. The kiss went on for a long minute, then he eased back down. "That brings me to what I was trying to say earlier, that we would—"

"No."

"Babe, you have got to rethink that word. It's not my favorite."

How could this man be amusing at such a difficult time for her? "You impossible."

"Okay. Add that to crazy, fun and hot."

"Not say hot," she told him, unable to keep the smile off her face.

"You wanted to though. I see the way you look at me and, by the way, I like it. You can ogle me all you want. I intend to ogle you just as much."

"I try be serious."

He inhaled so deeply, his chest lifted her up, then lowered her again as he exhaled. "I'm listening."

"I think no."

"Oh, no?" He rattled off, "You were born out of wedlock, crossed mountains for months to reach PK, found Nico on the way and adopted him. You made a deal to join Clan Boudreaux so you could bring Nico to live in America. You're gonna have to add being really smart to my list."

She snorted. "Add arrogant."

"Nah, we call it confidence where I came from."

"Clan Boudreaux?" she asked, hopeful.

His humor slid away. "That's not my home. So we need to figure out how to deliver you to that clan, get Nico sent over, then you can tell them you've decided to go on your own. I'll be there with you the whole way."

She didn't think any of the Louisiana male bear shifters would accept her, but would they allow her to stay with Justin?

Until meeting him, she had intended to fulfill her agreement, hope that all the potential mates would reject her, then demand Nico be sent. Once they got tired of her and Nico, she would just leave and live in mountains like this with him.

But now she had to consider Justin.

She could not put Justin in a difficult position that would be unfair to him. Would the alpha let Justin come live with them?

She considered slapping herself.

That alpha had been unkind to Justin as a child. If the alpha had not cared enough to keep a child, he would not treat Justin any better now, plus Justin hated them all. He used polite words, but the anger and hurt was clear to see by anyone who cared to notice.

Asking Justin to join her there would be cruel.

Also, he had some secret job to do.

She asked, "I agree to stay."

"I'm not standing by while anyone pushes you to do something you don't want to do," Justin said. Without taking a breath, he added, "You keep cutting me off, but I want you as my mate, Eli. I love you and your bear. If you don't want what I offer, I'll accept no, but not because some alpha thinks he can push you to stay in a clan that isn't yours."

"Oh, Justin. I make bad mess."

"No, you haven't. Just let me talk to my boss and—"

She said it fast, hoping it would hurt less once the words were out. "I agree to Clan Boudreaux mate."

She had been wrong. This was not better.

His silence crushed her.

CHAPTER 24

 ᴏʟ

JUSTIN'S BRAIN COULDN'T PROCESS ELI'S words.
She'd agreed to take a *mate* at Clan Boudreaux?
He stared at the fine features of her face as early daylight kept offering hints the sun intended to rise soon.

"What, Justin?"

He was trying to form something to say, but that lump in his throat made it tough.

"Please, Justin," she implored.

The sadness in her voice ripped little holes in his heart that struggled to keep pace with his pain.

"Please."

Time to suck it up.

How could he be angry with her when she hadn't even known he existed when she made that agreement? He couldn't, but that didn't stop him from being as hurt as he'd been every other time in his life when he wanted someone to care about him.

It felt as if his mate had turned her back on him and he knew that wasn't the case.

Drawing in enough air to force words past his thick throat, he said, "I'm not upset with you, Eli. I'm just ... I'm confused. Why did you—"

"Have sex?"

"Yes."

She gave him a sweet smile and watched him with dejected eyes. "I do not want other mate. I want you."

His heart surged with the shot of happiness her words gave him. "Then why did you agree to *mate* a Clan Boudreaux shifter?"

"You will not like."

Call him short on conscience, but he was glad for any reason she didn't want a mate from that clan. "You don't know that. Just tell me so I'll understand."

"Alexandre know I would not stay. He think mate will make difference. He said no mate, no Nico. I think I say yes to mate, no bond. I get Nico and run, but now ..." She looked away then back to Justin. "Now I know plan is bad. Many shifters here. Clan would find me. Maybe kill. I must keep Nico."

That fucker Alexandre.

What kind of father leaves a daughter to fend for herself all her life, then puts her in a bind to accept a mate she hasn't even met for any hope of seeing Nico again?

Justin was heartened that she had never intended to actually bond with a mate.

If her father thought this woman couldn't survive on her own, he knew nothing about Eli.

Justin skipped past the part about the clan punishing or killing her, because he'd destroy every clan member who dared to touch her. He asked, "Has the alpha here chosen a mate or is that your choice?"

"Do not know." She made a disgusted sound and shook her head. "Make stupid deal."

"Not stupid," he corrected her and rubbed his thumb over her lips. "Never call yourself stupid. You are bright, resourceful and beautiful. Agreeing to take a mate complicates things, but I'm not willing to admit defeat."

Hope stirred in her gaze. "How?"

"My boss is very powerful and it's important to him that each of his shifters end up mated." He wouldn't get into the mating curse all Gallize shifters faced. He still had a few years to go and he'd found a mate.

Not just *a* mate, the *only* mate for him.

He wasn't about to pass up having someone like Eli in his life.

She asked, "Your boss is alpha?"

"Not exactly. He's our leader."

"Not bear alpha?"

"No." Now Justin understood what Cole meant when he shared about the moment he had made the decision to tell Tess he was a

Gallize shifter before he had made her his mate. Cole knew Tess was his only choice, just as Justin now saw that Eli was his, but the doubt Eli's announcement raised had Justin hesitating.

The alternative was unacceptable though.

She waited patiently for him to explain.

Running a hand over his hair, he stared up at the sticks holding up their half-assed tent. Her fingers on his cheek brought his gaze back to her.

She ran her fingertips over the scruff that grew fast when he couldn't shave every day. He would be sporting a half-inch-thick, dark beard by now.

"I like," she murmured, brushing her fingers back and forth.

He could not give her up no matter what anyone said, even the Guardian. If he lost her, telling her about the Gallize would be the least of offenses he'd face with the Guardian.

Catching her fingers, he brought them to his lips and kissed each one then pulled her down to his chest. She came willingly and snuggled up to him.

Giving it one last thought, he launched into explaining.

"I did not meet my bear until I was twenty-one."

She moved. "Why?"

"Shh. Let me explain."

"Yes, okay. Talk."

Smiling at her new *yes* phrase, he said, "I am not a shifter like most bear shifters. I have blood of a very old line of shifters who were created through the magic of a druidess many, many centuries ago. Still with me?" He didn't want to confuse her with a lot of detail, but at some point he'd give her a better explanation.

"I understand words."

"This druidess bestowed the power of shifting and a little extra magic to the sons of five women who were all pregnant with boys at that time. Those sons would be the first Gallize shifters, which would be unlike any others. The druidess is the reason our animals have to be called up by a powerful guardian she also created."

"What is call up?"

"You know how an alpha can force the change on any of his clan, right?"

She moved her head in what felt like a nod.

"Our Guardian has that kind of power, but more." Justin recalled how he had been practicing special self-defense moves as part of the training his Guardian had them all go through, but he was impatient to shift. "When he had me brought to him, he explained that I needed to train until my animal was ready to appear. I trained, but I lost my temper one day for no real reason and tried to run to burn off energy. My trainer blocked my exit and called the Guardian. He ordered me to change. His power hits you like a ton of bricks. It wasn't easy the first time, but once I shifted into my bear I knew what had been missing in my life."

"This is boss?"

"Uh huh, the man I've been calling boss. He's not an alpha. He is way, way more powerful than alphas."

"What animal?"

"I'm not supposed to be sharing this much so I'm not going to tell you what he shifts into yet until I talk to him, okay?"

"Yes, okay."

"He's not a bear shifter and I have Gallize friends who are all different kinds of shifters. None of us belong to packs, clans, herds, flocks or whatever. We are like brothers who have trained and fought in battle together."

She lifted her head. "Brother like Nico."

"Yes, much the same. We would also die for each other."

Nodding in agreement, she laid her head on his chest again.

"We can't accept just any mate and we have too much power to bond with a human. The same druidess gifted five different pregnant women to have girl babies who would be as powerful as us, but the females are not shifters. They have unusual gifts, but to be honest we don't know exactly what gifts or powers each one possesses."

"Mate for you?" she asked with so much suspicion in her voice he hugged her.

"Those women are harder to find than someone special like you, but even if they lined up a hundred of those women in front of me and let me have my choice, I wouldn't take them now. Not when I know you are my other half."

Her fingers curled into a fist, holding a wad of his shirt. "How find mates?"

He sighed. "That's where things aren't simple. The females

are supposed to have their own guardian like we do, but their last guardian disappeared a long time ago. If she was around, she could help our shifters find mates. Because of how hard it is to find a suitable mate for my kind, my boss takes *any* potential mating as very important."

"Oh." Eli sounded so forlorn.

Justin put his hand on her cheek and whispered, "I don't know what we're going to do, Eli, babe, but I will never put you in a position of choosing Nico over me."

"I want both."

He squeezed his eyes shut at how sad she sounded. He wanted both, too. He would help her raise Nico if someone would just give them the chance.

But now that she admitted she'd agreed to mate a Clan Boudreaux bear, it complicated things. The Guardian took a hard line about not interfering with non-Gallize shifter groups.

Justin intended to take a hard line about not giving up Eli.

The first hint of light allowed his eyes to see the inside of their structure. They'd have to pack up and head out soon, but he needed a minute to make sure she didn't lose hope.

He said, "Just promise to give me a chance to talk to my boss and see what I can figure out."

"Yes. I like."

He smiled and started to say more, but her entire body went rigid. Her fingers turned white from twisting his shirt. She started breathing hard.

"Eli? What's wrong?"

He grabbed her shoulders and lifted her to face him.

Her eyes rolled back until all he saw was white. What the hell?

Sitting up, he turned her so he could hold her with one arm and pat her face with the other. "Come on, Eli. Talk to me."

Her hand grabbed his wrist. Her voice was sluggish when she said, "Stop."

Air rushed out of his lungs from where he'd held his breath. "What just happened?"

Her breathing calmed down and her eyes fluttered open. She murmured, "Vision."

"A *vision?* That looked like a seizure." He cupped her face, wondering what the hell kind of vision did that to someone.

"Yes." She stared at nothing. Her eyes moved back and forth. "Same vision."

Did she mean the same vision as in a repeat? "You've had this vision before?"

Seeming to shake off whatever had come over her, she looked at him with guilty eyes. "Yes. When first meet. You touch me."

He thought back over their time together and recalled the first moment of meeting her at the boat docks when she'd seemed so off and out of it. "It happened when I touched your arm to stop you from running into the dock steps, didn't it?"

In reply, she nodded and said, "I keep secret."

He heard the apology in her voice. "You didn't know me, babe. I can see why you wouldn't tell me then, but tell me now."

She started moving like she wanted up, so he lifted her and turned her to sit across from him. Brushing a handful of that cinnamon hair off her face, she described the vision of her running from a wolf and the first time Nico was part of it.

But she said this vision hadn't felt the same as the earlier one, only that it also had a wolf. Nico had been part of the last wolf vision, which she hadn't deciphered yet to know its true meaning.

Justin had no idea what to make of the visions, but he could tell she believed them to be premonitions.

Shaking her head, she said, "Is like other vision, but not."

"It's okay, babe. We'll figure it out."

She looked down at where she'd folded her hands in her lap. "Is not okay. My visions always true."

Hold everything. That gave what she was saying more gravity. "What do you think is going to happen, babe?"

Her fingers moved back and forth across his chest as she thought quietly. "In Russia, I have vision. I go to Nico, but grizzly in way."

Shit, did that mean she thought Justin was the grizzly? He didn't want to ask while she was talking.

"At dock, vision of running ... and you."

He asked, "Were you running *with* me?"

"Do not know."

She couldn't have been running from him. That would mean she feared him. He said, "That could mean what's happening now with us being chased by wolf shifters."

Her fingers stopped fidgeting. "Yes. I like." She sounded relieved and added, "Today vision blurry at end."

"Tell me more."

"You are in vision. Wolf attack person important for you. You must stop." Raising her gaze to him, she said, "If not, life for you not same anymore."

A wolf was going to attack Eli.

His pulse raced at the thought of not reaching her in time to prevent it, but that wouldn't happen. She was staying next to him until he had her in a safe place.

He still had to ask, "Am I successful? Do I stop the wolf before it hurts someone important to me?"

"Do not know. Dark fog at end. Last time dark fog, mother die. Could not save."

"When was that?"

"Day before leave Russia."

His heart ached for her. "You lost your mother right before you left? Oh, babe." He leaned over and hugged her close for a minute, then pulled back. "What happened?"

"Wolf shifters kill her. She would not give sex."

He cursed under his breath. "Are they dead?"

"Yes. I hide Nico and fight four, but strong and crazy on drugs."

He asked, "Have you ever heard of the Black River pack."

"Yes. They kill mother."

Eli had fought four of them. He could have lost her before she ever showed up. "Did you kill them?"

"No. I try. Alexandre and his bears kill them. Is why I make deal."

Justin would never hold any decision a woman made under that kind of duress against her. She was a survivor and used everything at hand to allow her to stand another day and protect Nico.

"Have you had many other visions, Eli, babe?"

"Yes. Have vision I find lost cub, then find Nico. Have had visions all life. All true, even if black fog at end."

Shit.

Rumors had floated forever through the bear shifter community about ursid hybrid shifters, though no one Justin knew had ever encountered one in person. The stories of their special capacities went from phenomenal abilities or strength to unusual gifts and powers.

Every time he learned something new about Eli, he was more convinced than ever she should be his mate.

First, he had to get her off this mountain before the wolves caught up to them.

Next, he'd ask her to alter her travel plans so he could go straight to the Guardian to plead his case. No question she would agree since she'd have the rest of her life to visit places such as Glacier National Park.

He now realized she'd bargained for five days to research a place to take Nico to live once Clan Boudreaux kicked her out, but he doubted that would happen. That Louisiana clan had too much sense to let her go.

They had to get their hands on her first, though, and Justin would be standing in the way.

Grabbing her hands, which had been warm earlier when they were generating their own heat in this little hideaway, he noticed they were cold now. "We're going to leave in the next few minutes and work our way off this mountain."

"Run past wolves?"

"We should be able to outwit two wolves." If there were only two and they hadn't called in reinforcements, because the fact that they hadn't hunted Eli down during the night meant they were not as familiar with this area as Justin.

Plus the wolves were packing titanium loads. With the rough terrain, those wolf shifters would likely wait for Justin and Eli to come off the mountain using the same path they'd taken hiking up.

That was the best descent option for that side.

Justin had another plan.

It would require covering a lot more mileage and the plan had holes, but any plan on the fly usually did.

He hadn't survived years in strange countries fighting for his life and that of his Gallize brothers, only to be defeated by two wolves in mountain terrain he knew.

Dawn had brightened enough to safely get out of their location.

Getting down to business, he instructed Eli, "Put your boots on. The minute we open this flap, all our nice warmth will be gone."

"Grizzly cold?" she asked in a teasing tone that took the edge off his dark mood.

She had grit.

"Me, cold?" Justin asked. "Not this grizzly. I've got a sexy grolar bear to keep me warm."

She angled her head in a quizzical look. "What is grolar?"

"You don't know? That's a mix between a grizzly father and a polar bear mother."

"No one say this before."

"Yep. Bunch of scientists probably came up with it, but I think it's cute. My own personal hot grolar babe."

"Crazy man. All things hot." Her voice had a smug happiness to it.

His woman liked being called hot and he would make sure she never doubted it again. "All things Eli-babe are hot."

When she was as dressed as she could be, he pushed the flaps open and stepped out first, getting slapped in the face with a brisk chill. He hadn't slept, but his body felt rested, which he attributed to the woman who had snuggled up to him for hours.

He could still feel a current of energy that had flowed between them during the night. It was only a guess, but he believed that energy played a role in keeping them warm, just as much as their body contact.

He assessed the area, then helped her out.

The direction he wanted to take would be no easy hike. If either of them fell and broke a bone, they'd have to shift and wait for healing.

If he was correct about the wolf shifters not having knowledge equal to his of this mountain, his plan could put the wolves at a serious disadvantage.

While he was up throughout the night, he'd had time to consider all the potential threats.

He considered his odds of success better than good unless they met up with one particular group of wolves—the Black River pack—but he couldn't imagine any reason why they would be after Eli.

Conversely, he couldn't come up with why *any* wolf pack would be after her except to hold hostage for ransom money.

Considering all that, this *could* be the Black River pack, especially if word had traveled to their headquarters in South America about the wolf shifter losses in Russia that Eli had mentioned. If that pack attributed the deaths to Eli and knew of her trip here, then this all made sense.

They would want vengeance, which could mean far worse than using Eli as a hostage for ransom.

Plus, during a recent operation in Spartanburg, Justin's team learned that the Black River pack was aligned with one of the five Power Barons. When shifters were exposed to the public eight years ago, the shifter community had no governing rules beyond those of local or regional alphas. Humans had panicked.

That had been a bloody year.

After a demonstration of magic by the Power Barons that scared the crap out of the US government, human politicians grasped at any power they believed could control what they considered a dangerous shifter community. They'd agreed to align with the Power Barons, and it just got worse from there.

The Power Barons loved their unthreatened position, because it allowed them to function without oversight.

One of them was now believed to be supplying magic to the Black River pack, which meant the wolf shifters hunting Eli didn't just have titanium bullets. They probably had magic at their disposal.

Going up against that would lower Justin's odds of getting her out of here safely.

He checked his weapon. Since his ankle holster had been left behind when they shifted after he'd been shot, he stowed the weapon inside the waistband at his back and led Eli away from their camp.

His mind continued to work through different scenarios for who had put the wolves onto him and Eli. He tried not to pin this whole thing on Clan Boudreaux.

Most of them were a bunch of assholes, but even if some individual in that clan *was* behind this, the clan itself would never get involved with wolf shifters who killed innocents and experimented on captured bear shifters to develop obscene drugs used against *all* shifters.

If it wasn't Clan Boudreaux, Justin would find whoever was behind this, and they would pay dearly.

CHAPTER 25

"WHY THIS WAY?" ELIANNA ASKED, trying to hide her hunger, but her stomach continued to voice complaints. With the sun blazing at midmorning, she enjoyed the cold and didn't mind the rugged terrain, but she could tell they had not descended much, if any, in the past hour. That concerned her. She still smelled a metallic odor from Justin's head wound.

The skin was trying to heal, but spots were still gray.

Justin tilted his head up, then looked around as if getting his bearings at this new ridge. "We need to make a side trip."

"Why?"

"We need to eat so we'll be able to traverse the course I have in mind. Plus, people on the other side of this mountain can hear your stomach growling."

Her stomach ached, but she was no stranger to being hungry. "I am good."

"You're hungry and I am, too. It's not safe for shifters to go without food for a long time."

He made a good point. She'd seen hungry shifters act out of their minds. "What of wolves?" She hadn't heard any howling since they'd headed out almost two hours ago.

Why would the wolves be quiet? Had they given up and left?

"We're not headed down the front side of the mountain where they're probably waiting for us. We will eventually descend on that side, but not close to where we first climbed up from the trailhead. That means today is going to be a long, hard hike. Those energy bars we ate last night aren't enough for the calories we're burning. If we eat a decent meal now, then we just have to worry about water along the way."

She trusted Justin to lead them.

Elianna stopped for a second. Justin was a physically strong man, sure. But he was more. If they were in PK, she believed he would trust *her* to lead. Because a confident man did not need to hold the power over a woman to feel stronger.

She had not realized this until Justin.

It was nice to share the burden of problems with him. She had fought all her battles alone for so long, she'd never expected to have a partner.

A mate.

That's what Justin wanted. She did, too.

He was worthy of her trust.

She still couldn't believe he had not yelled in anger when he found out what a bad deal she'd made. There had been no time to think it through. When her father said he was keeping Nico, she'd panicked and agreed to his terms for any hope of seeing the little boy of her heart again.

She'd had no idea that her snap decision might cost her the only man she would ever want.

Now, he might die because of her.

Mate special, her bear told her.

Oddly, her bear seemed quiet and content. Not yapping at her like normal.

Elianna silently answered her bear. *I agree, but is not our mate.*

Yes mate.

Why? Elianna asked.

Need us.

Where had her bear come up with that idea?

Justin had worked his way downhill while she'd been pondering her situation. He pushed back branches and turned to her. "Take a look at this."

Stepping forward carefully so she did not lose her footing and knock them both down the mountain, she stuck her neck out and peered at a body of water fed by small streams.

Fish! her bear told her.

Delighted, she turned to Justin and repeated her bear's word. "Fish?"

"Yep. In fact, it's called Trout Lake. We'll shift, eat our fill of fish in the shallows, and change back and get off this mountain."

She followed close, anxious to fill her stomach after all. While she *had* endured hunger in her life, she didn't enjoy it.

When the ground evened out farther down, Justin put his arm out, holding her back as he scanned everywhere, then looked up.

She followed his gaze. "What is in sky?"

"Nothing, babe." He hadn't sounded convinced, but after giving the area a long look, he said, "Let's move up this bank and change to our bears under the trees where we're shielded. Then stay in the stream where those tall trees on the opposite side shade a shallow area.

She bobbed her head in agreement and waved him on.

Justin led the way forward, but stopped short of where sunshine warmed the rocks and grass along the bank.

He said, "Here," and started shedding clothes.

This man was not the least bit self-conscious about his body and he had no reason to be. It was clear that he wanted them to appear only to be bears.

Herc would look natural here.

Not her bear. Elianna said, "You fish. I wait."

Her bear growled. *Want water and fish!*

Justin turned to her with a sharp look. "Why?"

Blowing out a harsh breath, she said, "You are grizzly. I am ... strange."

"You mean a grolar. You are not strange and ursid hybrid are not bad words," he said in a firm voice. "You look just as natural as I do here. It might be a little south for a polar bear and grizzly meetup, but you are as natural as I am in this environment. I just want you to stay close to shore around those trees." He pointed to the area he referenced.

Mate nice. Like mate. Her bear had already made up its mind about mating, but her bear did not deal with things like agreements and keeping Nico safe.

Giving up, Elianna shed her clothes and turned to Justin before she intended to drop down on her hands and knees. It had always been simpler to allow the change to come over her in this position because of how much her bear weighed.

He was just as naked.

She would never wear clothes if she had a body like that.

His lips tilted in the same smile he wore when he had sex on his mind. She was getting to know him that well.

She warned, "Do not say hot."

He held his hands up. "Monty isn't standing at attention for *me*."

Her eyes had no manners. They went straight south, to notice that, yes, Monty was happy to see her.

Justin started toward her.

Pushing a hand up as a barrier, she said, "No time to play."

"Sadly, you're right, but I need a kiss. It's been at least an hour since I had one."

Shaking her head at him, she lifted up and kissed Justin. She had intended a quick kiss, but he captured her face in his hands and turned his lips loose on hers. This man kissed with purpose.

This man did everything with purpose.

He ended it, then kissed her nose. "I love the color of your bear's coat, but to prevent it from catching someone's eye who would love to get a picture of a unicorn, don't let your bear wander off downstream."

"I understand." She hoped her bear had been listening and would behave since this was her animal's second time being free in less than a day.

Justin's eyes constantly searched around them. His gaze came back to her, sliding down her body then up to her face again. "Stop messing around so we can get out of here, eat a real meal and find a real bed."

She growled at him and he laughed.

Lowering herself to the ground so she could be on all fours, she called up her bear.

Energy boiled under her skin as she gave way to the change. Sometimes shifting dragged out painfully, but not today. It was as if her bear hurried the process along.

Or could the power that moved between her Justin last night be the reason? It had been odd, but had not bothered her. If anything, she felt closer to him now.

When she looked out through her bear's gaze, she glanced down at wide paws with long claws that belonged to the grizzly side of her blood.

Herc sidled up to her and leaned his big head over to rub hers.

Elianna's bear made such contented sounds.

Her bear had never been this happy and the fault belonged to Elianna. She had spent years in conflict with her bear.

It was obvious Justin could see the problem, but she did not think a name for her bear would fix their difficult relationship.

Giving a head signal, Herc led the way to the stream, took his time drinking, then went fishing with his head down.

While lapping up drinks of water, Elianna's bear searched for fish, chasing and jumping, but coming up empty.

Missed fish, Elianna said to let her bear know what it was like to be the one doing all the work with someone inside critiquing.

Not my fault, her bear said and growled when she missed another trout. *You no fish.*

Of course, the problem was because Elianna had not allowed her more time to learn how to fish. Elianna dropped it. She was going to carry all the blame no matter what and reminded her bear, *Do not wander.*

Growling low in frustration, her bear splashed at another trout then lumbered back toward the bank where they had entered.

A trout came flying past her and hit the bank.

She pounced on the trout, attacking it with vigor. When she finished eating, she looked over to the stream and found Herc grinning at her.

That was the same silly smile Justin sometimes wore.

Nice mate, Elianna's bear said and actually sounded as if she made a bear purr.

Elianna agreed. If only it were simple.

Herc sent another trout up, which she ate immediately, then caught one for himself. Another fish splashed near Herc. He jumped around, hitting it with his big paw.

Elianna's bear moved up the bank into the sun and sat on her rump.

She told her bear, *Go to water. Do not cause trouble.*

Warm sun.

You are stubborn bear, Elianna grumbled. She ordered her bear to get moving.

Sleep.

No. Wolves are coming.

Herc kill wolves.

Her bear dropped over on her side, content to warm herself after eating the fish.

Herc growled a warning sound.

Elianna's bear rolled up, immediately focusing on Justin's bear. Herc was not smiling anymore. He'd gone downstream about twenty yards, but lunged forward, running to her.

Hurry, Elianna told her bear, which moved quickly only because Herc had called to her.

That's when she heard the sound of a helicopter.

CHAPTER 26

J USTIN PUSHED HERC TO REACH Eli.
   His bear pounded through the water, making huge splashes
with each heavy step.

Justin's sixth sense, the one that kept military operators alive
in the field, had warned him not to expose their bears for long.
He knew Eli had understood the importance of his instructions.

Clearly, the grolar bear lacked discipline and Eli was unable to
manage her animal.

Justin should have spent more time talking to Eli about her
bear and what she needed to do to work as one.

No time for that right now.

Her bear was barreling toward them with worried eyes, but
she'd waited too long.

The helicopter flew over low just as Eli's bear reached the
stream, but short of the shaded area that would shield her coat.

When the helo circled around, Justin knew the pilot was clearly
taking a second look.

Justin kicked himself mentally over encouraging her to shift.
He hadn't liked the shame he'd heard in her voice when she'd
said she was strange. He'd thought if they stayed in the dark
shade cast over this side of the stream, it would be hard to make
out a grolar bear.

That plan would have worked if Eli had been able to control
her bear.

Herc ran up to Eli's bear, putting his big body in front to shield
her coat, but the damage had been done.

According to the emblem on the chopper, it belonged to the

park service. If that had been someone with the park service flying around for another reason and just happened to see Eli's unusual coat, then no problem.

But Justin had a bad feeling that wasn't the case.

Could the wolves hunting Eli have someone in the park service on their payroll? He hoped not.

Even if it was a casual flyover, by the time word of a possible ursid hybrid sighting got out, Justin had to have Eli far from here.

But that chopper had just wrecked his original plan to escape on foot taking the new direction he'd had in mind.

If wolves were clued in to his and Eli's current location, they would run them down before he could get somewhere to contact the Guardian.

Now, Justin might as well try crossing the mountain back to the side where he could reach his truck quickly. There was one decent route option from this point that would be open enough for him to scent and see someone coming, but he didn't like it. He couldn't stay on this side any longer, plus he had an additional phone and more than one extra weapon in his truck.

He didn't believe they'd shoot Eli, but they'd proven they had the means to kill him and that would leave her vulnerable.

When Herc and her bear reached the cluster of trees where Justin had left clothes and boots, he initiated his change. He pushed Herc to make the shift back to human quickly so that he wouldn't leave Eli unprotected.

By the time he stood upright and had his jeans zipped, Eli had almost finished her shift.

He gave her a hand up and started putting clothes on her.

She snatched them away. "I can dress."

"Hurry up, then."

Looking up at the sky then back to him, she said, "We are found?"

"Maybe. If the wolf shifters were behind that helicopter showing up, then they know our position. If it was someone in an official capacity with the park and unrelated to the wolves, we still have a problem if he saw your coat."

She buttoned up her shirt, which was looking rough, and grumbled, "I say my bear bad idea."

Stepping closer, he pulled her chin up so she faced him. "It is never bad to show your bear. We will just be careful while some-one is hunting you. Another thing. You had no control of your bear when it decided to lie down in the sun, did you?" When she shook her head, looking chastised, he tried to take it easy on her. "I'm only fussing because it scared me that we couldn't reach each other in time. That's what I was talking about this morn-ing. You should name your bear and work on having a better understanding."

She pulled away. "It is what is."

That just pissed him off more. "Not if you fix it."

Snatching up her boots, she sat on a rock and put them on, ignoring him. "Not so simple."

He pinched the bridge of his nose.

She sounded embarrassed and that had not been his intention.

This was not how he'd meant to talk to her about her bear, and it was not the right time. He was still suffering the after effects of panic over her being too far away from him. Even Herc had snarled at her bear, and Herc liked the stubborn grolar, which was saying something.

Kneeling in front of Eli, Justin waited until she had both feet on the ground and raised her disgruntled gaze to him. She plopped her hands in her lap and initiated a staredown.

He reached over and took her hands in his, pulling her palms to his lips where he pressed a kiss on each one, then placed her hands back on her knees.

Just that touch smoothed out the frown lines in her face.

This woman was so responsive to him.

When he spoke this time, he tried to do a better job of explain-ing. "I have a friend who is a wolf shifter. His wolf was called up when he was in college and had found the love of his life, so he was not happy to find out he was one of the hated shifters back when nonhumans first went public. He and his wolf didn't get along well. They managed to function for seven years, but their lack of connection almost killed both of them."

"What happen?"

"He fixed it, but only with the help of his mate. When we get out of here, I'll tell you the whole story, but right now I just want you to know I'm not criticizing you. The bond between human and animal for shifters is very personal and different for everyone.

Those of us who create a partnership with our animal live much happier—and safer—lives. I want you to enjoy the kind of trust I have with Herc."

"She is reason I live as outcast whole life."

His gut twisted at the misery in her voice. "It's not your bear's fault and it's not your fault, but allowing a wall to grow between you because some people are cruel is bad. You can fix this problem. You could start by naming her. Think about that while we walk out and we'll talk more in the truck. Okay?"

Heaving a sigh that sounded as if she carried the mountain on her shoulders, she said, "Yes. Will try."

"That's fair. Ready to go? We're going to move fast and use hand signals to keep sounds to a minimum." Justin went over a few more with her that he might need to use.

She jumped up. "Yes, okay. Go."

"Demanding little thing."

She'd been staring at the stream and turned to him. "What is little thing?"

"You."

"Eyes bad. I weigh like truck."

"Exaggerate much, Eli, babe?" He chuckled and herded her back the way they'd come so he could stay off the main trails, but parallel them in some places.

His head still pulsed with a dull throb, but the vertigo had backed off to where he didn't fear dragging her over a cliff if he lost his balance. This last shift to his bear form and getting to eat a solid meal had pushed his healing up a notch.

The bullet hadn't gone inside his body. He *hoped* he'd washed out enough toxins to not suffer any further issues, but Rory was the medic, not him.

They climbed uphill for almost an hour, then Justin blazed a trail for them through a thinner section of evergreens. Every time he recognized places he hadn't seen in more than three years, he felt encouraged, but he was forced to keep working his way toward the truck. The undergrowth had filled in some since the last time he came through here, but even a human could traverse it.

When he crossed over a known trail and dropped into a thick forest, he slowed a bit, but still followed a path he knew.

That's when Justin heard a sound that didn't belong out here.

Had that been a child's cry?

He turned to ask Eli if she'd heard it, but she was already turned in the direction of the sound.

She cried, "No," and went racing downhill through a gully of lush undergrowth of ferns and knee-high tree sprouts.

Tearing after her, he jumped down the cut she'd made, but she was still out of reach, oblivious to any danger.

Were the wolves close enough to hear the noise she made crashing through the woods? Justin had to get to her and calm her down. He looked beyond her bobbing head to find her target.

A small boy stood crying.

Then as Justin watched, the image changed to a woman. Eli.

Not slowing down, Justin drew in a deep breath.

Herc said, *No scent. Trap!*

His bear nailed it. Justin shouted, "Stop, Eli!"

Too late. She hit an invisible structure that pinned her in place like a giant spider web made of clear threads.

CHAPTER 27

JUSTIN SLOWED AS HE REACHED where Eli jerked and fought against whatever spell held her in place. "Eli, babe, you okay?"

"No. Am stupid. Think I see Nico. Is trap."

"I know, babe." Justin fought to keep from reaching for her and jerking her from the web, but he felt certain the spell behind that was probably set to capture anyone who touched her.

Whispering, he said, "Eli, I need you to calm down. The more you panic, the more it might entangle you. I don't want it to get caught around your neck. I can't pull you out yet, because it will probably trap me, too. Then I wouldn't be able to watch your back. Let me deal with whoever is coming for us, then I'll get you free."

"Sorry, very sorry," she started rambling, sounding sick that she'd run them both into danger. "Nico could not be here, but alphas are powerful. Do not trust. Saw him. Hear his voice." She was close to tears.

Justin wanted to gut the shifter behind this. "Stop apologizing, babe. That's a magic trap. I figured the little boy was Nico."

"What?"

"I'm guessing the spell made a general child sound, something any decent person would run toward. The minute you looked at it, the spell probably created a hologram from your memories of the one person you fear losing."

She was quiet and had stopped thrashing around. "You see Nico?"

"From a distance and only for a second, but when I focused on the image it immediately changed to you."

"Oh."

Another one of her loaded words.

He wanted to make sure she understood.

Keeping track of their surroundings, he said, "If you had not been right in front of me, I would have done the same thing to get to you. When emotions are involved, we don't always take the time to think through something unexpected."

"How to escape?"

"I won't know that until I know who is behind this, but I have my gun." He'd palmed his weapon while racing to catch her. "Just please stay quiet so you don't distract me."

Someone finally approached from the top of the trail he and Eli had thrashed their way through.

Wolf, Herc said.

Justin had recognized the shifter's smell, too.

Wolf hurt mate. Kill wolf.

Damn. That was the most he'd ever heard Herc say. Justin spoke mind-to-mind. *That wolf is dead meat walking, but we have to figure out how many wolves are here before we make any moves.*

Kill all.

His bear was jonesing for wolf blood and Justin would happily unleash his monster on everyone who had dared to threaten Eli, but this is where the human side had to rule.

He couldn't make a rash decision. He told Herc, *Just be patient. We both want to keep Eli safe.*

Herc growled, but stayed back to let Justin assess their situation.

The wolf walking downhill grinned. "Look what we've caught."

"Who are you?" Justin asked, but had a pretty good idea because of the magic used to trap Eli.

"Names are so boring. My title in South America is *El Cazador,* but you may use Cazador," the wolf shifter said accommodatingly.

Ah, hell. *The Hunter.*

Justin had heard stories about this ruthless killer. The Black River pack contracted this shifter for high-risk jobs in South America. But Justin had never heard of Cazador working on US soil.

Guess there was a first time for everything.

Cazador called out, "*Toro!*"

Evidently, Toro was the wolf shifter who popped up from his hiding place thirty yards away on Justin's right. The spell must have masked the area down here as well, because Justin hadn't scented the second wolf yet.

Toro waded through the lush undergrowth and low branches, knocking them aside.

He stood four inches taller than Cazador's six feet and out-weighed his leader by fifty pounds of muscle, but Toro was not the real threat.

Justin had spared shifter number two only a brief look and kept his true focus on Cazador, who held a Glock 17 9mm with an AAC Illusion suppressor in his left hand.

Eli still dangled from their invisible web.

Justin didn't carry titanium bullets as a rule, at least not unless he was hunting a criminal shifter. Using his weapon would only risk Eli getting caught in crossfire. When Toro walked up to Cazador, Justin shifted his stance so he stood between the wolf shifters and Eli, but no position allowed him to fully protect her.

Cazador asked, "Are we going to be reasonable, bear, or not?"

Buying time to get a handle on these two, Justin started in a conversational tone. "What do you want? If it's money, we can match—"

"Toro, take his gun," Cazador said, then told Justin, "If you make any sudden move, I will shoot her. She will heal, but not for days. She might have a body part rot off while waiting to heal and have to suffer through full regeneration. I've seen it. Not a pretty sight."

His lackey, Toro, held his hand out, not getting close to Justin.

With no better option, Justin handed over his weapon.

"Search him," Cazador ordered.

Toro hesitated.

Cazador said, "He will not harm you, Toro. I can see in this bear's eyes that he recognizes my name, don't you bear?"

Justin said nothing.

Following orders, Toro patted Justin down and located nothing else.

Standing, Toro said, "That's it." He handed the weapon to

Cazador, who stuck it in the back of his waistband.

The wolf clearly did not trust Toro to keep the gun from Justin. A wise move. Justin had fully intended to take it back.

Pointing at a spot on the ground, Cazador told Justin, "Move there."

"Why? What are you going to do?"

Cazador lifted his weapon. "You don't really expect me to explain everything I do to you, do you?"

Not really, but Justin had learned that engaging the enemy in conversation often revealed helpful information.

Waving his gun at the spot he'd indicated, Cazador warned, "Move now or I'll shoot her just to avoid arguments later."

Taking a step to the side, Justin complied, but kept up his questions. "If this is just a kidnapping for money, I'll work with you as long as you don't harm her."

Justin had no expectations that Cazador cared anything about his compliance, but since Cazador hadn't shot him first thing, he saw no harm in keeping the wolf talking.

Cazador shrugged. "I don't care if you help or not, because your life is expendable if you cause me any trouble."

"*No!*" Eli shouted.

Justin closed his eyes. Hadn't he asked her to stay quiet?

"No, what, princess?" Cazador asked as if sincerely interested, which was fouled by his mocking tone.

Calling her princess gave Justin another small piece of intel. That meant they definitely knew she was the daughter of the Romanov alpha.

But who was behind this, because Cazador was only a hired gun, albeit a very expensive one?

Still facing away, Eli said, "He is mate. We bond. Kill him and I die. No money for you."

Great lie, babe. Would these two believe that?

Justin cut his eyes over at Toro then at Cazador, who stared at Eli as if trying to decide if she was gaming him.

Cazador said, "You were sent here to take a Clan Boudreaux mate. Why would you mate this one?"

"He *is* Clan Boudreaux," she replied, sounding tired and bored. Justin could smell her worry, but only because he knew her scent so well. She was doing a damn good job of hiding her fear.

And ... she was selling her claim, because Cazador had lost his smile and now studied the situation silently.

Toro tried to look serious and mean, but Justin had already downgraded him to brainless muscle.

Cazador argued, "Bonding doesn't work like that." But he'd sounded unsure.

She made a scoffing noise. "This bond different. I am *special.*" She loaded the word special with arrogance.

Justin had not heard her sound like a snobby princess even one time since meeting her, but she owned it right now.

He was freaking proud of her.

Toro scratched his nose. "Could be true, Cazador. You said she's an ursid hybrid and they have weird abilities."

"Shut up, Toro."

But Justin figured out the rest. Cazador had warned Toro to be careful around her. Justin had to do some serious research on ursid hybrids if they got out of this.

When they got out of this.

Justin couldn't accept anything less than success, especially after shifting to feed in the stream. The shift and food had healed him enough to fight. He was ready to take on two wolf shifters, but Cazador had not earned his reputation by being careless.

Justin needed more intel. He had no idea if Clan Boudreaux knew Eli was a grolar. If not, then that might point at someone from Russia.

Addressing Eli, Cazador said, "I will not kill the bear for now, but if once we get off this mountain I find out you lied, he will pay."

Justin held his breath, hoping she didn't drop her arrogant façade.

She said, "My clan make sorry you harm us."

Justin held back a grin at her haughty and threatening tone. Her English was definitely getting better. He wanted to kiss her socks off for her threat until he took in Cazador's confident smile.

The wolf said, "Which clan would that be? The one paying the tab for this?"

She sucked in a breath and he laughed his head off.

Point to Cazador.

Justin would rip the guilty shifters apart, even if he had to

travel to Russia and fight every shifter in the legendary Romanov Kamchatka Clan.

"Put the collar on him first," Cazador said.

Toro eyed Justin and said, "Can you hit him with a tranquilizer
load first?"

Oh, hell. Justin did not want to get knocked out and leave Eli
to their mercy, which neither wolf shifter possessed.

"No. I told you, Toro, we are not carrying them off the mountain. It's too much trouble and will attract attention."

"You're right. I forgot."

Cazador's weapon made only a slight *chuck* sound.

The bullet tore a hole through Justin's thigh and exited the
back. He grabbed his leg and cursed.

"*Justin?*" Eli shouted in a panic. "Okay, yes?"

At the tiny twitch of Cazador's finger, Justin had moved fast,
but there hadn't been time to avoid being hit. Besides, the wolf
would have just shot him again.

"*Justin!*"

"It's okay, Eli." Or it would be once Justin pulled the wolf's
head off and shoved it up his ass. His leg burned like he'd been
stabbed with a hot poker. He'd bent over to press against the
wound on both sides of his thigh to stem the bleeding.

The pungent stink of titanium singed his nostrils again and the
wound burned like fire. This wound would fester in a day. He
could heal some if he shifted, but not as much as he needed to as
long as that much titanium remained inside his body.

Eli was shouting something in Russian.

Justin sucked in a breath and said, "It's okay, babe. Take it easy."

Cazador chuckled. "Now you can put the collar on him, Toro.
That's so much more effective than a tranq in this situation. Plus,
he now knows what she'll feel if I have to shoot her."

Blood ran through Justin's fingers.

Herc pounded to get out and heal Justin, then kill the wolves.

But shifting would end with Herc full of titanium.

The landscape swirled.

Justin blinked and shook his head. He could not pass out.

CHAPTER 28

W HO WANTED HER DEAD?
Elianna had given up thinking the wolves wanted to kidnap her for ransom money. This Cazador marching her and Justin through the narrow trail must have been sent by someone paying to deliver her.

That pointed at one of the clans.

She would not waste time thinking this was her father.

He dealt with issues himself and hated wolf packs.

No, Alexandre was not behind this. The only other group it could be was Clan Boudreaux. Why would they go to all this trouble to bring her over only to have her kidnapped?

Checking over her shoulder for Justin, she felt the chain snap against her back.

"Keep facing forward," Cazador ordered.

She hissed and drew her shoulders up, unable to rub the pain with titanium cuffs cutting into her wrists. The bloody patches burned, giving her a small idea of how much pain Justin was silently enduring.

She had never touched titanium before. It did not bother her healthy skin now, but the metal burned the abrasions on her wrists.

Toro had laughed at Justin earlier, saying, "That titanium bullet hurts, don't it?"

Her bear whined, *Neck hurts. Fix. Run. Run. Run.*

Elianna hated the collar, too, but nothing could be done. This was going down as the longest—and most miserable—Monday of her life. Speaking silently to her bear, she said, *Not possible.*

Must be patient. Justin is warrior. He will free us.

Herc kill wolves.

Elianna walked along, stumbling over rocks at times, trying to figure out how her bear and Herc had become close so quickly. Her bear had never recognized anyone in particular and definitely no other shifter's animal or name. Nico loved to play with Elianna's bear, but her bear had never once commented on Nico or his adorable polar bear cub.

Stop. Rest. Stop. Rest. Stop. Rest.

What had her bear so agitated? Elianna realized they were entering a level area for the first time in a while. The hike she and Justin had first made up here had been nice, but she didn't recall this spot.

Would Justin know this as well as the other areas he'd led them through?

Her bear said, *Herc like. Stop here.*

How would her bear know that?

Maybe her bear was thinking about Justin's wound affecting his bear and just saying they needed to rest, but again, that was more interest than her animal had ever shown.

Still, Elianna was just as concerned about Justin and agreed. She said, "Cazador?"

"Yes."

"Need water. Mate wound hurt me. Am tired."

"You want to rest?" he asked, sounding appalled any shifter would whine about being tired from walking.

Stop, stop, stop! Mate rest, her bear demanded.

Elianna wished her bear would go to sleep for a while and give her a mental break. She told Cazador, "Yes, please."

Wolf bad. No please.

Her bear's attitude change, from bumbling along without a care to sounding angry, was a complete about-face from all the years they had shared a semi-polite relationship.

Was meeting Herc the reason for this change?

The word please must have worked with Cazador, who said, "Fine. You can have your break up ahead."

When they entered the open space that overlooked miles of mountains and trees, wind whipped through with nothing to slow it down. Elianna stayed thirty feet from the edge of the cliff overlooking a valley thousands of feet down.

Cazador waved his gun at a specific area. "Stand there."

She hurried over and turned to watch Justin who walked ahead of Toro. Her face chilled at the blood that soaked his pants.

Hunched over, Justin moved slowly, in obvious pain. He stumbled, then dropped to his knees.

She ran toward him.

Cazador yanked her back.

Elianna spun around and snarled viciously at him.

His eyes narrowed. "You forget who is holding your leash, princess. We can continue just as easily as stopping."

"No. Sorry. Must see mate." She waited as Cazador watched Justin on his knees with his head down and arms trembling.

She had smelled the sick metallic odor coming from Justin's wound. Titanium was killing him.

He was dying because of her.

She would never have a chance to be with him if he died. She had destroyed a chance at life with him when she made a bad deal and now she was the reason he suffered.

Tears spilled down her face. She turned to Cazador. "Please."

He was unmoved.

A sob escaped her.

Finally, he shook his head in disgust. "I've got a deadline to meet tonight, princess."

She repeated, "Please."

Cursing lividly, Cazador said, "This is why you never want to be tied to a mate, Toro. All this blubbering. It weakens the male. Just look at that bear." Still shaking his head, Cazador said, "Fine. You have one minute with him, princess. If you annoy me in any way, I will shoot him again ... and again."

"I will be good."

He nodded for her to move and gave her twelve-foot chain leash slack. The links were the size of her finger and welded. Breaking steel chain that thick would be difficult, but snapping welded titanium links was impossible even for a shifter.

She dropped to her knees in front of Justin.

He didn't lift his head or acknowledge her. Another sob slipped out. She'd never cried as an adult, but seeing her strong and powerful Justin on his knees was too much for her.

She whispered, "Am sorry, Justin. Very sorry."

His warm fingers slid over hers and squeezed.

Her heart hiccupped, hoping for any sign that he would survive this.

As soon as Cazador and Toro started discussing the route down the mountain, Justin murmured, "If you accept the mating bond now, you'll have my power joined with yours."

It hurt to tell him no, but if she survived, she would not live with herself for letting Nico down.

Keeping her voice just as soft, she said, "I can not. I would lose Nico. Your love mean more than all power. I need only you to live."

"I understand." He finally lifted his head just enough to look into her eyes.

His gaze was as sharp as bear claws. Not the eyes of a man losing his grip on consciousness as she'd thought.

He whispered, "I'm not dying, but don't let them know. Be ready. When I give the signal, you run like hell. Don't argue or hesitate. If you do, we both die."

CHAPTER 29

JUSTIN REMAINED ON HIS HANDS and knees, continuing to look as if he struggled to remain conscious, which didn't require a lot of acting.

The titanium was doing its job to weaken his leg and zap his energy, but not enough to prevent him from taking a chance to free Eli.

He had his hand over Eli's small one when Toro yanked her chain leash to pull her back.

She yelped, falling over on her side.

Justin's fingers dug into the ground. Seeing anyone mistreat her sent him and Herc into a rage. He shook for real now, with the need to crush Cazador's skull.

But when he glanced at Eli to check on her, she gave him a calm face. As she made it to her feet, she lifted her cuffed hands to use a finger to rub the left side of her nose. That was one of Herc's physical signals. She was telling Justin she was going ahead and would wait on him.

That actually meant she would wait for him to get them free, which was a great idea if he had any chance of making it happen.

When she looked at him, it was clear she put all her confidence in him.

He'd be damned if he would let her down.

Until Cazador and Toro discovered she'd lied about their mating connection, the wolf shifters wouldn't kill him. But if he failed to get Eli out of here and escape himself, they'd hurt him bad enough he'd have to be dragged off the mountain.

Eli would end up in even more danger, because his alpha female would fight them to protect Justin.

Dammit. What a mate. He could not lose her.

Cazador said something sharp to Eli and she started walking ahead of the wolf shifter. The chain dragged behind her until Cazador looped a coil of the leash to hold and allowed the chain to become tight.

Herc was banging around, growling.

He wanted out to fight.

Justin silently told him, *I need you focused to help me, Herc. We will make the wolves pay, but not at the risk of harming Eli.*

Herc quieted immediately and waited for directions.

That was the partnership he'd had the entire time with his bear, one he would help Eli discover with hers.

Once Eli was out of sight, Toro slapped Justin across the back with the end of the chain. "Break's over. Get moving."

Justin wobbled getting to his feet and complained in a weak voice, "That fucking titanium is eating my muscle."

"Tough shit, bear. Move it." Toro tried to sound tough, but Justin could smell the wolf shifter's anxiety.

Good.

Weaving forward to appear off balance, Justin kept moving. As he did, he came up with a plan.

Not much of one, but Eli was depending on him.

All Gallize had an extra kick of power driven by their magic, but it didn't work the same for everyone. Cole could power up his arm or leg in human form to really blast someone with a fist to the head or roundhouse kick.

Justin's magic worked a little differently.

He and Herc were so closely joined in spirit that they both had to bring that extra power to the surface.

Justin silently said, *We need the Gallize power, Herc.*

His bear growled softly, agitated by the titanium collar preventing them from shifting and killing the wolves.

That didn't stop Herc from pushing power through Justin. Not even a Gallize could break titanium, but with his body feeling flush with an extra jolt of kick-ass, he was ready for the stunt he had in mind.

Herc kept up a deep rumbling sound in Justin's ear.

Justin warned his bear, *Stay calm. I'm going to try to free us.*

Kill wolves.

Getting there, Herc.

Justin paused, causing the leash to go slack as Toro kept walking. Lifting his hands to his head, Justin said in a weak voice, "Give me a minute."

"Fuck, bear. This is going to take all day."

"Your boss shouldn't have shot me."

"Quit your whining and move on. We need to catch up with that bitch."

Herc snarled a deep, deadly rumble that was normally the last warning before he ripped an enemy to shreds.

Justin wanted to free him right then.

Nobody called Eli a bitch.

"Okay, okay. Just a little dizzy." Justin nodded and acted as if he was going to move forward again.

Instead, he lowered his hands slowly from his head and curled the fingers of his left hand inside the metal collar around his neck.

That would save his throat, he hoped.

He spun hard, which took up slack in the chain, and gripped the leash with his right hand. His forearm muscles flexed, now increased in size and strength from the new surge of energy he and Herc had generated.

It all happened in seconds.

Jerking the chain to him, Justin loved the look of shock on Toro's face. Priceless.

Justin caught the wolf's throat in both hands and leaped left, shoving Toro downhill where the wolf landed sprawled on his back.

That only knocked the wind out of him.

Justin couldn't let him howl for his buddy. With a body that now weighed half again more than it should, Justin dropped his knees hard on the wolf's chest.

Ribs crunched. *Oh, yes. Love that sound.*

Blood oozed out of the wolf's mouth when he opened it to howl.

With his wrists locked, Justin slammed double fists down on Toro's throat, which gave easily.

Crushed windpipe.

Wolf eyes came forward, bulged in panic.

No more sound out of this one.

The wolf struggled for air, but he couldn't regenerate fast enough to get air into his lungs again. Not unless he shifted, which Justin realized the bastard was trying to do.

Dammit. Die already.

Justin grabbed the chain and looped it around the wolf's throat, pulling the ends tight.

Toro's head had already warped with snout and jaws widening, but the titanium did its job.

Finally, Toro's struggling ceased.

Sweat poured off Justin's face from the power overload and burning energy to fight this guy.

He hoped he wouldn't need an extra Gallize boost any time soon, because there was a limit to how much he could draw on at one time, and how often.

Basically, he couldn't do it again for a while. He would only be stronger in his bear form, which he couldn't use right now. He had to stay human to maneuver and communicate with Eli if need be.

Herc said, *Hurry. Save mate.*

"What the fuck do you think I'm doing?" Justin grumbled as he dug through the wolf's vest for a set of keys to his cuffs and collar.

Too slow.

"Save me the freaking commentary right now, would you?" Justin snarled, his big hands fumbling with the small keys.

Mishka need help.

Justin shook his head and stilled at Herc's words. "*Mishka?* Who is that?"

Bear mate.

"Who told you that's the name of Eli's bear?"

Mishka.

"Are you and Mishka talking?"

Stupid words.

Justin accepted the equivalent of Herc saying *duh.* Well, damn. Never a dull moment with his bear. After contorting his huge fingers to get the slender key in place, the cuffs snapped free. The collar popped next.

That felt good to get it off his neck.

Maybe his thigh would hold up until Rory could flush out the titanium.

Herc ordered, *Hurry. Find mate!*

"I'm on it." Justin kicked the dead wolf to the side where ferns and other plants covered him. Once he got out of here, he'd call in a cleanup team. His leg ached and he'd burned through a load of power, but Justin was ready to take on the world.

They should never have messed with his mate.

He didn't know how he and Eli would figure out the future, but they would. Their bears had clearly mated. Justin and Eli would bond then he'd bring Nico to Eli.

Justin intended to keep them both.

First he had to save her.

He had no weapon except this chain, but the minute he tried to use that on Cazador someone would be shot, probably Justin.

He fell back on what he did any time a mission went FUBAR, which many did.

Made it up as he went.

Discarding the idea of carrying the chain, which could also cause the tiniest noise Cazador might hear, Justin searched Toro and came up with a knife.

Not much help against a shifter unless he got close enough to slice Cazador's throat, but he'd take it.

Hurrying in the direction Eli had gone, adrenaline sharpened Justin's focus. He could take down the second wolf with his eyes shut if Eli wasn't involved.

Success would require stealth and the element of surprise.

After picking his way carefully along the path, he deviated to the side, away from the mountain face and into a more exposed area with piles of fallen rocks.

Moving silently, Justin finally heard Eli's voice.

She seemed to drag her feet, giving Cazador grief with each step.

Justin shadowed them with soft footfalls.

How could he let her know he was free so she wouldn't react when she saw him? The trail she and Cazador were taking curved closer to where the mountain fell away at a sharp angle.

There were deep holes on the other side as well, but he'd rather she stay away from that cliff.

She'd survive stepping off in a hole.

It dawned on Justin that he now had a direct line to her.

Justin asked Herc mind to mind, *Can you speak to Mishka and let her know we're close? Have her tell Eli not to react.*

Yes. Herc was quiet a moment, then he told Justin, *Mishka good.*

Eli slowed on a stretch of trail that was no more than eight feet wide and became very still.

Cazador whipped the chain up and down, jerking on her collar. "Get going."

"Must pee." She turned with careful movements to face him.

"You should have said something the last time we stopped. Pee where you stand."

She gave him a disgusted expression. "Is filthy idea. Russian shifter would not say such."

"Do you really think I'm going to let you go in the woods where I can't see you?"

"Yes. Over there." She nodded to the trees climbing gradually up the side of the mountain.

When the wolf looked where she pointed, Eli lifted her gaze past him, searching the trail behind.

Glad for the wind in his face, Justin had found two trees to stand behind. He stuck his head out from behind a trunk and moved his hand into view with his palm out. He wanted her to stay right where she was and not take any chances.

She lifted her chin enough to acknowledge the hand signal. A look of determination came over her.

Cazador said, "Nope. Not doing anything like that until my partner catches up and can watch my back."

Justin wanted to rush the guy, but Cazador carried that damn gun loaded with titanium-coated rounds.

A wild shot could hit Eli in the head and kill her quickly. That's the only thing that kept Justin going slow and steady, just like when he'd led the black ops mission into enemy territory to rescue Adrian.

He wouldn't let anyone else go first that time.

If someone was going to get caught or die, it had to be him.

Cazador glanced toward the trail Justin should have been walking down.

Leave it to Eli to draw his attention back to her with a question.

"Why you steal me?"

Angling back around to face her, Cazador said, "Why do think? Did you miss when I told you I'm getting paid big money for this?"

"Not money. What is reason?"

"Telling you isn't going to make any difference in what happens to you."

"Never mind." She lifted her head, looking down her nose at him. "You are cheap hand."

Justin kept easing around the few trees between him and Cazador to get a better approach to the wolf.

Scowling, Cazador snapped at her, "Who are you calling cheap labor? I promise you I'm not cheap, bitch."

She lifted a shoulder in dismissal and stuck her nose in the air in a perfect snooty pose. "You are like mushroom."

"Mushroom? What the hell are you talking about, princess?"

"Keep in dark. Feed sheep manure."

Justin almost snorted at that.

He would like to get more intel, but he didn't want Eli to push Cazador too much. This guy might be just as she had, so adorably, identified him. Nothing but a hired gun. But he was definitely not cheap labor. Finally reaching a place where Justin could slide into the open without stirring branches, he paused when Cazador made a slimy sounding laugh.

"You want to know why you're being snatched, princess?" the wolf shifter asked with a lilt in his voice as if all of sudden he enjoyed being the one to tell her. "First, my wolf client will run tests on you in lots of ways. Their people are making huge strides for shifters. I've watched their operation. Entertaining, especially when they bring in a female shifter and keep her conscious to see how far they can push her. Nothing slows those scientists down, not even loud screaming."

Eli had no comeback for that.

That fucking wolf was using terror tactics, looking for a way to break her psychologically.

She wouldn't break, but that didn't mean Justin wanted her listening to scum tout the abilities of a wolf shifter pack that preyed upon other shifters.

The Black River pack didn't research for the benefit of any

shifters, but development for profit. They created stronger pack mates by altering them in sickening ways, and screwed up other shifters both mentally and physically so the rogue wolves could rise to the top of the heap.

They were a purely predatory group.

Cazador smiled, clearly pleased with himself, narcissistic asshole that he was. He added, "Once those scientists get all they want, then the pack will hand you over to a Power Baron who supports them. I'll receive a bonus payment for you and the man financing this will get what he wants. Everyone's happy. Well, maybe not you." He laughed at his sick joke.

Defiance rose in Eli's voice. "Money not from clan."

The wolf started laughing. "Oh, sure. Dream on. How many people even know you're in this country? You work that out and the person behind this should be obvious."

Justin wished Cazador had named a specific clan, but the wolf shifter shared information only to weaken a captive.

Eli kept her attention on the wolf, but Justin knew by the subtle movements of those blue eyes she tracked his progress as well.

Cazador angled his head to the side, as if looking for Toro.

"Where do you take me?" Eli asked, like a teacher snapping the classroom's attention back to her.

Watching the trail, Cazador said, "You know what? Shut up already."

Lifting an imperial eyebrow at him that made Eli appear every bit the haughty princess she hated to be called, she said, "Ah. I see. Do not know. You are—"

"If you say mushroom, it'll be your last word for a long time," the wolf warned.

"Only ask where I go."

With evident exasperation, he informed her, "As soon as I get your slow ass off this mountain, I'm driving you to meet the pickup team. Be glad to be done with you. No. More. Questions. Got it?"

Did that stop Eli? Not one bit.

She said, "Mouth like pig."

"I'd really like to carve you up with a titanium blade, starting with your tongue. You should shut the fuck up while it's still your choice."

Justin had noticed right away that Cazador and Toro wore no communication gear, which pointed to the wolf shifter's arrogance over his ability.

Angling around, Cazador called, "Toro?"

Justin stood very still and far enough off the trail Cazador would not see him, but he was out of time.

Cazador gave the trail a long, thoughtful look then turned back to Eli.

Justin checked the wind. It still blew in his face. With his scent behind him, Justin stepped away from his cover, but still needed to ease into the open and quietly approach Cazador.

Eli's eyes did not move to give Justin away.

The wolf crossed his arms and the chain still securely in his grip jangled. "You have no idea how lucky you are they sent me. I'm the patient one. If they'd sent the backup wolf team that normally handles these situations, one of them would have broken your jaw by now. Not a bad idea, now that I think about it."

She gave him such a look of disbelief. "We have not same meaning for luck."

"Oh? Keep mouthing off at me and I'll show you how your luck can change. If you're such a badass ursid hybrid bear, you should heal by the time I dump you off."

Her face remained calm and full of disdain for Cazador. "Could be wrong."

"Not a chance, princess. I saw you change. If not for the shit load of money I've been promised, I'd kill you for your coat alone. It would be worth a fortune, but then I'd have a pissed off Power Baron to deal with *and* the Black River pack. See? You have no idea just how fortunate you've been."

Justin paused. That meant Eli's father hadn't given her away as an ursid hybrid, but it still didn't finger the person who had sent the Black River pack after her from the start.

Her father wouldn't have done it, because he could have killed her in Russia if he'd wanted to, and with no repercussion. He had nothing to gain by handing her over to wolves. Her father had killed Black River pack wolves that attacked her. If he'd wanted to trade her to a Power Baron, her father could have done that without involving the Guardian.

Anyone who had lived as long as her father had, and with a clan as old as he ruled, would be able to get word directly to a Power Baron.

The majority of the Power Barons hailed from Europe.

As for the alpha of Clan Boudreaux, Justin might be no fan of the asshole, but even he couldn't accuse that shifter of working with wolves to start a war with a Russian bear shifter clan.

Plus there was crossing the Guardian to consider.

Pissing him off would be worse than a war.

Justin took light steps, moving forward. Taking his time now could mean the difference in Eli not getting shot. When he was close enough, he'd lunge and wrap his arms around the wolf shifter, pinning his arms and gun to his body.

The wolf had been holding the weapon casually as he spoke to Eli, but now he pointed it at her head.

Justin's heart did its best to climb up his throat.

Without turning around, the wolf warned, "Been waiting for you, bear. If you touch me, she dies. I won't give up my life for any amount of money."

Eli's panicked eyes reached Justin.

How had the wolf realized he had company?

The wolf stepped over to one side where he had Eli and Justin in view, but kept his gun trained on her. "Wondering how I knew you were there? I smelled the fear on her. She's ballsy, but her heart rate jumped for no reason. Plus Toro never answered."

Eli's eyes reflected her disappointment, but only for a moment, then she was back to her solemn face.

Justin showed no reaction, waiting to see what the wolf would do now.

"I'm guessing you killed my partner," Cazador said, more thinking out loud than talking to Justin. Shaking his head, he said, "I had an excellent plan working. Now I have to rethink it. Didn't you pay attention when I said I'd put a bullet in her to get what I wanted? Looks like that's back on the table."

Justin didn't want to allow Cazador time to sort through his options.

He and Herc needed a minute to come up with an option as well. To buy time, Justin took a dig at the wolf's ego, as Eli had proved to be a good tactic. "Sure, you're a big man with a gun and woman on a chain. Is that how you earned the name

El Cazador? The Hunter? You didn't track us. Talk about luck. You're lucky we happened to hike past your trap."

"Think again, bear," Cazador spit out. "That helicopter pilot didn't find her by accident. He was up there looking to make the news with an ursid hybrid sighting, thanks to my tip. The minute I caught his radio transmission, I figured you'd go for the fastest way to get her out of here before the woods were flooded with people hunting a rare bear."

Justin had suspected that helo. "You can be smug all you want, but my people are searching for me right now. I haven't checked in on time. You have no idea what you're up against with my organization. Tell you what, I'll give you a head start if you release her now."

That soured the wolf's smile. He swung his gun at Justin.

"Do not shoot him ..." Eli started.

"I heard you the first time," the wolf snapped at her. "But I'm done dealing with having to get both of you off this mountain."

Justin wanted to tell Eli to stay calm and it would all be okay, but her bear surfaced and her eyes glowed bright blue before he had a chance to warn her to not interfere.

With fast reflexes, she reached up and grabbed her chain, yanking it hard as she ran and threw her weight backward down an incline.

Sure she would go rolling off the steep cliffs so close to that path, Justin yelled, "*No!*"

He jumped toward her.

The thunk of a suppressed gunshot sounded.

Heat ripped across Justin's head again, but he kept going.

Eli's yelling trailed off as she rolled backward out of sight.

The second bullet struck Justin's thigh. The same one still wounded. He hit the ground and the landscape around him blurred into a moving swirl. He struggled and blacked out from a double load of titanium.

CHAPTER 30

E LIANNA ROLLED OVER ROCKS AND sticks that stabbed
her. Her body would look like a black-and-blue human canvas
if she survived.

She kept expecting to roll off the mountain and plunge thousands of feet to her death.

She had to stop now.

Cazador had shot twice. Justin was hurt. He needed her.

Without thought to the risk of breaking a bone, she shoved a
leg out to use as an anchor. A tree whacked the back of her calf,
bringing tears to her eyes, but that slowed her momentum a little
and sent her rolling away to the side.

She hit a bush and flopped around it, but bent her knee to catch
her lower leg in the branches. That worked.

Struggling for air, she jerked her foot free and scrambled over
on all fours.

The chain snatched tight around her neck.

She looked up to find that the miserable wolf had her again.

Was Justin dead?

No, her bear grumbled. *Bear hurt.*

Her bear said Herc was hurt? That would mean Justin had lived.

Cazador's hand holding the weapon shook. Anger wiped away
his cocky calm. "Your mate's dead, but let's be honest. We both
know that bear isn't your mate."

How could this man know that? "He is mate." In her heart,
she would never have another.

"Bullshit. Your mate, or the one who was supposed to get stuck
with you, is the one flipping a bundle to keep you out of his hair.

It's now clear why spending that much money is worth every penny."

Clan Boudreaux wanted her dead? No, worse than dead. They sold her to a criminal pack of wolves.

"So it's just me and you." He swung the end of the chain back and forth. The side of his face bled where the chain had caught him when she'd jerked away. "Once I lock you in my transport van, you owe me some one-on-one time before I hand you off. Never fucked a princess before. Maybe I'll get my dick gold plated after that," he said, regaining his confidence. "Turn around and walk, princess. Every time you slow down, you will feel the burn of this titanium chain slashing your back."

"You die screaming."

He laughed. "Oh, big talk."

Kill wolf. Find mate. Kill wolf now, her bear demanded.

Elianna had never heard her bear in such a state of upset, but she could do nothing yet. *Patience,* she told her bear, needing to watch for a way to escape and get back to Justin.

No. No. No.

Now she could appreciate how that word rubbed on Justin. Elianna said, *I have collar. Can. Not. Shift.*

Her bear roared. It shocked Elianna.

"Get up," the wolf ordered.

She struggled to her feet and tried to push the hair out of her eyes, which was not easy with her hands cuffed.

He whipped the chain up, letting it pop her in the jaw.

She flinched and tears burned the corners of her eyes, but she would not make a sound.

"You are one tough bitch. Turn your collar around."

When she had the collar in place, the chain dangled from the back where she couldn't grasp it again.

Cazador said, "Lead the way."

She kept waiting for Justin to come running through the woods to reach her. Every minute that he didn't show up weighed heavily in favor of her bear being wrong.

Her mate could be dying back there.

Elianna took careful steps as they angled away from the mountain face and into a pocket of woods. If she did fall, she'd take the wolf with her.

That would be the only positive to dying.

Over the next twenty yards, she wove up and down through gullies where downed trees made passing more difficult. She was close to admitting defeat when she spied a dark gap in a shady area of the trees.

Was that one of those holes Justin had warned her about when they hiked up yesterday?

After giving it more thought, she believed she was correct. Maybe some deep area created when a hollow place in the mountain had caved in at some point. Small trees lay across one side of the fifteen-foot-wide gap.

How deep would it be?

Stepping more left each time, she shoved branches and limbs aside, determined to walk right past the hole. To keep the wolf from seeing it too soon or discovering why she was getting off track, she had to distract him.

She turned her head slightly then quickly faced forward again just as fast.

Her chain went taut on her next step, which meant the wolf had stopped to look at whatever she'd pretended to notice.

"What are you looking at, princess?"

"Nothing."

"Don't lie to me, bitch."

She turned a furious face to him and hoped he saw his death in her eyes. "I hear noise. That is all. You want look?"

"Not wasting time on stupid crap."

She started walking slowly again, allowing him enough slack to look around.

Every time the chain went tight, she knew he was not paying attention to where she was headed.

That was because he would never expect her to attempt suicide.

When she was three feet from the hole, she used her shifter speed.

First she leaned back.

Then she grabbed the bolt at the back of her collar where the chain was attached and lunged forward into the hole.

Her body weight caught four feet down and jerked her arms hard.

If she hadn't pulled him off his feet, she would choke to death once her arms gave out.

He growled and yelled.

Rocks and dirt sprayed over the edge, hitting her in the face.

In the next second, the chain dropped her fast as the wolf fell over the side. She had no idea what waited below her, but relaxed her legs for hitting bottom.

Unless this hole went on for a kilometer.

Her bear roared at her.

The fall seemed to take forever, but Elianna had made herself limp as a ragdoll and hit the ground thirty feet below the edge. Her next breath felt as if someone stabbed her lung. Her ribs? She rolled immediately to the side before the chain slapped the spot she'd left as gravity yanked it to the ground.

The wolf hadn't been as well prepared.

He smacked the ground next to her on his side.

His chest hit then his head bounced against a rock, cracking his jaw. It distorted out of shape.

Elianna taunted, "Use filthy mouth to threaten now, wolf."

She'd managed to free herself, but she had to figure out how to climb out with a cracked or broken rib.

Change, her bear told her. *I heal. Now. Change now.*

Elianna spoke out loud to her bear. "Can *not* change. Still have collar." She could feel her agitated bear ready to go on a rampage. Even if she could shift, she wasn't entirely sure she could control her bear with the wolf lying close enough to shred or to convince her stubborn bear to change back to human form when Elianna needed it.

Justin was right. She had to join better with her bear. Maybe they could start now. Elianna kept her voice soft when she told her bear, "Please, need calm. I try climb."

She got an angry bear silence for that, but it was an improvement over her bear's sulking in the past.

Small steps.

Reaching up, she found a handhold and picked around with her foot until she found a place to step. She had never been interested in rock climbing, but as she reached for the next handhold, she mused that it must not be so difficult after all.

She'd made it halfway up when the jutted out rock she'd been holding for support pulled loose from the wall, sending her and loose dirt tumbling to the floor.

Her back hit and her head bounced.

She feared a broken neck.

Testing, she moved her arms and hands, then her legs and feet. Felt like she'd been hit with a sledgehammer many times, but her body could still function.

The climb proved to not be as easy as it had looked five minutes ago.

Forcing herself back to her feet, she whimpered at pain fingering through her now and searched the walls for a better place to climb.

Nothing. The other walls were steeper, where this one had offered a slight angle.

CHAPTER 31

JUSTIN CAME AWAKE TO A pounding headache, leg on fire and the sound of Herc roaring inside his mind.

Mate hurt! Herc snarled, *Get up!*

Shaking off a disoriented feeling from too much titanium inside him, Justin wiped blood from his eyes and felt his head.

The bullet that struck above his ear had grazed him.

He was two for two in not having a titanium head piercing. He doubted he could avoid it a third time if Cazador got another chance.

Justin pushed up to his feet and took a step.

His leg gave out beneath his weight.

Ah hell! That bastard had broken his thighbone this time. He couldn't heal while titanium toxins attacked his blood-depleted body.

Justin shouted telepathically, *Herc, come forward!*

His bear rose to the surface faster than if Justin had called up the change. His body vibrated with unleashed fury.

Herc growled and snarled, wanting out.

No, Justin told him telepathically. *I need all of our power. Now.* What he intended to do was a dangerous idea, even for a Gallize. If a shifter called up his animal but stopped at over halfway and held his body there, the animal and human could end up stuck, unable to go in any direction.

Justin had faith in his bear.

Herc had faith in Justin.

He hoped that would be enough to prevent losing each other.

Without hesitation, Herc followed Justin's direction.   Power raced along Justin's arms. His body shook as if hit with a jolt of electricity. Teeth moved in his mouth. His face and hands began to change. Claws on his feet tore through his boots. He reached down and used the sharp claws now sticking from partially paw-shaped hands to rip his boots off.

His body pulled and twisted, trying to change shape.

He told Herc, *Hold up!*

His bear growled an ungodly sound.

Justin had to look like a monster from a bad B movie about now, but that was the least of his worries.

The real problem would be if Herc lost his mind and Justin couldn't maintain his control. This was a wild gamble that could cost both of their lives, because he needed both his bear strength and to stay human enough to function as one.

Lifting his arms that were now ripping out of his shirtsleeves, Justin shoved energy toward healing his thigh.

The bone began mending.

It wouldn't fully heal until the titanium was removed.

Testing some weight on his leg, he clenched his jaws at the pain shooting up from the still-fractured bone, but started forward in a hurry. Hairline fractures ruptured the bone still fighting to mend. He could hear it crack every few steps.

Pain blended with adrenaline.

Herc made more horrible noises Justin had never heard.

But one sound scared him above all that.

Eli's silence.

CHAPTER 32

E LIANNA'S BEAR RAGED TO BE freed. Even if she could shift with the collar still on, her bear could not climb the slick rock to get out of this hole any better than she could in human form.

Her bear did not want to climb. She wanted wolf blood.

Cazador had not moved since hitting the ground. Maybe he was dying. She would not touch him to find out.

Keeping an eye on him, Elianna searched for another way to use her chain to climb out.

"Ewri," growled from above.

She stepped back to look up at what she thought sounded like Justin, but his head, arms and legs were distorted into half human and half bear.

"You 'kay?" he called out through jaws too big for his face.

"Yes. But you ..." She had no words.

"I good." Then he stopped talking.

The next thing Elianna heard was her bear saying, *Collar off.*

What did that mean?

"Ewri!"

She looked up to see Justin holding something in his paws. He dropped it to her. She followed the tiny thing to the ground or she wouldn't have found where it landed in a crevice between two rocks. It was a key.

Her bear chanted in a roar, *Collar off. Collar off. Collar off.*

Elianna hurried with trembling hands and missed hitting the hole. She drew a deep breath and calmed herself, then unlocked her cuffs. Pulling the collar around, she jabbed the key until it went into a slot. The collar popped free.

Shoving the key in her pocket, she looked up at Justin.

But her bear told her, *Up, up, up. Throw.*

Elianna asked her bear, *Throw chain?*

Yes.

Are you talking to Herc?

Yes. Throw.

That's exactly what Elianna did. She looped the chain to make it more aerodynamic, swung it around two times and let go, slinging the chain up as hard as she could.

She jumped back in case it fell down again.

Justin used his two big paw-hands to catch enough to drag the chain backward out of sight. When he came back into view, he had the collar locked and looped over one arm.

The extra chain only reached halfway, but she'd made it that far last time.

"Weddy?" Justin called out. He waved a hand signal in the motion for up then grabbed the chain near the collar with both hands and set his feet wide.

Smiling, she said, "Yes." She started climbing again, but with a renewed sense of hope.

She grappled for any handhold and foothold, inching up little by little, never taking her eyes off Justin.

His eyes did not stray from hers either. Determination burned in that wild grizzly gaze. What happened to his face and body? It looked as if ... he'd stopped shifting halfway.

That was dangerous.

It could kill the human and the animal. He was injured badly and full of titanium. He must have done it intentionally to be strong enough to reach her. She pushed harder, closing the distance between her and the dangling end of chain.

As she grabbed the chain a foot up from the last link, a hand latched around her ankle and snatched her down.

She lost her grip and fell.

Justin roared, "*No!*"

CHAPTER 33

JUSTIN HAD BENT OVER TO get a new handhold on the chain to pull Eli up as soon as she had a grip.

That's when he saw the wolf leap up and latch onto her ankle, dragging her down.

The damn wolf lifted his weapon, too.

Without any thought to how it would turn out, Justin jumped over the edge, aiming his body at the wolf. He hit Cazador's shoulder, sending the gunshot wide. The wolf had clearly decided to kill both of them and walk away from this job.

Justin's bad leg folded as soon as he hit the ground.

A flash of energy buzzed the air. The fucking wolf was either shifting or using magic.

Shoving up on his arms and shaking his head, Justin dragged his supersized self around to deal with Cazador. That wolf had to die first so Justin could get to Eli.

But Eli's clothes had been shredded and Mishka stood in her place. The grolar shook off the remnants of shifting.

Then Mishka ripped into Cazador, who screamed. His fingers clawed for the gun, but it had landed against the wall, out of reach.

Mishka severed his head then finished him off using her claws and enormous fangs.

Heaving deep breaths by the time she finished, Mishka turned her blue-eyed gaze on Justin and moved over to rub her head all over his face and shoulders.

She made whimpering noises.

He lifted his hand to stroke the soft fur around her face. Herc still wanted out, but more to check on Mishka than to attack what was left of Cazador.

Justin had a sick moment of wondering if he could change at all.

Herc said, *Me strong.*

Yeah, you are, buddy, Justin answered silently instead of trying to force words through his screwed-up jaws. *Let's try to change all the way into our bear. We'll just take our time.*

Closing his eyes to focus all his energy internally, Justin called Herc all the way up.

His arms finished changing before his torso was halfway there. That wasn't a good sign.

His torso should have shifted form faster.

As his legs fought to make the change, bone scraped against bone. Justin wanted to throw up, but any distraction that stopped the change right now might end it all.

Warm hands covered his chest and energy soaked into his body, flooding his organs and limbs. The change began to move faster and finally, he could feel Herc whole again.

His head felt light with relief, but it could be the titanium and blood loss.

Opening his bear eyes, Justin looked at the most beautiful blue gaze in this world. Naked and dirty, his Eli kneeled in front of him.

He gave her a big lick across her cheek.

She laughed, a sound so pure and honest he was sure some angel had gifted her with it. But her laugh ended in tears.

She hugged his neck and rambled watery words. "You jump. Could die. Never do. Ever."

Justin told Herc to tell Mishka, *We will always protect our mate.*

He could tell when Mishka relayed that, because Eli's arms hugged him harder. "Do not die. I could not breath."

Those words circled around inside him and found a home in his heart.

They sat there, staring at each other, ignoring the wolf parts Mishka had tossed around. They had to get out of here before the smell went from fresh blood to spoiled meat.

Eli leaned in and kissed Herc, who literally sighed.

No one would ever be a bear tamer like Eli.

He asked Herc, *Ready to shift back so I can get Eli out of here? How?*

Good question. Looking up, Justin considered their options. He asked Herc, *How bad is the leg?*

In reply, Herc moved the fractured leg and gave the equivalent of a bear wince. But the leg didn't flop around, meaning it had started healing again.

Justin had a feeling Eli's energy had something to do with that. More questions to get answered about his unusual mate.

Gazing up at the top of the hole, Justin suggested to Herc, *What if we stand on the strong leg and use the bad one just for balance so it can keep healing?*

I like.

Okay, then you need to tell Mishka that when you lean against the wall, we want Eli to climb up until she can stand on your front legs. Then we can push her to the top.

Yes.

Eli had been stroking Herc's shoulder, which was above her head with them sitting down. Her hand stopped. She cocked her head and Justin figured she was listening to Mishka.

"We can do?" Eli asked.

Herc nodded.

Standing up, she said, "Do not hurt leg more."

Herc swung his big head back and forth.

Justin talked Herc through standing. His leg burned like crazy, but Herc never slowed from getting set.

On all fours in front of the place Eli had climbed last time, Herc walked his front paws up the wall instead of standing up on his hind legs. That prevented putting too much weight on the fractured bone all at once.

When Herc was ready, Eli pulled on her ragged shirt, which did little to cover her. She slid between him and the wall.

Following her original path, she worked her way higher until she did a contortionist act to get herself above Herc's forelegs, where she could put one foot on each thick leg.

She was still a foot short of the top edge.

Justin instructed Herc on what to tell Mishka so that Eli would put both feet on one leg.

Eli did as told.

Herc moved a paw away from the wall for her. When Eli stepped on the massive pad, he shoved her up in the air.

Justin hoped he hadn't miscalculated.

Eli landed with her chest against the top edge and grunted. Then she clawed her way over and out.

Hallelujah. Now how could he escape this stinking pit of death?

Herc eased back down and sat with the bad rear leg sticking out.

Justin said, *I'll explain to Eli how to get in the truck and call for help. More wolves?*

I don't know, Justin told him, not satisfied with that plan either.

Where had Eli gone? She hadn't stuck her head over the side yet.

Herc growled loud to get her attention.

Still no Eli.

Light was fading. If the sun vanished before she got down the mountain, she might not find her way. She might fall and hurt herself. She might ...

Justin told Herc, *We need to change back so I can talk to her.*

Herc blew out a weary breath, but did his part to make the shift from animal to human take place. It was easier this time, which Justin took to mean they hadn't damaged either of them permanently with the partial shift earlier.

Small blessings.

When he stood as a naked man again, Justin called out, "Eli?"

"Yes. Be quiet."

"What?" Okay, that sounded angry, but he'd had better days.

Her head popped over the top. "Sorry. Busy. Stay back." She went away again.

Grabbing his aching head, Justin counted to ten ... and then fifty. Now was not the time to get cranky.

A bear growled from above.

Herc had been resting, but hearing that brought him to attention. *Mishka!*

Why would Eli shift again?

Herc said, *Move to wall!*

That order had probably come from Mishka, so Justin put his back against the rock and dirt side.

A loud crack sounded and his heart fell.

Wait. That hadn't been a gunshot.

The sound of branches slapping around heralded a tree crashing down. Grunting followed that, and the next thing he knew a broken tree trunk with roots sticking out came into view over the edge above him, then it angled down.

Sliding slowly, the tree finally came to rest on the bottom.

He stuck his head out from his position to look up.

Mishka stared down with a happy bear grin.

And someone thought Justin would give up that woman?

They were betting against the wrong bear shifter. He made a move to climb and stopped, thinking about his weapon that Cazador had and where Justin had seen it against the wall of the hole. He dug through branches, starting to think it would be an impossible search, but his fingers grazed an object they knew well. Fishing the gun out of that mess, he felt better knowing he had additional defense. He had more weapons in the truck and, per his usual practice with any rental, had hidden a spare key in the engine compartment. His heart thumped with renewed hope.

Climbing against rough branches and snapped-off, sharp limbs would be generally ill-advised when naked, but Justin made it to the top with all the important parts unscathed.

He stepped off the log as Eli buttoned the shirt that had belonged to Toro.

She tossed jeans at Justin. "You much bigger."

"Glad you realize that," he quipped.

"Men." She shook her head but smiled. "Yes, much big, but same tall."

Dropping the jeans, he stalked her, never slowing until he had her pulled to him and was kissing her sweet lips. He didn't give a damn about how dirty they both were. After all they'd been through, he needed to feel her alive and safe in his arms.

She mumbled, "Missed kisses."

Like he needed any encouragement to keep going?

Hell, he'd stay right here for days and still not get enough of her. But dark would come quickly on this side of the mountain and his woman needed a hot bath, clean clothes and food. He did, too. Plus, he still needed Rory to get the damn titanium out of his leg.

With some effort, he let her go and stuffed his lower body into jeans that stank of wolf scent.

He owed Monty an apology.

Then he began picking their way off the mountain, grateful as the light diminished to offer them cover to reach his truck.

Justin did a quick recon of the area around the trailhead, but saw no sign of life. Fingers crossed that there was no more magic involved that could cloak a wolf, they walked up to his rental. Eli eyed the transport parked alongside it with hate.

Justin slashed the tires to prevent it from going anywhere. He already knew who had rented it, and that shifter would not be back to claim it.

First he had to ditch his truck, which would be too easy to track now that he knew he'd been followed here.

Once he and Eli found a place to eat and get a good night's sleep, he had to call the Guardian and fill him in. Justin hoped Eli would understand that they couldn't continue on their own for another two days. He needed Rory to tend his leg and hoped tomorrow was soon enough.

Besides, he was itching to make her his mate, but he couldn't do that until Nico's release and transportation were guaranteed.

The only guarantee he would accept was the Guardian's.

Justin knew how to keep a tail off of them, but he would stop only for the night.

He had to have her somewhere he knew he could protect her.

Without his mate, he had no life.

CHAPTER 34

WATCHING THE DARK HIGHWAY IN his rearview mirror for any suspicious change in headlights, Justin picked a straight stretch to go around another car. He put some distance between that car and his truck, then slowed to the speed limit now that he was ten miles down the road.

Watching for a tail should be easy. Monday night out in this part of the country should mean almost no traffic.

Eli had moved to the back seat where she could access her suitcase for clothes. The *thunk* of her hitting the ceiling was followed by what he'd come to recognize as cursing in Russian.

"You okay, Eli, babe?"

"Okay, yes."

He'd given her three bottles of water, a rag and a towel. She didn't want to put clean clothes over her dirty body.

Justin would clean up down the road. Eli had been in worse condition than he had after Mishka took vengeance on Cazador.

Eli kicked the back of his seat. She muttered, "Sorry. Arms and legs too long."

"Never. Every bit of you is perfect."

One of those spectacular legs, now covered in jeans, pushed between the seats and over the console, then the rest of her twisted into the passenger seat. She wore a dark knit pullover and old sneakers. Her new hiking boots had been destroyed on the mountain.

He'd get her all the boots she wanted.

She blew a strand of hair out of her eyes, which fell right back into place. Muttering, she grabbed her reddish-brown hair and twisted it into one of those knots only a woman could create.

When he glanced over, she eyed him with suspicion. "You have one opinion."

"About what?"

She gave him a saucy look. "Leg is perfect."

"Are you saying I'm not objective?"

"Yes, that."

"Not when it comes to you, babe. I know perfection when I see it. You should never doubt me."

"Crazy bear." She shook her head.

"Hot bear." He winked at her. "Remember, you like looking at my body *and* I like you looking at it."

"So modest." But she started laughing.

He'd gotten her mind off wolf shifters chasing her and Mishka's bloodbath in that hole.

Mission accomplished.

She waved her hand toward the windshield. "Where to?"

"Missoula Airport about two hours south so I can rent another vehicle."

Her smile fell. "Why?"

"Don't worry. We got away without being seen. Cazador said he had a deadline tonight, so that means he probably intended to contact his people this evening, but that could be any time. We have a good head start. I just want to rent a vehicle from a different company to make it really hard to find us."

"You pay cash?"

"No, they'll want a credit card."

"Credit card bad now."

"Normally, yes, but I work for a special group so I have an additional set of cards and ID just for this type of situation."

"Oh."

"I'm starving. We'll be in Kalispell pretty soon. I'll grab us some chow to take with us, then we'll eat a much nicer meal later on."

She waved her hand in dismissal. "Not need nice. All food good."

There was his down-to-earth princess.

He fell a little more in love with her every time she revealed a new piece of her personality. The way he figured it, he'd know all there was to know in a hundred or so years, but he would never tire of just being in the same space with her.

His mind chose that minute to remind him she'd refused to accept his bond, but she had a core of honor he couldn't criticize.

Two days left before she had to show up at Clan Boudreaux. He'd figure it all out by then.

After zipping through a fast food place where they ordered enough for four humans, he got her talking about Nico. Her face lit up and love bled through her words.

"My Nico too skinny and sick when find. Broke foot. Much cold. Clan leave to die."

"That's brutal," Justin said.

"True." She shrugged. "Is same all animals."

"Right, survival of the fittest, but natural animals abandon a weak or injured offspring because they have no way to save them. Shifters are part human, or are supposed to be. That's ... unacceptable."

She leaned over and kissed him.

"Not complaining, Eli, babe, but what's that for?"

"Would not leave weak child."

"Never. Tell me more about Nico."

Sounding at ease, she leaned back and talked about how Nico had been getting stronger. That he was a very bright six-year-old and would make a great warrior one day.

Justin had never spent this kind of time with any woman.

Herc hadn't been keen on bear shifters before meeting Eli, so Justin had kept his one-night stands to mature women who wanted the same. Human females mostly and they were all nice, but he could never be entirely himself around them.

His body felt at home with Eli.

And Mishka.

When Eli slowed down from talking about Nico, Justin brought up their bears. "Were you as surprised as I was to find out Herc talked to your bear?"

"Yes. Very odd. Never before."

"You know I said you should name your bear, but evidently she named herself." He looked over when Eli said nothing.

Her mouth was open. She closed it and asked, "What name?"

"She calls herself Mishka."

Eli frowned. "Silly name."

"Why?"

"Mishka mean bear. She hear others say bear in Russia."

"Well, she liked it and Herc likes her."

Turning toward him, Eli nibbled on her fingernail.

Justin didn't want to upset her, but he'd like to see Eli and Mishka connect better. "Tell me more about when you first learned you had Mishka."

Sounding as if her thoughts were far away, she said, "I thought bear fun as child. Then not fun. Coat wrong. Not polar bear. Clan mean to me and mother."

"That was wrong of the bear shifters."

She shifted her sad gaze to him. "Yes. They say I am bad mistake. Hate bear, hate me."

His grip tightened on the wheel, but he forced his voice to remain calm. She was talking about a painful subject. "You were never a mistake, babe. People who live in the remote area of Russia where you grew up just didn't know."

"What?"

"That ursid hybrids are a rare gift to our kind. Something to be appreciated and loved."

"You say good all time. I want believe."

Reaching over, he covered the hand she'd placed on the center console. "I'm telling you the truth. Those people weren't bad, just uninformed. Most people fear anything that is different."

Justin tried to sound positive, but he was disgusted over how many things Eli had been forced to survive. "Alexandre should have taken care of both of you."

She sounded wistful when she said, "Yes. Hate him long time. When he kill wolves we meet. He say mother would not live in safe place he offer. She want only mate. He had mate. I lose hate for that now, but not for him keeping Nico." She looked over to Justin. "Alexandre keep child as ... chess part."

"Using him like a pawn?"

"Yes, that. Nico cry when I go. I want hurt Alexandre."

He did, too. That might be the way the Romanov alpha operated, but he was putting Eli and Nico through hell.

Justin could not do the same to her. Lifting her fingers to his mouth to kiss them, he said, "I understand and I'm going to help you get Nico."

She kissed him tenderly. "Thank you." Then she sat upright and shook her head. "No."

That confused him. "What do you mean no?"

"Clan Boudreaux lied. *They* send wolf shifters."

He jerked around so hard the car weaved. He quickly regained control and said, "You think that clan paid them?"

"Yes." She told him about Cazador calling her a liar about Justin being her mate and claiming the mate she was supposed to end up with was paying to get rid of her.

The steering wheel cracked under Justin's grip.

Eli's worried glance at the steering wheel forced him to not grind it to dust. He'd find out who the alpha had promised Eli to and that bear shifter would suffer under Herc's claws.

Realizing she was still panicked about Clan Boudreaux, Justin said, "Don't worry. You're not going there without me so I can deal with the guilty party."

"Want Nico safe."

"You have my word he will be."

That was enough to give her relief, but she spent the rest of the drive to the Missoula Airport in silence.

After he was sure that he dragged no tail, Justin entered long-term parking at the airport and left her locked in the truck with a loaded gun.

He had pulled on a hoodie and tinted shooting glasses, just in case the wolves were smart enough to start hunting for him through multiple rental car companies.

He seriously doubted anyone could be that on the ball yet. He'd already sent a text to a Gallize cleanup team in this region that should dump Toro's body in the hole, strip all clothing and other materials away, then cover the naked bodies with enough rocks and dead trees to bury them where they would eventually turn into compost.

A fitting end for two pieces of shit.

Returning to his first truck in record time with a new gray sport utility, he transferred Eli along with their belongings.

Back on the highway, Justin set a course for the one place he could keep Eli safe for the next two days.

Wyoming.

Once he was in the area of the Guardian's land, he'd find a hotel so Eli could take a real shower and feel prepared to meet new people. Maybe let her sleep more than she would be able to during the drive.

He worked on what he'd tell the Guardian. He hoped his boss would make the trip to meet with him to discuss Eli and open the ward so she could pass.

Once Justin explained what a bear shifter in Clan Boudreaux had tried to do, he expected his boss to be equally furious. Justin could see the Guardian maybe using that breach of the contract to negotiate a deal for Eli to stay with Justin and have Nico, too.

Eli could spend the next two days seeing some of Wyoming.

Adrian would not harm her with Justin, Cole and Rory there.

Plus, Justin believed that the same man still lived deep inside Adrian who had wrecked many a bar when a guy treated a woman poorly. Also, Rory could flush the titanium out of Justin's wounds. He swiped sweat off his brow again, feeling the fever that had begun climbing across his skin during the drive. He'd washed the new head wound with bottled water as soon as they got to the truck, but he'd pushed past the normal deadline to get the residues out of his body. All the shifting was helping, but until the titanium was purged from his body, he'd have to take it easy on his bad leg to keep from breaking the bone again.

Rory would irrigate the wound and have to break the leg one more time to reset the bone properly.

Yep, that would be loads of fun.

He and Herc would be laid up a day or two for healing.

Eli would be there to kiss him and make it all better.

Six hours passed with Eli snoozing and Justin still mentally editing his conversation with the Guardian and making plans for his and Eli's future. She'd have plenty of input, because he wanted his mate happy.

Scratch that.

He wanted his mate ecstatic.

When he was an hour out from the north Wyoming warded area and sitting at a traffic light in the middle of nowhere, Justin sent a text to Cole.

Heads up. Need to meet G in WY after 0600 Tuesday for report and open ward. Future mate with me. What about A?

Justin didn't like bringing the Guardian around Adrian until the wolf was ready, but Cole and Rory could manage Adrian while the Guardian tweaked the ward. Justin would pull his boss back to the hotel to talk, thank him for opening the ward for Eli and say goodbye.

He hoped the Guardian wouldn't want to see Adrian then, but no one could stop it if his boss decided to take a look.

Justin wanted the four days they had left to get Adrian in shape. Justin was not losing Adrian, even if he had to drag his friend back to sanity kicking and screaming.

Adrian would do the same for him.

Justin relaxed for the first time since that first damn titanium round had grazed his scalp. He loved it when a plan came together.

Eli snored softly. A lady snore.

Yes, he found that hot, too.

If Cole was in human form, he'd reply to the text right away. If not, Justin would hear back by the time he got settled in the hotel.

His phone dinged with a message from Cole.

UR mate? Damn. Need details. Glad ur coming bc G is already on way here tonight to talk. Not sure why. A ... not much change. Going dark now w/A+R to keep driving A's wolf hard. Hope he sleeps thru G visit.

Justin sent back a *10-4* and suffered a wave of guilt over Adrian not improving.

Then he trounced that thought.

Cole and Rory were doing everything possible. Justin had no special cure. He just needed to be there doing his part to work with Adrian.

Why was the Guardian headed to Wyoming?

That was good news, right?

He couldn't muster any excitement. The Guardian had strange powers and shifted into a sea eagle. Had the boss been flying over Wyoming at night and seen how little progress Adrian had made?

Even so, the Guardian had given the three of them time off for this trip to be with Adrian. Their boss would never break his word, but all three of them *had* agreed to return to duty if something big happened.

Shit, that would mean Justin, too, when he finished his assignment with Eli, but things had changed. He had no idea what to expect when he saw his boss.

He'd been holding Eli's hand just because it made him happy to touch her.

Her fingers suddenly squeezed tight as a vise.

"Babe?"

One look told him she was having a vision. He stroked his thumb over her hand, just letting her know he was with her. When she came back to herself, she opened her eyes and sat up.

When she looked over at Justin, she said, "Wolf attack."

Recalling her last vision, he smiled at her. "That's all done, Eli, babe. You said I had to stop a wolf from killing someone I cared about. That's you and the wolf is dead."

She shook her head, looking panicked. "No. I say wolf attack person important to you. You must stop attack."

That did sound like her exact words, which he had interpreted to mean the vision had been about them and the wolf. "I don't understand. The person important to me is you." He thought back and said, "You had a dark fog last time. Did you have that again? Maybe this is just something left over from the first vision."

"No. I see much this time. Cazador wolf black. Wolf in vision red ... and attack eagle."

His hair stood on end.

Adrian had to be the red wolf and he was going to attack the Guardian.

Cole and Rory had gone dark and the Guardian would be airborne.

Chills covered Justin's heated skin.

Eli just had a vision of Adrian's death.

CHAPTER 35

JUSTIN BLEW SPEED LIMITS, TAKING advantage of scant traffic so early on a Tuesday. He was in northern Wyoming, but still had to reach the entrance to Guardian's warded land by six in the morning as he'd told Cole.

This time, Justin would park near the shortest route to the ward entrance.

So much had happened since his last casual stroll into the mountains with Cole and Rory, that his head swam when he thought about it.

The sun hadn't peeked above the horizon yet, but the lightening sky warned it would show up soon. Every second counted right now.

The Guardian generally flew in his eagle form at night. Would he still be airborne or already with the guys?

When Justin told Eli that he couldn't stop for food or to shower at the hotel, she'd shrugged and said, "Can wait."

She was a gem.

"What wrong?"

He glanced at her. "What do you mean?"

"More than worry."

Was she picking up on the guilt he'd been suffering since rescuing Adrian? It drove him to fix his friend, who had taken Justin's place.

He admitted, "I'm worried about a friend of mine. I was assigned to lead a mission, but my mother died so my friend, Adrian, took my place. He got captured." Saying those three words still knifed Justin in the gut. He spent the rest of the frantic hour-long drive filling her in on how Adrian and his wolf had been badly damaged due to Adrian being held prisoner in a small cage for weeks.

He hadn't shared so much of his deep thoughts with his buddies, and telling Eli actually helped some.

Her face turned greenish. "Would not live."

"Yes, you would. You're strong and so is Adrian, but he's had a bad split with his animal." He'd already told her about Cole and Rory. "My friends and I don't want to lose him. Our boss is coming in for some reason not to do with us," he said, indicating the two of them. "My boss wants to save Adrian, too, but if Adrian can't regain control ... our boss is the one who can call up our animal or ... put down a dangerous shifter."

He waited for anything from her, but she continued to listen with that quiet intensity. Justin said, "I'm not supposed to tell you anything, but I can't leave you alone while I deal with them and I want you to know what you're walking into."

"Yes, okay."

Justin gave his next words a lot of consideration then said, "You love me, right?"

"Yes. Love you much." She kissed his cheek.

He squeezed her fingers. "I love you, too, Eli, babe. More than you can ever know. That's why I want to make you my mate and get Nico for you."

Worry climbed into her face, but she withheld her thoughts and allowed him to explain.

"If I can absolutely get you Nico, will you agree to be my mate?" His stomach flipped over in the seconds it took her to answer.

"Yes. Want you and Nico."

"I know how important he is to you, babe. If it came down to a choice between us, I would never put you in that position."

"Thank you."

"I'm not supposed to tell anyone about our shifters and my boss, but we can tell our mates so I'm considering you my mate because I will never want another."

"I want no other. No share your words."

That was good enough for Justin.

"Like I said, all of us are different shifters," Justin began.

"Remember I told you about being twenty-one when my bear was called up?" When she nodded, he continued. "Adrian and Cole are wolves. Rory is a jaguar, but don't tell him I told you. He's kind of a loner when he isn't with us and likes to keep everything secretive."

"Like all cats."

"Yep. Our boss is known as the Guardian and he can shift into a giant sea eagle."

She gasped. "Wolf attack eagle."

"Yes, that's what I think your vision means and why I think you need to know more." Getting back on track, Justin said, "When we become mates, you'll receive a link to me and my power."

"Is power you try give on mountain?"

"Right. I told you about the druidess, and how we came to be Gallize shifters."

Her eyebrows went up. "Yes. You tell much. Ask odd much too."

"What did I ask you that was odd?"

"You ask birth month. Mean something, yes?"

"Ah, yes, I did ask about that. You've heard of the term blue moon?"

"Yes. Two moon. One month."

"Correct. Gallize females are born during a month with two full moons, but it's the thirteenth full moon that appears in a twelve month cycle. And they are always the second-born child, which you are, but we don't know your exact birth date."

"You think I am ... ?"

"That you're a Gallize? Maybe, but not exactly. Supposedly, the Gallize females are born with their own powers, but as far as we know, they aren't shifters. On the other hand, I was born into a grizzly clan and would have been a shifter either way. I shifted late because I was Gallize. So I'm wondering if you are a Gallize female, but like me, you were born a shifter, too. I don't know if you are a Gallize, but I've felt your energy and you've got some kind of extra power going on besides being a shifter."

Her voice was soft. "Yes, I have ... strange power inside."

He smiled at her. "I'm thrilled, because that's a winning combination for us even if you aren't Gallize. But know this, if I thought for a minute that your body couldn't accept my power safely, I would never ask you to be my mate." He glanced over, giving her a serious look. "I will never risk harming you or allow anyone else to hurt you."

She got a twinkle in her eyes. "I am ... special?"

He laughed. She didn't bat an eyelash at all of his concerns, but zeroed in on something *she'd* never realized her whole life. "You are very, very, *very* special, Eli, babe."

Her throat moved with a hard swallow. "You love me. Love Mishka. Show me you have love for Herc. I am make better with Mishka. Love her now. I am *special* for you. Only you."

Damn right. "That makes me happy for you and Mishka to start building a relationship. You'll never regret being close to your bear. I'll explain a lot more about my background and our group when we have time alone together. For now, just please let me try to sort this out with my boss."

"Eagle must not meet wolf." Her happy look fell away.

"I know, but that may be out of our control, babe. I'm trying to get to everyone before my wolf buddy attacks the eagle."

She grumbled, "Wolves. Much trouble."

"After all you've been through, I don't blame you for feeling that way, but these wolf shifters are my friends. They are brothers to me and will be to you and Nico. They'll be thrilled to meet you and they will always protect you, just as I will."

Of course, that was assuming the Guardian wasn't in the middle of putting Adrian down. Bile ran up Justin's throat at that visual.

Eli waited quietly as he pulled off the highway and drove the dog piss out of the rental to reach the access point in the ward. He didn't park at the usual stop, just drove over everything, bouncing them to hell and back.

He parked and jumped out. He had to grab the vehicle door for a second to keep from wobbling, and gritted his teeth over the aching leg, but the bone had mended decently while on the road. That wasn't helping his fever, but his adrenaline rush knocked back the headache and body aches from the titanium poisoning for now.

All that misery would come knocking.

Later, rather than sooner, he hoped.

His gut kept telling him that he'd be down for the count already if Eli hadn't been lending him some of her unusual power every time she touched him. He had no other explanation for why he was still upright with so much titanium residue in his body.

Eli met him in front of the truck. He took her hand. "Don't let go of me until I say we're inside. I'm going to stop when I'm close to the ward entrance and test it with our joined hands."

Had the Guardian arrived yet, and had Cole already asked him to alter the ward?

Eli stayed with his long strides as he hurried to the two gargantuan trees that marked the passage through the ward.

Slowing to make sure nothing harmed Eli, he stepped ahead and eased her toward him.

Sparkles glittered around their joined hands first, so he kept bringing her through. The sparkling outlined her body, then she was inside.

He asked, "Ready?"

"Yes. Run."

He released her hand and kept his speed so that she stayed with him. They raced down the path he'd walked only days ago with Cole and Rory. Straight through the woods was shorter, but he and Eli would make equal time running all-out on the hard-packed dirt road.

When he rushed from the woods to the open field where the cabin once stood at the top of the rise, he saw Rory and Cole shifting from their animals. Next thing, they stood stood nude in front of the Guardian, who was dressed like a Manhattan stockbroker as usual.

"Don't look at them," Justin said, catching a breath as he slowed their pace.

"Am shifter. See much naked."

"That doesn't mean I want you seeing *them* naked."

Nothing was happening yet, but the Guardian would have known the minute Justin entered the ward and sensed his approach.

That had to be why, in the next second, Cole and Rory were outfitted in T-shirts, jeans and boots.

Eli whispered, "Much magic. Old magic."

Justin would thank his boss later for that consideration for Eli, but it was not surprising from a man over three hundred years old who held to propriety.

Even twenty yards away, Justin could hear Cole arguing. More reserved, but no less opinionated, Rory chose his words and his moments to interject them.

Justin caught a flash of movement far to the right that burst from the woods behind the Guardian just as Eli said, "*Wolf!*"

Eli's vision was playing out before Justin's eyes.

Adrian's fierce wolf barreled across the open space straight for the Guardian's back.

Without a second thought, Justin released her hand to race forward. He exploded out of his clothes as he shifted to Herc on the run.

That was going to hurt later, but at least the shift to Herc gave his bad leg one more healing boost.

Cole and Rory looked at Herc, then at Adrian's wolf, and started to move.

The Guardian ordered them to stand down then turned to face the threat.

Adrian's wolf ran at top speed, hair standing up on his back and fangs exposed.

Fully shifted and eating up ground, Herc bellowed a warning, and everyone turned to him except Adrian's red wolf.

Suicidal damn wolf leaped. He was going for the Guardian's throat.

Herc pushed his massive bulk off the ground and met Red in the air mere feet in front of the Guardian.

Herc and the wolf crashed to the ground together.

Justin shouted at Adrian mind to mind, *Stop it, Adrian!*

Adrian's voice came from far away, begging Justin, *End it now. I ... can't ... hold him.*

If Justin gave in, the Guardian would do just that and terminate Adrian's life on the spot. Their boss hadn't so much as flinched over Adrian's blatant attack.

The Guardian was never in danger.

Everyone here knew that at the last moment the Guardian would have lifted a hand and used his power to slam the wolf down. His next move would have been what he considered a mercy killing.

To some degree, the Guardian would be right.

Eli's vision had been accurate.

If Herc didn't stop Adrian's wolf, Justin would lose a part of his soul that he'd never get back. His world would never be the same.

With only one option, Justin turned Herc loose to give that wolf a beatdown.

Fur flew, claws slashed and blood spilled.

In minutes, Herc faced a badly wounded wolf that continued to snarl even though he was clearly beaten.

The Guardian said, "Enough. Stop."

Herc took a step back, showing he had heard and obeyed their leader.

Adrian's wolf didn't have the sense it took to pour piss out of a boot right now.

Good job, Herc, Justin told his bear, who had run and fought hard in spite of the titanium draining his energy.

He felt for Adrian, who no longer had what Justin and Herc shared. If they could keep the Guardian from taking action this minute, Justin would plead for one last chance to get Adrian back to where he'd once been.

A man tightly bonded with his wolf.

That would happen only if the Guardian hadn't already decided that a few more days would be dragging out Adrian's misery.

Guttural sounds crawled up Red's throat.

Adrian had no control over that wolf.

The Guardian came into Justin's head. *I have tried to reach Adrian to help him return to us. I can hear him only in bits and pieces now. He's fought a hard battle, Justin. You all have, but I have to end this as I would for any of you.*

Justin begged, *Give me one minute in my human form first, Guardian. Please.*

The Guardian took in Justin and turned his head to where Eli stood quietly, staring at all of them. He asked Justin, *Is that the Romanov daughter you were tasked with delivering to Clan Boudreaux?*

Yes, but I can explain.

I will afford you the opportunity.

Then Herc told Justin, *Mate touch wolf.*

Mishka?

Not bear.

Herc had to be relaying a message from Eli.

Possibly thinking Justin's delay in replying was due to worry about Adrian going wild again with Eli near, the Guardian said, *Shift back, Justin. I'll watch Adrian's wolf.*

Justin did as told, standing at his full height once he was bipedal again, though his bad leg felt like it was ready to fall off. A set of clothes magically covered him as well, thanks to the Guardian.

Hurrying to get a handle on this disaster, which was all he could call it at this point, Justin said, "I will explain about the delivery, sir, but I need Eli ... Elianna here for that minute I've requested."

Pinching the bridge of his nose, the Guardian asked, "Why?"

"I think she can tell us something about Adrian that none of us are able to see, but ... she'll need to touch him."

"You would risk Adrian's wolf attacking her?"

Hitting the Guardian with a gaze that left no question of his intentions, Justin said, "I will not allow anyone to harm her. Ever."

Giving Justin a narrowed look in return, the Guardian appeared on the verge of dismissing all of them.

Then Eli said, "Please, sir."

That must have changed his mind. His boss signaled to her. "Elianna, please join us."

When she stepped up close, Justin immediately went to her side. He noticed Cole's congratulatory look, which he appreciated, and Rory's curious expression, which he'd expected.

Justin told the Guardian, "If you'll order Adrian's wolf to sleep, she can put her hands on Red."

Cole and Rory stepped forward to join the circle. Cole asked, "Is she a healer?"

Eli said, "No and she has voice."

Cole's eyes opened wide, surprised at her assertion.

Rory said, "Okay, then. What do you plan to do?"

"I have vision of wolf. Is why we come. Justin stop attack. Must see inside."

Clearly intrigued, Rory said, "What is it you expect to see inside?"

"If human there or ... all dark."

Justin smiled with pride at how she backed away from nothing, but that didn't mean Red and Adrian could still be saved.

She explained further. "I tell what I see. Maybe good. Maybe bad. Think vision important. I am here for reason. But only tell truth," she said, glancing at Justin.

He nodded, letting her know he understood that she would share exactly what she saw.

The Guardian had been observing Eli the whole time she spoke, but showed no sign of relent in his position on Adrian's fate.

Red chose that moment to make the sound of a demon ready to attack. His growls rumbled with fury.

Addressing Eli, the Guardian said, "You may place your hands on the wolf once I order him to sleep, but he will not sleep long. When he wakes, he will still be a vicious animal. I will still have to do what is best for him and this world. Understand?"

Nope, no second thoughts on Adrian's wolf.

"Yes," Eli replied.

All eyes were on the Guardian as he studied both her and the wolf for a long moment before asking, "Are you three willing to accept whatever she shares, even if it confirms what I've been saying?"

Cole and Rory exchanged guarded looks then turned to Justin, who had just as much trepidation in answering that question. His buddies waited to see what he said and would trust his judgment.

Justin clarified, "What if she indicates he can be saved?"

"We will discuss it," was all the Guardian would allow, which meant he had probably made up his mind and was just allowing Justin and his two friends time to accept the inevitable.

With a quick check of Cole and Rory, who sent him your-lead hand signals, Justin said, "Yes, we agree."

Turning to Adrian, the Guardian ordered, "Red wolf, look at me."

Adrian's wolf pulled back his lips and upped the crazy wolf sounds, but his eyes slashed at the Guardian who told him, "Sleep now, wolf."

Power rushed across Justin's skin. Eli gasped.

Justin held her anchored to him, but they both took a step back, pushed by the Guardian's energy.

Mad Red's snarling slowed. His eyelids drooped and he seemed to fall asleep standing up.

Turning to Justin, the Guardian said, "His wolf fights everyone even now. You must hurry. It may last one or two minutes at most."

Eli didn't hesitate, stepping past Justin, who rushed around her, dropping to one knee on the opposite side of the wolf.

"Your boss make sleep. No danger," she said pointedly to Justin.

"I'm making sure he *can't* be." Justin's heart pounded like a maniac on crack.

If Eli saw no hope for Adrian, it would be the last nail in the wolf's coffin.

CHAPTER 36

ELIANNA COULD UNDERSTAND JUSTIN TRUSTING her, but why had his friends?

And why had that eagle put this wolf's life in her hands?

Seconds were ticking away, but she would need less than one fourth of that minute if all went well.

If not, she would trust Justin to keep her head from the wolf's jaws.

Kneeling close, she wrinkled her nose at being near the tang of fresh blood that had already begun to dry across the wolf's coat after the fight with Justin's bear.

Giving Justin one last look, she tried to appear confident to answer the hope in his gaze, but knew she failed when he said, "I won't blame you no matter what, Eli, babe. Just tell us what you can."

Her eyes blurred for a moment with unshed tears.

She didn't know this Adrian, but she did not want to be the reason he received a death sentence.

Mishka said, *We see wolf. Not kill.*

Her bear was telling her they had not created this issue and they had no power over Adrian living or dying. Elianna wasn't quite ready to accept a lack of responsibility, but she had wanted to touch him to see what was inside. If he had only darkness and no glimmer of light, then perhaps letting him go would be better than forcing him to continue living a nightmare.

She finally realized how truly unfair she had been to Mishka by keeping her distance. *I am sorry, Mishka. You are good bear. Was not good shifter.*

You good. Me love.

Tears spilled at that.

Love you, too.

Justin frowned, "Eli, babe?"

She smiled. "Is fine. More later."

He nodded, still looking concerned but understood she'd explain when they were not here.

Extending her hands, she placed one on the wolf's head and one on his heart and closed her eyes to the outside world.

At first touch, waves of anger, hurt and chaos bombarded her. The wolf and man battled viciously. Images and thoughts flew at her in flashes of bright light and boiling black.

Her energy boiled up and flooded her hands, then left her fingers.

It was all too much.

She was kneeling by the wolf one moment and lying on her back the next, listening to Justin shout at her to wake up.

Opening her eyes, she lifted her fingers to his lips. "Too loud."

He pulled her up, so she sat with his arm around her back, but he breathed as though he'd run up a mountain carrying her. He dropped his forehead to hers. "I can't let you do that again."

"Yes. Will do again."

Sighing with resignation, he said, "I probably will, but not today."

"I am good. Must stand." She didn't like being on the ground as if she were a weak female.

When she was on her feet again, Elianna dusted herself off and took in all the expectant faces. All but the Guardian's. He seemed to wait for confirmation of his verdict.

Red started twitching and showing signs of coming out of his sleep state.

"Justin, your minute is up," the Guardian said quietly. "I'm sorry. I know the history between you two—"

Elianna shouted, "*No!*"

Cole muttered, "Oh, shit."

Rory's mouth gaped open.

The Guardian looked shocked that anyone would interrupt him. The other three had similar expressions.

Justin would be angry with her.

The Guardian said, "Pardon me?"

Mad Red snuffled and made some garbled sounds.

Elianna crossed her arms. "Mistake to kill friend."

Justin winced when she said his boss intended to take Adrian's life, but that was the truth.

The wolf shook his head and sidestepped on wobbly feet.

Cole said, "Heads up, everyone. Red is going live in seconds."

Elianna rushed to explain, "Wolf and human have terrible time. Much pain inside. Two life not happy." She looked to Justin who had to know she was talking from experience when she said, "Wolf and man must be one."

His sad smile encouraged her to continue.

She faced his imposing boss. That man had eyes too much like an eagle for his nice human face. Looking at his chin instead, she said, "Not have words."

"It's okay, Eli, babe," Justin said. "I'll explain anything they don't get."

Thinking hard, she said, "Man and wolf angry. Wolf not forgive man and man not forgive self. Wolf feel ... abandoned."

She noticed Justin staring at Red, then at her, because when the wolf's gaze finally lifted, those eyes searched for Eli. The wolf shivered as if in freezing cold, but the temperature was mild.

No fur stood up on his back. No snarling.

That was a hopeful sign, right?

Cole said in a half-joking voice, "You think she's a wolf whisperer?"

The wolf swung his demonic gaze to Cole. Back came the crazy sounds and he started forward.

The Guardian lifted his hand and the wolf ran into an invisible wall, which he hit several more times before backing off, still glaring at Cole.

Elianna asked Justin, "What is wolf whisperer?"

He explained, "Sort of like a healer who can reach inside a damaged person, or animal, to calm them and bring them back to control."

"Not healer," Elianna told Cole.

"But you think he can be saved, right?" Justin asked with so much longing it hurt her heart.

Elianna said, "Not what I say."

Cole and Rory cursed.

Justin called over, "Language, dammit."

She looked at Justin. "How is that make sense?"

He gave her a sheepish grin.

The Guardian barely spoke, but power drove his words. "Silence. Let her finish."

Gifting this eagle boss with a short nod, Elianna said, "What I say is not maybe save wolf. *Must* make live."

Drawing his brow down in tight lines, the Guardian asked, "Why must he live?"

"You are ... special shifters. Yes?"

The Guardian nodded, but cut a questioning gaze at Justin that Elianna read as Justin being in trouble, but she could not stop now. She said, "Have new vision when touch wolf. His life is much ... uh, need ... no, wrong word." She dug around for the English word and muttered it in Russian to jog her mind.

"You're saying this wolf is very important for us?" the Guardian asked.

"Yes. Speak Russian?"

"It's one of my languages," the Guardian said.

She finished her explanation in Russian, then the Guardian interpreted. "She says Adrian is the key to our future."

Rory asked, "All of us? Even you, Guardian?"

Frowning, their boss said, "Not me."

Elianna argued, "Yes. You. Wolf dies, key gone. Wolf alive, very good for special shifters."

Even the wolf quieted as everyone digested that.

Justin found his voice. "Are you saying he can go back into the world?"

Frustrated that they weren't grasping her point, she said, "Is simple. Wolf must live so wolf save life. Must save person necessary to shifters."

"You mean all shifters?" Rory asked.

"No." She pointed at each one of them as she said, "You, you, you, you. Gallize. Is what wolf call you." Justin had told her that name, but so had the wolf, which she hoped saved Justin from being in trouble.

Even Justin's boss had no words.

She turned to the wolf. His insane eyes relaxed and the wolf put his front legs out, sliding to the ground.

Justin asked his boss, "What's your decision, sir?"

The Guardian waited until the wolf looked up at him. "I will allow you the time you need to heal, Adrian, but I will also honor your request at any moment if you ask me to change my mind."

The wolf whined and dropped his head on his paws.

Justin kissed her cheek and said in a hoarse voice, "Thank you, Eli, babe. Thank you for saving our friend."

"My appreciation, too," the Guardian said. "I do not want to lose any of my flock."

"I did not much."

The Guardian corrected her. "You did quite a lot, Elianna, and I will not forget it. Now, we need to get you to Clan Boudreaux."

"What?" Justin shouted.

CHAPTER 37

JUSTIN HAD A MOMENT OF panic at the Guardian's announcement that Eli needed to go to the Boudreaux Clan, but he had
yet to inform his boss of all that had occurred.

That would be the same Guardian who currently stared at Justin with enough force he felt the ground tremble.

Cole and Rory stepped away from the Guardian, probably
expecting an apocalyptic explosion.

Shit, I so fucked up. "My apologies, Guardian. I haven't given
you my report and should have asked for you to hear that first."

"Ah, yes. Your explanation."

Justin caught them all up on what had transpired, leaving out
the part about being intimate with Eli, which he'd never embar-
rass her by mentioning in front of her. But if the Guardian pushed
the point, Justin would ask to speak to him in private and share
that development.

As he wound down, feeling tired by recounting every moment
of the last days, he said, "Bottom line is that Clan Boudreaux is
responsible for the attacks on her and I have asked Eli to be my
mate. She has accepted, but we are not bonding until we have
assurance of Nico's being sent here. I would like to propose that
if Clan Boudreaux makes the bear responsible pay for his actions
and they tell Alexandre Romanov they're okay with Eli staying
with me, that we are all willing to forego any vengeance."

In thinking through all he'd said, Justin felt like he'd laid out
a perfect case.

Something about the Guardian's lack of surprise over this information bothered Justin. Why wasn't the Guardian up in arms

over what Clan Boudreaux had done?

"The San Francisco wolf alpha tried to reach you, Justin, but it was evidently during the time you were on the mountain and without a phone. His message indicated two rogue wolves scented in the area of an attack on Elianna in San Francisco were traced to the Black River pack."

Justin grimaced over not being the one to inform his boss first about that attack, which seemed forever ago now.

Not slowing down, the Guardian continued. "I spoke to the Romanov alpha who convinced me he was not behind the attack and even offered to send a team to hunt down her pursuers. I was able to dissuade him from that action and convince him we could handle this. Upon my contact with the Clan Boudreaux alpha, he sent spies out among his people and discovered the person at fault. It was the shifter he'd offered Elianna to as a mate. The same man who had been put in charge of the Boudreaux warriors."

"T-Bone? The alpha promised her to T-Bone?" Justin's insides boiled at that thought. T-Bone was the worst kind of man whore.

Eli stood like an unhappy statue.

Nothing showed on her face for those who didn't know her, but he could feel her anxiety mounting.

Justin wanted to hug her and tell her all would be fine. That he would fight anyone and everyone for her.

"Yes, T-bone," the Guardian acknowledged. "The alpha felt it was time for him to settle down and figured the shifter would be honored to have someone like Elianna. Never did he expect the bear to be so dishonorable as to put her life in danger. He found out when one of his scouts reported back that T-Bone had secretly told some of the men to allow the Black River pack access through Louisiana to distribute their mind-altering drugs. It all unraveled at that point and T-Bone confessed."

"What'd they do with him?" Justin demanded, unable to shield his anger.

"The alpha dealt with him personally. Once the alpha felt T-bone had given up all the information possible about the sordid affair and the Black River pack contacts, he gave him a swift death."

Justin felt no sympathy for any torture T-bone had suffered.

That bear shifter would have faced worse from him. In fact, he felt cheated out of taking T-Bone apart, but at the moment he still had not heard the Guardian agree with his plan to keep Eli.

The Guardian continued, "The alpha wishes to make it up to Elianna a hundred times over—"

Feeling anxious, Justin cut in. "Good. He can do that by approving our mating."

"If you interrupt me again, you will no longer have a speaking role here," the Guardian warned.

Swallowing hard, Justin said, "Sorry. I understand, sir."

Inclining his head at Justin first, the Guardian addressed Eli. "Do I understand that you wish to mate with Justin?"

"Yes," she said in a whisper.

"I would consider it a huge honor for you to be Justin's mate," the Guardian began.

Justin let out the breath that had bottlenecked in his chest. He couldn't hold back his smile either.

"But I am the only person who can tell Alexandre to release Nico and I will not be able to do that until the alpha of Clan Boudreaux informs me you have fulfilled your agreement. He will have guards everywhere the minute you enter Louisiana, to keep you safe. I give you my word he is capable of protecting you and Nico. He says his other shifters were upset not to have a chance to court you, so it appears you will have your choice of Boudreaux mates."

Blood rushed from Justin's face.

This couldn't be happening.

Eli straightened her back. "I understand."

"No you don't," Justin argued. "Guardian, you can't do this. She's *my* mate. I won't let anyone else touch her. I promised ..." The rest of that rant stayed inside Justin's head when his mouth was sealed shut.

Eli touched Justin's arm. "Is okay, yes. I must show honor." Her eyes filled with tears. "Only love you." She pecked a kiss on his cheek and stepped away.

She couldn't accept another mate.

Justin was losing his mind. He reached for her and ended up frozen in that position.

The Guardian asked Cole to drive Eli to Clan Boudreaux and

told Rory to get started working on flushing the titanium out of Justin's leg.

With a sick expression on his face, Cole told Justin, "I'll protect her with my life and not leave until I know she's safe."

Herc railed, *Our mate! Mishka!*

Tears were stuck in Justin's eyes that couldn't fall, but his heart cried a river as Eli walked away. She glanced back with a sad wave one last time before she was out of sight.

CHAPTER 38

Three days later, Bighorn National Forest, Wyoming

HAVING SHIFTED BACK TO HUMAN form, Justin stretched his bad leg, which had gradually gotten better each day. Rory had flushed the poison out. Next time Justin should just tie his dick in a knot and drive a nail through it.

Had to be less painful.

Technically, he was healed. If not for sparing Herc more misery, Justin wouldn't care.

Life as he knew it was over.

Someone else had his mate.

Want Mishka, Herc said, his misery coming through in two words. He'd said little since their mate had left.

Justin murmured, "Me too, Herc. I'm sorry I lost our mate."

Herc withdrew, but not like when he slept. He just seemed to pull in deep and hole up.

Cole had returned two days after leaving with Eli and tried to explain that she was secure, but Justin couldn't hear it. He'd shifted and gone off on his own. His friend would understand Justin's need to be alone.

He and Herc had spent a long night roaming the rugged Wyoming country. Every thought centered on Eli.

She would enjoy seeing this spot.

She would ask a million questions.

She would smile and they'd be naked in the next breath.

He had to stop torturing himself by dwelling on her, but he

couldn't. He should be helping Adrian, but Justin was no help when he might be just as broken very soon.

Moonlight danced all around him as gently moving clouds flowed past. Eli would love that. Daylight wouldn't come for another hour. Then Justin would have to face a new day.

Without her.

His throat hurt from standing on the highest point he could find and shouting her name until he was hoarse.

Adrian and the guys were probably ready to rip his tongue out after that.

Justin wouldn't blame them.

He'd shifted and let Herc run as hard as he wanted until the big bear was ready to sleep. Instead of finding a dark cave, Justin had come back to this high spot and shifted back to human.

His human side felt numb.

He stared at everything and nothing.

Without Eli, the entire world was lifeless.

In the distance, a shadow flapped large wings and crossed between Justin and the moon. As the Guardian's giant sea eagle landed, power rushed around the hill and left a man wearing an elegant suit in the eagle's place.

Power rolled off the Guardian like heat off the sun.

Justin had used up his opportunities to mouth off. He was lucky the Guardian had not shipped him to a remote location and left him warded there until he relearned manners and respect.

He was glad that hadn't happened.

Justin held this man on a pedestal and, after three days, he could admit the arrangement that stole his mate had not been his Guardian's fault.

Standing to show the respect he owed his boss, Justin locked his hands behind his back and stood at ease even though he was naked.

Clothes covered his body next, which Justin appreciated.

"Thank you, sir." Justin had no problem being nude, but it was hard to face someone like the Guardian in his birthday suit.

His boss gave a brief nod and walked a few steps forward, then turned his head into the light wind. The Guardian stared out into infinity when he said, "I have an assignment for you."

Maybe that was just what Justin needed to get his head out of his ass. "Yes, sir."

"Are you healed?"

"Yes, sir."

"No loss of control?"

"No, sir. Herc and I are ready for anything you need."

Justin started to ask more, but the whole control issue was a little dicey, and he had to keep his yap shut if he wanted out of this warded territory.

Turning to face Justin fully, his boss said, "I'm sending you to Clan Boudreaux."

Justin's stomach hit the ground. He had to be fucking kidding. "Why?"

So much for showing some discipline, but Justin took that one right to the gut.

Overlooking Justin's lack of decorum, the Guardian said, "The alpha specifically asked to speak with you about Elianna's mating. He also told me about your childhood there. I believe he wants to patch things up."

"You have to be kidding me," spilled out before Justin could stop himself. The Guardian hadn't sealed his mouth shut again and had brought the past forward, so Justin took that as permission to speak candidly about the Boudreaux alpha. "Rey Boudreaux thinks we're going to hug and make up after years of treating me as something lower than a human? *Then* he expects me to smile and stand by while I watch *my* mate bond with another shifter? I can't even believe this is happening." Justin lost all sense of self-preservation and shouted at the Guardian. "None of that would be happening if I hadn't been stuck in this ward."

"My goal is to keep you *and* Elianna safe."

Justin's righteous anger dissolved. "Is ... is she in danger? Let me out. I'm killing anyone who tries to harm her."

Cocking his head in that odd, eagle-like manner, the Guardian said, "She is safe, but I have reservations about freeing you. However, I did agree to send you if you would go. Are you refusing?"

So this is what it feels like when your heart climbs up into your throat.

Justin choked down the thick lump and swallowed. Who was he kidding? He would give anything for just one more look at Eli. "No, I'm not refusing."

Admitting that cost him a chunk of pride, but Justin had no

pride left when it came to loving her.

Taking his time to share whatever was on his mind, the Guardian said, "I wish the guardian for Gallize females was still around. I sense that Elianna might be Gallize based on her power and gift, but I can't say for sure."

"Does it matter at this point, sir?" Justin asked, weary of the emotional drain he'd been through. "I never cared whether she was, because I knew she could take my power. But that's water under the bridge," he muttered, letting his voice trail off.

The Guardian must have been done with the topic. He said, "A vehicle has been delivered to the ward boundary. One of my jets is waiting for you in Sheridan and will transport you to Louisiana, where a vehicle has been delivered to New Orleans Lakefront Airport. No matter what you see or hear in Clan Boudreaux territory, I will have your word that you will show respect to the alpha and to Elianna. I want to know that you are ready to abide by all decisions made by me *as well as* those made by the alpha of Clan Boudreaux. You represent the Gallize."

Man, that was a tough one to accept, but Justin said, "Yes, sir. I won't disappoint you."

"Very well. I will allow you access through the ward again." The Guardian paused. "Don't judge her unfairly," he advised in an understanding tone. "She made a vow to a child who trusts her and she would never let him down. She's a strong and loyal woman."

"I hear you, sir. Thank you. Have a good flight back, sir."

"I'm not leaving yet. I wish to observe Adrian for a bit."

Justin cringed. "Now might not be the best time. Herc pissed off his wolf last night. I heard him howling, then Cole howling. Think I heard Adrian and Cole tangle it up with Rory."

Probably all Justin's fault for not letting them catch some sleep.

All except Rory, who preferred to prowl alone at night.

Sighing long and hard, the Guardian said, "I have never had a group of shifters who test me as much as your generation. I still have to locate a Siberian tiger shifter that Elianna described to Cole on the trip to Clan Boudreaux. Did he tell you?"

"No, sir. My fault. I've been MIA since Cole returned."

"She had a vision, which rattled Cole until she explained."

"It's freaky the first time you see it." Justin felt bad over not being there to soothe her. "What did she say about the tiger?"

"She claims it is one of ours and in this country. I question that because the last Siberian tiger Gallize shifter I knew of no longer exists."

Proud of her, Justin said, "If she said she saw it, then he's out there somewhere. Her visions are always true."

"I have not seen him in the New England area, which is what Cole thinks she was describing," the Guardian murmured in deep thought. Then he seemed to dismiss that and said, "You may take whatever time you need to get your head back together before I hand your team a new assignment."

"Yes, sir." Justin didn't need a head adjustment. He needed a heart extraction.

That was the only part of him unable to heal.

Justin didn't hunt up Adrian or the guys before he packed the gear Cole had brought inside the ward for him. Adrian knew the team would be coming back more often to work with him and Justin believed the Guardian would not actually show himself to the wolf at this point.

Hell, that sea eagle could probably observe from the stratosphere.

When he reached the private jet waiting for him at Sheridan County Airport, Justin was feeling more human as he entered the airplane cabin.

Then he saw someone sitting halfway inside the luxury aircraft.

Now he understood why the Guardian had warned him about accepting everyone's decisions. What was left of Justin's heart fractured and fell into a thousand pieces.

His boss had realized Justin was still in denial, and the person sitting in this cabin was the only one who could kill the last of his hope.

Walking slowly toward the child, Justin said, "Are you Nico?" He didn't really need to ask, but he was struggling to not lose his shit in front of this little boy.

"Yes. See Elianna?"

All Justin had to do was open his mouth and speak. It shouldn't be this hard.

He finally said, "Yes. I'll take you to your sister."

Joy filled the child's face.

Did this mean the Guardian had not sent him to talk to the alpha so much as deliver this child?

To find closure in this last act?

Justin had never known how difficult it was to be a man and do the right thing until now.

But he could do this. He had promised Eli he would bring Nico to her.

Once he did, he was putting in for an overseas tour.

Cole, Rory and Adrian would understand.

Justin needed an ocean separating him and Eli, because Nico was living proof she had taken a mate. *How can she do that when she loves me?*

Herc moaned, *Mishka. Want Mishka.*

Justin had tried to soothe his bear over the past few days, but clearly it was going to take a lot more time for both of them. The Guardian had made a good point when he said Eli had too much honor to not make good on her first commitment to a child. Justin understood and had told her he'd never make her choose. His boss expected Justin to prove he was the Gallize warrior he'd been trained to be.

No more refusing to accept reality.

As the engines powered up, Justin sat next to Nico and fastened the boy's seat belt.

Nico smiled because this child's world was coming together as Justin's fell apart. The kid had huge gray eyes. Eli had said he was a polar bear shifter. Nico's grin would light up a dark room.

"You Justin?"

"Yes. Who told you?"

"Eagle man."

Unable to hold back a warm smile for Nico, albeit one hiding pain, Justin nodded. This child sounded just like her. "Did she teach you English?"

"Yes. Said need be smart for survive." Nico's eyes shined with potential tears. He whispered, "Please tell."

"About what?"

"Elianna. Miss sister much."

Hearing the loneliness poured into those words, Justin fought his own tears and put his pain aside. He began to tell Nico all the good things that had happened from the day Justin met Eli.

He had to start telling her goodbye at some point. He might as well hand over his memories into Nico's good keeping.

CHAPTER 39

Clan Boudreaux territory, Louisiana

BY THE TIME JUSTIN TURNED off the last bit of pavement, onto a dirt road overhung with Spanish moss and with bayous on each side, he had come to terms with his loss.

Sort of. His mind had worked it out.

One day his heart would find a way to understand.

He would never get over Eli and it would hurt to see that she'd chosen a mate. For her, though, he would always show respect.

But the Clan Boudreaux alpha could bite Justin's boot.

As he peered ahead at the familiar territory, he knew Boudreaux's tight security had already announced Justin's presence to their boss.

He had no beef with this clan.

The ones who'd been the worst and treated him like shit had been his mother and the alpha.

A few clan members had persecuted him horribly, the way bullies tended to do. The rest had mostly ignored him.

Becoming a Gallize had given him the first real family he'd ever had, but he'd lose even *them* in a few short years.

Without a bonded mate, he and Herc would have to face the Guardian when the infamous mating curse took over. Gallize shifters had to mate, and that was that. If not, their animals took over and eventually the shifter lost his humanity.

Justin thought back on Eli's vision about Adrian saving a person who would be important to all of them, even the Guardian. His

Guardian had supposedly had a mate at one time, but she was dead and he didn't speak of it.

Just a crapshoot to find a female Gallize.

As if Justin cared anymore?

In truth, he did. There was no point in his friends not having mates, if possible. He would always help them, but he doubted he'd be of any use in tracking down mates after this epic failure.

Herc rumbled in anger, but he'd said little more than Mishka's name since Eli had left.

Nico snored softly, like his sister.

Justin smiled, surprised to realize his face could still move those muscles. The kid was worn out. He didn't think Nico had slept since the Guardian sent someone to retrieve him.

And that kid could talk. Justin had enjoyed Nico's stories about Eli and her silly bear. Wait until Nico saw Mishka again. The child would likely recognize a stronger bear and Eli would guide Nico into building a strong bond with his polar bear.

As Justin neared the wrought-iron gates to Clan Boudreaux, which had the name scripted in gold on a black plaque, he noted the armed guards in towers above each side of the entrance.

They would definitely stop or kill an unauthorized intruder, but those guards were more a show of force for visitors unfamiliar with Rey Boudreaux.

This clan protected its borders with claws and fangs, as much as tight security.

Only shifters were trained for their army.

That qualification had left Justin out when he'd lived here.

Now his bear would stand over the tallest one shifted, but this bunch would never know the truth about Justin.

Passing through the gates as they opened for him, Justin pulled up to the first building and parked. He left the truck running with the air on.

When he stepped out into heavy heat pulsing with humidity, someone said, "Cut the engine, dickhead."

Taking his time to turn, he faced a line of warriors decked out in their native gear for hunting and fishing the bayous. They looked like a bunch ready to sign up for Duck Dynasty.

No, a couple of them had clean faces.

Wonder why those two shaved?

Then he realized it was probably so they could make the best impression to court Eli.

You screwed up, guys. She'd liked Justin's scruff.

Cut it out, he told himself. *Stop bringing up those times.*

"I said to kill the engine, dickhead," the heavy one in the middle ordered. Damn if that wasn't Durand, a mean one who used to toss Justin into the swamp to see if he could outswim a gator.

Justin powered up his Gallize presence. Yes, it was an ego move, but who could blame him?

Durand's snarky, dark look faded to worry. All of them took a step back and stared at Justin with wary expressions.

Justin said, "A child is asleep in this vehicle. I need to talk to the alpha, who is expecting this child. If anything happens to this little boy, you won't get a chance to plead for mercy."

"He scarin' ya boys? Ya guard that truck with ya life, ya hear?" called out from the building.

"Yes, Alpha," rolled off every set of lips and all heads dipped in deference.

Justin prepared to face the man he'd told to kiss his ass the day he walked out of this place. Sucking it up for Team Gallize, he turned to face Rey Boudreaux.

Rey had to be pushing a hundred and ten. He'd aged well and appeared to be only in his forties.

Showing that he had returned a confident man, Justin said, "Hello, Rey."

"Welcome back to Clan Boudreaux."

"This isn't my clan," Justin made very clear.

His terse words bounced off the alpha. Rey stuck his hand out.

Justin looked at it with contempt, but as the face of the Gallize, he accepted the hand for a brief shake.

Crossing his arms, Justin said, "I'm here to deliver Nico."

"I told ya boss I want let's talk some."

"About what?"

Grasping his beard in a thoughtful way, Rey said, "Walk wi' me."

"Don't have all day."

"Won't take all day."

A muscle twitched in Justin's jaw. "Fine. Walk." With the alpha's orders in place for his men to guard the truck, Nico would be safer alone in that cab than he would in a padded bunker.

As Rey led them between buildings where Justin recalled his school years, then on past floating structures that housed private homes belonging to his clan, he started talking.

"I owe ya apology, son."

Justin kept from sniping back that he wasn't Rey's son, but he was going to prove he was the bigger man in all this. He refused to look at Rey, lest the man think Justin acknowledged his apology.

Too little, way too late.

"But I'd do it again," Rey admitted.

Justin stopped. That was over the top. "How can you apologize and say you'd do it again? Do you *not* see the contradiction?"

"I do." Rey continued walking, which meant Justin had to follow him for any hope of being done here today.

He caught up as Rey said, "I know ya think I treat ya bad as a child."

"Think? I lived it."

"I did want ya as my second," Rey admitted.

Justin refused to be swayed by anything at this stage, so he replied, "As if you wanted someone who had no animal to be your second."

"I did. I couldn't tho'. I would have if I hadn't thought someone would kill ya in yer sleep."

"Trust me. They wouldn't try that today."

"No, yer boss done told me how ya got a monster bear."

Okay, Justin forgave the Guardian a little bit for that plug, but this whole trip still sucked.

When they were crossing a long wooden walkway covered in trees and away from any buildings, Rey put his hand on Justin's arm. "A minute, please."

Pulling his arm away, Justin leaned back against the wooden railing on one side. He glanced around for any hungry gators.

None at the moment.

Taking a spot opposite him, Rey said, "I could not treat ya like one of the shifters or they'd have hurt ya in trainin'. I could not treat ya special or they'd have *killed* ya in trainin' or when ya slept. I pushed ya away to keep ya safe. In fact, I asked yer mama to take ya to live with humans and she refused."

Justin had never known that and wasn't sure how he felt about it. He quipped, "She wouldn't leave the clan where her brother is alpha."

"No, she wouldn't, but I do miss her."

In this one moment, Justin almost missed her too, but only to a point. He'd lived with a constant internal battle over his feelings about her for years until she died. She'd been embarrassed by his lack of ability to shift. A boy needed mom in *his* corner. Every kid did.

Damn, he hated the nostalgic feelings rising from seeing a place where he'd been happy at one time, but only as a very small child. Once he'd reached the age when even the late-bloomer bears should have shifted, it all went to hell.

His mother would never leave the security of her brother's clan. She had to have someone taking care of her all the time.

That had been Justin's full-time job even as she scowled at him for failing to shift into a bear.

His mother was nothing like Eli, who would brave anything to care for her family and would love any cub no matter what.

Justin wanted to punch his brain and make it stop defaulting to her. He had to find a way to make the constant thoughts of Eli stop. "So what do you want, Rey?"

"I'd like to be friends."

"Man, you don't ask for much, do you?"

Smiling, Rey said, "Ya always had more heart than all my males put together. I would like to see ya again."

So. Not. Fucking. Happening. "Well, there are things I'd like to have happen that will never happen, so welcome to the world of disappointment. I need to hand Nico off and get going." Justin would rather not sound like an asshole, but the longer he stayed here, the more that side was bound to show up.

Letting out a long sigh, Rey said, "Let's find the princess first."

Before Justin could snap at him that she hated being called a princess, Rey had taken off at his fast walk again. The man might talk as if he'd climbed out of the bayou last week, but he was dumb like a fox and a vicious fighter.

Justin could give credit where it was due, but that didn't change how he felt about being dragged here to witness Eli with her mate.

Follow that crazy alpha, or go back to get Nico?

Justin needed to know where to take Nico, right?

Herc snorted. *Big lie. Find mate.*

His bear was right. Justin itched to see Eli.

Find Mishka. Herc said that with anticipation that hit Justin in the solar plexus.

He wasn't sure he could do this. The end result would be more disappointment for him and his bear.

When he caught up to the alpha, Justin started to ask Rey to just point him in Eli's direction.

But then he heard her voice.

He followed Rey around the next bend until the alpha paused at a corner of the wooden building where Justin had lived when he'd been a member of this clan. He slipped up to the corner where Rey hid and was clearly eavesdropping.

Hearing Eli's voice, Justin could admit that *he* was not above listening in either.

"Well, I guess I win the lot'ry, Miss Princess," a male said.

Justin frowned. Was Eli still interviewing potential mates? If she hadn't committed to someone, why was Nico here and why hadn't the Guardian shared that information?

No way could Justin stay around and watch men fawn over her, but like rubberneckers determined to see a highway wreck, he couldn't turn away.

Able to look over Rey's head, Justin whispered, "Jasper? You would offer *Jasper* as a mate to the Romanov's daughter?"

Rey very quietly said, "Watch."

Jasper, who worked deep in the swamp for weeks at a time, who had never been seen without a beard to the middle of his chest, and who rarely bathed, stood with his arms crossed, grinning.

He was a decent guy, but not real quick when it came to women. Most of the females in the clan used to literally hit him over the head to make him leave them alone.

A male shifter stood on each side of Eli, fanning her with honest-to-God palm leaves.

What was up?

Clan Boudreaux had never fanned any woman, not even his mother, who had been a full-fledged prima donna.

Eli reclined in a chair that had been put up on stacks of wooden pallets. Had they made her a freaking throne?

She wore a long, shiny, silver dress with no sleeves, had her hair piled in a fancy 'do and a pair of strappy silver sandals on her feet.

Another male shifter painted her toenails.

Justin had to push his mouth closed.

"Well, Miss Princess?" Jasper asked.

"What is lot'ry?"

"Huh?" Jasper looked to one of the guys and said, "She don't understand our language?"

The shifter waving the palm leaf on the left told Eli, "Jasper is talking about a lottery, which is a game you play to win money."

"Oh. How to win?" she asked, sipping on what appeared to be iced tea.

"Uh, well, uh ... " Jasper said, and looked at the other men. "Can you tell her?"

"Hell, no," the shifter fan-slave on the right side said. "Last time I talked to her, I lost a bet to do this. By the way, I pass on courting her. You can have her. In fact, none of us want her."

That riled Justin.

Herc grumbled, *Kill all.*

Sighing, Justin said, *We can't do that, Herc. We owe it to Eli to show we're honorable.*

Herc miss Mishka.

I know, buddy, but if you talk to her please don't make this difficult for Mishka and Eli.

Herc huffed a noise of frustration.

Justin understood. While he wanted Eli for himself, he still didn't want anyone to say she was unworthy of being a mate. Why couldn't she be won in a battle?

Justin would unleash Herc and win their mate.

Rey lifted a hand, maybe to stall Justin from breaking out a bear this bunch had never seen. The alpha had always been intuitive about some things, but it still surprised Justin for this man to possibly be sensing Justin's fury.

Eli turned to the man who had complained and said, "You owe more hours. Four."

"Why?"

"You curse. No curse."

"Shit."

She added, "Eight."

Jasper looked at the other two guys. "You lose to her, too?"

"Yep."

"How?"

The guys smiled at each other then one told Jasper, "Just keep talking and you'll end up washing her clothes."

"Ain't doin' washin' for no woman," Jasper argued.

Eli looked down her nose with loads of arrogance. "You want princess. Think princess free?"

"That a trick question, boys?" Jasper asked in a conspiratorial voice.

They all nodded.

Justin grinned.

When the alpha turned to Justin, he said, "What I gonna do with that one?"

Instant smile kill. "Stop calling her princess for one thing."

"Justin!"

At Eli's shout, he stepped out into the open.

She pushed people away, pulled her dress up to her thighs and flew down from her perch, running to him.

He barely caught her when she launched into his arms, but his arms would always be open for her. His insides shuddered at the feel of Eli again.

This had been a mistake.

He couldn't live knowing he'd never have this.

She wrapped her legs around him and laid a kiss on him that brought Monty to attention. He didn't give a damn who it pissed off.

When she pulled her head back, she asked in an excited voice, "Why late?"

"You were expecting me?"

Her mouth drooped. "Yes. Every day I wait."

Sighing heavily, he said, "I wanted to be here, babe, believe me I wanted to, but I couldn't come until now."

The alpha cleared his throat.

Justin tried to put Eli down and she held on tighter. "No."

He never thought he'd be glad to hear that word again, but it was music to his bruised heart. "You have to, babe. You still have an agreement to fulfill."

"All males try. Jaxter last one."

"Jasper," he gently corrected.

"Okay, yes. Him."

"That means you still have a suitor." Justin hated saying those words, but he was proving himself worthy of the Guardian's trust.

Eli yelled over her shoulder, "Jasper?"

"Yeah?"

"You want mate?"

"Not if I have to do yer laundry."

"Laundry, cook, clean. Princess must not break nail."

"Nah, I'm out. Sorry, Miss Princess. You ain't suited to be a mate."

A round of agreement followed from the pedicure and palm-fanning team.

She spun her head to Rey. "More mates?"

"No, ma'am. You done gone through ever one of 'em I have faster'n Sherman through Atlanta."

Justin had expected her next question to be who was Sherman, but she surprised him and got down to business with Rey.

Holding Justin's gaze, she asked Rey, "What about deal?"

The old alpha got a twinkle in his eye and said, "Actually, I *do* have one potential male left. If he'll take you off our hands, he can have you."

Justin snapped, "Who?"

Rey said, "You're the only Boudreaux shifter I have left."

Eli grinned as wide as her pretty mouth would go. "I take. He is *mine!*"

Justin finally closed his mouth, then argued around his heart trying to strangle his words. "I left Clan Boudreaux a long time ago. I don't want Alexandre claiming a breach later on."

"Ya may a left us, son, but we didn't leave *you*. Yer still Clan Boudreaux, if you want to be."

Keep mate! Keep mate! Herc chimed in. *Mishka mine!*

Justin's insides shook with hope. He held everything he'd ever want in his arms.

To have this, all he had to do was accept that he was still Clan Boudreaux. Now he understood why the Guardian had been tight-lipped. His boss had no way of knowing whether Justin could overcome his past or not.

The Guardian had actually given him one more chance at winning this mate.

If Justin had to let go of the past to accept the future, he could do that for her, for them. He could do anything for her, and she had clearly fought her own battle for him.

"I accept," he told Rey. To be honest, Justin felt a weight lift that he hadn't realized he'd been carrying all these years.

Eli screamed in delight and kissed him again.

"You left me," a small voice accused from behind.

Hell, Justin had forgotten his delivery. He put Eli down just as Nico came running up to them.

She opened her arms. *Nico, Nico, Nico!* My sweet Nico."

She picked him up and swung him around, kissing his face and hair. He giggled and kissed her back.

Justin watched his family in quiet amazement.

His family.

This was just the start.

They'd have beautiful cubs with coats in all shades. He didn't care as long as they had a bunch of them.

When she calmed from seeing Nico and turned to Justin, tears poured down her face around her smile. "Thank you for my Nico."

"Anything for you, Eli, babe."

"Make me mate."

He couldn't wait. He had to figure out things like where they could live and how to keep this grolar treasure safe from ruthless kidnappers, but he could do that with her and Nico at his side.

"Stay for some gumbo, son. I want a look at those bears you two have."

Justin asked Eli, "You haven't shown them your bear?"

"Last ace. Save in hole."

He gave her a confused look. "What?"

Rey said, "The males who gave up courtin' her been tryin' to teach her cards. She's sayin' shiftin' to her bear was the last ace she had up her sleeve. Now why would she say that?"

Justin chuckled when he realized Rey was actually translating for *him*.

Pulling Eli to him with Nico between them, Justin said,

"Because you're never going to see another bear like hers and it'll blow your mind, but she's all mine now."

Eli hugged him and even Nico had a grip on Justin, physically *and* emotionally.

But by the time these Clan Boudreaux yahoos saw her bear, she'd be Justin's mate.

Eli said, "Mine. Only mine."

"Always, Eli, babe."

"Yes, okay."

THE END

ⓐ

THANK YOU FOR READING MY new League of Gallize Shifters series. I hope you enjoyed it and would appreciate a review wherever you buy books.

GRAY WOLF MATE (Book 1)
Available Now

and

STALKING HIS MATE (Book 3)
Coming Soon!

   All of these books are stand alones, so you can read them in any order. These books are being released at a discounted price that is good through the release month. If you'd like to be notified of each future release so you can grab them at the best price, just join my PRIVATE READER COMMUNITY. I DO NOT share anyone's information. I hate to have mine shared. All I do it send you occasional news and give you special deals and extra content.

LEAGUE OF GALLIZE SHIFTERS
Gray Wolf Mate
Mating A Grizzly
Stalking His Mate

OTHER BOOKS BY DIANNA LOVE

Q

DIANNA WRITES THE BELADOR URBAN fantasy series and the Slye Temp romantic thriller series (completed for those who want to binge read!). Keep watch for more Belador books and her new League of Gallize Shifters coming out soon.

Book 1: Blood Trinity
Book 2: Alterant
Book 3: The Curse
Book 4: Rise Of The Gryphon
Book 5: Demon Storm
Book 6: Witchlock
Book 7: Rogue Belador
Book 8: Dragon King Of Treoir
Book 9: Belador Cosaint
Book 10: Treoir Dragon Hoard (2018)
Tristan's Escape: A Belador Novella

★To keep up with all of Dianna's releases: sign up for her news-letter here.

THE COMPLETE SLYE TEMP ROMANTIC SUSPENSE SERIES

Prequel: Last Chance To Run (free for limited time)
Book 1: Nowhere Safe
Book 2: Honeymoon To Die For
Book 3: Kiss The Enemy
Book 4: Deceptive Treasures
Book 5: Stolen Vengeance
Book 6: Fatal Promise

For Young Adult Fans – the explosive sci-fi/fantasy Red Moon trilogy by *USA Today* bestseller Micah Caida (collaboration of *New York Times* Bestseller Dianna Love and *USA Today* bestseller Mary Buckham).

Book 1: Time Trap (ebook free for limited time)
Book 2: Time Return
Book 3: Time Lock

To buy books and read more excerpts, go to
www.MicahCaida.com

AUTHOR'S BIO

NEW YORK TIMES BESTSELLER DIANNA Love once dangled over a hundred feet in the air to create unusual marketing projects for Fortune 500 companies. She now writes high-octane romantic thrillers, young adult and urban fantasy. Fans of the best-selling Belador urban fantasy series will be thrilled to know more books are coming after Belador Cosaint plus Dianna is launching a new paranormal romance series – League of Gallize Shifters. Her sexy Slye Temp romantic thriller series wrapped up with Gage and Sabrina's book–Fatal Promise–but Dianna has plans for HAMR BROTHERHOOD, a spinoff romantic suspense series coming soon. Look for her books in print, e-book and audio (mosts series). On the rare occasions Dianna is out of her writing cave, she tours the country on her BMW motorcycle searching for new story locations. Dianna lives in the Atlanta, GA area with her husband, who is a motorcycle instructor, and with a tank full of unruly saltwater critters.

Visit her website at Dianna Love or Join her Dianna Love Reader Community (group page) on Facebook and get in on the fun!

A WORD FROM DIANNA...

ℚ

THANK YOU FOR READING *MATING A GRIZZLY*. I have to admit that this was one of my favorite books to write. I love the characters in all my books, but Justin and Herc will always hold a special place in my heart. I hope you enjoyed meeting them and Elianna.

As always, the first person I want to thank is Karl, who is with me every step of the way. I couldn't ask for a better partner to share my life. He is everything to me.

I appreciate the very early reads by Jennifer Cazares and Sherry Arnold, who catch the last few things that make it past me and my multiple editors.

Speaking of my editing team – you are amazing and I love the extra touch you put on my books without interfering with my voice.

My assistant, Cassondra, and her husband, Steve, have been with me through so many books. My husband and I treasure our close friendship with them. It's hard to put into words how much Cassondra catches that helps me keep the continuity true from book to book. I knew Judy Carney for many years before she offered another level of proofing my words. Once again, she's done a great job. Joyce Ann McLaughlin and I became friends while I toured so much and now she's one of my sharp-eyed early readers as well.

Thank you to all my early readers who post reviews the first week my books are out – you are so amazing. I wish we could meet in one location to enjoy a meal and drinks together. Until then, know that I say a special prayer for you and your families every night.

Here's a shout out to Kimber Mirabella and Sharon Livingston Griffiths, who are always willing to read plus send me encouragement. Leiha Mann has been in my corner for many years since my first book and her friendship is dear to me. Thanks for all you do.

I'm always bragging on the talented Xiamara Parathenopaeus of S Squared Productions, who makes me smile every time she surprises me with her beautiful creations.

I'm fortunate to have found Kim Killion way back when I did, because I love all the covers and additional graphics she's created for my books. I have no idea what I'd do without Jennifer Litteken (and Double D!) who spin their magic to format my pages – thank you for the many times you've helped me out of a tight spot. I've enjoyed a wonderful friendship with Karen Marie Moning for many years. Karl and I both appreciate the sage advice you shared with us this year in particular, which has impacted our lives in a major way.

A special thank you to Candace Fox, who stepped in from day one when I started a reader group page on Facebook, affectionately call the Love Boat Cruise. When a family crisis took front and center in my life at the same moment Demon Storm (Belador series) came out, I was offline for many weeks and skipped any promotion. Over a month later, when I got back to my writing cave, I realized Candi had picked up the ball and promoted that book on multiple sites along with holding a presence on my group page. Since then, she's managed online events on our community page and aided me in many other ways. I'm thrilled we got to meet during a trip I made to Florida. Thank you, Candi. Your friendship means a lot to me.

When I started writing, I had no idea how many terrific people I would meet in this business. If I had known that, I would have started much sooner. ☺

Thank you again to my peeps on the Dianna Love Reader Community group page on Facebook. You make every day wonderful.

9 781940 651637